Fractured Kiss

ALSO BY L.M. DALGLEISH

Fractured Rock Star Series

Fractured Hearts

Fractured Dreams

Fractured Trust

Fractured Kiss

Fractured Kiss

A Fractured Rock Star Romance

L.M. Dalgleish

Copyright © 2022 by L.M. Dalgleish

All rights reserved.

No part of this book may be reproduced in any form or by any electronic or mechanical means, including information storage and retrieval systems, without written permission from the author, except for the use of brief quotations in a book review.

This novel is entirely a work of fiction. The names, characters and incidents portrayed in it are the work of the author's imagination. Any resemblance to actual persons, living or dead, events or localities is entirely coincidental.

ISBN: 9798446701339

Cover Design: Wildheart Graphics

Photographer: Rafa G Catala

Cover Model: Jorge Del Rio Romero

Editing: Alexa Gregory Edits/Lawrence Editing www.lawrenceediting.com

To my beautiful mother, who has been with me every step of the way. Love you, Mum!

Chapter One

Zac moved his fingers over the heavy strings of his bass guitar in a pattern that had become as familiar as breathing over the last few months. The crowd let out a roar of approval as they recognized the distinctive thumping notes, and a corner of his mouth lifted. The song was a fan favorite from Fractured's last album, always guaranteed to bring down the house during their encore performance.

The smell of hot amps and the smoke from their pyrotechnics swirled around him. He breathed it in. The scent would linger on his skin, even once he'd washed away the sweat of performing after the concert. Not that he minded—or noticed most of the time. Like the smell of metal strings on his fingertips, it was ingrained in his synapses. He'd probably be smelling it years after he retired.

Not that he was planning on quitting this life anytime soon.

The noise in the arena rose higher, almost loud enough to drown out the mix from his in-ear monitor. The direct feed had cut out briefly during the last song but seemed to be working again now, thank god. Without it, the wall of sound from the crowd made it almost impossible to hear anything except the driving beat from Noah's drum set behind him.

As he played, Zac let his gaze wander over the tens of thousands of people who filled the stands. Most of them—those he could see through the blinding flare of the spotlights anyway—were now singing the words at full volume along with Connor, Fractured's dark-haired front man. He was center stage, gripping his microphone stand in one hand, while pointing his other at the fans, encouraging them to sing louder.

Zac focused on the deep resonant notes his fingers were drawing out of the cobra-blue Fender American Ultra J Bass he was playing. He had used the same instrument when they performed this song a week ago at the American Music Awards. That was just before Fractured won Artist of the Year for the fifth time in the band's thirteen-year-long career. His jaw tightened at the reminder of that night and who *hadn't* won. But he closed his eyes and breathed out slowly. He concentrated on weaving his bassline through Tex's squealing guitar riffs, the pounding beat of Noah's drums, and Connor's soaring vocals.

As they reached the chorus, Zac moved closer to the microphone stand in front of him and added his voice to Connor's. The resulting harmony roused the audience to new heights of frenzied excitement.

Movement to his right caught his attention. Tex, their long-haired, tattooed lead guitarist, grinned at him as his fingers flew over the strings of his custom Les Paul six-string in a lightning-fast riff.

Zac rolled his eyes at his bandmate's showboating, although he couldn't stop a return smile from breaking across his face. He stepped toward Tex and raised a brow, his grin widening at his bandmate's *fuck yeah,* when he realized Zac was accepting his challenge.

Unlike the lead guitar, the bass isn't intended to be flashy. It isn't meant to steal the spotlight. The bass is the backbone of the song, the glue that holds everything together. It's the pulsating rhythm beneath the melody that makes people *need* to move whenever they hear it. But just because the bass isn't meant to steal the spotlight doesn't mean it can't. And some situations called for making a point.

Zac waited for a gap in Tex's riff and jumped in, letting loose with a rapid-fire lick of his own. The deep tones of his J Bass thumped and growled through the air, rattling the amps as he punched the notes out. Tex threw his head back and laughed as the crowd surged forward in feverish excitement at the impromptu six-string versus four-string duel taking place in front of them.

Even Connor was grinning as he pulled his mic off its stand and strode to the edge of the stage. The fans transferred their attention back to him as they continued singing along, their voices rising in unison and filling the arena.

Now that he'd proven what his bass could do, Zac dropped his head and closed his eyes. He played that way for the rest of the song, feeling the vibration of the music through his fingers and the soles of his boots as much as hearing it. It took a few seconds after the song ended before the shrieks and catcalls brought him back from the place he sometimes drifted to when he was playing.

He stood there, a bead of sweat trickling down his temple as the wave of sound from the crowd broke over him again and again. Noah stepped up beside him, his blue eyes glittering, damp strands of his long, surfer-blond hair sticking to his temples. The drummer slung his arm around Zac's neck and gazed out at the crowd, a wide grin on his face. "Never gets old, does it?"

"No, it doesn't," Zac said. He might have been looking out at the heaving mass of fans too, but it wasn't their adulation he lived for. It wasn't the fame, or the money, or the women.

It was the music.

Whether he was playing bass with Fractured or singing as front man for his side-project band, Crossfire, it was always the music that came first.

In tandem with Tex, Zac flicked his pick into the crowd, threw the fans a final salute, and followed his bandmates off the stage. He pulled the strap of his bass over his head, disconnected his wireless belt pack, and pulled out his in-ear monitor, handing it all to Cassie, his guitar tech, with a smile of gratitude.

Her pretty lips tilted up. "Great show."

Zac ran a hand through his short, dark hair. "Thanks. Everything was good. But I did get a bit of disruption to the mix feed at the end."

"Okay, I'll have a look at it." She put the unit in question down on one of the equipment boxes that surrounded her, then turned away to rack the bass next to the three others already there. Involuntarily, Zac's gaze dropped to her ass, perfectly displayed in a pair of frayed denim cut-offs that hugged her curves and exposed the length of her slender, toned thighs.

He grimaced and looked away. He didn't want to be one of *those* guys. He didn't damn well need to be. He'd been in one of the biggest rock bands on the planet for the last thirteen years. Women weren't exactly an issue for him. There was no reason for him to be ogling his employee.

Especially not one with a fucking diamond ring on her finger.

And Cassie was a talented guitar tech, even if she was younger than the others he'd worked with in the past. She seemed to have an instinctive ability to understand the sound he wanted to get out of his instruments. In the short time she'd worked for him, she'd already developed an uncanny ability to anticipate what he needed before he had a chance to ask for it.

Cassie turned back and knelt in front of him, reaching between the larger equipment cases for the small one that stored his in-ear monitor. Like an asshole, he didn't step back to give her room. When she looked up at him—a sweet smile curving those full lips—he had a sudden vision of reaching out and tangling his fingers in her midnight dark waves, tugging her head back, and watching those deep-blue eyes change color as he unbuttoned his jeans and—

Zac stepped away. He needed to get laid. And soon. It had obviously been far too long between women if he was fantasizing about Cassie that way. Not that she wasn't attractive. She was. Attractive enough that when he'd met her before the tour, his first thought was that one of his bandmates—probably Noah—was having a joke at his expense. Young, gorgeous guitar techs weren't exactly common. She actually reminded him of the cover art from their third album, *Fallen*. The image was of a beautiful dark-haired, dark-winged angel, crumpled on the ground, face turned upward, and innocent blue eyes filled with tears as she reached one hand to the sky in supplication.

Cassie, with that hair, those eyes, and her full, pink lips, looked far too much like that fallen angel. It was exactly why he shouldn't fantasize about her. Because her type of sweetly sexy innocence wasn't something that usually attracted him. He made sure the women he spent time with were more hard-eyed than starry. The type who looked like they wanted to eat him for breakfast, not like they were going to start building white picket fences in their heads if he fucked them more than once. The ring on Cassie's finger left him in no doubt which group she belonged to. So even if she wasn't working for him, even if she wasn't engaged, he would never actually touch her that way.

No matter how good she looked on her knees in front of him.

Zac shoved the image out of his head, tossed another casual smile her way, then looked for his bandmates. He spotted them gathered around their manager, Drew, and made his way over, dodging the crew members pushing equipment cases toward the exit. Load-out started even before they sang their last song, but it really kicked into high gear after they left the stage. Zac stripped off his T-shirt as he walked and used it to wipe away the sweat that had beaded on his forehead.

Drew met his gaze when he got closer, a slight frown on his face. "I need to talk to you."

"Looks like that's our cue," Connor said. He tipped his chin at Zac. "See you back at the dressing room."

Zac nodded, but his attention was on Drew, who waited for the others to leave before saying, "We have an issue."

"Crossfire?" If there was a problem with Fractured, the other three would still be here.

"The label called. They want to bring the album forward by three months."

"What the hell? We've barely even started writing it yet."

Drew rubbed the back of his neck. "There's an opening at Abbey Road, and the label wants to schedule you in."

A slow grin grew on Zac's face. He'd been wanting to get Crossfire into the famous UK recording studios for a while. Drew's expression gave him pause, though. "So, what's the issue?"

"The opening is just before Crossfire's European tour. You'd have to have the album done and ready to go before then."

"Shit," Zac said. "So, we'll have to write it now while I'm on tour and they're back in LA."

"Yep. And there's more."

Zac raised his brows in query.

"That duet you were talking about doing for the album. Talia Harrison is available, and she's keen to be a part of it."

"Talia? She's huge in Europe, right? Not as much over here yet."

"Exactly. She's big everywhere but the US, so the label's looking to break her into the market. A duet on the next Crossfire album would be the perfect vehicle for her. And she's actually got a gap in her schedule the week before your tour. So, if you guys want to take advantage of both of those things, the album will have to be ready to go before you head to the UK."

Zac scrubbed his hand over his mouth. "Fuck. That's too good an opportunity to turn down."

"It *is* a good opportunity. That's why I told the label I'd speak to you rather than just telling them to fuck off. But it won't be the only opportunity. You really need to consider whether it's achievable with everything else you've got going on right now."

Zac laced his hands behind his neck and tipped his head back. He stared at the struts holding up the roof and considered the long days and nights ahead of him if he agreed to it. It wouldn't be easy; but getting to the top never was. He'd already done it once with Fractured. Crossfire deserved the same level of effort from him.

Maybe more.

His right hand found its way to the leather cord around his neck and the dull, scratched V of nylon that hung from it. He traced the outline of the pick, his dad's words echoing in his head. *Right place, right time, Zac.*

He met Drew's gaze. "Yeah. We'll get it done. I'll just need to schedule songwriting sessions with the guys at night after the concerts."

Drew studied him, concern filling his brown eyes. He took a step closer and lowered his voice. "If the fact that Crossfire didn't win an AMA last month is influencing your decision, it shouldn't. You know those boys were over the moon just to be nominated." Zac's spine pulled tight, but Drew kept going. "You are not solely responsible for Crossfire's success or failure, Zac. You need to stop putting so much pressure on yourself."

He shook his head, his eyebrows pulling together. "You know, when Fractured was on hiatus, throwing yourself into Crossfire was understandable. And there's nothing wrong with still having a side project now that you're out of hiatus. But being in Fractured alone would be enough work for most people. And no one, least of all, Beau, Devon, and Caleb, expects you to kill yourself trying to get Crossfire to the same level."

He pinned Zac with his eyes. "Now, I told the label I'd talk to you about bringing the album forward because that's my job as your manager. But I'm more than happy to push back on it. You can do the Abbey Road thing some other time."

Zac shook his head. "We can get it done." Drew opened his mouth, but Zac cut him off before he could say anything else. "We'll get it done. I'll take a break after the album's out."

The furrows in Drew's brow smoothed slightly but didn't disappear completely. "Okay, mate, let's make sure that happens. The last thing we need is you burning yourself out. You've got two bands and a whole heap of fans relying on you to stay in the game as long as possible."

Zac nodded, rolling his shoulders to release the tension. Long days weren't anything he couldn't handle; he'd just need to avoid any distractions for the duration of this tour. He needed to focus on the only important things.

His bands and the music.

Chapter Two

Cassie tilted her head to the side and closed her eyes as she plucked the strings of the dark purple bass guitar. The simple chord progression vibrated through the air, cutting through the clatter and shouts that were the chaotic soundtrack of load-in for a major arena tour.

She ran her fingers up the fretboard, her gaze catching on the glitter of her engagement ring reflecting the bright stage lighting. Warmth filled her chest, but she didn't let herself get distracted, adjusting the tuning pegs until she was satisfied that the instrument was ready for Zac to use that night.

The grizzled man sitting on one of the equipment cases next to her shot her a look of approval.

"You've got an excellent natural ear." Dan's voice was rough. Probably from the cigarettes he puffed on multiple times a day.

A smile tugged her lips up. "Thank you." She stood and carefully racked the bass, then turned back to watch Fractured's senior guitar tech finish tuning the one he was working on.

"There you go." Dan stood and handed it to her to rack next to the other three.

"I really appreciate you keeping me company," Cassie said, as she made sure all the nylon guitar straps were securely attached and the wireless transmitters were plugged in.

"I enjoy talking to you new techs. Makes me feel young again, seeing everything through fresh eyes." He chuckled.

Cassie smiled. "I'm not *that* new. I've been doing this since I graduated three years ago. Although this *is* my first national tour."

Dan snorted. "Three years is nothing. Talk to me again in thirty years."

Cassie turned away from him and fiddled with the guitar rack. She wasn't sure being a guitar tech in thirty years was what she wanted. But then again, she wasn't exactly sure what she *did* want to be doing. The only thing she was certain of was that she loved the music industry and wanted to stay in it. And it wasn't like she didn't enjoy being part of the backline crew. In fact, she loved the feeling of being part of something bigger than just her. Sometimes it was almost like what she imagined being part of a family might be like. Not a particularly close and loving family, maybe. But having so many people around meant she rarely felt alone when Bryan was busy.

Bryan.

Cassie surreptitiously looked at her watch. He and his band Blacklite were due on stage as the opening act for Fractured in just over an hour. Dan helping her out with the final check of Zac's bass guitars meant she'd finished early enough she might be able to spend a few minutes alone with her fiancé before he had to go on stage.

Dan must have noticed her checking her watch, because he grinned. "Got some spare time?"

Not wanting him to think she was slacking off, she gestured over at Fractured's other instrument racks. "Do you need any help with Tex's and Connor's guitars?"

"Thanks. But me and the boys have it covered. Why don't you go see that fella of yours? I know what these rock stars are like. I'm sure seeing you before he goes onstage will be just what he needs to help him relax." He waggled his eyebrows, and Cassie's face heated.

Not that he was wrong. Bryan was always a ball of nerves before a performance. Even more so now that Blacklite had gotten its big break—being signed by Hazard Records and touring with Fractured. Bryan hadn't stopped talking about what an incredible opportunity it was for months.

"Well, if you're okay with that? It's hard to get a lot of time to ourselves traveling on the bus with everyone."

"Off you go, then," Dan said. "I'll catch you during the show."

Cassie gave him a grateful smile, then headed backstage. Bryan and the rest of the band would probably be in their dressing room getting ready, but if she was quick, she might be able to steal him away for a little one-on-one time. Something that had been all too rare in the week and a half they'd been on tour.

Cassie made her way through the maze of corridors, dodging the crew members rushing past her on last-minute errands. She glanced at the door to Fractured's dressing room as she passed, a small thrill zinging through her. She still couldn't quite believe her fiancé was part of Fractured's opening act. Or that she was actually *working* for one of them.

She'd spent the last few years doing double duty as the tech for both Bryan, Blacklite's lead guitarist, and Toby, their bass player. So, when Bryan had told her the amazing news—that they would be opening for Fractured—she'd just assumed she'd keep doing it. But the label's tour manager had decided he didn't like the idea of Bryan's guitar tech also being his fiancée. Given that it was such a huge opportunity for Blacklite, Bryan hadn't pushed the issue.

Even though she understood, Cassie had been devastated, imagining lonely months at home without him. But a few weeks later, out of the blue, she'd received a call with the offer of working for Fractured instead. For *Zac Ford*. Only one of the most famous bass players in the world. His long-time bass tech had unfortunately had to pull out of the tour due to health issues.

It had been Dan who had called her with the job offer. Apparently, she had received a glowing recommendation from one of the band's audio engineers. Someone she'd worked with previously on one of Blacklite's regional tours. In the relatively small world of backline crew—the people responsible for taking care of a tour's instruments and electrical equipment—your reputation could make or break you, and word of mouth was king. And it seemed like they didn't have a problem with her working on the tour, as long as it wasn't directly for Bryan.

Plus, she was pretty sure that with the start date so close, and other guitar techs already hired for tours with conflicting schedules, she'd been the easiest option.

Whatever the reason, Cassie had been over the moon.

But meeting Zac for the first time had been nerve-wracking. He'd been gracious, if slightly reserved, and she'd seen the look he'd shot Dan after they were introduced. It wasn't like she didn't get it—she was younger than most other techs. And a woman. But she was good at what she did, and obviously, he trusted Dan's recommendation since she'd gotten the job.

Still smiling at the memory, Cassie reached Blacklite's dressing room and tapped lightly on the door. There was no answer, but the low beat of music came from inside, so she tried the handle. It swung open. No one was in the main dressing room. The guys and Stella, the band's lead singer, should've been prepping to go onstage by now.

Cassie looked around the vacant room, frowning. There were empty beer cans and what looked like a recently stubbed-out cigarette in an ashtray on the table. They must have been here recently. Cassie made her way to the adjoining wardrobe room, following the muted sound of the music. She tapped again. "Bryan?"

There was no answer, so she cracked the door open, keeping her eyes averted, just in case one of the other band members was changing.

"Bryan, are you in there?"

"Cassie?" It was Bryan's voice, but it sounded strange, almost strangled. "Don't come in, baby!"

Cassie wavered, not sure why he sounded so panicked. It couldn't just be that one of the guys was changing. Traveling on the tour bus with three men meant there wasn't much she hadn't already inadvertently seen.

"You said you locked the door!" Bryan's hissed words were so low she barely heard them. "Get off me."

Her stomach flipped over. Who was he talking to?

Cassie shoved the door open. It took her mind a

moment too long to process what she was seeing. Bryan, naked on the couch, trying to push an equally naked woman off him. The agony that ripped through her chest at the sight almost doubled her over.

"No." Cassie's lips made the shape of the word, but no sound came out, her lungs too compressed to function properly. She jerked her eyes away from her panicked fiancé to the woman sitting on top of him. It was Stella, Blacklite's sultry, red-haired lead singer who had all the men eating out of her hand whenever she performed. The woman Bryan claimed had become almost like a sister to him over the two years they'd played together. The woman who had never really seemed to warm to Cassie, no matter how friendly she'd tried to be. Stella's expression was almost apathetic, except for a flicker of what might be satisfaction in her gaze. She didn't seem at all interested in climbing off Bryan, even as he continued to push at her hips to get her to move.

Spots swam in Cassie's vision, and she clung to the handle of the door to steady herself. When she could finally breathe again, she ripped her gaze away from Stella and looked back at Bryan.

"Cassie," he pleaded. He gave up on trying to get Stella to climb off him. Or maybe he'd concluded that getting her to move would only put the evidence of his betrayal on full display. Instead, he held his hand out to Cassie. As if he wanted her to come to him. Did he actually think she would? While Stella was... while she was...

Acid burned up Cassie's throat. She clapped a hand over her mouth, even as a hot rush of tears flooded her eyes, thankfully blurring the sight of the man she loved with his dick inside another woman.

Cassie took a step back. Then another. She had to get away. As far away as she could. From him. From Stella. But where? Where could she go? To their bus? The bunk she shared with him? She couldn't. She couldn't ever step foot in there again.

With scalding tears blinding her, she whirled and bolted across the main room and out the door.

Chapter Three

Zac had just turned the corner into the hallway that led to Fractured's dressing room when someone ran into him so hard, it knocked him back a step. The other person rebounded off his chest and landed on their ass with a cry of pain that sounded more emotional than physical.

"What the hell?" he said, recognizing the slender form and dark waves of hair. It was Cassie on the ground in front of him. She had her head lowered so he couldn't see her face, but she was breathing hard. A second later, she scrambled to her feet, still not looking up.

"I'm so sorry." Her voice wobbled as she spoke. Fuck. Was she crying?

She edged around him, but he reached out and grasped her arm as she tried to get past. "Are you okay?"

Cassie nodded jerkily, gaze still cast down. "I have to go."

She tried to tug her arm away, but the tears he could now see glazing her cheeks made him keep hold of her. His neck and shoulders knotted tight. Had someone done something to her? *Hurt* her? There were as many assholes on tour as anywhere else, so unfortunately, it wasn't out of the question. He breathed through his anger at the thought, not wanting to react before he knew what had happened.

"I can see that, angel. But I need to know if someone's hurt you."

She gasped and shuddered, her reaction making Zac's spine snap straight. But before he could demand to know who the hell had put his hands on her, she shook her head in denial.

"Cassie, look at me."

She reluctantly raised her head, and he stared down at her, searching her face for the truth. Her lashes were wet and spiky, her eyes dark-blue pools of anguish. His stomach twisted.

"Cassie!" The yell came from down the hall. Bryan jogged toward them, bare-chested, no shoes, and struggling to button up his jeans. His guilt-ridden expression told Zac exactly what must have happened.

Zac's jaw tightened. Without letting go of Cassie's arm, he tugged her behind him and stepped forward. His hand slid down to bracket her wrist.

"What the fuck did you do?" Zac demanded as Bryan came to a stop in front of them.

"I need to talk to Cassie."

Cassie pressed herself closer to Zac's back.

"I doubt she wants to talk to you right now," he said.

"All due respect, man, but this has nothing to do with you."

"Considering you've got fucking lipstick marks on your chest, and your *fiancée* isn't wearing makeup, respect isn't exactly a word you should be throwing around."

Movement down the hall caught Zac's attention. Stella

was leaning against the dressing room door, a faint smile on her face as she watched the three of them. Disgust filled him. Had Bryan been screwing his bandmate? While his fiancée was on tour with him?

Cassie tugged at his grip on her wrist. When he didn't release her, she whispered, "Please let me go, Zac."

Zac looked over his shoulder at her but jerked around in time to slam his hand against Bryan's chest as he tried to get past. Bryan stepped back, his nostrils flaring and his fists clenched. Zac waited to see if he'd take a shot, but the guitarist took a deep breath and looked around Zac's shoulder. "Cassie, baby, I have to get ready to go on stage, but I'll come and see you afterward. We need to talk. I'm so fucking sorry. I never meant—"

Zac felt Cassie draw herself up at his back, a fine tremor running through the wrist he was still holding. "I don't want to talk to you. I don't want to see you. I don't want you near me ever again." Her voice cracked on the last word.

"You have to listen to me. It's—"

Zac turned his back on Bryan and pulled Cassie a couple of steps down the hallway. He lowered his voice. "Go out to our bus. Tell security I sent you and you need to talk to Maggie, our driver. You've got your crew pass, so they'll get her for you. Tell her what happened and that I said you could stay on the bus until we've finished with the after-party. It will give you some space to calm down, and this douchebag won't be able to get to you. I'll get Dan to cover for you tonight. Okay?"

Cassie swallowed, then gave him a grateful nod. He let go of her arm, and without another word, she spun on her heel and darted away from them.

He turned and stared Bryan down.

The man took a step back, running both hands through

his curly blond hair. "What the fuck is your deal, dude? She's my fiancée. I have a right to talk to her."

Zac's eyes flicked up to see Stella still leaning against the wall, her fingers playing with a pendant on a chain that hung between her breasts. When she noticed him watching her, she gave him a coy smile, dropping the necklace and trailing her fingers down her only partially laced corset to the waistband of her skintight jeans.

He kept his face expressionless, and obviously realizing he wasn't in the mood for her shit, she dropped her smile and straightened from her languorous pose.

Zac returned his attention to Bryan. "I think you lost any rights when it comes to Cassie as soon as you stuck your dick in someone else." He couldn't have kept the contempt out of his voice if he'd tried, so he didn't.

The muscles in Bryan's arms and chest tightened. Zac hoped this time the asshole would lash out. The record label wouldn't be happy at having to replace the opening act mid-tour, but Fractured was the moneymaker, not Blacklite. There were plenty of other up-and-coming bands that would be more than happy to step in and take their place. A strange sense of satisfaction pulsed through him at the thought of sending Bryan and Stella packing.

Unfortunately, the guitarist controlled himself. He scrubbed his hands over his face. "You don't know what you're talking about. Cassie and I... We've been together since we were teenagers. We love each other. This was just a... a... I don't know." He threw his hands up in the air. "A fucking misstep or something. We'll talk it through. I'll explain. She'll forgive me."

As devastated as Cassie had looked, Zac doubted it would be that easy. But he was well aware that people did stupid things in the name of love—staying together even when it tore them to pieces. For all he knew, the two of them would be back together tomorrow, though he hoped for her sake that wasn't the case. Either way, it wasn't any of his business what Cassie did.

He shook his head, not wanting to look at Bryan anymore. "Maybe. Maybe not. But the least you can do is give her some space. And I'd suggest you prepare to fucking grovel."

Bryan narrowed his gaze. "She'll forgive me," he repeated before turning and stalking back to his dressing room.

Zac watched him go, his lip curling when Bryan stopped next to Stella, inclining his head toward her. She put her hand up to his chest, but Bryan shot a look over his shoulder at Zac, then turned back to her, shook his head, and disappeared into the dressing room.

Stella stared after him for a second, then cast a quick look at Zac before following Bryan in. The door slammed shut behind her.

Zac pulled his phone out and texted Dan, asking him to do double-duty during their show tonight. The man was experienced enough to make it work for one night. Then he continued down the hallway to Fractured's dressing room.

When he went in, he found Connor, Tex, and Noah sitting at the table playing poker, several glasses of whiskey and bottles of beer scattered around them. It was their usual relaxed pre-show ritual. Lexie, Connor's pretty, dark-haired wife and the band's official photographer, was sitting on the couch behind them doing some work on her laptop—probably editing or uploading to the band's social media.

Connor looked up. "Hey, man. What was going on out there? I would have come out to see what was up, but I'm in the middle of wiping the floor with these guys."

"The hell you are," Tex said in his smooth Southern accent.

Zac dropped onto a chair and grabbed an unopened beer, cracking the lid and taking a long swallow before answering. "Just the damn opening act being assholes."

Connor snorted and looked back down at his cards. "Fucking amateurs. Do we need to do anything?"

"No. But Cassie's going to be on our bus when we finish up tonight."

The three men and Lexie all looked up and stared at him. Tex's brows drew together, his expression turning dangerous. "Is she hurt?"

"Not physically," Zac replied, the memory of Cassie's tear-stained cheeks and wounded eyes making him frown. What kind of fucking asshole treated his fiancée, the woman he'd apparently been with since he was a teenager, like that? If you're not prepared to fucking commit to someone, don't put a fucking ring on their finger. It was as simple as that.

"What happened?" asked Lexie.

"She caught him screwing Stella in their dressing room. Ran straight into me while she was trying to get away."

Lexie's gray eyes widened, then filled with compassion. "Should I see if she's okay?"

Zac shot her a smile. Lexie was one of the warmest, kindest women he knew. None of them had ever expected Connor to fall for someone. But he had, and at least he'd had the good sense to fall for Lexie.

"I think she probably just needs some time to compose herself. And I told her to ask for Maggie. If she feels like talking, Maggie will be there for her."

Lexie gave him a slow nod. With her brow still furrowed, she looked back down at her computer.

There was a knock at the door, and it swung open. Drew stuck his head through the gap. "Fifteen minutes before your pre-show guests arrive."

Zac and the other three men nodded their acknowledgment at him. Before most shows, the band spent half an hour hanging out with underprivileged kids who had been gifted tickets to the concert. They'd been doing it for years, as part of the band's commitment to various charities providing music therapy to children. It was one of the best perks of the job.

"I just need to get changed," Zac told Drew. The other three were already in their stage outfits, barely distinguishable from their street clothes. He stood and went through to their wardrobe room, quickly changing into fitted black jeans and a plain charcoal-gray V-neck T-shirt.

He was already wearing a leather cuff and chunky silver rings on both hands, so he didn't bother adding anything else. Leaving the room, he sat back at the table with the other men. He considered asking to be dealt in for the next round but instead reached for the bass he'd left propped against the wall earlier. Rocking back in his chair, he plucked a few chords, his mind drifting again to the devastation on Cassie's face when she'd looked up at him in the hallway.

Something constricted in his chest. That look right there was why he didn't have the slightest interest in getting involved with anyone. Guaranteed, someone was going to get hurt. Usually more than one person. Even his Fractured bandmates, all three of whom had somehow managed, against all odds, to fall in love, had gone through a world of pain first—or put their women through it. And even though things seemed to be going smoothly now, it didn't mean shit wouldn't hit the fan again sometime down the road.

Keep your distance, avoid getting emotionally involved. That was the best way to ensure you made it through life unscathed, while doing as little damage yourself as possible.

It was just a shame Cassie had to find that out the hard way.

Chapter Four

Cassie's eyes were raw. Her entire face burned. Not to mention her heart. She was curled up on one of the plush black leather couches on Fractured's tour bus. The dark wood paneling, massive wall-mounted television, and fully appointed kitchenette set it apart from Blacklite's much smaller, less well-appointed one.

Before the thought of Bryan had her dissolving into tears again, Maggie came over and held out a mug. "Here, sweetheart."

Cassie accepted it with a smile that trembled on her lips. She took a sip of the steaming hot liquid as the tall, slightly intimidating older woman settled on the seat next to her. She could sense Maggie's gaze on the side of her face, but she kept her own fixed on the mug in her hands.

"You don't have to tell me about it," Maggie said. "But sometimes it helps to talk. And I've been told I'm a good listener."

Cassie's eyes met Maggie's, noting the warmth in their brown depths. She looked away, letting out a dry laugh as more tears streaked down her face. "There's not much to tell. He told me he loved me. He promised he'd never hurt me." She wiped her wet cheeks with the back of her hand. "He lied."

Maggie nodded and leaned back in her seat. "How long were you two together?"

Cassie blew on her tea to give herself a few seconds before responding. "Since we were sixteen. But we were friends for two years before that."

"That's a long time."

"Yes," Cassie whispered. A hollow ache grew in the pit of her stomach. How could he do that to her? *Bryan.* The man she'd loved since she was just a teenager. How had this happened? It was surreal—like a nightmare. Like maybe she'd suddenly wake up back in the bunk she shared with him, his body warm and solid next to hers. He'd take her in his arms and tell her he loved her, and she'd breathe a sigh of relief and tell him she loved him too.

But the pain that raked Cassie's chest wouldn't let her hide from the truth. She stared sightlessly at the mug in her hands. "I'm such a fool."

"I don't think it's a bad thing to be foolish, even if it sometimes ends up hurting us." Cassie had almost forgotten Maggie was there. "It means you're taking a chance on something that could be amazing. True, it doesn't always work out. But when it does, well, it can make your journey through life unforgettable."

"But what if you believe you have something amazing, and then you just end up all"—her breath hitched—"all alone again?"

Maggie didn't answer her straight away, studying her face. "Were you alone, Cassie? Before him?"

Cassie swallowed past the lump in her throat and looked back down at her tea. She didn't really want to think about how things were before Bryan. She was struggling just to come to terms with how things were now.

After Bryan.

Fresh tears welled up, and she shook her head. Maggie seemed to understand that meant she didn't want to talk about it rather than answering in the negative because she patted Cassie on the shoulder and stood. "Well, I have to prep for heading out once the boys and Lexie wrap everything up. I'll leave you to drink the rest of your tea in peace." She reached up to a shelf above her head with a tattooed arm and placed something down on the seat next to Cassie. "Here's the control for the entertainment system if you decide you'd like a distraction."

Cassie's smile was watery. "Thank you."

Maggie gave her a sympathetic look. "You just relax here for a couple of hours, okay, sweetheart?" She turned to head to the front of the bus. Before she went through the doorway, she hesitated, then turned back. "You know, Cassie, being alone is far better than being with someone who doesn't appreciate your true worth. Just remember that when he comes crawling back." Without waiting for Cassie to reply, she left.

Cassie's fingers tightened around the mug. Bryan had been the only one who'd ever thought she was worth anything.

Bryan. Her heart lurched and stumbled in her chest.

Bryan and Stella. Nausea rose again, and Cassie curled forward over her tea, trying to ease the jagged wound in her chest. Was this really it? The end of all they'd had together? What did a life without Bryan look like? Without him, she had no one. She'd be all on her own.

Again.

More hot tears splashed down her cheeks. But it seemed

she was all cried out because soon, all that was left were dry, wracking sobs.

Eventually, even those tapered off.

Cassie stood on shaky legs, tipped her lukewarm tea down the sink, rinsed the empty mug, and placed it on the counter. She returned to the couch and curled into a little ball. She considered putting a movie on to distract herself, but suddenly the effort to even pick up the control seemed like too much. Her eyelids were heavy, and she let them drift closed, needing to rest for a bit. Wanting to escape this horrible day for just a minute.

She partially roused when the distant, raucous sound of excited fans leaving the venue floated into the bus. She needed to find somewhere to sleep. When the after-party was over, the band would be back. As kind as Zac had been, she couldn't bear facing him again right now, knowing he'd witnessed her life falling apart.

But exhaustion had her eyelids slipping closed again.

In a minute, she'd leave and find a spare bunk on one of the other buses.

She just needed a minute.

Just one more minute…

*　*　*

The steady rumble of the engine seeped into Cassie's consciousness. Her eyelids fluttered open, and she blinked into the dim morning light, wondering why her eyes felt so swollen and gritty. And where was Bryan? She always woke up curled around him.

Cassie's heart gave a hollow thump, and she buried her face in the pillow. Something was hovering. She could sense it ready to hammer down on her if she acknowledged it.

Maybe if she let herself drift off again, she could pretend for a few more minutes, a few more hours, that everything was still right in her world.

But it was too late. Her chest compressed. Her throat grew tight. There was no escaping the memory of what had happened—what she'd seen. No escaping that the one person she'd relied on since she was a teenager had betrayed her in the worst possible way. Cassie curled herself into a ball and tugged the soft blanket over her shoulders with shaking hands. But a sudden realization distracted her from breaking down again.

This wasn't Blacklite's bus. And she had no recollection of leaving and finding another bunk to crash in the night before. She might have been exhausted, but not enough to stay asleep while being carried off the bus and through the cool night air to another one. Which meant...

Cassie groaned quietly to herself. Which meant she must still be on Fractured's bus.

In one of their bunks.

Her cheeks flared hot, and she had to fight the renewed urge to pull the blanket over her head and pretend the world didn't exist. But pretending had never worked for her when she was a child; it wouldn't work now. The bus was still moving, so they hadn't arrived in Denver yet. Which meant she couldn't make a rapid exit.

There was only one thing to do. Get up, deal with the awkwardness, and graciously thank Zac and the other members of Fractured for letting her stay the night. The sound of muffled voices came from the living room, so at least a couple of people were awake.

Cassie sat up in the surprisingly spacious bunk and did her best to comb her fingers through her long hair. She still wore yesterday's clothes—a pair of jeans and a tank top. Not the most comfortable thing to sleep in, but not the worst either. And at least no one had tried to undress her. It was bad enough thinking that one of the band members had carried her to bed. Had it been Zac? The thought made her cringe with embarrassment.

She took a deep breath, pulled the privacy curtain open, and climbed out. She spent a couple of seconds straightening her clothes, then made her way down the short corridor.

The first person she saw was Zac. He sat on one of the couches, looking at his phone, his long, muscular, denim-clad legs extended out in front of him and crossed at the ankles. A vintage AC/DC T-shirt stretched across his broad chest, emphasizing the width of his shoulders and the toned muscles of his arms.

A quick scan of the rest of the area showed her that the only others currently awake were Connor, Fractured's lead singer, and his pretty wife, Lexie.

Zac noticed her first, his hazel eyes rising from the cell phone to meet hers.

The way his jaw tightened made Cassie wonder how bad her face looked after hours of crying last night.

"How are you feeling?" he asked.

Connor and Lexie both turned to look at her, and Cassie's cheeks warmed again. She forced a smile. "I'm okay, thanks. And, um, sorry for falling asleep on your bus. I know I was only supposed to be here until the end of the after-party, but, um..."

"Don't be silly." Lexie stood and walked over to her, a warm expression on her lovely face. "You must have been exhausted. And there was no way we'd kick you out without somewhere else to go."

Zac must have filled everyone in on what had happened

with Bryan. How else would he explain what she was doing on their bus? Cassie darted a look at him. He was leaning back, watching her, his brows drawn together. Her pulse sped up. She couldn't quite read his expression, so she gave him another little smile, hoping it conveyed her gratitude. He gave her a nod of acknowledgment.

"Would you like some breakfast?" Lexie put her arm around Cassie and led her to the booth-style kitchenette table where she and Connor had been sitting.

"Oh no, that's okay. I can wait until we get to Denver." She sat down opposite Connor, smiling an awkward greeting at him.

"Are you sure? We've got bread for toast and cereal. There's fruit and pastries as well."

Cassie's stomach prodded her, but she really didn't want to impose on them any more than she already had.

"Thanks, but I'm fine." Her gaze dropped to the cup in front of Connor as the heavenly scent of coffee reached her. God, what she wouldn't give for some caffeine, though. Her desire must have been obvious because Connor's green eyes creased at the corners as he laughed under his breath.

He called out to Zac. "Hey, man, stop leaving all your hosting duties to Lexie. Can't you see your guest needs a coffee?"

His soft Irish lilt almost lulled Cassie into not realizing what he was saying. When she saw Zac stand out of the corner of her eye, it finally registered. She looked up at him as he passed her on the way to the coffeepot. "Oh, no, honestly. I'm not... you don't have to..."

Zac shook his head, the corners of his lips curling up. "The fame hasn't quite gone to my head enough that I can't pour you a cup of coffee. Especially since you take such good care of my instruments."

Cassie shifted in her seat. What was it about this situation that she found so painfully embarrassing? Was it that everyone knew Bryan had cheated on her with Stella? Or that she was imposing on her very famous boss and his bandmates? Or was it that Connor and Zac were such huge stars, that having their attention focused on her, let alone fussing over who should offer her a cup of coffee, was overwhelming?

Probably all the above.

Zac reached up to the cupboard for a mug, his T-shirt stretching tightly over his shoulders and pulling up at the waist. From this angle, she could see the shadow from the deep V of muscle at his hip. She swallowed and looked away, catching Lexie watching her. Cassie gave the woman a faint smile. She hadn't been checking him out. She was in no state to feel anything like attraction for another man. Not with the pain of Bryan's actions still so excruciatingly fresh. But she had always been able to appreciate how beautiful Zac was, even though she was in love with Bryan. And it was hard not to admire musculature like that when it was right in front of you.

Still, she kept her eyes away from him until he asked her how she took her coffee.

"Just with a touch of creamer," she told him.

The movement of his arms as he poured the creamer and stirred was slightly hypnotic. When he finished, he brought it over and placed it in front of her.

"Thank you," she said, then had to shuffle over when he sat down next to her. She felt small beside him. She knew he was a big guy, of course—she'd been working for him for the last ten days. But she had only fully appreciated exactly how big he was when she'd pressed up behind him yesterday. He'd been like a wall between her and Bryan, and it had made her feel... safe.

Pain pulsed like a live thing behind Cassie's ribs, trying to break free. The need to feel safe from Bryan wasn't something she'd ever experienced before. She inhaled shakily, breathing in the cologne, or whatever it was Zac was wearing. She concentrated on the fresh, crisp scent that made her think of cool ocean breezes. Focusing on how good Zac smelled instead of thinking about Bryan helped her wrestle her emotions under control.

"Have you thought about what you're going to do?" Lexie's question brought Cassie's attention back from where it had wandered. "Do you know if you're going to stay on the tour?" the other woman clarified.

Anxiety flashed through Cassie as the reality of her situation hit her. How could she possibly stay and work around Bryan and Stella for the next two and a half months?

But what else could she do? She'd signed an employment contract when she joined the tour. She could get out of it, of course, but leaving wouldn't do any good for her credibility. It would be one thing if it were for health issues or a family emergency. Leaving because her fiancé had cheated on her was another. The industry was male-dominated and uncompromising. It wouldn't accept heartbreak as a valid excuse for departing mid-tour. Word would get out. Having the bad rep of someone who let her emotions impact her work would affect her ability to get another job. After all, the only reason she'd gotten this opportunity was through word of mouth. And she'd need another job quickly if she was going to have to move out of the apartment she and Bryan rented in Las Vegas.

The terrifying finality of that thought had her anxiety

growing until it was a ball in her throat she couldn't swallow past.

Cassie turned her head, her eyes meeting Zac's green-gold ones. The crease was back between his brows. "We don't want to lose you," he said. "But obviously, we'll understand if you think you need to go. Don't feel you have to decide right this second, though. There are still a couple of hours before we get to the next venue."

Cassie let out a shaky breath and gave him a small, grateful smile before taking a sip of her coffee.

What the hell was she going to do?

Chapter Five

Zac stepped off the bus, the cool, high altitude air bracing after the air-conditioned stuffiness they'd been traveling in overnight. The piercing screams started up immediately, coming from a group of die-hard fans pressed against the railings of the fence—the only barrier between them and the band.

Cassie came down the steps behind him, looking slightly rumpled but disconcertingly sexy in the T-shirt and denim cut-offs Lexie had loaned her. She brushed her long, dark hair back from her face, her eyes widening as she took in the mass of gathered fans. A few of them were holding up homemade signs declaring their undying love or proposing marriage. Pretty standard stuff.

Her gaze met his, and she came closer. "So, thank you again for, um..." She waved her hand in the bus's direction.

"It was no problem. Have you figured out what you want to do?" He didn't like seeing the way the brightness faded from her face at his question.

"I'm going to see if there's a spare bunk I can use on one of the other sleeper buses. At least until I can make a final decision. And I have to get my stuff off Blacklite's bus." Her throat worked. "God, this is all just"—she raised her hands and pressed the heels of her palms into her eyes, then took a deep breath before meeting his gaze again—"shit. This is shit." Her sad laugh tugged at his chest. He wished he could ease her pain. But apart from offering to punch Bryan in the face, there wasn't much he could do for her.

"Don't worry about getting your stuff. When you've found a spot, we can get one of our security team to grab it for you. No big deal."

Her bottom lip trembled, and she tentatively placed a small hand on his forearm. "I can't thank you enough. You really didn't have to do any of this."

Zac shrugged, doing his best to ignore the warmth of her fingers against his skin. "I'd be an asshole if I left you having to deal with it on your own."

Lexie walked over, her camera hanging around her neck. "I'm happy to keep you company this morning, Cassie."

"You don't have to do that." The relief on Cassie's face belied her words. The woman was hopeless at hiding her feelings.

"It'll give me a chance to take some photos of the load-in, anyway. The fans love seeing all the behind-the-scenes stuff."

"Okay, then. Thank you."

Cassie looked back at Zac, her lingering smile fading. The shrieks from the fans were getting louder as Connor, Tex, and Noah made their way toward the fence to sign autographs. "I'd better let you go," she said.

For a second, she looked almost bereft, vast loneliness darkening her eyes. He couldn't imagine what it would be like, stuck on this huge tour, suddenly cut loose, and left to

Fractured Kiss

drift without an anchor. He had a strange urge to reach out and touch her, reassure her she wasn't alone. But he didn't. Because the last thing she needed was false promises of comfort from someone like him. And he did have to go; he could hear some of the fans yelling his name. Duty called.

"When you've sorted somewhere to sleep, just grab one of us or one of the security guys if we're not around."

"Thank you, Zac."

He gave her a nod, then headed for the surging mob of people, their hands thrust through the railings clutching merchandise to be signed. As he reached them, some of the fans transferred their attention from his bandmates to him.

"Zac! Zac! Can you sign my shirt?"

"Zac! Will you marry me?"

"Zac! I love you!"

"Who's the girl, Zac?" That was from one of the paparazzi loitering about behind the crowd, obviously with nothing better to do in Denver on a Friday morning than ask stupid questions. Zac ignored him and smiled at a woman reaching through the fence, holding out a shirt with his face on it.

Tex looked over his shoulder and gave him a big, shit-eating grin. "Dragged yourself away, did you?"

"What are you talking about?" Zac signed his name on the shirt and handed it back to the fan. As he did, she reached through the bars of the fence and grabbed his bicep, her fingers gripping so hard, he wouldn't be surprised if she left marks. He kept the smile on his face but reached up and took her hand, squeezing it, then letting go and stepping away.

"You know, Cassie, your pretty guitar tech. The one you just spent the last five minutes talking to instead of being over here signing autographs for your loyal fans."

Zac rolled his eyes. "Really, man? She works for me. Even if she didn't, she had her heart ripped out yesterday. Do you actually think I was trying to hook up with her?"

"Why not? A bit of revenge fucking never hurt anyone."

He had a vision of Cassie, naked, skin slick with sweat as she arched up beneath him. His dick pulsed, but he shoved the image aside. "I think being with Eden has dulled your brain."

"Nah, dude. I saw the way you looked at her."

"You mean like an employee who needs help?"

Tex paused while a fan pressed their face up to the fence and stuck their camera through to take a photo with him. He turned his attention back to Zac. "I distinctly remember *you* telling *me* that the best way to get over someone was to get under someone else."

Involuntarily, the corner of Zac's mouth kicked up. "That's because you were being an idiot."

Tex laughed. "And your point is?"

Noah butted in. "I don't see the problem here. You're single, she's single. You both get off, and she gets to give Bryan a big fuck you."

The thought of taking Cassie to bed and helping her screw Bryan out of her system was a little too appealing. Too appealing to be anything but a terrible idea. He had to remind himself she wasn't his type. Okay, so she was beautiful and hurting, and maybe in another situation, he might just be tempted to break his rule about sleeping with women like her—ones who were after the happily ever after. But they were stuck on tour together for another few months, *with* her ex-fiancé. And at this stage, the ex part wasn't even definite. Cassie still wore her engagement ring, for fuck's sake. The whole thing screamed complicated.

And he didn't do complicated.

That was even truer now, with everything he had on his plate. So, proving to Cassie that she was better off without Bryan would have to be some other man's job. After today, they'd go back to having a strictly working relationship. And only if she didn't end up quitting the tour.

The thought made him frown. Cassie was good at what she did. She didn't deserve to be driven away from her job because her asshole ex couldn't keep his dick in his pants.

Zac looked over his shoulder. Cassie and Lexie were walking toward where the road crew was unloading equipment and pieces of the set from the fleet of trucks parked on the other side of the lot. He was glad Lexie had gone with her. The last thing she needed was to be alone right now.

His gaze fell to the sway of her hips as she walked, and he looked away.

Way too fucking complicated.

Chapter Six

Cassie walked across the parking lot next to Lexie. It was strangely comforting having the woman by her side, even though they'd barely had a chance to have a full conversation before this morning.

"Where to?" Lexie asked.

"I need to find Charlie," she named the tour's production manager, "and ask him if there's an empty bunk on one of the sleeper buses I can use."

"What will you do if there aren't any?"

Cassie exhaled shakily. "I don't know. There's no way I can go back on Blacklite's bus. I think I'll have to end my contract and deal with the consequences. At least it'll give me time to organize somewhere else to live while Bryan's still away."

Lexie frowned. "It doesn't seem fair that he screwed up, and you're the one who has to pay."

"No, it doesn't." Cassie flashed her a pained smile.

Lexie pressed her lips together but said nothing. She raised her camera and snapped a photo of some of the crew unloading massive pieces of stage set.

Fractured Kiss

Cassie finally spotted Charlie. He was overseeing the movement of cases of audio equipment into the venue. Nerves fluttered in her stomach as he noticed them. He held his radio up to his lips, spoke something into it, then walked over.

"Cassie, Lexie. Can I help you with something?"

"I hope so," Cassie said. "I was wondering if there might be a spare bunk on one of the buses."

He eyed her. "Why are you asking?"

She did her best not to let the rawness of her wounds show. "Um, Bryan and I... well, uh... we've..."

Charlie grunted. "I can't move people around just because you and your fiancé had an argument."

"No, it's more than that." She drew in a steadying breath. "We're not together anymore, and I can't stay on there. I can't—"

Charlie cursed under his breath. "This is why I don't like having couples on tour together."

Cassie frowned. Lexie was listening to Charlie with a little crease between her brows.

With a long-suffering sigh, he pulled out his phone and tapped on it a few times. He scratched his chin. "According to the crew manifest, the sleeper buses are full."

Cassie's stomach dropped. *Shit*.

"You can blame your fiancé and his band for that. They wanted to *go big or go home*." She thought she saw his upper lip curl as he made air quotes with his fingers. "So, now we have extra pyrotechnicians and lighting techs on board."

A knot of worry was rapidly forming in Cassie's chest, but Charlie continued. "Look. There's a small chance I might be able to find you a bunk. It's not unusual on tours like this that people hook up." She tried not to flinch at how painfully accurate his words were. "Someone might not be using their own bed. I can ask around, see if anyone's willing to give theirs up."

The knot behind her ribs loosened a little. It certainly wasn't outside the realm of possibility. "Thank you so much. That would be amazing."

He nodded. "But just so you know, it's a long shot. Most people aren't willing to make a bet that a casual hook-up is going to last the whole tour, so they probably won't want to lose their bunk permanently. You'll have to consider an alternative plan." He raised his brows. "Or get over whatever it was Bryan did. Or you did. Whatever. One of you just apologize and move on."

Indignation stole Cassie's voice. The only person who needed to apologize was Bryan. And getting over what had happened wasn't possible. Not right now, anyway. Maybe never. What she'd seen yesterday had forever changed her belief in who Bryan was. In a few seconds, he went from the hero of her story to the villain. All the promises he'd made, all the whispered declarations of love, asking her to spend forever with him, it was all meaningless. All her imaginings of a future with him now seemed like the silly daydreams of a lonely little girl, desperate for someone to love her.

"Thanks Charlie," Lexie said when she saw Cassie struggling to respond. "We'll try to figure something out in case you don't have any luck."

Charlie only grunted, gave a nod and strode off.

Lexie's smile was sympathetic. "Let's get you some breakfast and have a chat. I might have a solution for you."

Before Cassie could ask what it was, Lexie started toward the catering truck parked at the far end of the lot. Sighing, Cassie followed her.

The catering truck was huge. It had to be to service over one hundred crew members supporting the tour. And the food was first-rate. Though they were surrounded by loud yells, the clang of metal against metal, and the rumble of trucks moving around, it was still pleasant being outside in the sunlight.

Cassie ordered a breakfast burrito and an orange juice, while Lexie, having already eaten on the bus, just grabbed a smoothie. They sat down at a table farthest from the noise.

"Do you really have a solution?" Cassie asked.

Lexie nodded. "I was wondering..." She paused and studied Cassie.

Cassie had picked up her burrito but stopped just short of taking a bite. "What?"

"If Charlie can't find you a spare bunk, would you consider using the extra one on our bus for the rest of the tour?"

Cassie's brows rose, and she put her food down on her plate. "I can't stay on Fractured's bus."

"Why not? Because you'd rather just leave and be done with it, or because you're worried about imposing?"

"I don't *want* to leave. As much as I hate the thought of having to see Stella and Bryan every day for the next few months, quitting isn't a great option for me career-wise. I hate the thought of my personal issues causing a problem, and obviously if I leave, they'll have to organize a replacement tech for Zac. But I—"

A sudden thought occurred to her, and her stomach did a sickening swoop. "Oh, shit." She looked at Lexie with wide eyes. "If there's nowhere for me to sleep, there won't be anywhere for a replacement, either. I can't leave Zac in the lurch like that."

"Don't worry about Zac," Lexie reassured her. "There's no way anyone's going to risk him being left without a tech.

If you go and they need to fill your position, Charlie will just have to hire another sleeper bus."

Cassie felt sick. Hiring another bus and a driver, not to mention all the logistics that went along with that, just for one person, would cost a fortune. There was no way she'd ever be hired again if she was responsible for that.

Lexie sat back in her chair. "Look. I know staying and having to face Bryan and Stella every day will be hard. I completely get it. But sometimes the hardest things to do are the ones most worth doing. Your career and reputation in the industry are important. Don't let someone else's selfish choices ruin that for you. You need a bunk. We have a spare one. Why not use it?"

"Because... because the band won't want to have a random woman staying with them for the next couple of months."

Lexie smiled. "I was once the random woman staying on their bus. It didn't turn out too badly."

Cassie choked out a laugh. "I don't think it would end up working out quite the same for me."

Lexie's expression turned serious. "But you'll still have your job, you'll still have your reputation, Zac will still have you as his bass tech. And Bryan won't have screwed you over any more than he already has."

Cassie looked down at her plate. Lexie was right. As awful as the whole situation was, her staying was the best thing for the tour, and for her. She might not want to be a guitar tech forever, but until she figured out what she did want to do—or even what she *could* do—it was her job. One she was good at. Staying made the most sense. She also wasn't quite prepared to pack up and leave the tour, find a new apartment to live in—and potentially a new career if

Fractured Kiss

her leaving pissed people off—and start a new life all by herself. She wasn't ready for that.

She wasn't ready to be adrift and alone again.

A memory surfaced, catching her by surprise.

The hot sun beat down on her head. Her mouth was dry, but her sweaty hands left damp marks on her notebook as she wrote and wrote just to pass the time. A boy said hello from behind her and she turned...

Cassie's breath shuddered out of her, and she quickly took a sip of her drink. She would have to figure out her life after this tour ended, but right now, she wanted to keep this job. Bryan wasn't in her corner anymore. There was no one in her corner now, except her. And if she had to suck up her pride and accept help from Fractured, then that's what she'd do.

She swallowed, then looked back up at Lexie. "Are you sure me staying on the bus will be okay?"

Lexie smiled. "I'm pretty sure the guys won't have a problem with it."

"Can you... can you ask them? I don't want to get my hopes up and have them absolutely hate the idea."

"I'll ask them when they get back from their interview this morning. That way, at least you'll know you have the option if Charlie isn't able to find you anything."

Cassie hated the thought of begging her boss to take her in like a stray dog. Even if that's how she'd felt so often before. Desperate for someone to care about her enough to want to keep her.

She forced a smile. "Thank you, Lexie."

Lexie smiled back, but Cassie leaned over the table and put her hand over the other woman's. "I mean that sincerely. I don't... I haven't had many people..." She swallowed. "*Friends.*" It wasn't easy for her to admit that to someone she'd only just met. But something about Lexie made her want to be honest. "Thank you for helping me."

Sadness filled Lexie's eyes, and she clasped Cassie's hand. "I know what it's like to feel lost and alone, Cassie. Just know that it won't always be that way. I'd like to be your friend. And one day, you'll find someone who'll be there for you. Always."

Cassie's throat tightened. "Thank you," she whispered.

Lexie squeezed her hand, then let it go. Cassie finished her breakfast, and they made their way back toward Fractured's bus and the venue. Cassie could see Fractured's gear being unloaded and wheeled into the arena, so it was time for her to head in and start checking over the instruments and equipment. At least that would hopefully keep her mind off the horrible situation she'd somehow found herself in.

Before they parted ways, Lexie surprised Cassie by giving her a hug. "How about I track you down later. Maybe we can grab lunch together?" she said.

A lump formed in Cassie's throat, and she blinked back grateful tears. "I'd like that. Thank you."

If Lexie noticed Cassie's overly emotional response to her offer, she was gracious enough not to show it. "Great! It's always nice to have some female company on tour. Apart from when Summer and Eden fly in to spend time with Noah and Tex, I'm usually overwhelmed by the testosterone on the bus."

Cassie's laugh was choked but genuine. "I'm sure there are more than a few women who would happily trade places with you." Her eyes widened, and she slapped a hand over her mouth. "I'm sorry. I probably shouldn't say that."

Lexie laughed. "It's the truth, though. I'm very lucky." Her voice was soft and full of affection.

Longing pulsed through Cassie. Longing for the time before yesterday when she'd felt lucky like that. Lucky to have found something special—to have found the one. But apparently, she'd been wrong. Bryan wasn't the one. Or perhaps he was, and this was just how the world worked. Perhaps she was naïve to think that when you meet the love of your life, he sweeps you up and carries you away from all your problems, and you live happily ever after. Maybe she'd been stupid to believe there was such a thing as a knight in shining armor.

With a wave, Lexie walked off and Cassie made her way into the venue, dodging the crew members lugging cases of equipment.

She dreaded seeing Bryan and Stella, but there was no way to avoid them if they were around when she was doing her checks. She'd had a reprieve last night thanks to Zac, but that wouldn't last. Probably sooner rather than later, she was going to see the two of them together. Talking, laughing, touching….

Cassie jerked to a halt, all the oxygen in her lungs leaving in a rush. The mass of people that normally comforted her was suddenly making it hard to breathe. She needed to get away for a minute. To be on her own. Turning, she slipped down a corridor and pressed herself into an alcove. It wasn't much, but she was away from the manic rush of load-in. A moment of solitude before she had to take her broken heart and battered pride out there for everyone to see.

Cassie let her head drop back against the wall. It's funny how things change. She'd always hated being alone. But it had been a long time since she'd truly felt that way.

Not since Bryan had found her—since he'd saved her. But this time, Bryan hadn't been the person saving her. He was the one she needed to be saved from.

It was Zac who had saved her this time.

His intense hazel eyes flashed through her mind. Even though she'd worked with him every night for the last week and a half, their actual one-on-one contact had been relatively limited. She'd never expected him, and the rest of Fractured, to be so down to earth. She didn't know what she'd expected, really. For them to be full of themselves or fucked-up on drugs and alcohol like so many of the super successful bands seemed to be.

But they weren't like that. Not at all.

And Lexie was lovely too.

A tentative smile trembled on Cassie's lips. Making friends had never been something that came easily to her. It was hard when you were considered an outcast just by association. Being judged before you even had a chance to talk to someone made it difficult to make a good first impression. After a while, she'd given up trying. But things were different after Bryan came into her life. He saw something special in her, and that was enough to convince others she was worth something after all.

A tear slid down her cheek, and she closed her eyes.

She hadn't been worth his fidelity, though.

Cassie brushed the tear aside. Enough. She had a job to do, at least for now, and she didn't want Bryan or Stella—particularly Stella—to see her cry.

Cassie gave herself one more minute to push the hurt down as far as it would go. She wished she had her notebook, but it was on Bryan's bus. There was no way she was going to risk going to get it. She'd have to do without it until she hopefully found somewhere to sleep and could move her stuff.

Straightening, she took a deep breath, stepped out of the alcove, and walked back into the hive of activity with her head held high.

Chapter Seven

"We're so excited to have you here today, guys!"

Zac pasted a friendly smile on his face. He swore radio show hosts were getting younger every year. The two sitting across the studio's audio console from him and his bandmates looked like they were barely in their twenties.

Or was it just because he was getting older? He was almost thirty-one now. After thirteen years in the industry, it was more and more exhausting trying to match their level of enthusiasm during on-air interviews.

"We're excited to be here." Tex gave the expected response.

Not that Zac didn't appreciate the fact that their fans were still interested in hearing what they had to say after all this time. But after so many interviews, all the questions seemed to blend into each other. Which was probably why there was an increasing focus on the band members' relationships—or lack of them—than their music.

At least this one seemed to start the right way.

"So, a sold-out arena tour. You guys must be pleased," said the bouncy blonde sitting opposite Zac, who'd introduced herself as Amy.

"We're happy that we'll be able to give as many fans as possible a chance to come and see us play," Connor answered. "We know a lot of people have missed out over the last couple of years, during our hiatus, and then with some of the smaller tours we've been doing."

Amy nodded. "Right. That was a conscious decision you came to as a band, wasn't it? To focus more on intimate performances?"

Connor nodded. "We've been in the business a long time. Touring year after year can be exhausting after a while. Going on hiatus allowed us to refresh ourselves as a band, spend some decent time with our loved ones, and come back with a whole new passion for what we do. And one of the things we wanted to do was show a more personal side of us. Doing those smaller tours allowed us to share that with our fans."

"So why are you going back to bigger shows now? An arena tour this time. Will you be expanding back up to stadium tours next?" Michael, the dark-haired male host, asked.

"The energy you get from a big venue concert is incredible. It's something we obviously enjoy. The albums we released coming off hiatus were personal. They were intimate. They suited those smaller venues. This latest one throws back a little more to our earlier stuff. It suits a bigger venue. We certainly won't rule out stadium tours again in the future, but we'll let the direction of our albums dictate what we do going forward."

The hosts nodded, then Amy turned her attention to

Zac. "Zac, as arguably the busiest member of the group, how are you finding being back on a national arena tour?"

"It's great. Whatever venue we're in, the love from the fans is the same. Connor's right, the music should dictate where we perform, but the upside of getting back into arenas and eventually stadiums is that more of our fans get the opportunity to attend. Giving back to the fans will always be a priority for us."

She smiled benignly before hitting him with the question he'd been dreading. "And how are you feeling after Fractured's win at the AMAs last month? Particularly since your other band, Crossfire, missed out on an award?"

Zac didn't allow his expression to change. "Obviously, I was disappointed for my Crossfire bandmates that they missed out. We've worked hard, and we're incredibly proud of the albums we've produced. Being nominated is always a win. But the fans vote for the AMAs, and Fractured's been around a long time. We've been lucky enough to attract a lot of very loyal followers. Having proof that we're still making music they love is fantastic. And I'm sure if Crossfire keeps going, we'll all be standing up on that stage one day too."

Michael jumped in. "So, there's a chance Crossfire won't keep going?" His eyes were bright, as if he thought he was getting a scoop on the air.

Zac shrugged. "As much chance as any group has of disbanding. But we certainly don't plan on going anywhere. We've got our European tour coming up and another album in the works. We'll be around for a while."

The host looked disappointed, which sent a spike of irritation through Zac.

Amy reverted to her earlier line of questioning. "Do you feel like Crossfire's success rests on your shoulders because you're the front man? Does it make losing more personal?"

Fractured Kiss

Zac's pulse kicked into high gear. He stopped his hand halfway up to the leather cord hanging around his neck. *Right place, right time.* The words echoed in his head.

He leveled a look at her, and the smile on her face withered slightly. "No," he forced out through gritted teeth.

She continued to wait expectantly. With the base of his skull pounding, he continued. "I try not to take anything personally. Crossfire is a group effort, just like Fractured. We all have equal responsibility. We all contribute to the music and any major decisions. And at the end of the day, winning awards isn't what's important. Making music that we love—that our fans enjoy—that's our priority. Not collecting statuettes to put on our mantelpieces."

She nodded, her eyes narrowed and probing as if she was trying to detect the lie in his words. Unfortunately for her, he'd spent years perfecting his poker face.

Apparently satisfied, she directed her next question to Noah, asking about his recent engagement. As always, the drummer was more than happy to talk about his relationship with Summer. Zac tuned out. There was only so much gushing about love he could take. Since all three of his bandmates had partnered up over the last few years, he was used to thinking about other things when they went on about it.

His mind drifted to Cassie, all the talk about relationships making him think about how spectacularly hers had just fallen apart. He wondered if she'd made a decision about staying. He hoped she didn't end up leaving, because while he could understand why it would be hard for her, he liked having her as his guitar tech. As much as it had disappointed him when Duncan, his previous tech, pulled out of the tour, having Cassie take his place had been a very pleasant surprise. He couldn't guarantee it would be the same with a replacement.

He was brought back to the interview when Amy said his name. "So, Zac, what's it like to be the last man standing now that the other guys are all coupled up?" He'd been asked variations of the same question for the last year, ever since Noah and Summer had started officially dating. It was getting old. Actually, it had been old the first time someone had asked him.

"I'm okay with it. As you said before, things are busy for me at the moment, and it's not really fair to try to maintain a relationship when my focus is on the music. Maybe sometime in the future, I might have time to meet someone." His stock answer rolled off his tongue.

"You're notoriously private about your dating life," she persisted. "Are you sure you're not keeping some lucky lady tucked away?"

Noah jumped in before Zac could reply. "Actually, Zac had a female guest on the bus just last night."

Zac slitted his eyes at the drummer, who gave him a smirk in response.

"Really? Wow, lucky girl," Amy said with an avaricious expression. "So, there's definitely still hope for all the Zac Ford fans out there."

"Absolutely." Tex joined in. "But ladies," he drawled, "you never know when some lucky woman will snap up this prime example of manhood, so if you want a chance to ride the Zac express before that happens"—Connor snorted a laugh—"then you need to put the effort in. Be aggressive. Don't let his surly demeanor put you off. If he tells you to stop touching him, he's just being shy. Double down and go for the full-frontal grope. It's the quickest way to his heart." Tex shot a broad grin at Zac.

The others were laughing hard, including the two hosts. Zac shook his head, but he couldn't stop his own smile at their antics. "Quickest way, huh? I knew you weren't listening in biology class. It does explain why you shove your hand down your pants every time you tell Eden you love her, though." For all that they were now in their thirties, one of them married, one of them soon-to-be, sometimes he was vividly reminded of the teenage boys they'd all been when they met.

"Well, there's *something* trying to beat its way through my fly when I'm talking to her," Tex said. "But I can guarantee you it's not my—"

"Okay, okay, guys. Don't forget this is a family-friendly show," Michael interrupted with a chuckle. "It's good to see your friendship has survived all these years. How do you keep it going traveling on the road together for months at a time?"

The rest of the interview passed quickly. In the downtime between questions directed at him, his mind wandered to the songs he—*Crossfire*—had to write, to the logistics of getting it done with the tight schedule he had over the next few months, to Cassie again and what she was doing at this moment, if Bryan had cornered her yet. If he'd groveled.

Zac rolled his neck to ease the tension from it.

"Thanks for hanging out with us this morning, guys."

Zac blinked at Amy's words and stood, realizing the interview was over. He could only assume he hadn't missed any questions aimed his way. He thanked the hosts and followed the others out of the studio.

"What was up your ass at the end?" Connor asked as he fell in beside him.

Zac shot him a look. "What do you mean?"

"You looked like you wanted to strangle someone."

He'd been thinking about Cassie. About whether Bryan had found her. "Just thinking about a tough song the guys and I are working on," he lied.

Connor frowned. "You know if you get stuck, we're more than happy to help."

"Thanks, but we've got it."

Connor put a hand on his shoulder and stopped, forcing him to stop too. "You're putting a lot of pressure on yourself and the rest of Crossfire. You don't have to do everything on your own, you know."

"I appreciate that, man. I really do. But I've got it. *We've* got it."

Connor looked at him searchingly, then he nodded and dropped his hand, continuing out of the building. Zac rubbed the back of his neck before following him.

Twenty minutes later, the car pulled up next to where their bus was parked outside the arena. When he entered the living room, the first thing he did was scan it. He wasn't even sure what he was looking for. Or *who* he was looking for. What he found was Lexie sitting at the table, fiddling with her camera.

Her gaze immediately went to Connor, a beautiful smile making her pretty face glow. Connor headed straight for her, cupping her cheek and dropping a soft kiss on her lips. A pang of some unfamiliar emotion tunneled through Zac's chest at the sight of them.

He shook the feeling off and headed to the kitchenette to make himself a coffee. With his steaming mug, he settled at the table across from Lexie.

She smiled at him. "How was the interview?"

"Same old, same old."

She nodded and went back to pressing buttons on her

camera. The silence stretched on. Zac took a sip of his coffee and gazed out the window.

Without looking up, Lexie spoke. "Just in case you're curious, it's not looking good for Cassie. She's not likely to find a bunk."

He noticed the slightest upturn of her lips. "Doesn't seem like something you should smile about."

"Well..." This time she looked at him. "I was thinking, if you guys are okay with it, that she could stay with us."

He put his cup down and studied her.

"I mean, we've got the spare bunk. It would be a shame for it to go to waste when there's someone who needs it."

"She works for me. It'd be weird for her."

"She'd get used to it."

He drummed his fingers on the tabletop. He didn't know why he was hesitating. Lexie was right. It'd be a shame if Cassie had to leave when they had a perfectly good bunk available. Connor's old one was just going to waste, with him and Lexie sharing the small bedroom at the back of the bus. And the thought of Cassie having to leave her job because of Bryan pissed him off.

"Yeah, okay, makes sense," he said, trying to ignore his unease over the thought of being stuck in close proximity to Cassie for the next few months.

Lexie beamed. "Good, because I've already spoken to her about it. I'll check with the others, then let her know that if Charlie can't find something, she can move in with us."

Zac grunted in reply and turned to look out the window again, suddenly wishing there was any other solution to Cassie's problem than the one he'd just agreed to.

Chapter Eight

Cassie sat on an equipment case behind one of the big amps at the side of the stage. She'd fallen into her normal routine of checking and tuning all of Zac's gear. The tightness in her back and shoulders had loosened as she made sure everything was working as well as it had been when she'd packed it away the night before. She was so absorbed in her task she jumped when Bryan's voice cut through the air from behind her.

"Where the hell were you last night?"

Cassie's hands tightened around the bass she was holding. She schooled her expression and twisted around to look up at him, her lungs deflating at the concern on his face. The hurt and anger that stabbed through her at seeing him warred with an urge to throw herself into his arms. To pretend yesterday had never happened and just go back to the way things were. To when she felt safe and loved.

Before she could give in to the impulse, a vision of him and Stella flashed through her mind, and the urge shriveled up and died.

Fractured Kiss

Cassie looked back down at the instrument and ran her fingers over the thick strings. "I was on Fractured's bus."

He let out a growl and her gaze jerked up to meet his. "Where did you sleep?" The anger in his voice confused her until she understood he thought she might have been sharing someone's bunk. The hypocrisy infuriated her.

She lifted her chin. "None of your damn business."

Bryan huffed, his face reddening. Then his shoulders sagged. "Damn it, Cassie. I was worried about you when you didn't come back last night."

She narrowed her eyes at him. "Did you honestly expect that I would willingly spend the night on a bus with you and"—Stella's name caught in her throat—"and *her*?"

"No, I—" He blew out a breath. "I just wish you'd let me know you were okay, that's all."

"I didn't think you'd care. After all, it just gave you two more time to screw."

"Fuck, Cassie." He speared his hand through his hair. "I don't want Stella. I promise. It was just a crazy one-time thing. A mistake. My head's been all over the place lately, but I love you. So damn much. *Too* much. I messed up, but we can get through this. I know we can. You and I are meant to be together."

Her throat grew thick and hot, and she blinked back tears. That's what she'd always believed—that it had been fate that brought him to her on that long ago afternoon. She stared up at him, her gaze tracing the familiar contours of his face. Was it really possible that it was just a one-off? That it would never happen again? If she forgave him, would this all be forgotten one day? Bryan had always been there for her. No one else ever had. Was it wrong of her to not even consider giving him a second chance?

Cassie bit her lip. Bryan read her uncertainty and sat

down next to her on the case, his denim-clad thigh pressing against hers. She breathed in the woodsy scent of his cologne and wavered further, her body instinctively listing toward his.

"Bryan!" Stella's husky voice cut through the bubble that surrounded them. Cassie jerked upright. What the hell was she doing? Was she really that weak-willed?

"Bryan." Stella's voice was louder now. "Get over here. I need you to check the levels on your mic."

"Dammit." Bryan stood but didn't move away.

Still angry at herself for almost falling back into his arms, Cassie couldn't meet his gaze.

"We can fix this, baby. I know we can." His voice throbbed with sincerity.

"Bryan!" Stella appeared around the corner, her eyes going straight to Cassie.

Cassie stiffened her spine and raised her chin, wanting to appear unaffected, even though unaffected was the last thing she felt right now. The red-haired singer's expression tightened as she looked her over, then seemed to dismiss her, shifting her attention to Bryan.

"Bryan, did you hear me? I need you to come test your mic levels."

Bryan kept his gaze on Cassie. "Just remember that I love you. We can talk more later."

Cassie didn't respond, and Bryan sighed, ran his hand through his hair again, then headed toward Stella.

She watched them go. Stella moved closer to Bryan, so close their arms brushed together as they walked. Cassie's chest tightened painfully. It was no use. She'd never be able to forget what had happened. Never be able to wipe the vision of the two of them naked together from her mind.

Particularly knowing they'd be spending countless days and nights with each other for the foreseeable future.

She had to let go.

Of Bryan.

Of everything he'd meant to her.

Of her dream of them being together forever.

She wrapped her arms around Zac's bass and pressed it against her aching chest.

She just needed to figure out how.

Chapter Nine

Zac made his way backstage. They'd just finished meeting with the venue management, and the others were heading to the bus for a break before they had to come back in for sound check. He should be with them. Instead, he found himself winding his way through the crew members busily setting up, keeping a lookout for long, dark hair.

He just wanted to check on her, make sure she was doing okay. See whether Charlie had got back to her yet.

He spotted Bryan first, and his fingers curled into fists when he saw Cassie staring up at him, her face pale. Her hands were tightly clenched around Zac's bass, and the line of her spine was taut. He watched as Bryan walked away to join Stella. The asshole's eyes narrowed on Zac when he noticed him.

Zac ignored him. He grabbed a second equipment case and dragged it over next to the one Cassie was sitting on. She must have been deep in thought because it was only when he dropped onto it that her head jerked around.

A hand flew to her throat. "You startled me."

Fractured Kiss

"Sorry. Just wanted to check on you and make sure you're doing okay."

He studied her face. Her eyes were tinged with red and slightly swollen, but it didn't seem as if she'd been crying recently.

He nodded at the bass she was holding. "It's still in one piece."

She looked down at the instrument, then back up at him. "Did you think I was going to hit him over the head with it?" Amusement threaded through her voice.

He smiled. "I think you're too professional to smash something so expensive. But I imagine the thought ran through your mind."

Cassie laughed softly, her fingers smoothing over the body of the bass. Zac had a vision of them stroking over his skin the same way, and a shudder rippled down his spine. *Jesus.* It really had been far too long since he'd gotten laid if he was reacting that way to the sight of a pretty woman touching his instrument. He suppressed a grin as he imagined Tex's or Noah's response if he said that to them.

"Have you heard from Charlie yet?" he asked.

A breath puffed out of her. "No, not yet. I'll track him down once I'm finished here and see if he's had any luck. It's not looking good, though."

She darted a nervous look at him, probably wondering if Lexie had already mentioned the idea of her staying with them.

"So, if Charlie can't find you something, you're going to use our spare bunk?" He asked, to let her know Lexie had spoken to him.

She bit her lip. "Only if that's okay."

She looked pretty damn uncomfortable with the idea. That made two of them. But all he said was, "No problem."

"I really appreciate it. Thank you." The smile she gave him was self-conscious. "And you never know. Charlie might still be able to find me something."

Zac just nodded as he watched her put the bass she'd been tuning on the rack, then get another one out of the case. She sat back down with it and went to work, seemingly okay with him sitting there with her.

Rather than leaving her alone to do her job as he should, Zac stayed and listened to her pick out a melody. He cocked his head. The instrument wasn't out of tune, but the tone was slightly dull. Knowing when to change strings while you're on tour is a fine art. New strings were too twangy for his taste, he preferred the more mellow sound after they'd been broken in. But being played every night meant that it only took a week or so before they became too dull. Keeping them in that sweet spot was a constant balancing act. Instead of saying something to Cassie, he waited and wasn't surprised when she came to the same conclusion as him.

"I'll restring it," she said, looking at him to check he was okay with the decision.

He nodded and held out his hand to take it from her so she could grab the spare strings.

While she was doing that, he played a few lines of a song he'd been working on for the album, modifying it to adjust for playing it on a bass instead of a six-string.

He glanced up when he realized Cassie was standing next to him.

"That's lovely," she said, with a soft smile.

He handed the instrument back to her. "Thanks. It's a work in progress."

She sat down and quickly restrung the bass, her hands moving gracefully as she did.

"Did you always want to be a guitar tech?" he asked.

Backline crew were predominantly men, although as with most things, that was slowly changing for the better.

She kept her focus on what she was doing as she answered. "It made the most sense when we were deciding what I should do after high school."

When *we* were deciding? "In what way?" he asked.

"By the time we graduated, Bryan knew he was going to make a go of being a musician. He thought if I was a guitar tech, it meant we could work and travel together." Her voice wobbled on the last word, but she kept going. "So, I went to vocational college and did an Associate Degree in guitar repair and worked part time in a guitar shop while I studied. I teched for Bryan at night when he played, and then when he joined Blacklite, I started looking after Toby's bass as well."

"Didn't you ever want to be a musician yourself?"

She looked at him then, a pretty smile on her lips. "Not really. I mean, I love music, I love the industry, but I'm not really an *in-the-spotlight* kind of person. I prefer being behind the scenes."

"But you obviously learned to play."

"Not incredibly well. Definitely nowhere near as well as Bryan. Enough so I can play along for fun and do this job." She gestured to the rack of bass guitars. "Not well enough to play professionally."

"So, what I'm hearing is that you chose a career that supported Bryan's dream." His voice came out sharper than intended, and her eyes widened. Annoyed at himself, he softened his tone. "What was your dream? What *is* your dream?"

Cassie's fingers paused on the tuning pegs. He wasn't sure why he was asking her all these questions. Maybe to distract her. Or himself.

She was quiet for so long, he thought she wouldn't answer him. But then she sighed. "It sounds terrible when I say it out loud. But for most of my life, my dream *was* Bryan. Now... Now I don't know what it is."

Irrational anger prickled up his neck. Why would anyone make being with someone else their goal in life? Why would anyone build their life around what someone else needed and think it would make them happy? "Your life should never revolve around one person. They're usually not worth it." She cut her gaze to him, but he met it unflinchingly. "As you found out."

Cassie's head dropped, her dark hair falling down and curtaining her face. "Sometimes there's no one else to revolve around." It was almost a whisper.

"Friends? Family?" Not that he could talk about family. Well, apart from his sister, anyway.

Cassie just shrugged, her face still shielded by her hair. He had a strange desire to reach out and brush those dark waves away, so he could see her expression.

"Are you saying you don't have anyone other than Bryan in your life?"

When she finally looked back at him, it was with a flash of fire in her eyes. It sent a jolt up his spine. "I appreciate you helping me out yesterday and today. But I'm not really up for a game of twenty questions right now."

Amused by the unexpected snap in her voice and the flush in her cheeks, Zac held up his hands. "Sorry."

She stared at him for a second, then licked her lips and let out a deep breath. "No. I'm sorry. I'm just... on edge." She gave him a quick smile. "See, not really an in-the-spotlight type of person."

"Me neither," he said.

She arched her brows and pointedly glanced around the

arena before meeting his gaze again. The corners of her mouth kicked up. "Obviously not."

He could have made a joke about it, but he didn't. "That's different. It's not about sharing myself with people. It's about sharing the music."

She angled her head to the side, considering his words, then nodded. "I get it, I think."

Thankfully, she didn't probe further. She just gave him a smile and went back to what she'd been doing.

The silence stretched out between them. But it wasn't uncomfortable. It was almost peaceful. Zac listened to her play, adjust, then play again. The hustle and noise around them faded, and he rested his elbows on his knees, his head dropping forward. He closed his eyes and let the calm wash over him.

Unfortunately, it only lasted a few minutes before his phone vibrated in the pocket of his jeans. He pulled it out and checked the screen. It was a reminder notification for a phone interview in fifteen minutes. *Rolling Stone* was doing an article on successful side-project bands and wanted to talk to him about Crossfire. He needed to get back to the bus to take the call before sound check.

Still, he sat there for a few more minutes, watching her—her graceful movements, the soft curve of her cheek, the gloss of her hair. He had no interest in having a woman share his life, but if Bryan *was* that kind of person, he was an idiot for trading Cassie in for someone like Stella. Blacklite's lead singer was all attention-seeking surface glitter and no depth. At least, not that she seemed interested in showing anyone, anyway.

Zac checked the time. He needed to go. He looked around and spotted Bryan glaring at him from across the stage. What's the bet the asshole would rush over here again the second Zac left?

A heavy hand landed on his shoulder, and he looked up to see Dan standing next to him. "Thought I might join young Cassie again. We had a nice chat yesterday. Wouldn't mind a bit more company while I work."

Cassie gave the older man a warm smile. "I'd like that."

Zac nodded gratefully at him and received a wink in reply. Dan hadn't questioned Zac when he'd asked him to step in for Cassie last night, but he obviously knew something was up. He must have figured it out since Zac had spent the last twenty minutes loitering by her side. Not to mention Bryan was being anything but subtle as he moved restlessly around the stage, his attention on her.

"Yeah. I've got to get going for an interview," he said. "I'll leave you two to finish up."

Cassie's sapphire-blue eyes caught his as he got off the case to let Dan take his place. He was strangely reluctant to go, but he had a busy afternoon and a late night ahead of him. He needed to get moving. "I'll see you later." Hopefully, that would be the case and she wouldn't end up throwing it all away and leaving the tour.

The memory of her parting smile lingered with him as he headed back to the bus for his second interview of the day. He tried to put it out of his mind. He had far more pressing things to think about right now. Like writing a whole damn album in the next couple of months with his band half the country away.

Thank god staying focused was never a problem for him.

Chapter Ten

Cassie plugged in the new cable for Zac's in-ear monitor system and placed it carefully back in its case, ready for tonight's performance. A throat cleared behind her and she turned, looking up—and up—at a mountain of a man. Cassie stood, trying to equalize their height slightly. He must have been at least a foot taller than her.

He held out his huge hand. "I'm Will. Fractured's head of security. Lexie asked me to come and assist you in getting your things off Blacklite's bus."

"Oh, hi," Cassie said. His hand engulfed hers as she shook it. Nerves quivered through her. This was really happening.

Charlie had found her half an hour ago and broken the news that he hadn't been able to find anyone willing to give up their bunk.

"There's nothing to stop the same thing that happened to you, happening to them," he'd said. "Then they'd be the ones on their ass." She'd thanked him and when he'd asked her if she'd figured out an alternative plan, she'd let him know she'd be moving onto Fractured's bus. His eyebrows had shot to his hairline, but he hadn't said anything.

Not long after that, Lexie had swung past to check on her and to grab some lunch. As soon as Cassie had let her know what Charlie had said, the photographer had told her that she'd get someone from Fractured's security team to help her get her stuff off Bryan's bus.

She hadn't been expecting their head of security though.

Suddenly, what had only been hypothetical a few short hours ago was now all too real. She was removing herself from Bryan's bus—from him. Cassie steeled herself for the pain to hit, and it did, a part of her rebelling against the thought of never touching him again. But the burn of her anger was stronger. She blinked back any tears that threatened to fall. She didn't need tears. She needed to be strong. She needed to remember the lessons she'd learned when she was young. The lessons she forgot when she met Bryan. Comfort, security, love; you couldn't rely on those things.

Cassie's spine stiffened, and she gave Will a tight smile and a nod, then hurried to catch up with him as he strode off.

She walked next to his stoically silent form until they arrived at Blacklite's bus. It was smaller than Fractured's, with no band name written on the side. She hesitated, but Will didn't, thumping loudly on the door of the bus.

A few seconds later, it opened with a hiss, and Terrence, Blacklite's driver, stared out at them blearily. Cassie felt guilty for waking him from a much-needed nap after he'd been driving all night, but his face brightened when he looked over Will's shoulder and saw her standing there.

"Good to see you're okay. Bryan was worried about you last night."

Her smile was strained. She wondered if he'd known—if they'd all known—what Bryan and Stella were up to behind her back. Bryan had told her that last night was the only time he and Stella had slept together, but you don't just go from zero to one hundred overnight. There must have been something between them for a while. "I've come to get my stuff," she said.

Terrance's face sobered, his gaze drifting to Will. "Right. Does Bryan know—"

"Bryan will figure it out," she cut him off, feeling bad again when his forehead creased. But he didn't hold them up any longer, moving back up the stairs to make way for her and Will.

As she stepped back onto the bus, memories wormed their way into her chest: sitting with Bryan's arms around her as the bus rumbled underneath them, cuddling together in his bunk, watching him as he joked with his bandmates and loving the thought that he was hers and she was his.

But other memories flooded back, too. The hushed conversations and laughter between Bryan and his bandmates that so often excluded her. Being brushed off with *it's band business* when she tried to join in or offer her thoughts. Stella's subtle condescension. All of those things had rubbed Cassie the wrong way, but she'd said nothing. Now, there would be no more making excuses for the band and how they'd made her feel.

Cassie hurried to the sleeping area while Will stood in the living room, which was smaller by half and far shabbier than the one on Fractured's bus. Thankfully, none of Blacklite were there.

She grabbed her small suitcase out of the storage cabinet and started gathering her clothes and dumping them in. Normally, she was a neat packer, but she didn't want to linger any longer than she had to. The last thing she wanted was to risk a run-in with any of the band members.

She emptied her drawers, then dug her hand down the side of the bunk where she kept her notebook. She hadn't wanted to leave it out where one of the others could potentially find it. It was too private to let anyone see. She'd only ever shown it to Bryan a couple of times. And after the second time, she hadn't bothered again. Not when he'd been so dismissive.

Back then, she'd excused his lack of care. He simply didn't understand what her writing meant to her. He didn't understand that before she'd had him to share her feelings with, there was only her notebook. But now, her rose-colored glasses were off—or more like smashed on the ground. She could finally admit what she hadn't then. His lack of interest had hurt.

After that, she mainly wrote when he wasn't around, preferring to keep that one little part of herself separate. She'd been all in with him in every other respect. But not this. Not this essential part of who she was.

Cassie gave the bunk one final check but stilled when voices came from the front of the bus. Her breath caught when she recognized Stella's aggravated tone, followed by Bryan's deeper voice.

She squared her shoulders, slung her bag over her shoulder and stepped out of the sleeping area. Will, bless him, stood before Stella and Bryan, blocking their view of her. It gave her a few seconds to compose herself before she walked out from behind him. She looked up at Will, doing her best to ignore them.

"Thanks. I'm done."

His eyes swept over her face, obviously reading the tension there. He slid her bag off her shoulder, slung it over his, then put his hand on her back and guided her toward the front of the bus.

Stella snorted. "Oh my god. Dramatic much?"

Biting her lip to hold back the scathing words that wanted to erupt, Cassie looked straight ahead. Unfortunately, that meant she was staring directly at Bryan's chest as he blocked the doorway.

"Cassie, c'mon. You don't need to do this. We can talk about it. We can figure it out," he said.

The pressure of Will's hand on her back kept her moving forward. "There's really nothing to talk about, Bryan. You two can have at it."

Sudden tension radiated from Will as he understood the situation. His big body swelled up even larger. Bryan took his life in his hands by not moving out of their way, forcing Cassie and Will to slow down.

Cassie made herself look at him. At the face she'd traced loving fingers over a thousand times. The hurt there sent pain stabbing through her and her steps faltered. But Will's didn't. All he did was say mildly, "I suggest you move. And if you fancy taking a swing, just know that I'll have to defend myself. And I wouldn't want your band to have to find a new guitarist on such short notice."

Cassie was surprised to find her lips twitching as Bryan scowled but sensibly moved aside.

Will got her going again, and she looked up at him. Her mouth curled into an actual smile when he winked at her.

"Come on, babe," Stella said. "Let her go. You're better off without her."

Cassie almost stumbled hearing her call Bryan babe, but once again, Will's steadying hand kept her moving.

"At least tell me where you're going," Bryan demanded, irritation and frustration making his voice rough.

She wanted so badly to say something cutting, but she held her tongue. She needed to be the bigger person. Apparently, Will didn't have the same concern. "She's been upgraded," he said, without turning around.

Cassie was grinning as she stepped off the bus.

Chapter Eleven

Zac extricated himself from the clutches of an overenthusiastic fan whose hands had wandered south far too often for his liking. It wasn't as if he wasn't used to it after so long in the business. Or that he didn't sometimes welcome fans and groupies making advances. But he wasn't in the mood. Tonight, he was impatient to get back to the bus for another songwriting session with Beau, Devon, and Caleb.

A vision of midnight hair and sapphire eyes whispered through Zac's head, and he drained the rest of his beer. It was Cassie's first night officially staying with them. Hopefully, she'd settled in okay.

Security was finally ushering all the fans and VIPs out. Zac caught Connor's gaze from across the room and jerked his chin at the door that would take them out the back. Connor nodded and said something to the others. Tex downed the last of his drink, and by the time Zac was heading out, the other men and Lexie were behind him.

Noah caught up to him as they made their way out into the cool night air. "You okay with Cassie staying with us?"

Zac gave him a look. "Why wouldn't I be?"

"Because Cassie is very pretty and newly single. And you're the only one of us without a woman warming your bed or waiting for you at home."

"And you think having access to a pretty, single woman is all it takes for me to lose control of myself?"

Noah snorted. "I don't think I've ever seen you lose control."

"So why are you asking, then?"

Noah barked out a laugh. "I'm not going to get a straight answer out of you, am I?"

"I don't have any issue with Cassie staying with us. Happy?"

Noah smirked at him, and Zac shook his head, a smile twitching his lips. "Don't get your matchmaking panties in a twist. Just because the three of you are all coupled up doesn't mean I want to be. I'm happy we can help Cassie out, but that's all this is."

"You don't know what you're missing, man. Being coupled up is amazing."

"I know exactly what I'm missing, and I'm good with it." That seemed to shut Noah up, and they walked the rest of the way in silence.

Still, the first thing Zac did when they boarded the bus was look around the living room for Cassie, wondering if she might have already gone to bed. She hadn't. She was curled up in the corner one of the couches, a notebook and pen in her hands, looking up at them with a shy smile as they all filed in. Seeing her sitting there, so small and alone, an echo of sadness still showing in her eyes, made his chest ache unexpectedly.

She stood up, clutching the notebook to her stomach. "How was the after-party?"

Fractured Kiss

"Same shit, different day," Tex answered as he stretched his tattooed arms over his head, his fingertips brushing the ceiling of the bus.

Maggie walked in behind them, checking they were ready to go, then headed up to the front. The rumble of the bus engine started a few minutes later.

Zac sat down at the kitchen table with his phone in his hand as the others spread out around the living room, talking about the show and how enthusiastic the crowd had been. They made an effort to include Cassie in the conversation, but while she made the occasional comment, she seemed mostly happier just listening.

When he realized he'd been watching her long enough to give Noah the wrong idea, Zac looked down at his phone. He scrolled through Fractured's various social media feeds, replying to some comments, only half-listening to the conversation.

Eventually, Tex announced he was going to hit the sack, and the others echoed the sentiment. Zac didn't budge as everyone said good night and made their way to their bunks. He'd organized to call his Crossfire bandmates in about ten minutes' time to run through some of the songs they were working on for the album.

"Are you staying up?" Cassie's voice startled him. She was still sitting on the couch, but while he'd been distracted with his phone, she'd changed into what was obviously her sleep outfit. A little white camisole top that clung enticingly to her full breasts and tight, pale pink sleep shorts, which did far too good a job of showing off her legs.

Zac dragged his eyes away from all that smooth, exposed skin. The last thing either of them needed was him eye fucking her, even if she looked as sexy as hell sitting there in her pajamas. He had no interest in proving Noah right.

"Yeah, I've got to fit in a songwriting session with the guys back home."

"Aren't you tired?"

"Aren't you?"

She smiled. "I didn't perform on stage and party all night."

"You've had a pretty rough twenty-four hours, though."

He regretted saying it when her smile faltered. She looked down at her notebook and rolled her pen between her fingers. "If I go to sleep, then I have to wake up and remember what happened all over again." She met his gaze, her eyes shadowed, expression somber. "Would it bother you if I stayed up? I'll be quiet, but I'd like to write some more before I go to bed."

"What are you writing?"

She hesitated, her fingers brushing the open page. "Just some thoughts."

Zac understood the need to get what was in your head out onto a page. His therapy had always been chords and notes. Apparently, hers was writing.

"I don't mind," he said.

She gave him a solemn little nod before returning her attention to her notebook. He studied her for a few more seconds, then dialed Beau.

"Hey, man!" Crossfire's bass player had a grin on his face as he answered. "We have to stop meeting like this."

Devon, their guitarist, and Caleb, the drummer who'd replaced Noah when he left Crossfire the year before, appeared over Beau's shoulders.

"I was half expecting you might cancel tonight," Caleb said. "It's been a couple of weeks since the tour started. I thought this might be the night you gave work a miss and let little Zac out to play."

Zac's lips quirked. "There's nothing little about it." He might be a man in his thirties, but he was still a guy.

Devon snorted. "Yeah, we heard all about it when you took that blonde woman back to your hotel room on our last tour. I think the whole fucking floor of the hotel heard about it."

Zac's gaze locked with Cassie's. A pretty flush infused the skin of her cheeks, and she quickly looked back down and started writing intently again.

Zac bit back a chuckle. She was lucky that was the worst thing Devon had said. He probably should warn the guys that Cassie was there, though. Not that it would be any guarantee they wouldn't come out with something even more inappropriate.

"So, we have someone staying on the bus with us," he said. He felt Cassie's eyes on him again. "She's sitting out here with me at the moment."

"She, huh? Who is this mysterious she?" Beau pasted a fake expression of shock on his face. "Don't tell me you've become so pussy deprived, you've actually invited a woman to spend the night on the bus with you."

Zac winced internally. "Cassie's my guitar tech, and she needed somewhere to stay. I'm just telling you so you know there's someone else here who can hear you." Time to move things along. "Now, I was thinking we could—"

"Hold the fuck on," Devon interrupted him. "You don't get to drop that kind of information and not introduce us to the lady in question."

He clenched his jaw. Why the hell had he said anything? He should have known they wouldn't let it go until he introduced them to Cassie.

Zac looked over at her. She'd pulled her knees up to her chin and was hiding her smile behind them. He raised a brow. Understanding his silent question, she rolled her eyes with a huff of laughter. She stood, placed her notepad and pen down carefully, and came over to him. When she got close enough, he turned the screen toward her.

"Well, hello there, Cassie."

Zac could almost hear the flirtatious grin in Beau's voice.

Cassie gave a little smile and a wave. "Hi."

"No wonder Zac wanted to hide you away." That was Caleb.

Zac turned the phone back toward himself, giving her an apologetic look. But she just laughed quietly again and walked back to where she'd left her notebook.

He dragged his gaze away from her tight ass in those little shorts. Three faces smirked at him from his phone screen.

He ignored their gleeful expressions. "So, as I was saying, I think we should start with—"

"Why do my guitar techs never look like that?" said Caleb.

He kept talking as if Caleb hadn't spoken. "Tearing it Down. I think it's missing something in the transition to the second verse."

"You realize this conversation isn't over, don't you?" Beau had a grin the size of Texas on his face.

Zac pinned him with a stare, and Beau sighed. "Okay, fine. Let's write some music."

An hour and a half later, they'd finally wrapped it up for the night. Zac rubbed his gritty eyes and looked over at Cassie.

She'd fallen asleep, her head resting against the corner

of the couch, long, dark lashes lying against her cheeks, her hands lax on the notebook in her lap.

Zac slid his guitar into its case and latched it. His eyes shifted back over to Cassie.

She looked so peaceful.

His legs moved of their own accord, and he found himself next to her. He stood there, his gaze roaming along the curve of her breasts, the smooth skin of her arms, her slender fingers resting against the lined pages of her notebook.

A part of him was a little too curious about the thoughts she spilled onto those pages. Would her words reveal all her dreams and fears? Would they explain why she'd tied herself so closely to Bryan? A man who obviously hadn't deserved that level of dedication.

Then again, why did anyone commit themselves to someone when love was so easy to abuse?

Not wanting to invade her privacy, and strangely reluctant to learn the answers to those questions, anyway, Zac didn't look too closely as he eased the book out from under her hands. He closed it and tucked it into the back of his jeans beneath his shirt.

Stooping, he slid his arms under her and lifted her gently. She curled into him, her hand resting against his chest. The sweet scent of apples and vanilla teased his senses. He closed his eyes and stood there for a second, holding her against him, breathing her in. Did she taste as sweet as she smelled?

He forced his eyes open. What the hell was he doing? Yeah, she smelled good; most women he met did. Most women hadn't just had their lives implode around them. Most women didn't work for him. And most women definitely wouldn't be living on a bus with him for the next couple of months. Connor might not have resisted Lexie's pull when she was staying with them, but this wasn't the same situation. Zac knew better than to complicate his life by giving into something that was just a fleeting temptation. Or worse, something that wasn't as fleeting as it should be.

At the corridor leading to the bunks, Zac turned sideways to keep her legs from hitting the doorway. Her bunk was on the bottom, opposite his. The curtain was open, so he bent down and laid her gently on top of the covers. He didn't want to disturb her by trying to get the blanket over her, and it was warm enough on the bus that she shouldn't get too cold.

Zac straightened, not letting his gaze linger on her this time. He pulled her notebook out from his jeans and tucked it down by her side, then drew the curtain shut and went to wash up in the small bathroom. He looked at his reflection, at his bloodshot eyes. There were a lot more late nights stretching ahead of him.

Maybe Cassie would stay up with him again.

He grimaced, turning away from the mirror and going to his bunk. He slid under the covers, but before he closed his curtain, he glanced over at her bunk, remembering how her slender body had curled against his chest.

After snapping his curtain shut, he flung his arm over his eyes and concentrated hard on filling his head with music, the way he always did when he was trying not to overthink.

He had a feeling it was going to be a long tour.

And not just because of the album.

Chapter Twelve

Cassie mouthed the words to one of her favorite Fractured songs as the band played it on stage. She stood to the side, behind one of the big amps, holding Zac's bass, ready to change it out with the one he was using as soon as the song was over.

It had been three nights since she'd moved onto Fractured's bus. Some of her awkwardness around the band had eased. Some. Not all. They were doing what they could to make her comfortable, but she couldn't help but feel as if she was intruding. They were obviously a close-knit group, and she'd found herself watching their easy interactions with envy.

Things hadn't been like that with any of Bryan's bands over the years. Not even Blacklite. Not for her anyway. Bryan had never had any issues. He was one of those people who had no problem fitting in with different groups.

But while she'd tried, things never seemed to click with her. She'd often wondered if it was because she was *the girlfriend*. So many of the musicians Bryan spent time with were single and enjoying the party life. They probably thought she cramped his style.

Or maybe it was just her. Maybe the thing that prevented her from making friends as a child had left an indelible mark. One that stopped people from wanting to get close to her.

Everyone except Bryan.

Her thumb slid over the smooth band of her engagement ring. She needed to take it off, but she hadn't quite found the resolve to do it yet. Part of her knew it would be the final step. Once she slipped that diamond off her finger, she was acknowledging the end of everything she'd once dreamed of.

Bryan hadn't taken her move onto Fractured's bus well. He'd tried several times to corner her to explain himself. The first time her traitorously weak heart forced her to listen. As if she still thought there was something he could say that would make everything right again. But when he reached out and pulled her against him, whispering that he loved her, that it was all a terrible mistake, she lost it. His arms, once so safe and familiar, felt wrong now. His woodsy scent didn't bring any comfort. She couldn't stop picturing Stella naked on top of him.

She'd shoved him away. "I can't. I can't." Tears blurred her vision, and she'd rushed off, finding Dan and making herself useful near him. After that, whenever Bryan tried to get her alone, Dan or Lexie miraculously turned up.

Since then, Bryan had been giving her increasingly irritated looks. She had to talk to him eventually, regardless of how she felt right now. They had a whole life they'd built together that would have to be dismantled.

She understood Bryan's scowls, but Stella's increasingly

venomous glares were a mystery. Cassie had done nothing to the woman.

She was doing her best not to think about Stella. Or Bryan. It still hurt too much, and she needed to concentrate on her job. Right now, that meant listening to Zac playing onstage and making sure his instruments and all the equipment were working as they should be.

Zac stepped up to the mic, adding his smoky voice to Connor's for the chorus, his hands still moving smoothly over his bass. He gazed out over the crowd as he sang, and she wondered if he was looking at all the women reaching their hands out toward him, screaming his name, wanting the opportunity to be close to him, even if just for a moment.

His head angled to the side, and his eyes met hers. Unexpectedly, a buzz of energy danced over her skin. She didn't have time to analyze her odd reaction before he looked away again.

The band finished the song with a pulse-pounding crescendo. To the sound of the screaming fans, Zac came toward her to change his bass out. Ready for the switch, Cassie was holding out his next one by the time he got to her, and she waited for him to strip off the one he wore. They only had a few seconds to make the swap before the next song; Noah was already banging out the intro on his drums.

Their fingers brushed, and a zap of static electricity sparked between them. She almost jerked her hand back with the shock, her eyes darting up to his face. He looked slightly bemused, and she wondered if he felt it too. It was the first time that had ever happened during a performance. She'd double-check his body pack afterward and make sure there weren't any more faulty connections.

He gripped the neck of the bass, handed her the one he'd been using, and with one final enigmatic glance at her, strode back out on the stage, his fingers already moving over the strings as he walked. Cassie blew out a breath, wondering why her heart was beating so hard.

* * *

Cassie sighed, looking away from Zac sitting at the kitchenette table and back down at the notebook in her lap. The words on the page, the ones she'd written before her eyes had been drawn to him like a magnet, stared up at her.

A crackle of sparks,
The world falls silent,
One heartbeat, an indrawn breath,
Then you are gone.

She cringed. God, what was she thinking? Writing poems about something as ridiculous as static electricity. Annoyed with herself, she looked over at Zac again. She'd caught herself doing that more and more over the last few days.

Cassie's breath hitched when she found Zac's eyes fixed on her. "Oh, are you done already?" she asked.

A shard of disappointment pricked her. This part of the day had quickly become her favorite. The peaceful moments when she was alone with her thoughts. Not lonely, though. Because Zac was there.

His voice as he spoke to his Crossfire bandmates, and

the quiet strum of his guitar, eased the tightness in her shoulders and soothed her the way nothing else seemed to.

Although after that first night, she'd done her best to avoid falling asleep again. The last thing she wanted was to wake up in her bunk in the morning, knowing he'd had to carry her there. Unfortunately, it was easy to linger a little too long. Sitting out there with him was so much more pleasant than tossing and turning in her bunk, unwelcome memories crawling through her head.

Zac laid his guitar down next to him on the bench seat. "Not yet. Just taking a break."

"How's it all going?" she asked.

"Okay. Slower than I'd like," he responded. "It's harder not being in the same place. We always work better when we're together and can pick up on each other's energy." He rolled his neck and rubbed at one of his shoulders.

"Why are you doing it this way, anyway? It seems like you're pushing yourself so hard."

"We've got to get the album done before we head to the UK for our European tour. We're going to be recording at Abbey Road the week before the tour starts."

"Really? Where the Beatles recorded?"

One side of his mouth kicked up, his eyes crinkling at the corners. "Yep."

"That's awesome. Will it be the first time you've been there?"

"We recorded Fractured's fifth studio album there. But the other guys in Crossfire haven't been, so I want to make sure they get the chance."

She pulled her knees up to her chest and wrapped her arms around them. "Do you always work so hard?"

He laced his hands together behind his neck, a small smile on his face. "Not always."

She laughed under her breath. He was definitely a man of few words when he wanted to be, and she was finding herself increasingly curious about him. In the space of a few short weeks, he'd gone from this abstract figure of a huge rock star to her boss to a man she enjoyed spending time with every evening. "So, how do you relax when you aren't working so hard then?"

He didn't answer straight away, the small smile growing into a grin that spread across his face.

She cocked her head. "What? Why is that funny?" Then she gasped. "Oh my god, I'm so stupid. It's sex, isn't it? Sex is how you relax."

Zac threw back his head and laughed. Cassie blinked at the sight, not sure if she'd ever seen him laugh quite that unrestrainedly before.

It was nice.

She was so used to seeing him composed and in control. *Focused.* That was the word. Even when he played on stage, even when the fans were screaming and chanting his name, he was always so focused. On the music. On something deep inside himself. She liked seeing him this way. He was more real somehow. More approachable. Not the aloof, unobtainable rock star.

"Actually," he said, the humor still in his voice, "I was going to say karaoke."

She let out a surprised laugh. "Really? Karaoke? I'd love to see that." She smiled to herself, picturing him singing an off-key rendition of "Bohemian Rhapsody" on a smoky little stage in some dingy dive bar somewhere. Not that it would be off-key. Zac had an amazing voice. But for the purposes of her mental imagery, he was definitely singing out of tune.

He watched her, an odd grin twisting his lips. "I'm sure there are some videos up on the internet somewhere."

Fractured Kiss

"And I am *definitely* going to look those up."

Still smiling, Zac stood and stretched, reaching his arms over his head. Cassie's eyes dropped to where his shirt had pulled up, revealing a strip of tanned skin and the faint line of a happy trail that dragged her gaze down to the low waistband of his jeans.

Her throat suddenly dry, Cassie looked away, hoping he hadn't noticed.

Zac rolled his neck again, and she heard the crack from across the living room. She put her notebook and pen down on the couch next to her and walked over to him. He watched her approach, raising his brows as she stopped in front of him.

"Sit down." She pointed at the bench seat he'd been sitting at before. The one that had space behind it for her to stand.

He eyed her with curiosity but did as she asked. "What are you doing?"

She moved behind him. "I'm going to give you a shoulder massage. I used to do it for Bryan all the time when he was stressed."

He twisted to face her, his brows drawn together. "You don't need to—"

"I want to. You can consider it a thanks for helping me out."

"I don't need to be thanked."

Apparently, he was stubborn as well as being a workaholic. "Then just consider it part of my job as your guitar tech. How can you play your perfectly tuned basses to their full potential if you're all tense?"

He gave a low laugh. "Well, when you put it that way." He turned around, then glanced over his shoulder at her. "Is it okay if I take my shirt off?"

"Oh, uh, of course."

Cassie's cheeks heated when he stripped his T-shirt off and held it balled in his hands as he leaned back against the seat.

She let out a quiet breath, then placed her hands on his shoulders and pressed her thumbs into his muscles. He said nothing, just let his head drop forward so she could work.

It didn't take long for Cassie to regret her offer. She was so used to giving Bryan massages, she hadn't thought how different it would be to have her hands on another man. A man who—as much as she was trying not to notice—felt a little too good under her fingers. Her thumbs made small circles up the back of his neck, brushing the tiny velvet strands of hair at his nape. Her breaths grew uneven.

He smelled good too. Obviously, he'd showered after the concert. The fresh, masculine scent filled her senses. It was slightly intoxicating.

She worked her hands back down, her thumbs rolling over the leather cord he wore around his neck. She'd seen the pick that hung from it a couple of times when it had slipped out from under his shirt. She wondered what sentimental value it had. Was it his first pick? Did it once belong to an idol of his?

It wasn't the right time to ask. Not when she was trying incredibly hard not to notice how smooth and warm his skin was. She was suddenly all too aware of his broad shoulders and the densely packed muscles that covered them.

Zac's breaths deepened as she worked, and when she pressed her fingers into a particularly tense knot, he let out a deep groan. The kind of groan that conjured up visions of sweaty bodies and tangled sheets. Heat unfurled low in Cassie's belly, and her fingers trembled.

The muscles that had loosened under her ministrations

tightened. Had he noticed her reaction? After a frozen second, it appeared he was merely shifting position. He tilted his head a little to the side, allowing her to work her way back up his neck.

Now Cassie was hyperaware of him. His every breath, his tanned skin, the warmth emanating from him. It was shockingly intimate. She'd never been with anyone but Bryan. He was her first and only. But her mind suddenly filled with visions of Zac. What would it be like to be naked with him, running her hands over every inch of his body, not just his shoulders?

What would it be like to have his hands all over *her* body?

She imagined the rasp of his stubble against her sensitive skin, the wet heat of his mouth on her breasts, the hard press of his hips between her thighs. Would he fill her so completely, she wouldn't be able to think of anything but him? Would he make the same groan when he—

Cassie inhaled sharply at the arousal that blasted through her. Her nipples tightened into diamond-hard peaks, and she jerked her hands away, almost stumbling in her haste to step back from him.

Expecting him to turn around and ask what was wrong, she crossed her arms over her chest to hide her physical reaction. Her mind reeled, preparing to give him some lame excuse about her hands getting tired.

For a few seconds, he didn't move at all. He faced away, his spine a rigid line. When he finally turned to look over his shoulder at her, his hazel eyes were dark. They raked over her, and she licked her lips and took another half-step back.

They stared at each other. Could he see the thoughts written on her face? Was she looking at him exactly the same way all those other women did? Cassie's cheeks heated. *Please don't see it.*

Zac cleared his throat. "Thanks. That was... good." His voice was a little rougher than usual, but that was it. He couldn't know she'd been fantasizing about what it would feel like to have him inside her.

The tension gripping the back of Cassie's neck loosened a little. Maybe it wasn't as obvious as she feared. Maybe she was just overly sensitive to her body's reaction because she hadn't expected it. Not so soon after Bryan.

She gave him a tentative smile. "No problem. I'll, uh, let you get back to it."

She retreated to a safe distance, picked up her notebook, and slumped down on the couch. A quiet breath gusted out of her. That was surprising. Not that she didn't find Zac attractive, but she'd never fantasized about him. Not like that, anyway. She might have occasionally glanced at his firm, masculine lips or a snuck a furtive look at his abs when he pulled his T-shirt up to wipe the sweat off his face after a performance. But certainly nothing like the vivid imagery that had made her body react as if they were actually naked together.

Her eyes slid back to Zac. He'd picked up his guitar and his fingers danced over the frets, his mouth moving silently through a song. Heat crept over her skin again as she watched the muscles in his forearms flex.

She let her head thunk back against the wall of the bus.

Great. Just what she needed. A silly crush to make this horrible tour even more hellish.

Chapter Thirteen

Zac had felt it in her hands first. The moment when the simple massage turned into something else. Her fingers quivered against his skin. Her breathing quickened, even as her movements slowed. Her strokes became more of a caress. He couldn't stop his body's reaction, knowing what she was imagining.

Because he was imagining it too.

He knew having her hands on him was a bad idea. But he let her do it, anyway, knowing she just wanted to help. Sensing she was still trying to find her feet traveling with them. He could hardly tell her it had been weeks since he got laid. That having a beautiful woman touch him would probably do the complete opposite of what she intended. And for some reason, he decided to make it harder on himself and take his shirt off.

The last few nights, having her sitting out with him was surprisingly relaxing. Even if he was sometimes distracted when she crossed and uncrossed her legs or pulled her knees up, revealing tantalizingly shadowed glimpses of her inner thighs and the curve of her ass.

It was easy enough to push aside those momentary distractions with her safely on the other side of the living room. But when she stood so close behind him, her apple-and-vanilla scent surrounding him and her hands stroking along his skin, it was all too easy to picture more. To close his eyes and imagine peeling her out of those little pajamas and exploring every inch of her soft skin. With his lips, his tongue, his hands. Then unzipping his jeans, releasing his straining cock, and pulling her down onto him so she could ride him until they both exploded.

And fuck. Wasn't that a damn tempting image?

But it wasn't going to happen.

Not tonight.

Not any night.

He'd had to wait until he was composed enough to face her after she jerked herself away from him. It was why he pretended not to see how blown her pupils were, or how she crossed her arms over her breasts, or that her chest and face were flushed. He'd ruthlessly suppressed the urge to yank her back to him so he could press his lips to her skin and feel the heat of her arousal.

Now, she sat on the other side of the room, and he'd somehow forced himself to concentrate for the last forty-five minutes while he kept working with the other guys. That was forty-five minutes of ignoring the sharp impulse to ditch his guitar and make what he'd imagined real.

"It has to be more emotional," Caleb was arguing with Beau. "It's a duet. I want to feel the fucking poignancy in my gut when Zac and Talia sing it."

"Yeah, well, it's hard to feel the emotion when we're all damn tired," Beau responded. "Zac looks like he's actually fucking daydreaming for the first time in his life. And if he's zoned out, then I think we can safely say it's time to call it quits for the night."

Zac realized his focus had drifted. Again. "Beau's right. It's been a long night. We can pick this up tomorrow. We'll try to work on strengthening the lyrics for the second verse. Hopefully, we can nail it soon."

Ignoring the moaning and groaning from the other end of the line, Zac said goodbye and disconnected. He finally allowed himself to look over at Cassie. Just like the first night, she was asleep, and he let out a sigh of relief. He could carry her to her bunk without any further enticement, then go to bed and try to put this night out of his mind.

He approached Cassie and stood looking down at her. He didn't know what he found so compelling about watching her sleep. Maybe because it meant he could actually let himself look at her without worrying what assumptions people might leap to.

From the very first time he'd met Cassie, he knew she wasn't someone he could let himself touch. He'd told himself she was too starry-eyed and innocent for him. Not innocent in the virginal sense. Innocent to the harsh realities of life. Was that still true? Or had what Bryan done stripped that from her?

She still looked damn innocent, though. With her long lashes brushing the creamy skin of her cheekbones and her soft, pink lips slightly parted, she looked like that damn angel, fallen from heaven just to tempt him. Waves of silky dark hair cascaded over her shoulders, leading his gaze directly to her full breasts. Her nipples were still half-hard, pressing against her top, and he wondered if they'd stayed that way since she'd had her hands on him.

His dick swelled as he took her in, pressing against his fly. He resisted the urge to palm it to relieve some of the pressure. He felt like enough of a damn pervert standing over her and getting hard just from watching her while she slept.

Get a fucking grip. She's just a woman, like any other.

Her notebook on the couch next to her drew his gaze. He wanted to know what she wrote in there every night. He'd almost asked several times over the last few days, and every time, he'd stopped himself. He wasn't sure why he was so reluctant to give in to his curiosity. What was he worried would happen if he let himself find out more about her?

These late nights were scrambling his mind.

He exhaled. Unfortunately, he still had to get her to her bed. He grabbed the notebook and shoved it in the back of his jeans again, slid his arms underneath her, and straightened.

He took a few careful steps toward the bunks when Cassie's eyelids fluttered open, and she blinked up at him.

"Zac?" Her voice was husky with sleep.

"Shh, angel," he said. "I'm taking you to bed."

Maybe it came out the wrong way. Or maybe it was the rasp in his voice when he said it because her eyes widened, her lips parted, and she tried to sit up in his arms. He swore under his breath and let go with one arm so she could slide down his body.

It was a mistake.

They ended up pressed against each other, her staring up at him with her hands trapped against his chest, and him with his arms wrapped tightly around her waist.

The position was too intimate. And yet neither of them moved. Zac's heart was pumping hard in his chest, and Cassie's breaths came fast and uneven from her parted lips.

He was fixated on those lips—soft, full, and naturally

pink. He couldn't stop staring at them, knowing that all he had to do to get a taste was to lower his head. The tip of her tongue darted out to wet them and he almost broke. He needed to wrestle back some control before he did something stupid.

Zac forced himself to remember all of the reasons why kissing Cassie would be a terrible idea. His arms fell away from her, and he stepped back.

"Sorry." His voice was rough. "I was just taking you to your bunk."

She blinked slowly, still half-asleep, the sweep of her long, sooty lashes hypnotizing him.

"It's my fault," she said. "I shouldn't have let myself fall asleep. I'll make sure to go to bed earlier so you don't have to worry about me."

"I have no problem taking you to bed." There were those words again. Was he saying them deliberately? He enjoyed the flicker of awareness in her eyes when he said them a little too much. He was definitely doing it on purpose. Zac cleared his throat. "Are you still having problems sleeping?"

"Once I'm asleep, it's okay. But it's hard to turn my thoughts off to get there. And waking up still isn't great." A sad smile pulled at the corners of her mouth.

"It'll get better soon." The platitude fell from his lips without thought.

She tilted her head to the side. "Do you say that from personal experience?"

"If you're asking me if I know what I'm talking about, you got me."

"You've never had your heart broken?"

"That would require getting emotionally involved. And I don't."

"Why not?"

Zac was all too aware that they were still standing close to each other, their proximity imbuing the moment with a sense of intimacy it shouldn't really have. Still, he wanted to keep talking, just so she would stay where she was, looking up at him with those beautiful blue eyes.

His gaze dropped to her lips again, but he looked away just as fast. Best to nip this thing in the bud now—if this was even a thing. After all, he didn't really know her. He could be completely misreading her.

But he didn't think he was.

Her attraction to him might be reluctant, she might be confused she was feeling it so soon, but he was sure it was there in the flush of her cheeks, in the rapid rise and fall of her chest, in her dilated pupils.

There was no point lying to himself. He'd felt the attraction since the first day Dan introduced her to him. It didn't make sense then. It didn't now. She was exactly the type of woman he'd spent his life avoiding. The type who wanted more than a few nights of passion. The type who was looking for a commitment he wasn't prepared to give them. He'd seen the damage done when love turns selfish and twisted. When the realization comes too late that you're not prepared to make the kinds of sacrifices happily ever afters require.

Seeing the glitter of light reflecting from her ring finger that first day had almost been a relief—confirmation she was off-limits. If he'd known she would end up broken-hearted and staying on their bus, he might have asked for a replacement. She was too much of a risk to the rules he always stuck to when it came to women. The rules that would make sure he never became a person who ruined other people's lives.

Cassie was still waiting patiently for an answer to her question, an expression of open curiosity on her face.

He told her the truth. At least enough of it to make sure she knew nothing could ever happen between them. And maybe to remind himself too. "Because I have no interest in giving up music for a relationship I don't want or need. If I feel like having sex, I have no shortage of willing women. They know the deal. One night, a few weeks if we hit it off physically, but never a commitment. I'll never do to anyone what Bryan did to you because I'll never tie myself to someone when I know I'm not capable of giving them what they want. If that makes me an asshole, then..." He shrugged again.

Cassie's brow creased, but she surprised him. Instead of walking away, she stepped closer and put her hand on his chest, directly over his heart. "I think I get it. I used to believe being alone was the worst thing in the world, but now I'm wondering if you might have the right idea. Maybe for some people, alone is just how they're meant to be."

It was stupid, but he didn't like hearing those words come out of her mouth. Didn't like thinking that Bryan's selfishness had damaged that hopeful, innocent part of her. The ache in his chest tightened, sharpened until the only thing he could feel was his heart pounding against her palm.

He reached out, tipped her chin up, and held her gaze. "Not you."

She blinked, her lips parting. Before he did something even more stupid, he stepped back. Her hand fell away from his chest.

Zac needed some distance from her. Even his bunk was too close right now. He needed some distance from himself too. But there was only one escape from the thoughts in his own head. "Go to bed, Cassie. I'm going to stay up a bit longer." Not waiting to see if she listened to him, he turned his back on her, went to the table where he'd left his guitar, and pulled it out of its case.

He was relieved that she didn't follow him. When he looked over his shoulder to see her gone, his breath came out in a rush.

It shouldn't have mattered that she'd agreed with him. But it had. Was it just Bryan who had made her feel she was better off alone? Or had someone else hurt her?

And why the hell did the thought of Cassie believing she was meant to be alone bother him so much?

Chapter Fourteen

Lexie grabbed Cassie's arm and tugged her up the stairs to the club's VIP section. "I'm so glad you came with us," she said.

It had been almost two weeks since Cassie moved onto Fractured's bus, and she'd finally gotten used to the strangeness of spending so much time with the band members outside of her work.

Mostly.

And now she was here at a club with the men and their significant others. She'd met Summer, Noah's fiancée, and Eden, Tex's girlfriend and Noah's younger sister, after that night's concert. They'd both flown in from LA to spend the weekend with their men.

Cassie felt awkward at first. The obvious affection between everyone in the group made her feel like an outsider. Thankfully, Eden and Summer were as charming and easy to get along with as Lexie. After the almost painfully touching reunion between the couples, Eden and Summer had turned their attention to Cassie, effortlessly drawing her into their conversation. It had fascinated

Cassie to discover that both of them worked at Eden's non-profit, Sharing the Spotlight. The organization connected recording artists with music-based charities in need of support and endorsement. They had chatted about the work and then Cassie's job with the band. Soon, they changed topics to that night's scheduled PR event. All three women had worked together to convince Cassie to join them.

That's how she'd ended up here. The VIP section was one level above the main part of the club. The strobe lights from the dance floor flashed erratically, reflecting off the massive low-hanging crystal chandeliers, and making her blink. The place was packed with beautiful people dancing, mingling, or standing at the bar looking glamorous. Music thumped through the speakers so loudly she could barely hear Lexie talking to her as they made their way through the crowd.

The guys, along with Summer and Eden, followed behind her and Lexie, and several of the bands' security detail surrounded the group.

Lexie led them over to a couple of oversized plush red velvet couches that fit the opulent style of the club. She pulled Cassie down to sit next to her. Connor sat on his wife's other side, and the three other men sat opposite them, with Eden and Summer tucked in between Tex and Noah.

Cassie's gaze caught Zac's across the low table between them, and a tingle of warmth flushed her skin.

It wasn't the first time it had happened. Since the night she woke in his arms, she was all too conscious of his presence. This morning she had walked out to the living room to find him standing there in just a pair of low-hanging jeans. Her eyes had drifted over his broad shoulders, past the ridges of his abs, to the defined V of muscle that disappeared into the waistband of the jeans that hung low over his hips.

A bloom of heat unfurled in her stomach. The flush that began at her chest crept up her neck and burned hotly in her cheeks. The way his eyes had seared into her when he'd caught her staring—even though she'd tried to pretend she hadn't been—made her think her body's response hadn't gone unnoticed.

This painfully new reaction to him had to be gratitude. It had to be. She was just grateful he'd helped her. She was grateful to Lexie and the others too, but it was different with Zac. He was gorgeous, obviously. And single. She'd have to be blind not to appreciate how attractive he was. That's all it was—a combination of gratitude and female appreciation for a good-looking man.

Of course, that was really selling him short. Because it wasn't just the way he looked that made him attractive. There was his talent too. He wasn't considered one of the best bass players in the world for nothing. And he wasn't exactly a slouch with the six-string either. Though, perhaps the thing she found most appealing about Zac was the way he wove words and music together. Watching him do it every night resonated with something deep inside her. Sometimes she liked to just close her eyes and listen to him as he took a few lyrics, just the seed of a song, and made magic out of it.

A waitress approached with a tray of drinks and carefully placed them on the table. Her breasts almost popped out of her low-cut top as she bent over. Her butt, barely covered by a short black skirt, was pointed straight at Zac, and Cassie caught herself wondering if he was looking. Her stomach twisted.

God, what was wrong with her? What did it matter if

he was? The number of body parts that got aimed in his direction on any given day was ridiculous. Cassie forced her gaze out to the dance floor and focused on the dancers.

She reached for a glass of champagne and took a sip. The crisp, effervescent liquid, flavored by the cut strawberries that floated in it, fizzed down her throat, relaxing her. Her attention wandered back to Zac again. He was watching Noah and Summer laughing together, the hint of a smile on his face. The drummer had his beautiful strawberry-blonde fiancée on his lap and was nuzzling her neck while she giggled and tried to wriggle away from him.

The flashing lights reflected from Zac's eyes, and Cassie couldn't stop herself from staring at them. They were mesmerizing. She had never seen more beautiful eyes on any man—a piercing green with a ring of golden-brown around the pupil, and lashes so long and dark they wouldn't look out of place on a woman. When he turned those eyes on her, it was far too easy to get lost in them.

Cassie took another sip of her champagne and looked away.

Right at Bryan.

She sucked in a sharp breath. Bryan was there with the rest of Blacklite. Stella sat next to him, looking like a pin-up model in a skin-tight, black corset and jeans, with her red hair flowing in waves over her shoulders.

Bryan's eyes were narrowed and fixed on Cassie. It made her feel as if he'd caught her doing something she shouldn't. Which was ridiculous. But Bryan's jaw set, and he slid his gaze toward Zac, his mouth twisting into a scowl. Zac stared back at Bryan, his expression revealing absolutely nothing.

Lexie put her hand on Cassie's arm. "Are you okay?"

Cassie couldn't quite catch her breath, but she gave a

jerky nod. Bryan's presence had sucked any sense of enjoyment out of the night.

As perceptive as she was, Lexie noticed the tense exchange between her, Zac, and Bryan. She grabbed Cassie's hand and tugged. "Come on. Let's dance."

Her heart still beating a little too hard, Cassie stood and nervously smoothed down her dress. Lexie caught Summer's and Eden's attention and pointed at the heaving mass of dancers. The two women joined them.

They walked out onto the dance floor, and just having the other women with her helped Cassie to relax. Lexie discreetly filled Summer and Eden in on the Bryan and Stella situation, but now that Cassie knew her ex was there, she just wanted to forget about him. She was so tired of thinking. Remembering. She just wanted it to all go away. Her thumb brushed over the bare skin of her ring finger, and she was grateful that she'd finally taken her ring off.

Closing her eyes, she let the driving beat of the music pulse through her and began to move. The other women dancing around her was reassuring. She was a part of their group. For once, she was surrounded by friends.

Cassie danced for a while, undisturbed and freer than she'd felt in a long time. Sensing someone behind her, her eyes popped open. Eden grinned at her, amused as a man's hips—and something else—brushed against her ass. For just a few seconds, she let him grind up against her. Why not? She was newly single. Bryan was here with Stella. Zac was... Zac. Her boss. Why was she even thinking about him?

But the thought of Zac did the trick. She snapped out of it and stepped away from the man, a little rattled.

"Let's get a drink at the bar." Eden flashed Cassie a

wink as she gathered her long, blonde hair off her neck and fanned her flushed cheeks.

Cassie followed the other women off the dance floor, suddenly desperate for a big glass of champagne.

Maybe two.

Chapter Fifteen

Zac downed the last of his whiskey and thumped the empty glass down on the table. He fixed his eyes on Cassie standing at the bar.

From the second he saw what she was wearing tonight, he *knew* it was going to make his night hell.

The long-sleeved shimmery black dress covered her from the base of her throat to mid-thigh, clinging to every curve along the way. That wasn't the issue. Not the main one, anyway. It was the back of the dress that was the problem—it plunged low, to just above her ass.

If he thought she looked like a fallen angel before, tonight she was his very own version of heaven and hell: innocently sexy from the front, fucking sin personified from the back.

All he wanted to do was bend her over the table and run his tongue from the base of her spine to the nape of her neck. Then smack her on the ass for making him lose control.

He had cracked open a beer right there on the bus and downed half of it in one go.

At least she'd finally taken that damn engagement ring off. It had started to bug him that she was still wearing it. Her naked ring finger had been the second thing he'd noticed when she'd walked out that evening. He hoped it meant she wasn't considering taking Bryan back anymore. Not that it was any of his business what she did or who she was with, but she deserved better than her ex. Then it had occurred to him that there might be a reason she'd taken it off just before heading out to a club. Was she planning on proving something? That thought had him draining his first beer and immediately opening a second.

Once they were at the club, Zac relaxed. At least there were plenty of other things to look at that weren't Cassie. He didn't let his gaze rest on her for more than a few seconds. But when he'd spotted Bryan and Stella making their way through the club with the rest of Blacklite in tow, his eyes went straight to Cassie. She obviously hadn't noticed them. She was deep in conversation with Lexie, pretty lips curved in a smile and looking happier than she'd been since that night in the hallway.

Bryan had seen Cassie, though, his head turning in her direction as they passed by. His mouth had set in a hard line, even as Stella tugged his arm to lead him to a set of empty couches.

Zac had looked back at Cassie, wondering if there was anything he could do to keep her from realizing Bryan and Stella were there. As if she'd sensed his attention on her, their gazes had met. Her smile lingered on her face as those blue, blue eyes burned into his.

Zac's heart had lurched uncomfortably in his chest.

She'd blinked, licked her lips, then looked away, breaking the connection.

Not wanting to draw attention to Bryan's and Stella's

presence, Zac turned his attention to Noah and Summer sitting next to him. He couldn't stop a slight smile crossing his face at seeing them laughing together. It was good to see Noah so happy after the hell he'd gone through to get Summer back.

The visible stiffening of Cassie's body in his peripheral vision distracted him from his thoughts. She'd noticed Bryan. A wave of protectiveness surged through Zac and he pinned Cassie's ex-fiancé with his eyes, fucking daring him to try anything with her. Bryan had screwed her over once. Zac wasn't going to let him do it again.

And then when Cassie had headed out to the dance floor, he'd watched her. The sway of her hips was almost hypnotic. With her head tipped back, her hair rippled like a dark river down her spine, the ends almost brushing the top of her ass. When a man moved up behind her, Zac's jaw clenched, but after only a few seconds, Cassie stepped away from him. He only realized how tense he'd been when his shoulders noticeably relaxed.

Zac scrubbed a hand over his face. Cassie was fine. She had Lexie, Eden, and Summer to keep her company and look out for her. He didn't need to take personal responsibility for her emotional well-being. He glanced at the glass in his hand and swirled the small amount of whiskey left at the bottom. Maybe he'd had too much to drink. He was nowhere near a lightweight, but all those late nights were kicking his ass. He wasn't a fucking teenager anymore who could stay up all night, every night, for weeks at a time and not suffer the consequences.

He was just tired and pushing himself hard to get this damn album done. That was why he was overreacting to this whole Cassie situation.

He looked for her again and saw her at the bar, talking

to the three other women. She threw back her head and laughed, revealing the smooth column of her throat. Something warm uncurled in his chest.

Spending every night of the last week together, him working with Crossfire, and her quietly writing nearby, was messing with his head. He didn't want to admit that those hours—when it was just the two of them alone—had become something he looked forward to a little too much.

He would watch her while she wrote, only half-listening to the other Crossfire members as they talked intros and verses. Instead of focusing on what he should be, he would wonder what words she was filling that notebook with. Was she writing diary entries? A book? Was she a songwriter? He wondered if she used to sit like that with Bryan while he composed songs for Blacklite.

The thought sent a flare of something a little too close to jealousy through him. For some reason, the time he and Cassie spent together in their little bubble every night had taken on a significance that was raising red flags in his mind. Maybe that was why he couldn't bring himself to ask her about her writing. He couldn't afford for there to be that kind of connection between them.

Zac closed his eyes and took another sip of his whiskey, concentrating on the burn of the liquid trickling down his throat to distract himself from thoughts he didn't want to be having.

But a minute later, his gaze was drawn straight back to Cassie. Tension gripped his back and shoulders when Bryan materialized at her side. Damn. He hadn't even noticed the man leave his seat next to Stella.

Noah leaned toward him. "Cassie can handle herself. You can stop worrying about her."

"I'm not worried." His focus remained on Cassie and Bryan.

"Bullshit. Your problem is you spend far too much time worrying about what you think everyone else needs and not enough worrying about what you need."

Zac cut his eyes toward the drummer, who for once didn't have a smile on his face.

He didn't offer a response, just turned back to the bar.

Bryan leaned closer to Cassie and said something. She recoiled, shook her head, downed the rest of her champagne, and headed for the dance floor. Lexie, Summer, and Eden looked at each other, then at Bryan, and followed her into the mass of dancing bodies. Bryan stood stiffly, watching Cassie go, then stalked back to where the rest of his band was sitting, a frustrated scowl twisting his face. He leaned down, planted his hand on the back of the couch next to Stella's head, and whispered something in her ear. A second later, she was up on her feet and following him out on the dance floor. They disappeared into the crowd surrounding Cassie.

"On what grounds can we fire an opening act?" Tex was only half-joking.

Connor snorted. "I don't think actively disliking them counts."

"Shame," Noah said, then leaned forward to track Bryan and Stella through the throng of dancers. "What the fuck is he playing at?"

But Zac was watching Cassie. He saw the moment she must have spotted Bryan and Stella. Her lithe movements stuttered to a stop and her lips parted. The next moment she'd clamped her eyes shut to block out the vision of whatever it was Bryan was doing to make his point. She started dancing again, but her movements were jerky. Any relaxation she might have been feeling was obviously gone. Another man moved up behind her, and she didn't step away. She let him put his hands on her hips and pull her close.

The heat of Zac's anger, fueled by the whiskey he was drinking, burned through him like wildfire. Fuck Bryan. Someone needed to teach that asshole a lesson on how to treat the people you're supposed to love. He downed the rest of his drink, slammed his glass down on the table, and stood.

"Oh shit," Noah said from behind him as Zac stalked toward the dance floor.

He shouldered his way through the crowd until he saw what Cassie had seen: Stella with her back to Bryan's chest, rolling her ass into his dick while he held her hips against him.

The fucker was staring directly at Cassie.

Zac's anger flamed hotter. That asshole had hurt Cassie badly, and when she didn't fall back into his arms—when she wouldn't give him the forgiveness he so obviously thought he deserved—he proved what a petty little shit he was by torturing her more.

Zac's hands fisted, and he suppressed the urge to punch the man. He didn't need to. He knew what would hurt Bryan more than a fist to the face. Emotional pain always did more lasting damage than physical.

He should know.

So, instead of jamming his fist into Bryan's face, Zac made a beeline for Cassie.

The man dancing behind her must have seen Zac's determination and he quickly melted away into the crowd. Zac barely noticed. All he could see now was Cassie, body

Fractured Kiss

stilling, eyes widening as she watched him approach. He wondered if she sensed his intention.

If so, she didn't retreat. She stood frozen, gaze fixed on him.

Waiting for him.

He reached her. Didn't stop. Didn't second-guess himself. He knew what he needed to do. What he fucking *wanted* to do.

He buried his hands in her hair, tilted her face up, and crashed his lips down on hers.

Zac didn't know what he'd been expecting—hesitation, maybe, possibly resistance. If so, he would have stopped. But that wasn't what happened. Cassie opened for him, her tongue meeting his, the taste of champagne and strawberries and *her* exploding through him. He tugged her head farther back and slid one hand down to bracket her neck. Her pulse jackhammered under his thumb as he pressed it lightly against the hollow of her throat. What would she taste like there if he flicked his tongue over her skin?

"What the fuck!" Bryan's enraged voice seemed to come from a distance behind him, but Zac didn't stop. Couldn't stop. The reason he started kissing Cassie faded from his mind until all he could think about was tasting more of her, thrusting his tongue deeper, claiming her, taking her.

She moaned into his mouth, and he felt the vibrations under his thumb where he was stroking it across the satiny skin of her neck. He dropped his hand to the small of her back and dragged her against him so he could feel the softness of her breasts against his chest. Their hips were pressed together, and there was no way she could miss how hard he was. He didn't care. Didn't care if she knew he wanted to take her somewhere right now, bend her over, and fuck her until they were both crying out in release.

Someone bumped against him, and he finally broke away. But he didn't look to see who jostled him. Or to see Bryan's reaction. He kept his gaze fixed on her. He watched her eyelashes flutter open, revealing pupils wide and black. Her lips were still parted, swollen from the intensity of his kiss.

And he fucking *liked* it.

Bryan yelled something, someone behind him swore, and finally, Zac turned. Tex stood in front of Bryan, who glared at them over Tex's shoulder. Connor and Noah were flanking Bryan. The bands' bodyguards held the crowd back, but many of them had their phones up, recording the moment for posterity.

Reality hit him like a bucket of ice water to the face. *Fuck, what was he thinking?* He'd lost his cool in front of everyone and did something he promised himself he wouldn't. Zac's heart slammed in his chest, all too aware of Cassie's presence at his back. He had no idea what she was thinking, but he needed to wrestle back some of the control he lost the second his lips had touched hers. Fuck, the minute he'd seen her in that dress. He stepped toward Bryan, leaned close, and said, "It's about time you learned what it feels like."

He turned, catching Cassie's stricken expression. A stab of guilt made his stomach clench. He somehow had to explain why the hell he'd kissed her. He needed to justify his actions to her. But not right now, and not here.

He averted his gaze. "Let's go," he barked at the others. He headed for the exit without waiting to see if anyone followed.

Chapter Sixteen

The ride back to the bus in the stretch limo was beyond awkward.

Cassie somehow ended up sitting between Summer and Noah, diagonally opposite Zac, who was silently staring out the dark-tinted window the whole time. A muscle flexed in his jaw. Was he angry?

Her pulse was still racing, her lips tingled, and a confusing mixture of hurt and arousal simmered inside her.

Seeing Stella and Bryan dancing together like that had been painful. Two weeks just wasn't enough to get over losing the person you'd thought you were going to spend the rest of your life with.

But her anger was stronger. The Bryan she thought she knew would have *never* stooped so low as to rub her nose in whatever he and Stella had going on now.

Rather than succumb to the hurt, she'd shut her eyes to block out the sight of them and kept on dancing. She'd let that stranger pull her to him. It beat feeling her anger and pain.

When his hands had suddenly dropped away and the

cool air at her back told her he'd gone, her eyes had blinked open.

Zac.

Coming right for her.

Even now, the memory of the look on his face as he'd stalked toward her had heat flaring low in her belly.

She didn't think anyone had ever looked at her like that before. The intensity in his gaze had sent a bolt of need sizzling through her. Desire curled hot and heavy in her stomach, triggering the sudden desire to know what it would be like to have his body against her body, his hands on her skin, his mouth pressed to hers.

She'd stood there, forgetting everything and everyone around her, forgetting Bryan.

She'd waited for him.

And that kiss.

Her fingers were halfway to her lips before she realized what she was doing. She lowered her hand, resisting the urge to touch the swollen, tender flesh. To close her eyes and remember the way he tasted, how he felt, the hard press of him against her stomach.

Cassie let out a soft, shuddery breath. She needed to stop these thoughts in their tracks. She'd heard what Zac said to Bryan after: *It's about time you learned what it felt like.*

He'd been teaching Bryan a lesson. That was all. He'd punished Bryan for doing something hurtful to her. Because apparently, Zac was protective like that. So why wasn't she happy about it?

Why had pain stabbed through her when she realized he'd only done it to mess with Bryan?

"Zac, man, you are full of surprises." Noah's voice, brimming with mirth, finally broke the silence.

The blond drummer grinned over at Zac, whose own expression was coolly unreadable as he looked back at him. For a second, Zac's eyes flicked to hers, caught, held. Without conscious volition, her body responded: nipples tightening, lips parting as she inhaled shakily, cheeks heating.

Zac didn't react, turning his attention back to Noah. "The guy's an asshole. He deserved a taste of his own medicine." Then he went straight back to looking out the window.

If Noah was disappointed he couldn't rile up Zac, he didn't show it. He just grinned over at the others sitting opposite them.

Summer gripped Cassie's hand and squeezed it. When she met her gaze, the pretty strawberry-blonde gave her a reassuring smile. "Are you okay?"

She didn't want to make a big deal about what had happened. Because it wasn't. It wasn't a big deal. It was just a thing that had happened.

With her boss.

The man she was living with.

The one who awakened all kinds of inappropriate thoughts.

She forced a smile to her face and nodded jerkily.

Summer squeezed her hand again. When she let go, Cassie laced her suddenly cold fingers together. She slid her eyes back toward Zac. The sharp angle of his jaw as he looked out the window made her feel as if she'd done something wrong. Even though she hadn't.

Although she was surrounded by people, she suddenly felt alone again.

* * *

Cassie was acutely conscious of Zac's entrance into the living room the next morning. There was a subtle shift in the air pressure, a prickle of awareness at her nape alerting her to his presence. She raised her head at the same moment his eyes landed on her.

Cassie's breath caught. She wasn't sure how to react. She wanted things to go back to normal but wasn't sure how to make it happen. Last night, she'd thought Zac might take her aside after they got back to the bus. He owed her an explanation, after all. But he hadn't spoken a word to her. He disappeared into his bunk, and she hadn't seen him again until now.

Zac looked at Tex and Eden, who were sitting next to each other at the table drinking coffee. Obviously reading his expression, they both stood up and took their coffee cups back into the bunk area. Eden threw Cassie a reassuring smile over her shoulder.

As soon as they were gone, Zac approached her. He stopped in front of her and shoved his hands in his pockets.

He was silent for a long moment, then he cleared his throat. "I owe you an apology."

It felt too much like a disadvantage having him looming over her, so she stood, wanting to be on an equal footing with him.

That put them closer, though. Close enough that she had to tilt her head back to look up at him. God, she was far too aware of him now. Too familiar with how his body felt against hers. "I understand what you were trying to do. You were just... looking out for me. Proving a point to Bryan. You don't need to apologize for that."

Her pulse was speeding up, her lips tingling with the memory of his mouth on hers. She hated that her body was reacting to his proximity like never before. She hated even more that she'd responded so enthusiastically to a kiss he'd only given her to make a point.

At her words, something flashed in his eyes, but his expression didn't change. He was completely composed. Nothing like the man who had stalked toward her through the crowd like some dark, dangerous jungle cat last night.

"Still, I shouldn't have done it. Particularly not when you work for me. It won't happen again. I promise."

Her heart did a strange stutter of disappointment. But this was exactly what she needed, wasn't it? Reassurance that everything was okay and what happened was just a one-off. So why did she have to fake a smile? "Okay."

He searched her face for one long beat, nodded, and headed for the kitchenette without another word.

Cassie let out a breath and sank back down onto the seat. She watched him move around as he made himself a coffee. The memory of his hard muscles under her hands and something even harder pressing against her stomach sent a shiver through her. She looked away.

That damn kiss. She wished it had never happened. She understood his reason for doing it. Sort of. But now there was something physical between them that hadn't been there before. Or maybe it *had* been. The memory of how her body had reacted to touching him the night she'd given him a massage tugged at her. Things were all muddled up in her head now. How could she be attracted to anyone so soon after what had happened with Bryan? Particularly an attraction this intense. Shouldn't she be in mourning for the death of the only relationship she'd ever had?

Eventually, the others came out from the bunks, and conversation flowed around her. But Cassie remained lost in her thoughts until they pulled into the parking lot of the arena they'd be playing at in Fargo, North Dakota. The bus shuddered to a halt with a hiss of hydraulic brakes. They were barely stopped a few seconds before the door swished open and someone thumped up the stairs.

Drew strode toward them, scowling. "What the hell were you thinking?"

Cassie's stomach lurched.

"What's going on?" Zac responded.

Drew held his phone up for everyone to see.

Cassie sucked in a sharp breath. The headline of the website article screamed out at her: *Is Fractured's Bass Player Fracturing Relationships?*

And below that was a dark, blurry, but unfortunately clear enough photo of her and Zac on the dance floor. His hands were buried in her hair, hers were clutching the shirt at his chest, and their mouths were fused together. Bryan was beside them, rage on his face, with Tex clearly fending him off.

"Oh my god," she whispered, pressing a hand to her stomach as nausea swelled and rolled.

"And it's not the only site that's picked the story up," Drew said. "You two made quite a scene last night." He flicked through a few more websites, all with variations of the same photo.

"Fuck." Zac squeezed his eyes shut and rubbed the bridge of his nose. Tex and Noah laughed hysterically, and even Connor was grinning. Summer and Eden exchanged small smiles of amusement with each other. None of them seemed to be bothered by the article.

A touch on the back of her hand jerked Cassie out of her tailspin. Lexie's expression of concern was probably in response to whatever emotion was showing on Cassie's face. But she, Drew and Zac were the only ones who looked less than amused.

"You two can stop laughing." Drew pointed at Tex and Noah, then looked back at Zac. "It's not you I'm worried about."

His gaze slid to Cassie, and dread swirled through her. "I'm sorry, Cassie, the articles aren't very flattering."

Zac's spine snapped straight. "Give it to me."

Drew handed his phone over, and Zac scrolled through it, his expression growing stonier by the second.

"What does it say?" Cassie's voice was choked.

He didn't lie to her or try to soften the blow. "They identified you by name as Bryan's fiancée and mention you're working as a guitar tech for Fractured." He looked up at her. "It basically insinuates that you're a bed-hopper who cheated on your fiancée with me, and that it's causing issues on the tour."

Dizziness hit her. *Bed-hopper?* They were suggesting she was a... a... whore. Just like her mom... just like—

Cassie's gut churned. She squeezed her eyes shut and swallowed through the constriction in her throat. Ending up with the same label as her mom wasn't what she should be worrying about the most right now. If staying on the tour was supposed to protect her professional reputation in the music business, she might as well have packed up and gone. Now everyone was going to assume she was just sleeping her way through the rock stars she worked for. Who would want to hire her if they thought she was causing those kinds of issues? She'd be passed over for all the good jobs and probably only end up getting hired by musicians who thought she'd be up for a little fun on the side.

"Let me see." Connor held his hand out for the phone.

Zac slapped it into his palm, then looked back at Cassie. "I'm sorry."

Cassie gave a little head shake, her mouth too dry to speak.

Drew cleared his throat. "I think there are two ways we can play this. Ignore it and wait for the media to move on to something else, which, honestly, won't take long. There's really no story here. Or we get the label to make a statement that Cassie and Bryan broke up before this photo was taken and leave it at that."

Lexie regarded Drew with a frown. "The problem with both those plans is that they're fine for Zac—he's a rock star. He can do whatever he wants, and no one cares. Cassie is the one being painted badly in this, and neither of those strategies does much for her. People will assume the worst, and even if the media attention goes away quickly, we already know industry word of mouth is going to tear her apart. And while it might help a bit having it out there that she wasn't cheating on Bryan, it still doesn't look great for her if she's seen as jumping from Bryan's bed to Zac's. No one wants someone who's going to cause problems on tour."

Cassie slumped in her seat, her neck and skull throbbing with tension. "But that's not what happened. Can't we tell everyone it was just a kiss? Can't we force them to print a retraction or something?"

"No." Zac's voice was flat.

She looked at him. "Why not?"

"They're not interested in the truth. They won't report it. If we make a statement, we're on the defensive. They'll smell blood in the water and be more interested."

Drew nodded. "And we can't sue and make them retract what they've written. It's all insinuation. They never come right out and state anything as fact. Even the headline is a question, not a statement. It's enough to do damage, not enough to hold up to a defamation suit. They know exactly how to walk the line."

Anger and frustration flooded through Cassie. "So, there's nothing I can do? One kiss that didn't even mean anything and my career could be ruined?"

Zac's eyes flashed to hers. "I'm not going to let what I did ruin your life." His voice was low, tension vibrating through it. For a second, it distracted Cassie from the nausea in her stomach. She wasn't sure why Zac was taking this so personally. Yes, he'd been the one to kiss her, but she hadn't exactly pushed him away.

"There is another way we could play it." Drew's cautious tone made Cassie sit up straight. His gaze met hers, then swung to Zac. "I wouldn't have suggested this a few years ago, but considering everyone else is in a serious relationship now, it will seem more believable." Zac's brows lowered, his jaw tightening as if he knew what his manager was going to say. "And since you're usually so private about your dealings with women, I don't think it will be questioned."

Cassie looked between them. "Please tell me what you're talking about."

Drew's hand rasped across the stubble on his chin. "The only thing we let slip to the media is you and Bryan weren't together. Zac's right. They don't care about the truth, and it will just make them more interested. Instead, you and Zac act like you're a couple. It won't fix everything. But if you act as if you two have a genuine connection, you'll look less like the bed-hopper they're suggesting you are. Once the tour is over, and you have your next job lined up, the two of you quietly go your separate ways."

A knot formed in Cassie's chest. Why would Drew even suggest something so ridiculous? "Musicians get away with sleeping with people they work with on tour all the time," she whispered.

Drew nodded his sympathy. "It's a huge double standard—one I'm not condoning in any way. Rock stars are pretty much expected to screw around. But if women crew members are thought to be sleeping around with the musicians, they get labeled pretty quickly. And regardless of how unfair that is, it's not something we want happening to you."

Zac slumped back against his chair and scrubbed his hands over his face. "Fuck," he muttered again.

"I don't want to do it," Cassie said quickly, and everyone turned to look at her. She couldn't meet Zac's eyes. She didn't want to see the relief shining there.

"Cassie—" Lexie started.

Cassie shook her head. "Can we just go with the option where we let everyone know Bryan and I had broken up before the photo was taken? At least it won't look like I'm a..." She shook her head and swallowed hard.

"Are you sure that's the way you want to play it?" Drew asked.

Cassie hesitated for a fraction of a second and was about to nod when Zac spoke. "No."

Cassie met his gaze, frowning.

"It was my fault. You shouldn't be the one to suffer the consequences." His expression was unreadable.

She gave a humorless laugh. "There's no way you want to pretend to be in love with me for the next few months."

"We don't have to be in love. Just together." His voice was tight.

She didn't know why that hurt. But it did. She shook her head but stopped when Zac leaned toward her.

"Cassie," he said, more softly. "Let me make this right."

For a few erratic beats of her heart, she forgot the

others were there as she stared into his eyes. She almost thought she could see a plea in their beautiful hazel depths.

Cassie blew out a breath. Would it be so bad to go along with it? As much as she needed to learn to stand on her own two feet, that didn't mean she shouldn't accept help. And Zac obviously felt guilty about the kiss and wanted to make up for it.

He reached out and touched the back of her hand. "Cassie—"

"Okay." It came out slightly choked.

Zac nodded and sat back in his chair. She couldn't read his expression, and sudden misgivings hit her. He was only doing this because he thought he had to. Because he felt obliged to.

But Drew had already leaped into action, typing rapidly on his phone as he spoke.

"Okay. So, neither of you makes any statements to the media about this. I'll let the record label know you two are together. The information will get out there soon enough." He smirked before looking over at Zac. "This is where your privacy when it comes to the women you... ahem... *date* comes in handy. The fact that you're making this public makes it look more serious. Which makes it more believable. People are always more willing to forgive transgressions if they think it's true love." One corner of his mouth twitched up, and he shook his head as if he couldn't believe what he was saying either.

"I could take some photos of you together and put them up on your social media," Lexie said to Zac. He nodded absently.

"Cassie's already staying on the bus, so that lends credence to the idea that the two of you have fallen for each other," Drew said. "Just make sure you're seen together regularly, and that'll be it."

Cassie gripped the edge of her seat. This was all running away from her. And she still couldn't read Zac's expression. All the confusing emotions of the last twelve hours descended on her. She stood suddenly. Everyone stopped what they were doing and looked at her. "I just... I want to... I just need a second," she said and squeezed out from behind the table.

She pretended she couldn't feel Zac's gaze burning into her as she headed for the front of the bus. She might want to just crawl into her bed and pull the covers over her head, but she didn't really have that luxury with her job waiting for her. So, she'd take a few minutes away from everyone. Just a few minutes to hide away from the reality of her life now. And to try to figure out just how it all kept falling apart around her.

Chapter Seventeen

How the fuck had he gotten them both into this situation? Zac speared his hand through his hair, looking around the crowded after-party to see if Cassie had arrived yet. He couldn't see her, and relief trickled through him. It was closely followed by a stab of guilt. This wasn't her idea. The whole thing was on him. Losing control, kissing her when he knew better. He'd even been the one to convince her to go along with Drew's suggestion, just to absolve his guilt and minimize the damage of his impulsive act. Had he even stopped to consider what she might want?

Zac sighed and rubbed his hand over his face.

A woman wearing a Fractured tank top approached, clutching a pen. Given that she wasn't holding any merchandise, Zac figured she was going to ask him to sign her top. Or what was under it. Based on previous experience and the fact it was pretty clear as she walked she wasn't wearing a bra, his guess was it was going to be the latter. She was attractive, so it wouldn't exactly be a hardship. But even signing a pretty woman's tits stopped being exciting after you've done it a thousand times.

She stopped in front of him. "Hi, Zac." Her voice was breathy, but he recognized the look in her eye. It was the look he normally sought out. The one that said she'd be more than okay if he wanted to use her body for a little stress relief. That she wanted to use him too. That was the way he liked it—mutually assured satisfaction with no expectation of commitment. He might have even taken her up on the offer implicit in her expression if things were different. But they weren't. He ignored the invitation in her gaze and gave her a practiced smile. "Hey there. What's your name?"

"Camille."

"Hi, Camille. Did you enjoy the show?"

"I loved it so much. You guys are amazing! Especially you. The way you play that bass is just, mmm..." She gave a little shiver.

"Well, thanks, I appreciate that. You want me to sign something for you?"

"Yes, please." She held out the pen.

Zac took it from her and cocked a brow. She smiled coyly and pulled her top down. She didn't quite bare her nipple. Not quite. Just a sliver of pink areola showed above where her fingers were hooked into the fabric.

He leaned over her, put the tip of the pen against her skin and scrawled his signature, then capped it again and held it out for her. She stared at him, lips parted, apparently surprised he was so quick and efficient. As if she wanted him to cop a feel. As if he hadn't seen tits just like hers almost every night since they'd hit the big time. Her face fell when she realized that was it.

"Are you going to get the others too?" He tipped his

head toward Tex and Noah, who were standing with Eden and Summer.

She glanced over at them. "Um, yeah. I just wanted to get yours first because I—" Her words cut off as her gaze darted over his shoulder, her eyebrows pulling together.

Without even turning, Zac knew who she was looking at. He'd sensed her, a frisson of awareness skittering down his spine. He glanced over his shoulder. Cassie stood a few feet behind him, her big blue eyes uncertain, hands tugging at the hem of her crew T-shirt as her gaze ping-ponged between him and Camille. Drew was standing by the door and gave Zac a nod. He'd obviously sent Cassie over here, but it looked like she had no idea what to do next.

She wasn't the only one. How the hell were they supposed to play this? During this morning's discussion and his and Cassie's awkward interactions since then, they'd failed to discuss if they were going to act any differently than usual. The pause stretched on a little too long, and Cassie's expression froze more with every second that passed. Zac took a deep breath and held his hand out to her.

She swallowed hard but lifted her chin and stepped toward him. Almost without realizing he was doing it, he slid his arm around her waist and tugged her against him. Instinctively, her arm looped around his back. There was an infinitesimal pause as their eyes met. There were storms in hers. For the first time, he really stopped to think about how difficult this must be for her. Two weeks ago, she'd been happily engaged. Now she had to pretend she'd forgotten all about her ex-fiancé and moved on with Zac.

He tightened his arm around her and did his best to give her a reassuring smile. She wet her lips, then gave him a shaky one in return. He tried not to stare at her mouth. The last thing he needed to do was start remembering the way it had felt under his.

He looked back at the woman standing in front of them. She'd covered herself back up, and her face was alight with recognition.

Her eyes moved between the two of them. "Oh my god, are you two actually together? I saw the article and thought—"

"Looks that way," he cut her off before she said anything that might piss him off. And it wasn't exactly a lie.

The woman's gaze drifted up and down Cassie, and tension vibrated through the slender form under his arm. God, they really hadn't thought this thing through at all. Fans took ridiculous liberties sometimes. The four of them had learned to cope with the invasion of privacy over the years. He could put up with a lot of shit, but if Camille tried to say anything about—or to—Cassie, she'd learn his patience only went so far.

If Camille had an opinion, she kept it to herself. She gave him another smile, a slightly disappointed one, but seemingly genuine. "Well, thank you for..." She gestured to her chest before her eyes widened and darted toward Cassie. Her cheeks turned red as if she suddenly realized she'd just asked Cassie's boyfriend to sign her breast. "Um, yeah, thank you." With a last glance at Cassie, she headed toward Noah and Tex.

Zac loosened his arm, and Cassie stepped away from him. The side of his body cooled with the space that opened between them.

"I'm sorry if that was weird for you," she said quietly. "I'm not really sure how we're supposed to do this."

He gave a low laugh. "It's not exactly something I'm familiar with either."

She shot him a self-conscious smile. "I guess we just play it by ear, then. But if I do something, or say something you don't like, just tell—"

"Hey." He gripped her chin between his thumb and forefinger. "You're not going to do or say anything I don't like. Look, I know this situation is less than ideal, but it's only for a couple of months. Then you'll find another job, and we'll be out of it. Okay?"

The smile she gave him this time was stiff. He probably could have phrased it a bit more tactfully, but it was true. This wasn't something either of them had wanted. But since he was the one who had caused the problem, he was going to do what he needed to do to fix it.

A group of fans approached. Without thinking too much about it, Zac reached out and linked his hand with Cassie's, pulling her toward him again. There was an upside to this. He'd be less likely to be groped and propositioned all night. He might be used to it, but right now his only focus was on getting through these after-parties as quickly as possible so he could get back to the bus and work on the album.

The next forty-five minutes passed quickly. He was right. Having Cassie by his side seemed to calm the more enthusiastic fans down. Not all of them. But enough that he was actually enjoying interacting with most of them rather than trying to guess which one was going to stick their tongue in his ear or slide their hand down the back of his jeans while they were taking photos.

When the party finally wrapped up, the eight of them headed back to the bus. Lexie and Cassie were walking in front, talking quietly. Zac couldn't hear what they were saying, but the sound of Cassie's soft laugh made him smile.

"Hey, Tex, do you recognize that expression on Zac's face?" Noah asked.

Zac didn't give the drummer the benefit of acknowledging his comment.

"Not sure I do," Tex drawled. "Don't think I've seen that one before."

"You know, I think it could have something to do with the woman who was glued to his side all night long." Connor got in on the act.

Now they were starting to bug him. He shot a look at all of them where they were walking to his left and grinning like fools. He didn't have a problem with them giving him shit, but he didn't want Cassie overhearing and reading something into it. Not that he really thought she would. She knew the truth just as much as he did. But he couldn't be too careful. He'd spent his life avoiding emotional entanglements. The last thing he wanted was to get caught up in one with Cassie.

"Nope, it's gone. Back to the usual inscrutable one now," said Noah.

Connor snickered. "Don't make us call Cassie back here."

"Cut it out, assholes," Zac said through clenched teeth.

"Don't get your panties in a twist." Tex couldn't hide the laugh in his voice.

"Stop talking shit, then."

Tex held up his hands, but he still sported a wide grin on his face. Zac shook his head. His friends were having far too much fun with this situation.

Around them, the remaining trucks and buses were rumbling to life, filling the air with the smell of diesel. Most of the convoy had already headed out on their way to the next venue.

Fractured Kiss

Zac watched Cassie walk in front of him and wondered whether she would still join him tonight. Or if she'd hit the sack early, having worked all day and night, then come to the after-party to be with him.

He'd gotten used to the soft scratch of her pen across the paper while he worked. It formed a calming backdrop to the sometimes-heated conversations that occurred—common enough when you were trying to write music with four different personalities.

As soon as everyone was on the bus and sprawled around the now crowded living room, Maggie got them on the road. Thirty minutes later, the others headed to bed. Cassie, who'd been chatting with the three other women, collected her notebook and sat in her usual spot. She rested her back against the padded armrest of the couch and pulled her knees up so she could lay her notebook on her thighs.

He watched her with a faint smile as he waited for the other three Crossfire members to get their shit together on the other side of the video call. Tonight, she was wearing little gray shorts with pink hearts and another clingy white cami top. On her feet were a pair of fluffy pink socks that only emphasized the smoothness of the skin above them. Zac shifted in his seat. Jesus, was he actually getting a semi from a pair of socks?

Cassie's dark hair was piled in a messy bun on top of her head and her eyes were cast down at her notebook. Her long, dark lashes threw spiky shadows across her cheekbones, and her full lips were wrapped around the end of her pen as she read over whatever she was writing.

Fuck. Those lips. Damn it. He'd spent all day and night trying not to think about her mouth. Because remembering how she'd tasted last night, how she'd felt pressed up against him, was too fucking dangerous. He needed to stop. It would only make this thing more difficult. But his dick hadn't got the memo. It was throbbing against his fly as he remembered the sound of her moan when he kissed her. Would she moan the same way if he pressed his mouth to other parts of her body?

What was worse than his physical reaction to her was the part of him that wanted to know what made her tick. The part that wanted to blow off this session with the guys, sit down next to her, and ask her about herself. Ask her what her hopes and dreams were. Find out the joys and sorrows that had shaped her life.

He needed to resist both urges.

"Zac!" The voice emanating from his phone jerked his mind back.

Cassie cocked her head and raised her brows at him. Damn, he was still staring at her.

Zac shifted his attention to his phone. "Sorry, just running through some ideas for chord changes in my head," he lied smoothly.

Devon eyed him skeptically, and Zac wondered how long they'd been trying to get his attention. Normally he was the hyper-focused one, having to pull their attention back from whatever shiny object had distracted them back in LA.

He rolled his shoulders. He needed to get his head back in the game and off Cassie. Getting this album finished was his priority. He'd do what he could to get Cassie out of this mess with her reputation as intact as possible, but that was it. Crossfire was at the top of his priority list right now. He wouldn't let them down because of a woman.

Even one as distracting as Cassie.

Chapter Eighteen

Cassie carefully tightened the tuning peg, running her finger along the string to test the tension. Footsteps alerted her to a presence, and she turned with a smile. A part of her was hoping it might be Zac coming to talk to her again, like he had the morning after her first night on their bus. A weight settled on her chest when she found Bryan watching her instead. His eyes were dark, his face almost as unreadable as Zac's normally was.

She looked back at the bass, a strange numbness settling around her. She wasn't angry, and even the searing pain seeing him had evoked in her a few days ago was nothing but a dull ache.

"Is it true?" His voice was rough.

"Is what true?"

"You and Zac. You're together? That didn't take long."

She whipped around to glare at him. "Excuse me? It took a hell of a lot longer than it took you, considering we were still together when you shopped around for a better option."

A muscle in his jaw pulsed. "How many times do I have to say that I'm sorry? I love you. Only you. I..." He let out a frustrated breath and rubbed both hands over his face. "I don't even know why I did it. It wasn't cold feet or anything. I wanted to marry you. I *want* to marry you. I..." He shook his head and looked at her with a helpless expression.

"It doesn't matter how many times you say it, Bryan. It doesn't make it go away. Sorry doesn't erase the betrayal. Telling me you love me doesn't make it hurt less."

"So, you still care about me then? You wouldn't say it hurt if you didn't still care. If you're with Zac just to get back at me, I get it. Okay? I don't like it, but I get it. But if you still love me, then when you're over this... this thing, you and I can try again, right?"

Cassie let herself really look at him. Like probing a sore tooth, she let herself remember all the good times, made herself think about everything he'd meant to her over the last ten years. Could she get past the hurt? Could she put the anger behind her? Would she ever be able to look at him the same? This *thing*, this fake thing, between her and Zac, wouldn't do what Bryan thought it would do. It wasn't about evening the score, bringing their relationship back in balance. It was nothing. A favor Zac was doing for her. It was on the tip of her tongue to tell him that, but the words wouldn't come. If she told him, he wouldn't let it go. He'd keep pushing her to try again with him.

I don't want to be with Bryan anymore.

The thought scared her. It shouldn't, but it did. A few short weeks ago, the idea of not being with Bryan was inconceivable. It had been her and him for so many years. The last time she'd known what it was like to feel truly alone was when she was fourteen. She'd thought she would never have to feel that way again. Was she really prepared to face it at the end of this tour?

Cassie suddenly recalled the words of advice Maggie had given her that first night on Fractured's bus: *It's better to be alone than with someone who doesn't appreciate your true worth.*

Her chest cinched tight, her hands clenching around the bass she was holding.

"What about you and Stella?" Her voice came out more evenly than she expected.

He grimaced, obviously not wanting to talk about it. But Cassie just sat there looking at him, waiting for his answer. She needed to know.

He cleared his throat. "She says she wants to keep things going between us. Nothing serious, just a—a physical relationship. But if you're willing to try again, I'll tell her nothing else can happen between us."

"*Nothing else?* You mean nothing else except for that one time I caught you two?"

His slight hesitation was telling. Guilt pulled down the corners of his mouth. If she'd thought she was beyond being hurt, she'd been wrong. Barbed fingers clutched at her heart.

Bryan blew out a harsh breath. "After the other night at the club. You and Zac. I was in a crazy headspace. I didn't mean for it to happen, but with the alcohol, seeing you kissing him. It didn't mean anything. I promise. I—"

"So, all this time, you've been telling me what a mistake it was. That you love me and want me back. That it was a one-off and would never happen again. Were those lies?"

"You and Zac—"

Her choked laugh cut him off. *If he only knew the truth about her and Zac.*

She stood, turned her back to him, and racked Zac's bass. She took that time to compose her expression before facing him again.

"That's twice now something happened with Stella that you didn't mean to happen." And she wasn't sure she believed him that nothing had happened before that, either.

"So that's it? Because I got drunk and jealous over you having your tongue down someone else's throat, we're done?"

"I think you need to take a good, hard look at the choices you've made over the last couple of weeks and ask yourself if those are really the actions of someone who wants to be with me and only me for the rest of his life. Or if you're clinging to something just because it's familiar and comfortable."

He shook his head and persisted. "So, we're done?"

She took in the soft, golden curls she used to run her fingers through, the beautiful blue eyes, now dark with emotion, the slightly petulant droop of his lips. All so familiar. She knew exactly where her head would fit under his chin. Exactly how strong and warm his arms would feel around her. She knew exactly how he would smell, and if she tilted her head back and pressed her lips to his, she knew exactly how he would taste.

But if she clung to those things as a reason not to let go, she was no better than him. Familiar and comfortable wasn't everything. There *had* to be more than that.

Bryan wasn't hers anymore. He'd proven that. He wasn't the person she'd thought he was. The familiarity and comfort were a lie. And she didn't want to keep living a lie just because it was less scary.

She closed her eyes and took a breath, then met his gaze

and nodded. "Yes. We're done." Then she turned and walked away.

Chapter Nineteen

Zac walked into the hotel suite, Cassie trailing behind him. He leaned his guitar case against the wall and threw the keycard onto the table, then scanned the large living area, breathing out a sigh of relief. There was a luxurious couch, plenty big enough for him to sleep on. That meant Cassie could have the separate bedroom. It made more sense for her to take it, anyway, since she'd be able to go to sleep if she got tired while he stayed up working on the album with the guys. Not that she often went to bed before him. He wasn't sure if it was because she still had trouble getting to sleep, or if she'd started enjoying their time together as much as he had.

It had been three days since they'd begun this thing. Since they were performing at the same venue two nights in a row, they were staying at a hotel overnight. When Drew mentioned that he and Cassie would share a room, Zac had let out an internal groan. If being on the bus with her had become distracting, sharing a hotel room was going to be worse.

Cassie had asked Drew why she couldn't just get her

own room, but he'd reminded her that all the rooms for the tour had been booked months in advance. Trying to organize a last-minute room for her would look odd, considering she was already living on the bus with Zac. People paid too much attention to stuff like that when you were in a world-famous rock band. She'd nodded, understanding the logic.

Zac tried to ignore the part of him that was a little too pleased that she'd be with him tonight.

They'd wrapped up the after-party half an hour ago and driven straight to the hotel. While he stood there, looking around, Cassie dropped her purse on the table and sat down on the couch. She bounced a few times to test the softness, and Zac tried to avoid staring at her breasts under her shirt as they bounced right along with her. It'd be easier if they weren't such fucking nice breasts.

Cassie slipped off her shoes and lay down, closing her eyes and letting out a little sigh. Zac's pulse sped up. She was a far too tempting sight lying there with her hair a dark cloud around her head.

Zac's imagination took over. He saw himself closing the distance between them and skimming his fingers along the smooth skin of her legs, up toward the apex of her thighs. Would she stop him? Or would she let her legs fall open in invitation? He clenched his jaw and took a deep breath.

Cassie turned her head, her gaze finding his. She gave him a happy smile, and something twisted behind his ribs. He cleared his throat. "What are you doing?"

She sat up and gave him a strange look. "I'm testing the couch."

He shook his head. "I'll take the couch."

"Um, no, I don't think so."

"It's big enough, and believe me, I've slept on far worse in my life."

She frowned and pierced him with her eyes. "So have I."

Zac suppressed a smile. The more comfortable she was around him, the more confident she was becoming. "I'm not making you sleep on the couch."

She stood, her delicate jaw hardening. "*You* are the famous rock star. *I* work for *you*. I'll sleep on the couch."

This more assertive version of Cassie drew him in. He stepped closer, fascinated at how her pupils dilated as he got within touching distance.

"How are you going to make me?" he said. "Pick me up and throw me on the bed?" The corners of his mouth curled up.

Frustration danced in her eyes. "You're making this about me being a woman."

She didn't need to point out she was a woman. He was all too aware. His gaze dropped to her full bottom lip, and he fought the urge to lean down and nip it, then run his tongue across the tender skin to soothe the sting. Irritation at himself sharpened his tone. "What should it be about then? Your willingness to sacrifice your needs for the man you're with?"

Her face blanched.

Fuck, where the hell had that come from?

"You don't get to say things like that. You don't know anything about me." Her voice shook, and Zac was pissed at himself for bringing her down like that.

He scrubbed his hand over his face. She was right. He had no right to comment on her life. They were employer and employee, even if they were in this ridiculous situation together.

"I'm sorry, Cassie. I shouldn't have said that."

They stared at each other for a few seconds until she

nodded her acceptance of his apology. Then she gave him a mischievous smile. "Apology accepted. If"—she held up a finger—"you agree to let me sleep on the couch."

Still, he hesitated, and this time it was Cassie that stepped closer. Suddenly, they were standing so near each other he could smell the sweetness of her scent, see the faint freckles scattered across her nose. He swore he could feel the heat emanating from her body.

She laid her hand on his arm and looked up at him. "Please, Zac. I know you're trying to do the right thing, but I'd hate every second."

He could have said something about wanting the space to work on the album while she slept. She'd agree if he told her that. Whether or not she wanted to acknowledge it, she was a giver. She'd give up what she wanted for him. But he already knew how defeat would change the shade of her eyes, and he didn't want to be responsible for that.

He gave a curt nod, and her face brightened into a delighted smile at having gotten her way. Only when she turned away from him did he let his own lips quirk with amusement.

"You want a shower?" he asked. He'd already showered before the after-party, but he figured she might want one. Working the backline of a concert could be a hot, sticky job.

She glanced at him over her shoulder, obviously undecided. Her lower lip was caught between her teeth, a lock of dark hair partially covering one eye. The unintentionally seductive look set his already half-hard dick throbbing.

Fuck, he was far too on edge around her. And he couldn't even fuck someone else to get some relief while he was in this fake relationship. Even if it wasn't real, he'd never humiliate Cassie that way.

That meant no sex for the next couple of months. No

sex and spending all his time with a beautiful woman who had already made him lose control once.

Cassie nodded, answering his question. "I'd like that if you don't mind."

"I don't mind. I'll get the guys on the line and get some work done while you're in there."

She scanned the room, and realizing what she was looking for, he added, "Your bag will be in the bedroom. Don't forget, everyone thinks we're fucking."

He didn't know why he said it. Or why he enjoyed the slow flush that darkened her cheeks so much. Maybe he had a previously undiscovered sadistic streak. Or was it masochistic? Because the heat that flared up his spine made his body pulse with a hunger he had no way of satiating.

"Okay, I won't be too long." She went into the bedroom, shutting the door behind her.

Zac blew out a breath and pushed Cassie out of his mind. He grabbed his guitar out of its case and settled himself down on the couch. After propping his phone up, he dialed LA.

As always, the guys were waiting for his call, but with notably muted enthusiasm.

After about ten minutes, Zac put down his guitar. "What the hell is the matter?"

"We need a break, man," Beau answered. "Even if you don't. We've been doing this almost every night that we don't have an event scheduled."

"You know the timeline—"

"Yes, we know the timeline. But missing a day or two here and there won't make a difference. Burning out will."

Zac leaned back against the couch, frustration flaring to life inside him. Didn't they realize he was pushing them hard for their own benefit?

"Cassie, sweetheart. You need to help your man relax," Caleb said, his focus shifting over Zac's shoulder.

Zac twisted around to see Cassie standing behind him. His gaze drifted over her. She'd washed her hair, and it was hanging in a still-wet streamer over one shoulder. Her skin was dewy and flushed from the heat of the shower. The tank top she'd changed into clung to her breasts, while her sleep shorts accentuated the smooth curve of her hips and the length of her legs. For a second, all he could think of was how those legs would feel wrapped around him as he thrust into her. His whole body tightened in response, and he had to force himself to turn back around.

All three of his bandmates stared over his shoulder at Cassie, and he didn't like it. He hadn't told them the whole thing was fake. One of them was bound to get drunk and think the situation was hilarious enough to spill to some random person. But even though Cassie wasn't actually his girlfriend, he didn't want them looking at her like that.

"Fine." His voice came out with a snap, causing the three men to focus back on him. "You can have the night off. You can even have tomorrow off. But then it's back to business. The label's going to be pissed if they've organized the studio and time with Talia and we don't get this finished."

"No problem, dude. Don't stress. We'll get it done. Now fucking hang up and pay some attention to your woman. You both look like you could do with some relaxation."

"Yeah, you guys should definitely relax tonight. In fact, you should make sure you relax multiple times." Caleb laughed.

Assholes. He ignored their smirks. "I'll see you in a couple of days." He hung up before they could make another dumbass comment.

Cassie came and sat down on the couch next to him.

The intoxicating scent of her body wash wafted over to him, and he did his best to ignore her proximity. And the sudden vision of what she could do to help him relax.

"I'm sorry if I interrupted you," she said.

"It wasn't you. They just needed a break." He rubbed at the tightness in his neck.

"I think you probably need one too. You do look tense."

His eyes drifted over to her again. She made it hard to look away, sitting there looking completely innocent but still so damn tempting.

His very own fallen angel.

"You going to help me with that?" he asked, then silently cursed himself. Something about Cassie just made him act without thinking. Still, he was pleased with the way her creamy skin turned pink.

Zac cleared his throat and stood, walking over to the wet bar. "You want something?" he asked as casually as he could.

"Yes, please. Just a vodka, thanks."

He nodded and poured them both a drink, then carried the glasses back to the couch. She scooted to the end and leaned against the armrest, tucking one foot up underneath her. When he handed her the glass, her fingers brushed his, whispering across his skin in an accidental caress that sent a bolt of heat through him. Jesus, it was like he was fifteen again.

He sat down as far away from her as he could and took a sip of his drink, closing his eyes to savor the burn of the bourbon sliding down his throat.

When he opened them again, Cassie was watching him, a small smile on her lips. He raised his brows.

"So, I know you like karaoke, but what else does a famous rock star do when he's not on stage, writing his next hit album, or, you know, kissing random guitar techs in night clubs." Her eyes sparkled, and he liked this more relaxed, playful side of her.

"Sometimes I mix it up and kiss a drum tech."

She laughed. "I wondered why Pete looked so happy a couple of weeks ago."

Pete, Noah's drum tech, was grizzled, fifty-something, and covered in tattoos that looked like he'd inked them on himself. Zac grinned. "Lucky the media didn't get a hold of those photos. The view wouldn't be half as nice right now."

There was that blush again. She looked down at the tumbler of vodka resting on her thigh. Her thumb traced the side of the glass in a caress he could almost feel on his skin.

Zac put his own tumbler down on the coffee table a little too hard and reached for the guitar. He needed something to do with his hands to keep from reaching for her.

He picked out a simple melody. "What about you? What do you do to relax?"

"Okay, Mister Private, don't answer my question."

He heard the amusement in her voice and his lips curved in response.

"I like to read," she said.

He nodded. He'd seen her with her e-reader a few times on the bus. "What do you read?"

"I can't turn down a good thriller."

"Hmm. Okay, what else do you like to do?"

"I enjoy gardening," she said. "Back h-home I have planter boxes out on the balcony." He didn't miss the stumble over *home*. It reminded him that her life was in turmoil at the moment. "One day I'd like to have a garden. A big one. Full of flowers." She smiled self-consciously. "Maybe a vegetable patch."

What's the bet there's a white picket fence around that garden.

The thought sent a pang through him. Regardless, it wasn't exactly something she could have when she was on the road for months at a time.

His voice was softer when he prompted her again. "What else?"

Her eyes darted over to her purse. He knew it would have her notebook tucked away in it. "Well... You already know I like to write."

"Are you writing the next big thriller?"

Her smile was self-conscious. "No. I love reading them, but I'd never be able to write anything like that."

"So, what do you write?"

She bit her lip. Her gaze met his, and she swallowed as if it was difficult to share. "I write poetry."

The information didn't really surprise him. "I can see you as a poet."

Surprise flitted across her face. "Really?"

"Yeah. Sometimes, when you're in the middle of writing, you stop and get this far-off look in your eyes and a dreamy smile on your face. I can imagine lyrical phrases running through your head."

She laughed. "I guess you're a poet yourself."

His fingers played over the strings of his guitar. "All song writers are poets. They just set their poems against a backdrop of musical notes instead of white space."

"Is that right?" Her eyes sparkled.

A smile slipped out as his fingers moved over the instrument, playing a pretty little tune he made up on the spot. Then he sang, his voice coming out low and husky.

"She walks in beauty, like the night
Of cloudless climes and starry skies;
And all that's best of dark and bright
Meet in her aspect and her eyes;
Thus mellowed to that tender light
Which heaven to gaudy day denies."

"Oh my god, you're singing Lord Byron!" Her bright smile was fucking gorgeous.

His return smile faded, and he searched her face. "Didn't you ever help Bryan with his songwriting?"

She blinked. "Well... he didn't really like having any external input. You know, he wanted the music to be organic to the band. He and S-Stella had a process." She shrugged as if it hadn't mattered to her that her fiancé didn't want her help.

"So, will you read me some?" he asked.

"Some of my poetry?"

He nodded, and she looked down, fidgeting with the hem of her tank top. When she looked back up at him, her expression was guarded. Was it Bryan who had dented her confidence so much?

Zac waited, and eventually, she nodded. She walked to her bag, pulled out her notebook, and brought it back to the couch. She flicked through the pages, searching for something to read him. Finally, she stopped, her slender fingers curling tightly around the cover.

Her gaze darted up to meet his, and he nodded. She took a deep breath and started reading.

"Your love echoes in the hollows of my bones."

Zac closed his eyes to listen. Her shaky voice was almost too soft to hear.

*"The slide of your hands on my skin chases the dark away,
You wrapped yourself around my heart long ago,
When sunbeams flared too bright in my eyes,
You wrapped me around your heart just as tightly,
And now, entangled, we stay."*

The words had to be about Bryan. He was the only man she'd ever been with, and it was too personal not to be based on her own experience. He wanted to ask her about it, about Bryan. About what had been between them. But he wouldn't. He was already more invested than he should be. He didn't want to know what might happen if he let himself get too curious.

The draw he felt toward her was already too strong.

He opened his eyes and found her watching him nervously. He nodded. "It's good."

Something like disappointment flitted across her face. As if she were hoping for something more. Zac could imagine Bryan telling her the same thing. Right before he went back to doing whatever it was that was more important than Cassie sharing a part of herself with him.

She closed the book and went to stand, probably to return it to her bag.

"Wait," he told her. He shut his eyes again, remembering her words. He turned them over in his mind, looked at them one way, then the other. Something clicked and his fingers moved. He started singing one of Crossfire's new songs. One that until now hadn't quite been working. He made some changes on the fly, adding some of Cassie's words.

"I've gotta feeling you know this isn't right.
Got a feeling our hearts are wrapped up too tight.
We're fighting a cold war with the words we don't say.
But we're in too deep now, so entangled we stay.
You gotta know I'm feeling this isn't right."

It needed a bit of massaging, but he liked it. It fit. He smiled and opened his eyes. Cassie was staring at him with parted lips.

He put his guitar down. "It's rough, but it's good. If you let us use it, we'll give you a songwriting credit and a royalty payment."

"Wh-what?" She sounded winded.

"I'll run it past the guys and see what they think. But if they like it, we'll pay and credit you."

Cassie's laugh was slightly hysterical. "It was a couple of words. You don't have to credit me. Or pay me."

He leaned forward and reached over to grab her wrist. "Yes, I do. *We* do. Your words, Cassie. Not mine. Not Devon's, or Beau's, or Caleb's. Yours."

She looked down at where his fingers curled around her arm. "You could have just as easily come up with them on your own."

He let go and leaned back. "Yeah, we might have. But we didn't. And now this song is done, and we can move on to the next one. So, you just saved us some very valuable time."

She opened her mouth, but he cut her off. "We're done arguing about this. If we use your words, we'll credit and pay you. Now it's late, and we should take advantage of having an early night. Are you sure—"

"I'm sure, Zac. This is very comfortable, and more than big enough for me."

He nodded and stood, looking down at her sitting there so small on that big couch. The sight warmed him in a way he didn't want to examine.

"Good night, Cassie," he murmured.

He didn't know what the expression was on her face as she said good night in return, but the chaotic mix of emotions that swirled through him as he walked away told him it meant trouble.

He couldn't let Cassie's beauty, her sweetness, her poet's soul, make him lose sight of what was important.

He'd only end up hurting her

He was his dad's son after all.

Chapter Twenty

Cassie stared hard at the bedroom door, willing it to open and for Zac to walk out. But it remained the way it had been all night, slightly ajar.

She was dying to use the bathroom, but the only one was off the bedroom. Zac had left the door open for her. So why was she so reluctant to go in there?

She stood, fixed up her twisted tank top, then made her way over to the bedroom door. She gave a soft knock, in case he was awake, but there was no answer. Easing it open, she slipped through.

The room was dark, but not so dark that she couldn't make out his long form lying on the bed. She made her way quietly toward the bathroom. With a mind of their own, her eyes slid back to where he lay.

He must be a restless sleeper because the sheets were tangled around his legs. He was only wearing a pair of black boxer briefs, leaving his chest bare. Her steps slowed as she let herself drink him in—his broad shoulders, defined pecs, the curves and the ridges of his six-pack, and the far-too-enticing V etched at his hips.

Her gaze slid lower to the bulge in his briefs before she jerked it away and increased her pace. She made it into the bathroom and closed the door behind her. Leaning against it, she blew out a breath.

Why did he have to be so gorgeous? It was distracting in the worst possible way. She was technically free to look now, but Zac definitely wasn't who she should be looking at.

She considered taking another shower, given the hotel one was so luxurious, especially after weeks of bus life. She didn't want to wake Zac up, and she hadn't thought to bring any clothes with her. The last thing she wanted was to try to sneak past him, clutching a towel around herself. Or to have to rush and get dressed out in the front room.

Cassie contented herself with tidying her hair with her fingers and brushing her teeth.

Ready to sneak out again, she startled. Zac was awake and sitting up with his back against the headboard.

Once again, her eyes disobeyed her and dropped to his muscular chest. She snapped them away before he could see. "I'm sorry if I woke you," she said.

"You didn't. This is about when I usually wake up." His voice was husky and deeper from sleep. It sent a little shiver through her.

"Well, I'll let you get dressed." She quickly retreated to the living room before she lost control of her eyes again.

After Zac showered and dressed, they headed down to the restaurant for breakfast. All the others were already there, sitting at a booth large enough for their group. Cassie smiled at them and slid in behind Zac, realizing too late how the constraint of space meant they were pressed together. She tried to ignore the hard length of his thigh against hers.

"Sleep well?" Lexie asked.

"Yeah, the couches in those suites are ridiculously

comfortable," she said. "I've been missing out in those cheap rooms we were staying in." She gave Zac a teasing smile.

"You made Cassie sleep on the couch?" Tex was outraged.

Zac leaned back in the seat, his bicep brushing her shoulder. "Hey, man, I offered. She insisted on staying on the couch. Twisted my arm behind my back and everything."

Noah snorted. "She must be stronger than she looks."

Zac's gaze met hers, humor glinting in the depths of his hazel eyes. A little shock of something sparked through her, but she forced herself to look back at the others. "To be fair, I had to coerce him into agreeing to take the bed."

Lexie laughed. "Cassie, you're a woman after my own heart."

Connor draped an arm around his wife's shoulders and dropped a kiss on her dark head.

Cassie gave her a shy smile, then checked out the menu.

After they ordered, the conversation continued around the table. Cassie looked around at the four men and one woman, and warmth spread through her. This was what she'd always imagined having a group of close friends would be like. The banter, the laughter. It didn't seem to matter that four of them were mega-famous rock stars. There was an ease about them, a confidence in who and what they were that didn't require being pandered to.

And they'd accepted her into their circle without hesitation, in a way that Bryan's friends and bandmates never had. Those people had never gone out of their way to make her feel welcome. In fact, sometimes, it seemed like they'd tried to exclude her as much as possible. Bryan had done little to change that. She didn't know if he'd even noticed.

Or cared. And she didn't know why she'd never said anything to him about how it made her feel.

"You're coming with us, aren't you Cassie?" Lexie's question jolted her back into the conversation.

"Sorry, where?"

"To the hospital this morning."

Zac had mentioned that the band was heading to a local hospital as part of their involvement in children's charities. He hadn't specifically invited her, and she'd assumed she'd head back to the venue and get to work while the band did their thing.

The weight of everyone's attention made her self-conscious. This was something she still wasn't used to. Suddenly being confronted with having to navigate this non-relationship with Zac. She never really knew what he expected or wanted from her. "Oh, no, that's okay. I can catch a ride-share back to the venue."

"You should come." Zac regarded her steadily.

"Well, I don't want to intrude, and I should probably get back and check on everything."

"You don't need to do a load-in check today. Everything should be fine how you left it last night since you didn't pack it up for transport. You can do a check after we get back if you're worried." His intense hazel eyes swept over her face. "And as my girlfriend, you're not exactly intruding." His voice deepened as he said the word girlfriend and Cassie's mouth popped open. She shut it quickly at the quirk of his eyebrow and the slight uptick of his lips. It was the first time he'd used the word, and she didn't know what to think about it. Everyone at the table knew it wasn't real.

She felt the amused stares of the others and flushed. "Well, if you put it that way," she managed to get out.

"I do," he said. This time, his smile was wider. The pressure against her leg increased, and she didn't know if it was deliberate or not. Questions raced through her head. He didn't make it easy to know what he was thinking. But misreading his friendliness as more than that was a sure way to have this whole thing explode spectacularly.

She just needed to remember it was all fake. That in a couple of months she'd be back in Las Vegas.

On her own.

Chapter Twenty-One

Zac balanced his bass on his lap as Connor asked if there were any more requests. The group of children sitting in front of them called out a couple of different suggestions. Connor nodded. "Sounds like most of you want to hear 'Holding Out'." Both Connor and Tex had their acoustic guitars, while Noah had the hand drums he liked to use when they were doing acoustic performances.

The kids cheered. Even the one little girl in her hospital bed at the back of the group. Zac smiled at her, and her eyes got big. She ducked her head shyly. A few feet away from her, Lexie and Cassie whispered to each other. Cassie's smile was stunning. Even in the jeans and T-shirt she was wearing, she was sexy. Too sexy for his peace of mind.

He turned his attention back to where it should be, on the eager young faces staring up at them.

Noah counted them in for the song, and they began to play "Holding Out". It was one of their most popular songs from a couple of albums ago. Zac joined in with Connor for the chorus.

*"Your love is an oasis
And I've been living in a drought
I want to fall to my knees and quench my thirst
But I'm forced to go without
My heart is begging for just one taste
But I know without a doubt
That the only way I'll survive you now
Is by holding out, holding out."*

His gaze caught on Cassie's as he sang, the lyrics suddenly taking on a whole new significance. Pink stained her cheeks, and she looked adorably flustered. But she didn't drop her gaze. And neither did he.

He shouldn't have to keep reminding himself that she wasn't the type of woman he let himself be with. The ones who only wanted to ride a rock star for a night, or see how many ways he could think of to screw them before they both got bored and moved on. Those were the women he chose. The ones who wanted the same thing as him, discrete, short-term, fun-while-it-lasts fucking.

And there was a damn good reason for that.

The last thing he wanted to do was to follow in his dad's footsteps.

Cassie's heart may have taken a beating, but she'd never be one of those women. He could still see the hope in her beautiful blue eyes. Heard it in the sweetness of her laughter. He remembered the look on her face last night when she'd read him her poetry. The need for approval. The need to feel like she mattered to someone. That her heart, and her soul, and her dreams mattered. What must her childhood have been like? Had no one encouraged her? Supported her? Someone along the way should have shown her she was worthy of anything and everything.

If he touched her—if he let himself take her the way he wanted to—when he walked away, it would break her heart again. He was the last person who could show a woman she mattered because no one would ever matter more than the music.

A rush of regret tumbled through him, and he averted his gaze. He kept his eyes off her while they finished the song.

Afterward, they hung out with the kids. They listened to their stories. Some of them were damn heartbreaking. That was always the hardest part of these visits. As rewarding as they were, it was difficult for him and his friends to walk out of here and go back to their insanely privileged lives. These kids faced weeks, sometimes months of tests and treatments. If anything in this world should keep you humble, this was fucking it.

Zac made his way around the room to speak to as many of the kids as possible. Cassie was standing by the hospital bed, talking to the girl he'd smiled at before. He stopped a few feet away and listened to their conversation, curiosity getting the better of him.

"It's... nice, I suppose." Cassie sounded uncomfortable, and he wondered what the question had been.

"Are you going to marry him?" the little girl asked wistfully.

"Noooo! Um, I mean, getting married is a very important decision. One you should spend a long time thinking about. Zac and I haven't been together very long, so..."

He suppressed a laugh at her awkwardness.

"Well, if you don't marry him, when I grow up, can I?"

Zac rubbed his hand over his mouth to hide his grin.

"I think when you grow up, you should take your time and make sure you find someone who loves you more than anything or anybody in the world. If you love them the same way, you can marry them. Only if you want to, though. You don't have to get married at all if you don't want."

"I want to!" She was indignant.

Cassie reached out and smoothed her hand down the girl's arm. "Then you should get married. You should do anything you want, sweetie. Just make sure you have adventures too. Make sure you find something you love to do and do it. Don't let anything hold you back. And when you find someone who wants to have adventures with you, who loves that you have something you're passionate about, who sees you for the amazing person you are and celebrates that, you marry that person and share your adventures with them. Okay?"

A strange pain twisted behind Zac's rib cage. Was that how it was supposed to work?

"Okay," the little girl said. "I think that person's going to be Zac. I hope you won't be sad about it." She was so earnest that he laughed. Cassie swung around with wide eyes, an embarrassed smile pinching her lips. The little girl gave an excited gasp.

"Zac!" she exclaimed. He stepped closer to them and tempted fate by pressing his arm against Cassie's. He held his breath as he waited to see if she'd move away.

She didn't.

"Hey there," he greeted the girl. "What's your name, sweetheart?"

"Annika." She'd turned shy on him now, her name coming out as more of a whisper.

"Hi, Annika. I'm Zac. It's nice to meet you."

"Nice to meet you." It was still a whisper.

He and Cassie shared an amused glance.

"So, I hear you and I are going to get married," he said.

She nodded, brightening.

"Do you know who I am?" She was young enough that he didn't know if she actually knew the band or was just there as part of the hospital's music therapy program.

"Cassie said your name was Zac. And I think you have nice eyes and a nice voice."

Apparently, that was all the child needed to know before deciding on marriage.

"Well, thank you, Annika. You have lovely eyes too. And I bet you have a lovely voice."

She preened, as only a young girl can. He had a sudden memory of his little sister doing the same thing when they were younger.

When she wasn't crying in his arms.

"You know," he said. "By the time you're old enough to get married, I'm going to be way, way old. Like, an old man old. I'm not so sure you're going to want to marry me when I'm all old and wrinkly. What do you think?"

"Um, I don't know?"

He hadn't convinced her yet.

He lowered his voice. "And you know, when you *are* old enough to get married, there's going to be someone out there who is perfect for you. Someone who isn't old and wrinkly. Someone who's going to adore you, who'll want to give you the sun, the moon, and the stars. Someone who'll want to marry you more than anything else in the world. And you won't want to disappoint them by already being married to wrinkly old me, will you?"

She giggled. "I guess not."

He nodded. "Good, it's settled then."

"I was only pretending, anyway," Annika said.

"You were?"

Fractured Kiss

She nodded. "Yeah, I think you have to be a grown-up to get married. So, I don't think I'll be able to."

Cassie stiffened next to him, sudden tension radiating from her arm to his.

"Why won't you be able to?" he forced himself to ask.

"I heard the doctors talking to Mommy. They said I might not get to be a grown-up. So, I won't get to be married." She sounded disappointed rather than upset.

A fine tremor quivered through Cassie, and she leaned slightly against him. Zac looked around. Where was the girl's mom? Shouldn't her mom be here? A nurse across the room caught his eye and started walking over.

He forced his voice to stay as steady as Annika's. "Well, getting married isn't everything."

She shook her head. "Nope, it's not. And if I go to heaven, I'll get to play with Puddles. He's my guinea pig that went to heaven last year. Mom says you can do whatever you want in heaven. So, if I go, I'm going to play with Puddles all day and let him sleep on my bed all night."

Cassie was shaking like a leaf now. And he wasn't too damn steady himself. The nurse made it over to them, a worried look on her face.

Zac smiled reassuringly at the girl, then asked the nurse, "Where's Annika's mom today?"

The nurse's gaze darted from him to Annika and back. "She had to go to work."

"What about her dad?"

"My dad doesn't live with us anymore," Annika piped up.

Zac sought confirmation from the nurse, who looked pained. "She's a single mom."

Cassie leaned against him. He felt the tremors passing through her in waves. She was going to break; he sensed it.

"Annika," he said. "You know, Cassie has a guinea pig too. She's called, uh, Rainbow. And it's Rainbow's lunchtime, so Cassie has to go feed her. She'll have to say goodbye now, okay?"

Annika looked at Cassie. "Okay. It's important to feed guinea pigs. Otherwise, they get cranky and bite you. I think they think your finger is a carrot. You don't want Rainbow to bite you."

Cassie shook her head a little wildly. Her lips were pressed together, eyes glossy.

"I really liked talking to you, Cassie. You've got nice eyes too. I'm glad you and Zac are getting married."

"Thank you." It was a choked whisper, but Annika didn't seem to notice.

"Bye, Cassie. Give Rainbow a hug for me!"

Cassie reached out and squeezed Annika's hand. "I will. The biggest."

Annika beamed as Cassie pivoted on her heel and fled through a side door. Zac turned his attention back to the little girl smiling up at him. "So, tell me about Puddles."

Ten minutes later, Zac shouldered his way through the same door as Cassie. She sat in a hard, plastic hospital chair at the end of the corridor. Her knees pulled up to her chest.

He headed toward her. "Cassie," he murmured when he got close.

She lifted her head, her face awash with tears. They played tricks with the blue of her eyes, deepening their hue.

"I'm sorry," she said, her face crumpling.

"What are you apologizing for?"

"For leaving. I should have stayed, like you. She's just a little girl, and she's braver than me."

He reached for her, tugged her up, and wrapped her in his arms. "Don't you dare be fucking sorry for caring."

She laid her head on his chest, and hot tears soaked through his T-shirt. After a few minutes, she let out a shuddery breath. "Did you find out anything more?"

"I spoke to the nurse. Apparently, she has a rare form of lymphoma."

"It's not fair. She's so young," Cassie sobbed. "And her poor mother."

"Shh, I know." He stroked his hand slowly up and down her back. "But the nurse said they're going to be trying some new treatments, and they think they'll have a good chance of success." Zac didn't mention he planned to call the charitable trust Fractured contributed a percentage of its profits to and organize to have Annika's treatment paid for.

Cassie's arms tightened around him, and she exhaled shakily against his chest "That's good."

He didn't say anything else, just kept stroking her soothingly. After a few more minutes, her tears slowed. His arms were still around her, his chin resting on the top of her head. The apple scent of her shampoo teased him, and he closed his eyes and breathed in. Another few minutes and she shifted in his arms and tipped her head back.

"Thank you," she whispered.

His heart stalled and unease trickled down his spine. He shouldn't be doing this. It shouldn't be him giving her comfort. He shouldn't be pretending he was a man who could give her what she needed. Because sometimes it was all too easy to start believing the lie.

He let his arms drop and stepped back from her. She didn't try to hold on to him. She let him go. He wasn't sure if it was disappointment that flashed across her face or something else. Whatever it was, she just gave him a shaky smile and walked away from him down the hallway.

He released a ragged breath, then turned to follow her.

Chapter Twenty-Two

Cassie followed Zac into the hotel suite. Her skin was hot and sticky after the concert and after-party. She was dying for another long, indulgent shower, since it had been four days of sleeping and showering on the bus since their first hotel stay. Zac stopped suddenly, and she almost ran into his back. She stepped around him, confused. It took her a few seconds to realize what the problem was.

No couch.

In its place, there was only a series of uncomfortably modern-looking single and double chairs arranged artistically around the suite's living room. None were big enough to stretch out on comfortably. Where was she going to sleep tonight?

Zac turned to look at her, his brows pulled together.

"I can sleep on the—" she started.

"You're not sleeping on the floor."

She scanned the room again and pointed at the biggest of the chairs. "I can curl up on that one."

He scrubbed his hand over his mouth. "It was bad

enough when I was making you sleep on the couch. I'm not making you sleep on a hard-as-fuck seat that's barely large enough for two people to sit on."

Cassie looked around the room, as if a big, comfortable couch would miraculously appear. "Could we ask for a different room?"

He crossed his arms over his chest and arched his brows. "And tell them to make sure the next one has somewhere comfy you can sleep that isn't next to me?"

She bit her lip and looked away.

"We can share the damn bed, Cassie. We're both adults."

Her gaze shot back to meet his, but he looked coolly unconcerned. Of course, why *would* he be concerned? It wasn't like he wouldn't be able to control himself just because she was in the bed with him.

It had been three days since the hospital. Three days since she'd stood there, skin flushing as Zac's green-gold eyes stared into hers while he sang that song.

She'd forgotten about it after talking to Annika, too torn up by that brave little girl to think about how flustered she'd gotten at a song he'd sung hundreds of times before. Probably while staring into the eyes of a hundred different women.

It made her nervous, how barbed that thought was. Things were complicated enough without her attraction spiraling out of control and making everything worse.

"You're right," she said. "I'll just jump in the shower if that's all right?" She spoke over her shoulder as she went, not wanting him to see her face and realize exactly how *not* coolly unconcerned she was at the thought of sleeping next to him.

"No problem. I'll get some work done with the guys."

She escaped into the bedroom, eyeing the huge king-sized bed with relief. She'd have plenty of room to make sure she didn't end up pressed up against him. Because if there was one thing she knew, it was that she was a cuddler. Bryan had sometimes complained that she would make him too hot. It wasn't something she could consciously control. What if her body mistook Zac for Bryan, and she curled into him out of habit?

Would Zac think she was ridiculous if she asked to build a pillow barrier between them? She laughed to herself, imagining his face. She bet no woman had ever asked him something like that before.

Somewhat reassured, she relaxed and had a long, peaceful shower, soaping up every inch of her skin and washing her hair.

Twenty minutes later, she was out, squeaky clean and feeling much better. She donned her sleep shorts and cami pajama top, but as an extra, completely useless form of clothing barrier, she pulled on her long, fluffy knee socks. She'd keep her bra on tonight too. When she was on the bus, she usually only took it off once she got into her bunk. She felt a little too vulnerable parading around in front of Zac with only the thin material of her top covering her nipples. Her bra was only thin satin, but it was better than nothing.

When she finally came out of the bedroom, Zac was absorbed in a discussion with his bandmates. They were talking about changing the key of the song they were working on. She went to her bag and pulled out her notebook.

She turned around and found Zac's eyes on her. They scorched a path down her body, the flames of his gaze licking over her skin, leaving her breathless. He stared for a long beat at her knee socks, and his throat worked on a swallow.

He didn't look away from her. Just continued to torture both of them, dragging his heated inspection all the way back up again, pausing at where her nipples were apparently trying to pierce their way through her bra and top.

Without so much as a nod of acknowledgment or a smile, he returned to his discussion.

Cassie's legs shook as she made her way to the chair farthest from Zac. Putting some distance between them was a wise move. Though probably pointless, considering they would soon be sleeping together. *Sleeping in the same bed.* Not *sleeping* together.

She shook her head and scolded herself for letting her imagination run away with her. God, she really needed to get a grip. Anyone would think she was sixteen, not twenty-four. She and Zac were adults. Apart from some heated looks, and that one kiss which had meant nothing anyway, he hadn't done anything to indicate he was planning to rip her clothes off and have his way with her. And why would he? He'd dated some of the most beautiful women in the world. And *dating* was definitely a euphemism in this case. She was nothing to him. An employee, someone who needed his help, a distraction from what he should be focusing on. That was all. That was all she would ever be.

She tried to ignore the tightness in her chest as she bent over her notebook. Nothing was going to happen between her and Zac.

Not tonight when they were sharing a bed.

Not ever.

* * *

Zac's fingers skimmed lightly up the length of Cassie's inner thigh, and she sighed. Anticipation and heat built in her core as she waited for him to touch her where she needed him to. "Zac," she moaned as he finally moved his body over hers.

His hand swept higher, higher, finally reaching the ache between her legs. She shuddered as he skimmed her clit, then circled her entrance. He brushed a kiss against her hip.

"Cassie?" It was the first time he'd spoken to her, but strangely, he hadn't raised his head from where he was pressing his lips to her skin. The sensation of his touch faded. It was as if he were slipping away from her, even as the heat from his body burned hotter against her side. "Don't stop," she whimpered in protest.

"Cassie." It wasn't a question this time. The deep, gravelly tone jolted her out of what she suddenly realized with almost crushing disappointment was a dream. A dream about Zac. A *sex* dream about Zac. When he was sleeping in bed right next to her.

Cassie's eyes flew open in horror. It wasn't the dream Zac who had spoken to her; it was the real one. The one leaning over her right now, his knitted brows just visible in the dim light.

It was obviously the middle of the night. The room was dark, only a little shimmer of moonlight making its way through the curtains. Thank god, because her skin flared hot in an instant.

"Just a dream," she muttered, turning her face away and hoping he'd accept that and go back to sleep.

The silvery light from the window made his eyes glimmer. "What were you dreaming about?" His voice was low and rough. It wasn't a casual question. The air rushed out of her lungs. Did he know?

"I... I don't remember."

"You moaned."

"Did I?" It came out on a weak breath.

"You said my name."

Cassie didn't think she could burn any hotter than she already was, but she was wrong. As if he knew she was thinking about just rolling over and pretending that *this* was all a dream, Zac's hand came to rest on her hip. His fingers curled into her flesh, holding her in place. At his touch, a firestorm of goose bumps erupted over her skin.

"What was I doing to you?" The grit in his voice had nothing to do with sleep, and her core clenched.

"I don't remember," she tried again.

"Yes, you do."

Cassie shook her head, covering her eyes with her hand as if she could somehow block out her humiliation.

"Tell me what I was doing to you." His fingers tightened.

"You were touching me." The words tumbled out of her.

"Where?" he growled. "Where was I touching you?"

God, why was he torturing her like this?

"Cassie—"

"Between my legs."

For a second, the only sounds in the room were his jagged breaths. "Did you come?"

"What?" she choked out, pressing her hand tighter over her eyes.

"When I was touching you. Did you come for me?"

Cassie's lungs weren't working properly; she couldn't seem to get enough air. The only thing she could hear was the whoosh-whoosh-whoosh of blood pumping too fast through her veins.

She sensed him lean in close, even though she couldn't

see him. His fingers left her hip and wrapped around her wrist, pulling her hand away. She kept her eyes closed, hoping if she just ignored him, he'd give up and go away.

No such luck.

"Look at me." His tone didn't brook any argument. She swallowed and did what he said.

Even in the dim light, she could see the tic in his jaw.

"Did. I. Make. You. Come?"

His heated skin and the bulk of his muscular body looming over her, sent a shiver rolling through her. It was so close to what he'd been doing in her dream, it had her arousal spiking again.

"No." It was almost a whimper.

They stared at each other, the tension between them mounting. He still had his fingers wrapped around her wrist. Now he adjusted his hold until his hand covered the back of hers then pressed her palm to her stomach. He slid it slowly down until her fingertips rested just above the waistband of her shorts.

"Show me," he said, the rough edge to his voice sending a full-body shiver through her. "Show me how I was touching you."

Cassie couldn't catch her breath. There in the dark, this whole situation was taking on an almost surreal quality. For a second, she wondered if this was just some crazy continuation of her dream. But she couldn't quite believe it. Goose bumps hadn't covered her skin in her dream the way they did now. She hadn't felt the slippery dampness of arousal between her legs the way she was right at this moment. And dream Zac hadn't stared at her with hungry, half-hooded eyes the way he was now.

Her body was hot, achy, and tight. She was burning with need, desperate for the release that was denied her in her dream. With only a few whispered words, Zac had built the tension humming low and deep inside of her into a hot, sharp live wire of desire. It buzzed and sparked beneath her skin. But even as her fingers flexed under his hand, she hesitated. She didn't know if she was prepared for how this would change things between them.

Zac leaned down until his mouth hovered just above hers. She thought he might kiss her, but instead, he murmured, "I've never left a woman unsatisfied. I'm not about to start now." His voice deepened as a thread of steel wound through it. "Even if it was a fucking dream. Now show me how I was touching you."

With a sigh almost of relief, Cassie slid their hands into her shorts, her fingers finding her slippery center. Her clit was already swollen and sensitive. She was so turned on, she doubted it would take much to make her come. And suddenly, she didn't want this to be over too quickly.

With Zac's hand still on top of hers, she gently brushed her fingertip over that sensitive bundle of nerves. Not enough pressure to give her any relief, only drive her arousal higher.

"Is that what I was doing?" His voice was a deep, bass growl.

She licked her lips and nodded. Their hands moved as she did it again. And again.

"Was that all I did, Cassie? I find it hard to believe that's the only place I touched you." His tone was pitched so low it sent a slow pulse of heat through her. She bent her knees, letting them fall apart so she could bring both their hands farther down. Her fingers—*their* fingers—circled her entrance, barely dipping inside. Her breaths were coming in ragged pants as she teased herself—teased both of them.

Zac muttered a curse at her wetness. When she let out a

shivery little breath that turned into a moan, he growled and pushed her hand away, taking over and sinking two fingers into her.

Cassie gasped at the sudden fullness. She was already slick and ready for him, his fingers sliding in and out effortlessly.

"Was all this from your dream, or from now?" he ground out.

"Both," she admitted. It was far too late to be embarrassed. Not when he was easing a third finger inside her.

Cassie dragged her hand out of her shorts and, desperate for even more sensation, slid it up under her top and cupped one of her breasts, rolling the hard nipple between her fingers as she arched into her touch.

"So fucking tight and wet." Zac pushed himself closer to her. The long, hard ridge pressing into her hip told her he was anything but unaffected by what he was doing to her.

With one arm braced next to her shoulder, he dropped his head and closed his mouth over her other nipple where it strained against the confines of her bra and top. Even through the two thin layers of material, the heated suction of his mouth drew it into a diamond-hard point. Something light dragged over her ribs as his lips and tongue worked her nipple and he continued thrusting his fingers in and out of her. A small part of her brain registered it was the pick he wore around his neck. The larger part could only focus on the jagged shards of pleasure that zinged along her nerves when he rolled his thumb over her clit. Cassie knew it was only a matter of seconds before he flung her over the edge.

"Zac." She moaned his name, just as she'd done in her dream. But this time, the incredible sensation didn't fade away. It only grew stronger, pushed her higher. Zac bit

Fractured Kiss

down on her nipple and curled his fingers, finding a spot that caused every muscle in her body to tighten.

With a few more firm strokes of his thumb over her slick, swollen bud, Cassie's body detonated. She covered her mouth with her hand to muffle her cries as her back bowed off the bed and her inner walls clenched around the fingers he was pumping into her.

Zac let out a harsh burst of breath against her breast as his thumb continued to work her clit, dragging more and more pleasure out of her until she couldn't take anymore.

Her body sank onto the mattress, boneless, and Zac pulled his hand from her shorts. He reached up and yanked her top and bra down. Cassie gasped as his mouth descended on her now naked breast. He drew one nipple deep into the heat of his mouth, sucking on it hard and rhythmically while his fingers, still glistening with the evidence of her orgasm, worked the other, pinching and tugging it. The twin sensations shot straight to her already over-sensitized core. She cried out as a fresh round of spasms jolted her hips off the bed.

Zac swore and ground the steel rod of his cock hard against her hip. "Did you just fucking come again?"

"Y-yes," she panted. "I've never... That's the first time..."

Her admission did something to him. He jerked upright, his expression so pained it was almost angry. Cassie's gaze dropped to the intimidatingly large bulge in his gray sweatpants, and she reached for him, wanting nothing more than to wrap her fingers around him. To give him the same ecstasy he'd given her. But before her hand could make contact, Zac grabbed it and held it away from him.

"Don't," he snapped.

Her eyes shot up to his. "You just made me c—"

"I told you. I don't leave women unsatisfied. That's all it was."

A wave of hurt and embarrassment crashed over her. She yanked her hand away from his.

"You're not responsible for a *dream*, Zac," she hissed at him. Feeling too exposed with her breasts spilling out of her top, she covered herself, the material clinging wetly where his mouth had been.

His gaze followed her movements, his eyes dropping closed for a beat before he looked back up at her. Any evidence of desire had been carefully wiped from his face.

"Go back to sleep, Cassie," he said, then stood and strode to the bathroom. She hated that even with the conflicting emotions coursing through her, she still noticed how the moonlight gilding his body made him look like a walking piece of art.

She sat frozen on the bed as he slammed the door behind him.

Flopping down on the mattress, she huffed and turned on her side so that he'd only see her back when he came out. Her body was still buzzing from her two orgasms. She'd never had two in a row before. And she'd definitely never had one just from having her breasts played with. But now she was back to being embarrassed again because he hadn't wanted her to touch him in return.

In the heavy silence of the room, Cassie heard a groan, long and deep, from the bathroom. Her breath shuddered out of her. He'd gone and jerked off in another room rather than have her touch him. Hurt and confusion rushed through her, along with a new surge of arousal at the image of his hand wrapped around his cock. But fury at him for putting her in this position closely followed.

They needed to talk. This *thing* they were doing wasn't

going to work. How could they possibly carry on after tonight? But she couldn't face him now. Not with her panties still wet with what he'd done to her. Not with her body still humming with the pleasure he'd given her. She'd tell him tomorrow morning.

So, she didn't move when he exited the bathroom. She pretended to be asleep when he strode across the room and went out to the living room. She lay staring into the dark as she listened to the strains of his guitar coming from the other side of the door. He was still playing when her eyes drooped closed, and she finally drifted off into a thankfully dreamless sleep.

Chapter Twenty-Three

Zac blinked himself awake, the muscles of his shoulders twinging. He groaned. Why the hell was he so cramped?

He looked around and realized he was sprawled in one of the uncomfortable chairs in the living room.

Fuck.

The memory of last night came crashing back, and he let his head drop against the chair. He closed his eyes, reliving the moment he'd woken to the sound of his name hanging like the whisper of a promise in the air. He sucked in a breath as he remembered sinking his fingers into Cassie, then let it out on a strangled groan at the memory of her hips bucking up against him as she came.

And then when she came again.

His erection was a heavy ache that his sweatpants could barely contain. He palmed it, squeezing as he inhaled deeply. He'd already jerked off last night after it had happened. He had to. If he hadn't, if he'd taken her up on her offer and let her wrap her fingers around him, he would have broken his rule and fucked her.

Fractured Kiss

Even now, the urge to storm into the bedroom, pull those tiny shorts down, and bury himself in her tight little body was almost overwhelming.

He let go of his dick and sat up, forcing aside the memories, shoving the impulse down as far as he could.

He couldn't sleep with her.

Kissing her at the club was a mistake. Touching her last night was a moment of insanity. He refused to let it go any further.

The door to the bedroom opened, and she stood there.

As much as he knew he shouldn't, he drank her in—from her dark, tousled waves, to her sleepy eyes and full, pink lips. The thin straps of her top only emphasized the delicate line of her collarbone. And fuck, those full tits with nipples that even now were jutting through the material covering them. The memory of how they'd tasted on his tongue made his mouth water.

Her arms folded over her chest, and he met her narrowed gaze. She was pissed. Was it wrong that he enjoyed seeing her blue eyes snapping with anger?

Zac pushed himself up from the chair and closed the gap between them, watching her lips part and her pupils dilate.

"I'm sorry," he said once he was standing in front of her.

She blinked, as if she expected him to blow her off or pretend last night hadn't happened. But there was no pretending he hadn't felt her come on his fingers.

She licked her lips. "Why?"

"Why am I sorry?"

She huffed out a breath. "Why didn't you let me touch you?"

So, she wasn't pissed he'd put his hands on her—or not just that, anyway. She was pissed he didn't let her do the same for him. He should have known not being able to give back would bother her more than the fact he shouldn't have touched her in the first place.

"If I'd let you touch me, it wouldn't have stopped there. I would have fucked you, and we both know you'd have let me. That can't happen."

She bit down on her full lower lip, and his traitorous cock pulsed. "Why not?" she asked, her cheekbones tinting pink.

"Because I can't give you what you need." His tone was gruffer than he intended.

Cassie's mouth turned down. "And what is it you think I *need*?"

"Love, a family, happily ever after. The fairy tale." Tension rippled through his voice.

Her delicate brows pulled together. "You make those sound like bad things."

He sighed and ran a hand through his hair. "It's not a bad thing. It's just not something I'm interested in."

Her back stiffened. "And what, you think that if we slept together, I'd expect you to propose?"

"Would you be happy with a one and done? Or for me to screw you a few times, then walk away? Because that's all this could ever be." Her lips pressed together at the harshness of his tone. He softened his voice. "I'm not the man for you, Cassie. I'm never going to be the man for you."

"Then why did you even touch me?"

He barked out a laugh. "I woke up to you moaning my name, so yeah, I went a little crazy."

Hurt bloomed across her face. "Crazy?"

Damn it, that wasn't what he meant. He cupped her jaw and tilted her face up. "Not crazy for wanting to touch you, Cassie. Fuck, I'd be crazy not to. Crazy because I lost control with you. And losing control is not something I let myself do."

Not before he met her, anyway.

Cassie's eyes widened, then darkened with something that looked an awful lot like satisfaction. She liked knowing she'd made him lose control. His dick jerked in his sweatpants again, and he cursed. It was safer seeing dreams of white picket fences in her gaze than the awareness she had that kind of power over him.

He dropped his hand and stepped back.

"I'll say it again. I'm sorry. I shouldn't have touched you last night." He laced his hands behind his neck. "It won't—"

"Happen again." She crossed her arms over her chest once more. "I've heard that before."

"I mean it this time."

She studied him silently, then nodded. "Okay."

"Okay?" His pulse kicked up. Was that disappointment he was feeling? Had he actually wanted her to push for this thing to happen between them when he wouldn't?

Cassie pursed her lips and raised her chin, one eyebrow cocked almost defiantly. "You're right. It's too soon, anyway. I'm newly single. I'm not in the headspace to be with anyone. This?" She waved a finger between them. "This would only complicate things. Let's just forget..." She faltered for the briefest of moments. "We should just forget it ever happened."

She left him standing there and walked back into the bedroom.

Zac let out a harsh breath. Yeah, forgetting wasn't going to happen. There'd be no way to erase from his mind the memory of her arching up under him.

But it was better for both of them to pretend he could.

* * *

"See you tomorrow night." Zac hung up with a chorus of goodbyes from the rest of Crossfire ringing in his ears.

His attention was on Cassie, writing in her favorite spot on the bus. With the tension simmering between them since last night, he'd half expected she would retreat to her bunk with the others.

But she hadn't. Without looking at him, she'd grabbed her notebook, and begun writing while he'd called Beau, trying not to acknowledge just how relieved he was.

At least the songwriting sessions were going well. Everything was finally coming together. The four of them were in a rhythm now, and he had a good feeling about this album. It could be the one that sent them to the top. But his thoughts weren't on the music right now. Instead of doing the sane thing, which was packing up his guitar and heading to his bunk, he was watching Cassie scribble away.

"What are you writing?" he heard himself ask.

He didn't like the cautious shade of blue her eyes turned when she looked over at him. He thought she was going to blow him off, but he should have known she wasn't like that.

"Just something about… I don't know." She flashed a ghost of an embarrassed smile. "Bryan, I suppose."

Zac's jaw clenched, but he forced himself to relax and lean back in his chair. "Can I hear it?"

She looked down at what she'd written, then back up at him. "Do you really want to?"

"I wouldn't ask if I didn't." As a songwriter, her words called to something inside him, an essential part of who he was. And maybe it was also a way to find out more about her without admitting how much he wanted to.

She searched his face. "Okay." She dropped her gaze to her notebook and licked her lips. He tried not to remember the feel of his mouth on hers. With a sudden stab of regret, he realized he hadn't kissed her last night. It had been the smarter move, but it suddenly grated on him that he hadn't. That he hadn't gotten a chance to taste her again. That he hadn't taken the chance to taste her everywhere.

She started speaking, her voice shaking a little. The same way it had last time. It tightened his chest that she was so nervous about letting anyone hear her poetry.

"You took what was empty and filled it
Took what was shadowed and made it bright
You took my hurt and healed it
Took what was wrong and made it right

I let you be the one to fill me
Let it be you that made me bright
Never tried to heal my own hurt
Never tried to make my own wrongs right

I'm empty again now that you're gone
My bright turned dark, right turned wrong
The stitches that sealed my wounds torn open
Seems I was still broken all along."

Questions hovered on the tip of Zac's tongue. No wonder Bryan's betrayal had hit her hard. He'd obviously meant more to her than just a high school-sweetheart-turned-fiancé. But he'd let her down, the way the people who are supposed to love you always seem to do.

Zac knew all too well the damage that could result from that kind of betrayal. How it could claw at you until it stripped away your sense of self-worth. She'd needed Bryan, entrusted herself to him, and been left hanging when it all went to hell.

He swallowed his questions, closed his eyes, and let her softly spoken words play in his head. He could feel the aching sadness woven through them. It echoed something deep inside him he didn't want to think too much about.

Zac picked up his guitar and let his fingers idly play with the strings as he ran her words through his head again. He didn't sing, just let his fingers find the melody that unfurled in his mind.

Cassie didn't talk or interrupt him. He didn't hear her pen against paper. She just sat there, her soothing presence helping him focus, not distracting him.

When he finally stopped and opened his eyes, her soft smile hit him square in the gut.

It took him a moment to find the words that had fled his mind at the sight. "Can you sing?"

Her brows winged up, and she gave a self-conscious shrug. "I can hold a tune. Why?"

Zac ignored the cautionary voice in his head and crossed the living room. He sat on the couch and angled himself toward her. "Sing the words for me."

She shook her head. "I—"

"Don't think about it. Just go with the melody." He started playing before she protested again. At first, he watched her as he played the same chords a few times until she nodded that she had it. He kept watching her when her lashes fluttered shut, and she started to sing. But when her voice emerged, hesitantly at first, then a little stronger, he breathed in and let his eyelids drift closed.

She could do more than hold a tune. She had a beautiful voice, pure and melodic. Hearing her sing the words she'd spoken before, weaving them through the notes he was playing, sent a different kind of pleasure humming through his veins. When she got to the end, she opened her eyes, but he just nodded at her and kept playing. "Again."

She started from the beginning. This time their gazes stayed locked the whole time, and the music and words flowed together effortlessly.

Zac's pulse kicked into high gear. It was fucking intense looking into Cassie's sapphire blue eyes as she sang about her pain to the music her words had drawn from him. Maybe even more intense than when he'd watched her orgasm with his fingers deep inside her.

She reached the end again and stopped singing. His fingers stilled on the strings, and they stared at each other. A slow flush spread over her cheeks.

Zac's gaze drifted to her lips. They parted, formed his name, though no sound came out.

Hunger pulsed through him. A hunger to be closer to her. To touch and taste her again.

Fuck the consequences. He wanted her. She wanted him. They both knew this wasn't real. But that didn't mean they couldn't take advantage of the situation. Everyone was passed out in the bunks, and Maggie was driving. He could have her right here. He could get as close to her as was physically possible, and it didn't have to mean anything more than two consenting adults giving in to their attraction.

He knew he was only trying to justify what he wanted to do, but right that second, he was beyond caring.

Zac put his guitar down on the couch behind him and reached for her. He dragged his thumb along her full bottom lip, then slid his hand into her hair, cupped the back of her head and tugged her toward him. She came with a breathy sigh of surrender, her fingers curling into his shirt.

He held her there, his mouth hovering just above hers as he pushed against the familiar bonds of his control. Her eyes were wide and imploring, tempting him with everything he shouldn't want. Need shone brightly in them. Not just need for his touch or for his mouth on hers—though that was definitely there. It wasn't the need for a quick fuck. It was a deep-seated desire for connection, and it was fucking terrifying how much he wanted to throw caution to the wind and give in to it.

Zac's heart crashed against his rib cage at the soft vulnerability in Cassie's expression. This was wrong. He knew that. But he'd already made the mistake of kissing her once. Just one more taste couldn't hurt, could it?

He never got the chance to find out. Before he could either close the distance between them or come to his senses and let her go, his phone vibrated on the table behind him. Cassie startled, her blown pupils urging him to ignore it and just fucking kiss her.

But the disturbance cleared his mind—the fog of desire he'd been stumbling around in lifting. He swore under his breath at what he'd been so close to doing.

Furious with himself, he jolted to his feet and stalked over to his phone, wondering who the hell was calling him at this time of night. Or rather, morning.

Concern hollowed his gut when he saw his sister's name on the screen.

He turned his back to Cassie. "Is everything okay, Tori?"

"Dad's in the hospital, Z. He's had a stroke." Her voice vibrated with tension.

Nausea swirled in his stomach, followed by an icy numbness. He stayed silent, not sure how she expected him to respond.

"Zac, did you hear me?"

"Yes."

Tori sighed. "I know things aren't great between you and Dad, but I'd really appreciate it if you could come."

Zac rubbed his hand over his eyes, knowing he wouldn't say no to Tori. Even if going to see his dad in the hospital was the last thing he wanted to do.

"I'll be there as soon as I can," he said. "Which hospital is it? I'll get Maggie to divert the bus to the nearest airport and organize a charter." It would take too long to get one of the label jets to pick him up.

He let out a heavy breath. He'd have to talk to Drew and the tour manager about arranging a substitute bass player too. In case he couldn't get back in time for the concert that night.

"I'm sorry. I know it's difficult for you to get away," Tori said. "It's just, Mom's not coping well, and I'm..." Her voice wavered, and he felt like shit for making her feel guilty.

"It's not a problem, T. I'm just figuring out what I need to do."

"Okay." She took a breath. "So, you'll let me know when you'll get here?"

"Yeah, as soon as I get the charter flight booked, I'll let you know my ETA."

He said goodbye, hung up, and stared down at his phone. He only remembered Cassie was there when her small hand smoothed tentatively down his back.

"Are you okay?"

A line of concern drew her brows together.

He relaxed his jaw enough to tell her. "My dad's had a stroke. He's in the hospital."

Her eyes filled with sympathy. "I'm so sorry." She

wrapped her arms around him and rested her cheek against his chest.

Zac stilled, not reacting as his pulse drummed loudly in his ears. Just as her arms loosened at his lack of response, he folded his own around her slender form and pulled her tighter against him. They stood there for a minute, the only sound coming from the engine of the bus and the rumble of the road passing underneath its wheels.

He didn't even know why he was holding on to her so tightly. He didn't need comfort. His care factor when it came to his dad was minimal. But holding her—having her hold him—felt good. It wasn't until his heart rate began to slow that he even realized how fast it had been racing.

He allowed himself a minute of having her against him, then forced himself to step away.

"What can I do to help?" she asked, looking up at him.

He checked the time on his phone. It was almost 2:00 a.m. He needed to find the nearest airport with charter options and book one. After that, he'd call Drew and let him know so he could line up a substitute. The last thing he wanted was for one of their shows to be canceled because of his dad.

Cassie was still waiting for him to answer her.

"Go to bed, Cassie. It's late. You need to sleep, and I need to sort this out."

Disappointment clouded her clear blue gaze. "Are you sure? I can help you find a flight or something."

He shook his head, and she caught her lower lip between her teeth as she took a step back.

He felt her absence before she even took that one step away from him. He reached out, grasping her wrist. She stopped, eyes searching his face.

"Will you come with me?" he asked, his voice low.

Fractured Kiss

He didn't know where the desire had come from. But suddenly, he wanted her there with him. Maybe he was just looking for a distraction from the fact he'd have to see his dad again. Whatever the reason, it felt like a screw was slowly tightening in his chest as he waited to hear her answer.

He didn't miss the surprise that flickered over her face. But she only gave him a soft smile. "Of course."

His heart tripped in his chest, and he dropped his hand from her wrist as if her skin had burned him. "Go get some sleep. I'll wake you up when we're close to the airport. I'm not sure if we'll be back tonight or not, but we won't be gone longer than one night. Don't pack much."

Her brow creased, eyes filling with questions. Was she wondering why he wasn't planning to stay longer? He braced himself to deflect her when she asked. But she didn't, just gave him a nod, then headed for the bunks.

Zac watched her go. Forcing his mind away from her, he started his search for the nearest airport.

Chapter Twenty-Four

Cassie's stomach twisted in a knot of worry as she followed Zac into the hospital. The bodyguard Drew had organized to meet them when they arrived in Ohio—a big, burly man called Paul—trailed behind. Zac wore a cap pulled low over his face and a pair of dark aviators. So far, he seemed to have gone unnoticed, though Cassie couldn't understand how when his presence was so damn magnetic.

He walked up to the nurses' station and took his glasses off. "I'm here to see Cal Ford." The young nurse did a double take. Cassie wasn't sure if it was because of how good looking he was, or if the woman recognized him. Or both.

The nurse's eyes widened and her mouth fell open, but she quickly regained her professional demeanor. "N-name, please?"

"Zac Ford."

Her head bobbed up and down in a daze. "Yes, of course, Mr. Ford. I'll let the doctor know you're here." She pulled herself together and pointed to a pair of swinging doors. "There's a more private waiting room through there if you'd like to take a seat. Someone will be out in a minute."

Zac nodded, put his glasses back on, and headed for the waiting room the nurse had indicated. Cassie gave the wide-eyed woman a grateful smile, then followed him. He sat down, and Paul took up a position at the back of the room. Cassie sat next to Zac, unsure what she should do to help him—what he needed from her. Outwardly, he appeared calm, but his knuckles were white around the phone he was clutching in his hand. She wanted to ask him if he was okay, but ever since she'd hugged him after he heard the news, he'd been distant.

After waking her this morning, he'd barely said a word except to tell her Drew was arranging one of the Hazard Records' jets to fly them back when they were done. Cassie didn't know whether to leave him alone or try to distract him. Something was obviously off between Zac and his father—his tension didn't seem to be related to worry about his dad's health. Which was what made it so hard to know how to help him. The only thing she knew was that Zac wanted her there, so she let him feel her presence without intruding on his thoughts.

But worry gnawed at her. His big body was coiled tight, his shoulders almost up at his ears. He'd completely withdrawn into himself. Her fingers itched to reach out and smooth over the creases in his forehead, but she wasn't sure he would welcome her touch. He might have had his hands on her intimately, but that was purely physical. Anything that smacked of real emotional intimacy between them seemed to make him uncomfortable.

A different door to the waiting room opened, and a doctor came out, followed by a pretty woman with wavy, caramel-colored hair and hazel eyes so like Zac's that she had to be his sister.

Zac stood and Cassie followed suit, her palms suddenly damp.

"Z!" His sister rushed forward and threw her arms around him. He didn't hesitate. He enfolded her in his arms and hugged her tight, some unknown emotion crossing his face.

"Hey, Tori," he murmured.

The doctor cleared his throat, and Zac and Tori stepped back from each other. Zac looked at the doctor, while Tori studied Cassie. Cassie gave her a small smile, uncomfortable at intruding on this family moment.

"So, Mr. Ford," the doctor said. "As I've already explained to your mother and your sister, your father had an intracerebral hemorrhagic stroke. We've operated to remove pooled blood and repair the damaged blood vessels. He's currently stable, but he is still at risk for further hemorrhages. We need to monitor him."

Zac nodded at the doctor's words, but that was his only reaction.

"He's recovering now, but he'll sleep a lot. He may or may not be lucid when he wakes. If you want to go in and see him, you can."

A muscle pulsed in Zac's jaw, but he just gave a curt nod.

The doctor went back the way he came. Tori glanced once more at Cassie before following him.

Cassie sat down, ready to wait however long she needed to for Zac to spend some time with his family. Zac started forward, stopped, stared at the ground, then pivoted and held out his hand to Cassie.

"I don't know how long I'll be in there. I don't want you waiting out here on your own."

"Oh, well…" She glanced over at Paul, who was an expressionless statue in the corner.

Zac kept his hand extended. For a second, Cassie thought she saw a glimmer of an entreaty in his eyes. She stood and slipped her hand into his, a shaky breath leaving her as his fingers tightened around hers.

They followed Tori and the doctor down a few hallways before stopping outside a closed door. Tori eyed Zac's and Cassie's clasped hands, her gaze assessing. Cassie pretended not to notice. His sister was probably wondering what the hell a stranger was doing outside their dad's hospital room. But Tori said nothing. Instead, she touched Zac's arm. "Do you want me to come in?"

Zac shook his head. "Is Mom in there?"

"She went home to have a shower and get a change of clothes. She'll probably be back soon."

Zac nodded, then opened the door and tugged Cassie in after him.

The beeping of the machines was the first sound she heard. Zac's grip tightened as he stood there, his breathing fast and uneven. After a few seconds, he dropped her hand and walked over to the bedside.

She took a step closer but didn't know if he wanted her near him, so she turned her attention to the man lying in bed.

It was clear he was Zac's father. He had the same facial structure, though his face was weathered and currently very pale. His hair had obviously been as dark as Zac's at one stage, though what she could see of it was well peppered with silver. Faded tattoos covered both his arms.

Cassie's eyes strayed back to Zac. He had his hands

shoved in his pockets and his head was lowered. She wanted nothing more than to go over there and wrap her arms around him, to give him some comfort. But she doubted he wanted that.

They stood like that for a while. Zac silent. Cassie watching him. She jumped as the machines began beeping more rapidly. Zac's dad's eyelids flickered, then opened. He blinked dazedly at the ceiling before his gaze drifted backward and forward across the room. It landed on her first, a frown creasing his brow, then moved to Zac.

The frown disappeared, but it wasn't replaced by a smile. The unreadable expression rivaled Zac's. The increased tension in the room made the back of Cassie's neck prickle and she crossed her arms, her eyes bouncing between the two men.

When Zac's dad finally spoke, his voice was slurred but still discernible. "What the hell are you doing here?"

Cassie's breath caught. Zac stood stiffly by the bed, his spine a rigid line.

"Tori asked me to come," he said.

His dad grunted. "Damn girl."

"You should be grateful she cares enough about you to bother being here herself."

The ailing man curled his lip—or tried to. The partial laxity of his face twisted the expression into one of pure disdain. "I never asked her to be here."

"You wouldn't, since you never wanted us around at all."

The man looked over at Cassie, but his words were aimed at Zac. "Didn't bother taking my advice, I see. You gonna ruin your own life too?"

Cassie inhaled sharply, and Zac moved between her and his dad.

"I didn't ask for your opinion. But obviously, you're fine, so I'm going to head out."

Zac pivoted, his gaze catching Cassie's, his expression stony.

"You ruined my life!" his father half-slurred, half shouted at Zac's back before coughing and sagging against the bed. Zac's steps faltered, but he recovered, still focused on Cassie.

"We're leaving." Zac grabbed her hand and tugged her toward the door. Cassie fell in behind him, leveling a look over her shoulder at Zac's dad. She couldn't believe he would say that kind of thing to his son.

"You ruined my damn life!" The words echoed in the room behind them as Zac closed the door.

Tori waited in the hallway, her arms wrapped around herself, tears shimmering on her cheeks. "I'm so sorry, Zac," she said, obviously having overheard. "I hoped he might have changed. I thought he might have finally realized what he's been missing out on."

"The only thing Dad has or will ever care about is himself." Zac's tone was icy.

"Zac?" A woman's voice rang out down the hallway.

Cassie turned to see an older, bottle-blonde woman rushing toward them. "Zaccy?"

Zac didn't move as the woman approached. Even when she threw her arms around him, he didn't react straight away. Just like when Cassie had hugged him earlier, he hesitated before returning it. He didn't hold on, though. After a few seconds, his arms fell away.

That's when she noticed Cassie. "Who are *you*?"

"It doesn't matter, Mom," Zac said before she had a chance to reply. She did her best to ignore the stab of hurt.

Now was not the time to worry about her deep-seated feelings of rejection.

Zac's mom dismissed her, turning her attention back to Zac. "Have you been in to see him?"

"Yep. And apparently, he'd much rather I hadn't. So, we're going to head out."

His mother's mouth dropped. "You're not going to stay? He's your father!"

A shadow descended over Zac's face. "He's never been a father to me. Or Tori. So, I don't see why I should hang around. I've got a tour to get back to."

His mom's eyes narrowed. "Maybe if you hadn't chosen the same career just to spite him, it would have made things easier."

"You know what? You might be prepared to put up with his shit in your fucked-up, toxic relationship, but that doesn't mean I have to."

"You're just like him," his mom spat. "The only thing you care about is your damn music." She turned to Cassie. "Enjoy him while you can, honey. I doubt I'll be seeing you again." She opened the door to the hospital room and slipped inside.

Zac's anger smoothed away into a mask of indifference, but his throat worked. He turned to his sister. "Tori, can you look after Cassie? I need a minute."

"Of course." Tori's voice was watery with tears.

"Zac?" Cassie didn't want him to be alone after what she'd witnessed.

"I shouldn't have brought you." It was all he said before stalking down the hallway and rounding the corner.

Pain speared through her, but she pushed it away, turning wide eyes on his sister. She felt completely out of place in the middle of such tense family dynamics.

"I'm so sorry about this, Cassie." Tori sniffed and wiped the tears from her cheeks.

"It's not your fault. I just... I'm not sure what's going on."

Tori sighed. "I'm not sure how long he's going to be. Do you want to sit down while we wait?"

Cassie nodded, and they returned to the private waiting room, which was thankfully still empty apart from Paul. The bodyguard's gaze narrowed slightly when he saw Cassie and Tori come back out on their own.

"Should I tell him to go find Zac?" she asked Tori.

Zac's sister shook her head. "He just needs some time on his own. He'll be safe enough. This is a private hospital. I don't think he's likely to get ambushed by crazed fans."

They sat next to each other. Cassie studied the other woman as she dabbed at her cheeks with the backs of her hands.

Eventually, Tori gusted out a breath. "He doesn't mean it, you know."

Cassie frowned.

"Zac. He wouldn't have brought you if he didn't want you here."

Cassie's throat tightened. "I'm not sure why he wanted me here, to be honest. I haven't been much help, and it only upset your mom and dad."

Tori was silent for a moment. "Has Zac told you anything about..." She gestured in the general direction of their dad's room.

Cassie shook her head. "I don't think he's ever said anything about his parents."

"We had a... rough childhood, I guess you could say."

Cassie nodded. She had some experience with less-than-ideal upbringings. But she only had one parent to deal with. It seemed like Zac and Tori had two.

"It's not my place to tell you what Zac went through. I hope he'll talk to you when he's ready. But I can tell you that our dad is a very"—she paused, searching for the word—"*unhappy* man. He has been for as long as I can remember. What you heard today, well, it isn't the first time Zac's heard that. Or me. But Zac bore the brunt of Dad's bitterness growing up. He did his best to protect me from the worst of Dad's moods." Her gaze turned inward. "Hearing that kind of thing day in and day out. There's no way it doesn't affect you."

Cassie's heart ached for Zac. And Tori too. She pictured Zac as a little boy, being told he'd ruined his dad's life, and all she wanted was to wrap her arms around him and hold him tight. She shifted uncomfortably on the seat. Should she even be listening to this? Would Zac see it as an invasion of his privacy? Even if it was his sister telling her these things?

Tori must have sensed Cassie's unease because her gaze focused back on her. She reached out and clasped her hand. "I'm telling you this because it was Zac who kept me smiling when things got rough. Because of him, I came out of everything, not exactly unscathed, but much better off. Even when he left for Fractured's first tour, he checked up on me constantly. I'm not sure he would've even gone if I hadn't convinced him I was okay with it. And I was, because I had a good group of friends, and I knew I'd be out of there as soon as I turned eighteen."

Cassie squeezed Tori's hand. It sounded a little like her experience. As soon as she'd been able to, she'd left home too. Not long after that, she'd followed Bryan across the country.

"Zac showed me what having someone really care about you and look out for you feels like," Tori continued. "But he didn't grow up with the same experience. *I* loved him of course, but I was younger, so I relied on him. He didn't have anyone that he could rely on. And our parents didn't set a great example of a healthy, mutually supportive relationship."

Tori sighed. "I worry about him, Cassie. He hides a lot of scars under the surface. He's this famous rock star who acts like he's got it all together. But it's hard for him to really let people in. He's convinced himself that being needed, or needing someone else, will only drag him down. The way it dragged our parents down. And then they dragged us down with them. I'm pretty sure it's why he's never been interested in a serious relationship before. As far as I'm aware, he's never spent more than a few weeks with any woman. Even then, I'd put my money on the fact that it was probably just a temporary physical thing. He's never brought anyone home. Never talks about the women he's with. I've never even seen him hold a woman's hand before."

She smiled at Cassie, her eyes turning glossy again. "But now there's you, and I can't tell you how happy I am that he has someone to care about him. Someone to show him it's okay to let himself be needed." She reached out to squeeze Cassie's hand. "And to let himself need in return."

Cassie had grown more and more uncomfortable as Zac's sister spoke. But at Tori's last words, her stomach flipped. Zac hadn't told his sister the truth about them. Tori had shared all this thinking she and Zac were actually a couple. She wrapped her arms around her waist. "I'm so sorry, Tori. I thought Zac had told you. He and I aren't together. This"—she took a breath—"this thing between us, it's not real." She fought a sudden urge to cry. "It's hard to explain."

Tori's brows shot up, then she let out a sad laugh. "No, he didn't tell me that." She exhaled. "I love my brother, and I know he loves me, but he rarely lets me know the details of his life." She studied Cassie carefully. "But honestly, that makes more sense to me than you two being in an actual relationship."

"It does?" Although, after everything Tori had just told her, that kind of made sense.

Tori let out a long, slow breath. "I told you that Zac doesn't really let himself get too emotionally involved with anyone. Even with his friends, he keeps a little distance between them. He holds himself aloof, and that's particularly true with women. I already mentioned that he's never brought a woman home; it's not how he works. But if you and he aren't really in a relationship, I can see why he would think he could bring you."

Cassie shook her head in confusion. "I don't understand."

"As crazy as it sounds, I think the fact he can tell himself it isn't real is why he allowed himself to be vulnerable in front of you. Kind of like, um"—she squinted up at the ceiling for a second—"plausible deniability. That's it." She gave Cassie a little smile. "What you have may not be real now, but it doesn't mean that will always be the case."

She hated having to douse Tori's hope. "I don't think that's going to happen."

Tori cocked her head. "Why not? I can see you care about him."

"You said he doesn't want to be needed, and apparently..." The words caught in Cassie's throat. "Apparently, I need too much."

Fractured Kiss

Tori held her gaze. "Zac might not admit it, but he needs someone who can show him that deep emotional connections make you stronger, not weaker. Maybe you can be that person, maybe you can't. But the fact you're sitting here next to me tells me you've got a better chance than any other woman he's ever spent time with."

Cassie was about to protest when the door opened, and Zac walked in. He stopped in front of her. "The jet's ready to leave as soon as we get there."

Tori and Cassie both stood. His sister's expression had saddened again. "I *am* sorry, Zac. I really thought things might be different—"

"It's okay," he cut her off, his smile softening his words. "You always did believe in miracles."

Tori hugged him again, then Zac held his hand out to Cassie. "If we get to the airfield quickly, we might get back in time to make the show tonight."

Cassie interlaced her fingers with his, a movement that was becoming far too comfortable. But she wasn't going to stop.

Not now.

"I'll call you soon, T," Zac said.

Tori nodded, gave Cassie a smile, then headed back toward their father's room.

Zac's eyes met hers. "Let's go."

Chapter Twenty-Five

The bright white Hazard Records jet waiting for them on the tarmac stood out against the overcast sky. The weather matched Zac's mood.

When they boarded, Zac sank onto one of the cream leather seats, signaling to the flight attendant for a drink. Cassie sat in the chair opposite him. He was grateful that the ride to the airfield had been quiet. He didn't feel like answering questions right now. And he was sure Cassie would have them. How could she not?

The attendant came over and Zac asked him for a glass of whatever top-shelf scotch the label had in stock. Cassie ordered a vodka tonic. The man soon returned with their drinks, then disappeared back through the door at the front of the plane as the jet pulled away from the terminal. It was impossible to talk over the roar of the engines as they taxied down the runway and took off. They sipped their drinks in silence.

Zac kept his gaze averted from her, watching the patchwork quilt of the ground below out the window as the jet banked.

He didn't know what had come over him. Why had he invited Cassie along to what he knew would be a shit show? Maybe he'd been hoping his dad would be out of it enough for him to get in, do his duty, and get out. He should have known his old man would never let him get away unscathed. He should have known he risked Cassie seeing a part of his life he didn't want anyone to see. He gripped the armrest. Or maybe that's exactly why he'd done it?

He took another swig of his drink just as the jet finally achieved cruising altitude. The roar of the engines suddenly diminished, and his thoughts resonated too loudly in his head.

Immediately, Cassie spoke, "Zac, I'm so sorry."

He shook his head sharply, not wanting her pity. "No, I'm sorry. I should have known better. I shouldn't have asked you to come."

"I'm glad you did." Her voice was soft.

He stared down at his glass, watching the ripples from the plane's vibrations subtly distort the smooth surface of the liquid. His skin felt too tight for his body, tension clawing up his spine to coil at the base of his skull.

You ruined my life.

He inhaled sharply. It had been a while since he'd heard those words. He wondered if they would replace the other phrase that played on repeat in his head. *Right place, right time, Zac.*

His ribs compressed, his hand tightening around the glass.

The click of Cassie's seat belt unbuckling jerked his head up. There was no seat beside him, but that didn't stop her. Cassie sank to her knees and placed her hands on his thighs. She squeezed gently, trying to catch his gaze. Zac had to control a sudden visceral reaction to her looking up at him from between his legs. She was only trying to offer comfort. And yet, it painted a far too pretty picture.

"I don't know who my dad is," she said. Zac's stomach twisted as he took in her distant expression. "He bailed as soon as he found out Mom was pregnant. Or at least, that's what she always told me. But part of me wonders if *she* even knows who my father is."

Her eyes focused back on him. "I don't remember her ever holding down a job for longer than a few weeks. She told me once she just wasn't cut out for it. But from the number of boyfriends who visited, I soon figured out how she made the little money we did have."

Zac curled his hands over the top of hers but said nothing. He just let her talk.

"When one of them came over, which was most days, Mom would yell at me to get out of the house. I'm grateful for that now, I guess. I don't think all the men who visited would have been averse to making it a two for one deal." A breath shuddered out of her, and his fingers tightened, his heart constricting then lurching erratically against his ribs. "But at the time, I wasn't grateful. I was just sad and scared and alone. I used to run out to the fields behind our house. There was a tree there that was far enough away to feel safe but close enough that I could see when the men left. When I was little, I'd be out there for hours, sometimes all day. It's why I eventually started writing poetry, to help pass the time and get my feelings out." Her eyes met his and the openness in her gaze tugged at something in his chest.

"Things got a little better when I started school because I was comfortable and had company, at least for those hours. Sort of." Her full lips pressed together. "Any friendships I made soon faded away. I saw the looks the parents gave me. I eventually figured out what the issue was."

Fractured Kiss

Zac growled through clenched teeth at the thought of young Cassie, shunned because of her mother's activities.

She turned her hands over underneath his, so they were clasped. "It's okay. It was a long time ago."

"You shouldn't have had to go through that."

She nodded and exhaled. "When I was fourteen, I was sitting under my tree after school, writing in my notebook and waiting for Mom's visitor to leave. It was summer, and I remember how bright it was. How thirsty I was because I'd forgotten to bring any water with me. I heard someone say hello, and I remember turning and the sun beaming in my eyes. I had to squint to see who it was. A boy, about my age." A faint smile touched her lips.

Zac's stomach plummeted. "Bryan."

"Yes. His family had just moved into a house on the other side of the field. He kept me company until the car outside my house left, and I could go home. Then he was there the next day. And the next. He was my first real friend. My only friend really. He didn't care who my mother was. He just cared about me." Her gaze dropped.

Fuck. No wonder she fell hard for Bryan. He was the only person who was ever there for her. And then he betrayed her too. Fucking asshole.

"Are you still in touch with your mom?" he asked.

"I tried to keep in contact when we first moved away. She's still my mother, you know?"

He nodded. You couldn't choose your family. And as much as you might want to cut ties, sometimes it was hard to let go of the hope things might be different if you just kept trying.

"She didn't want to know," Cassie continued. "I think she was just glad not to have me getting in the way anymore. I stopped trying after a while."

A weight pressed down on his chest. "Cassie," he murmured.

She shook her head. "It's okay. I'm okay. I just wanted to let you know all that because"—she gave him a small smile—"well, because if you want to talk about your family, then I'm here for you. And I understand that sometimes the people who should love us the most let us down the hardest."

Zac stared at her, his heart thrashing against his ribs as she looked up at him with those big, blue, fallen angel eyes. She didn't deserve to deal with that shit. And she was trying to comfort *him*. Offering to listen to his sordid fucking family history so that they could commiserate. But he didn't want the sort of comfort words provided. Suddenly, the only comfort he wanted was the taste of her on his tongue, the feel of her skin under his fingers, the sound of her moans in his ears. He wanted her, the way he couldn't ever remember wanting a woman before. He wondered if she wanted him just as much. If his touch could soothe some of her hurt. At least for a short time.

He slid his hands up and wrapped his fingers around her delicate wrists, his thumbs stroking along the sensitive skin of her inner arm. Goose bumps rippled out from under his touch.

His breathing deepened as need pulsed through his veins—a need to let go. To pretend for just an hour or two that this was all there was. Just her and him and the energy that seemed to crackle between them. The energy that flared even brighter now. He tightened his grip, then stood, pulling her to her feet so quickly she overbalanced and fell against him.

"Zac?" Her voice was breathless with surprise.

He let her wrists go and tangled his hands in her hair,

tilting her head back. "I don't want to talk right now," he said, his voice dark and laced with heat. "Do you want to talk, Cassie?"

Her breaths were coming fast, her eyes wide as they bounced between his. The compassion that had filled them before slowly being drowned out by the black of her pupils. "Do you want to talk?" he pressed her.

She licked her lips. "No."

He lowered his head, so his mouth hovered over hers. "What do you want?"

Her lips parted, and she exhaled shakily. He ran one hand down her throat until he could feel her pulse fluttering like a hummingbird under his palm. "I don't want to talk," he said again. "I want your body against mine. I want to know what it feels like when you come on my cock." She let out a ragged little moan that had him hard and throbbing inside his jeans. "Tell me what you want, Cassie."

Her throat worked against the hand that bracketed her neck as she swallowed. "I want that too," she finally got out.

He didn't crash his mouth down on hers the way he wanted to. The way he thought he was going to. Instead, he eased them closer, so close her frantic breaths washed over his skin. He held himself there, letting the anticipation build between them until she was swaying toward him, her lips almost brushing his with every silent plea. He held them there, on the edge, until he couldn't take it anymore. Only then did he allow himself to close the final distance between them and press his mouth to hers, slide his tongue between her lips.

She whimpered, the sound sending desire pounding through him. The desire to forget what had happened at the hospital today. The desire to see her gaze filled with something other than sadness. The desire to wipe Bryan and what he'd done to her—what he'd *meant* to her—from her mind.

With their mouths still locked together, he maneuvered her to the door at the back of the cabin. He fumbled with the latch, then shoved it open, backing her through it and letting it swing shut behind him. Cassie pulled away to look around the small but luxurious bedroom.

"Label VIPs like to travel in style," he murmured against the skin of her neck before gripping her jaw and turning her head back to his so he could claim her mouth again.

She scrabbled with the bottom of his T-shirt, pulling it up so they had to break apart for him to drag it over his head. She stepped back, her gaze roaming over his chest, her luscious bottom lip clamped between her teeth. When her gorgeous blue eyes met his again, he almost groaned from the heat blazing in them.

She wasn't thinking about Bryan now.

"Take your clothes off," he demanded, need riding him too hard to be soft and gentle with her. Even if that's what she deserved. With a startled jolt, Cassie obeyed. She pulled off her shirt and stripped out of her jeans until she stood before him in only a black satin bra and panties. Her midnight waves tumbled over her shoulders and curled around her breasts.

It was the first time he'd gotten a good look at her without clothes on, and he drank her in. "Fucking gorgeous."

His fingers skimmed her creamy skin. One hand dropped to the small of her back, the other palming her through her bra. Her nipple strained against the confines of the thin material, allowing his fingers to tug and roll it.

Fractured Kiss

Cassie gasped and shuddered, her head falling back so the ends of her hair brushed over his knuckles.

He remembered how she'd come for him the other night in the hotel room, once from his fingers, and then once more from his mouth and hands on her tits. Would she do it for him again?

Still holding her firmly with his hand on her back, he pulled her bra down and flicked his tongue against a tight peak before sucking it deep into his mouth. He bared her other breast too, kneading it, then pinching and pulling on the pretty pink tip.

Cassie let out a breathy moan. Her hands came up to dig into his hair, nails lightly scraping his scalp. She felt so fucking good; he couldn't get enough. He kept it up, mouth and tongue working one nipple, fingers tugging and rolling the other.

She panted, rocking her hips against his thigh where it pressed between her legs, giving her the friction she needed. "Oh my god." She gasped. "Don't stop. Don't stop."

You couldn't have fucking paid him to stop. He scraped his teeth over one hard peak while pinching the other. She squirmed on his thigh, then, with a sharp cry, she came, bucking against his leg and shuddering in his arms. Holding onto his control by his fingertips, Zac unhooked her bra and let it fall off her shoulders. Then he dragged her panties over her hips and pressed her backward, so she fell onto the bed. He knelt between her legs, pulling her underwear all the way off and flinging them aside.

Desperate to finally taste all of her, he put his hands on her knees and jerked her thighs apart. She raised her head, eyes wide, cheeks stained pink, and tried to close them. But when he narrowed his gaze on her and gave a stern shake of his head, she stopped resisting.

Fuck. So damn pretty. He rubbed his throbbing erection through his jeans with the heel of his hand. If this was the only time they did this, he intended to enjoy every inch of her.

He leaned forward and swiped his tongue across her folds, the sweet taste of her arousal exploding on his tongue. His mouth pressed to her petal-soft skin, and he groaned in approval. An answering shiver wracked her body.

With steady licks and swirls around her clit, he built her back up until she was panting again. She fisted the bedspread in one hand and tugged on his hair with the other. Only then did he push one finger deep inside her, her hips jerking against him. She was so wet and ready for him, he quickly added another finger.

Cassie was far beyond hiding herself from him now. He took the hand that had been holding her open and used it to tilt her hips toward him. He worked her clit with his tongue, circling it, flicking it. His fingers stroked into her, rubbing against her front wall, finding that sweet spot that made her moan. As soon as he sucked her swollen bud between his lips and bit down gently, she exploded again.

"Zac," she cried out, loud enough he wouldn't be surprised if the steward at the front of the plane heard her. Beyond caring, she was almost sobbing as her hips rolled up against him. Her release coated his fingers and tongue, and he groaned, drunk on her sweetness.

He wanted to keep going, wanted to taste her orgasm again, but his dick was throbbing painfully in his jeans. When she gasped out a desperate, "Please, Zac. I need you," he was done.

Standing, he kept his eyes fixed on where she lay, pliant and wide-open for him on the bed. He made quick work of his jeans, stripping them and his briefs off in record time.

He fisted himself and squeezed. Cassie's eyes widened as she saw him, rock-hard and ready.

"Holy shit," she whispered when she noticed the apadravya piercing at the head of his cock, the one he'd gotten instead of tattooing himself like his bandmates had back when they first got famous. He'd wanted to do something that didn't involve being covered in ink like his dad. It wasn't a choice he'd ever regretted.

"Don't worry, angel. It'll feel good. I promise." The words came out rough with desire.

She bit her lip. "Can I—Can I touch it?"

He almost let out a groan but nodded, and she pushed herself upright. Having a gorgeous, naked woman staring intently at his dick made it jerk as it hardened further. Something he would have thought was impossible. She reached up with hesitant fingers and stroked them over where the piercing entered the smooth flesh of his crown. The movement of the barbell stimulated his already aching shaft, and he cursed under his breath.

Cassie's eyes snapped up to his. As soon as she saw it was pleasure that made him react, a faint smile crossed her face. She did it again. And again.

"Cassie," he growled.

Before he realized what she was planning, she leaned forward and slid him between her lips.

"Fuck," he choked out as the wet heat of her mouth engulfed him. He tangled his hands in her hair and held her head still. It wouldn't take much for him to blow right now, and he needed to be balls deep in her pussy, not her mouth when that happened.

She couldn't move her head, but Zac was still at her mercy. Her tongue stroked over his piercing, and he bit back a groan. Instead of pulling her off him, he bent over her, the movement pushing another inch of him between her lips, so he hit the back of her throat. "You can either swallow me now or lie back on the bed so I can show you just how hard you'll come with my cock deep inside you."

Cassie moaned around him, almost sending him over the edge. She pulled off him with a pop, leaving him engorged and pulsing, one hard stroke away from painting her pretty face.

"Lie back," he gritted out.

She did. All shyness gone now, she spread her legs and invited him into her body.

He reached down to his jeans on the floor, pulled out his wallet, and extracted a condom. He sheathed himself, then climbed onto the bed, bracing himself over her with a hand next to her head.

He ran the tip of his erection over her glistening flesh, getting it slick with her arousal. She twitched and whimpered whenever his piercing bumped against her clit.

"Ready?" He searched her face for any hesitation, but she only nodded.

He lined himself up with her entrance, then hissed out a breath as he sank the first few inches of his cock into her. Fuck, she was tight. She was petite to start with, and he was definitely on the larger side of average. Add in his piercing, and it was enough to have her wide-eyed and clutching at his biceps.

"I told you I'll make it feel good. Do you trust me?"

"Yes." No hesitation. A surge of satisfaction hit him.

He went down onto his elbows, cradled her face with his hands, and claimed her mouth. With each sweep of his thumbs against her cheeks, with each thrust of his tongue, he worked another inch of himself inside her. Finally, with a guttural groan, he was seated as deep as he could get.

He broke the kiss, resting his forehead against hers as they both gasped for breath. She felt incredible; her body gripping him so fucking tightly he had to force himself not to start driving into her immediately. He closed his eyes and breathed deeply, until he'd grappled back some control.

Zac withdrew slowly, then surged powerfully into her. She arched her back and cried out. That was it. That's what this was about. Losing themselves in the pleasure of each other's bodies. Forgetting all the shit they'd have to go back to worrying about once this plane landed.

He did it again. And again, unable to get enough of her reaction as he stroked inside her. Her head was thrown back, slender neck bowed. Her breasts bounced with each thrust, her nipples tight and straining upward. He dropped his head and took one of the hard peaks into his mouth, rolling his tongue around it, then sucking it deep.

"So good, Zac. That feels so good," she panted.

She felt so good. Too good. His heart was slamming against his rib cage, pressure was already building at the base of his spine. But he didn't want it to be over just yet. He didn't want to have to stop touching her. He pulled out.

"Roll over. Hands and knees," he ordered, and she did it without hesitation.

He notched his cock at her entrance, then palmed her ass, his fingers kneading her smooth skin. Before he pushed back into her, he ran his hands up her rib cage and over her shoulders. Twisting up her dark hair in one hand, he loosely circled her neck with the other.

With his hold on her hair, he tugged her head back. She let out a breathy whimper, her body quivering around him where he was pressed against her. The need to be back inside her was like a physical ache in his bones. He slid his other hand up her throat until he could press two of his fingers between her lips. His eyes almost rolled back in his head when her tongue curled around them, and she instinctively sucked. She was so fucking perfect.

Zac slammed his way home.

He started a steady, driving rhythm, his shaft and his piercing rubbing against her sensitive inner walls. Every stroke sent heat flaring up his spine.

Cassie moaned around his fingers, and he knew he wasn't going to last much longer.

"You like my cock in you, Cassie? Do you like me filling you over and over?"

The ripple of her body around his was her only answer.

"I can feel you squeezing me. Are you going to come for me?"

He tugged her head back further, removed his fingers from her mouth, and pulled her upright so her back was flush against his chest.

The hand in her hair dropped to palm her breast while his wet fingers circled her clit, the slick, swollen bud throbbing under his touch.

"Answer me, Cassie. Are you going to come for me?"

"Yes!" She let out a strangled sob. "God, yes."

The walls of her pussy spasmed as she pushed herself down onto him. She flung her arm back and curled it around his neck, pressing her head against his shoulder as she cried out her release. Her delicate internal muscles clenched around him, released, clenched again.

"Fuck," he growled. "That's it, angel. You're going to make me come too. *Fuck.*" With a last hard thrust, he buried himself inside her. Ecstasy boiled up from the base of his spine, and he let out a hoarse shout as he exploded into her. His fingers tingled as his shaft pulsed, the pleasure almost agonizing as it radiated through every inch of him.

He stroked his hands over her, gripped her hips, withdrew, and thrust hard again, wanting to drag the moment out as long as possible. The feel of her around him, the sounds she was making, her scent, the taste of her that still lingered on his tongue, the blood that surged through his veins. It was all conspiring to make his head spin.

Having her like this could get addictive. She'd be right there for the taking for the rest of the tour. He imagined her in his bunk every night, sharing his bed during every hotel stay, waking up with her body wrapped around him every morning. Holding her hand in his, kissing her, listening to her talk and laugh and share her poetry with him.

He wanted that. Right then, he wanted that so fucking badly, it almost hurt.

The last of his orgasm shuddered through him. He clenched his eyes shut against the ache in his chest.

Jesus fucking Christ, what had he done?

Chapter Twenty-Six

When Zac finally loosened his hold on her, Cassie fell forward onto her hands and knees again. Her head hung between her shoulders as she struggled to catch her breath.

She expected him to pull out straight away, but he stayed, rocking slowly into her as his own breaths came loud in the cabin. He curled his fingers over her hips, his thumbs stroking the small of her back. Tiny aftershocks rippled through her in waves.

Finally, he eased out of her and disposed of the condom in a small trash bin stowed in the side table.

Cassie lay down on her stomach, then rolled onto her back, shyness suddenly making her skin burn. She couldn't believe they'd ended up in bed. She'd only meant to share something of her past with him. To let him know he could talk to her if he wanted.

But he *really* hadn't wanted to talk.

She suppressed a slightly hysterical laugh.

Zac turned his head toward her. They were both still naked, and Cassie's eyes dropped to his still impressively half-hard penis. To his piercing. She didn't know why she was so surprised that he had one. Maybe because he didn't even have a single tattoo, and that he came across as so reserved. Then again, they do say it's always the quiet ones...

And it was so good. *He* was so good. She pressed her thighs together.

Wanting to feel his warm skin again, she reached out to him just as he swung his legs off the bed and stood with his back to her.

Cassie pulled her hand back. Her pulse sped up as he stooped down for his jeans and dragged them on. Still, he said nothing.

Her skin chilled. *He regretted it.*

She should have known he would. He'd already told her he didn't want complications. And no matter what Tori thought, that's what she was to him. A complication.

She climbed off the bed, keeping her head down as she gathered up her clothes. The silence grew thick, and she struggled to catch her breath.

Anger hit her next. Was it just the convenience of her being there that had made him decide he wanted her? Even knowing he was a rock star, she'd never expected him to be the type of person who'd screw the nearest available woman. But it seemed like that was exactly who he was. Now reality had hit him again, and he realized he was stuck with her. Stuck having to pretend that whatever there was between them meant something when it so obviously didn't.

Or maybe he thought she was going to fall for him the way she had for Bryan. Her brand-new knight in shining armor. Was that what she was doing? Clinging to the first person who seemed to care about her?

Zac wasn't her boyfriend. Cassie's throat tightened. He

wasn't even her friend. He was her boss. She'd let the time they'd spent together and what Tori had said at the hospital convince her there was something between them when there wasn't. She was still alone. As alone as she'd been that day in the field before Bryan had found her.

Zac finally turned toward her as she was sliding her panties up her legs. She could sense his gaze on her while she pulled her jeans on. Her movements were jerky as she struggled to contain her anger and hurt.

"Cassie," he said, as she reached behind her back to do up her bra. Her movements slowed, but she couldn't bring herself to meet his eyes—to see the regret in them.

"Fuck," he muttered, scrubbing his hand over his face.

Finally, she faced him, tensing her jaw so her chin wouldn't wobble. He'd told her he didn't want complicated. She should have listened. Now here they were, hundreds of miles in the air on a luxury jet, standing next to a rumpled bed and staring at each other with no words to say.

Zac reached out and brushed a tendril of hair from her face. She forced herself not to react, even as her pulse leaped at his touch.

His hand fell away. "I'm sorry."

How often was she going to hear those words? Her lips were numb, but she made herself reply as casually as she could. "What for?"

His gaze swept over her face. For a beat, his eyes dropped closed, and he swallowed. "For this. For taking advantage of your kindness. I told you I didn't want things to go this far, and then I did it, anyway."

Cassie steeled her spine and took a steadying breath. "I guess we both took advantage of this situation, then. You needed a distraction. I needed a push to see if I was truly over Bryan." She tossed the words in his face, ignoring the muscle that jumped in his jaw. She reached down for her top and yanked it on over her head, giving herself a few more seconds to compose herself. He was still watching her, his beautiful hazel eyes that had been burning with intensity a few minutes ago now shuttered against her.

"If this has made things too awkward, then we can just end this whole relationship thing." Cassie worked hard to keep her voice steady. "I don't know what we were thinking, going along with it to start with."

Several emotions flitted over his face in quick succession. "There are only five weeks left of the tour. We might as well see it through."

She exhaled, some of her composure crumbling. Maybe he saw it because he stepped forward and cupped her cheek so he could study her expression. She tried to meet his gaze steadily and not let her hurt show on her face. Tried to keep herself as self-contained as he so often was.

His eyes searched hers, then dipped to her mouth. It was his turn to take a jagged breath. "Let's finish the tour. We'll just make sure to keep it platonic from now on. That way, no one gets hurt. Okay?" Something flickered across his face. Regret? Desire? She had no idea. And right now, she didn't have the energy to care. He'd made his feelings clear. He'd had her, but he didn't want her. Just like everyone else in her life.

"Okay." Cassie stepped back, forcing him to drop his hand. She turned away from him, pulled the door open, and stepped out into the main cabin. A single tear escaped, but she wiped it away before he could see it.

Chapter Twenty-Seven

Cassie walked down the jet's steps ahead of him, her spine ramrod straight, slender shoulders stiff. She'd barely looked at him for the rest of the flight, and he couldn't blame her. What he'd done was unforgivable. He hated not being in control. And Cassie made him lose control more than anyone else ever had.

Instead of opening up and letting her in the way she'd obviously hoped, he'd treated her like a groupie. Just someone to take him out of his head for a while. Not someone who'd had her heart broken a few short weeks ago. Not someone who, through his own lack of control, he'd gotten into this situation. Not the woman who shared her poetry with him. Who'd revealed to him her deep-seated pain.

He'd waited for her to accuse him of using her. Or to ask how many other women he'd screwed on one of the jets. Because if she asked, he wouldn't lie to her. There'd been other occasions before. When fame hits you, you tend to take advantage of every opportunity that comes your way. At least until the novelty eventually wears off.

But there were some things he wouldn't tell her. That he *couldn't* tell her.

That this was the first time his heart almost crashed its way through his ribs at the touch of a woman's skin. This was the first time it was more than just a way to scratch an itch with a willing partner. It was the first time he saw fucking stars when he came.

And it was the first time he'd ever had to force himself to let go when it was over.

It scared the shit out of him.

His hands clenched into fists. He couldn't deny he felt a connection to Cassie. One he hadn't experienced with any woman before. He liked having her with him. He liked listening to her poetry and hearing her sing the words she'd written. He wanted to write more songs with her. To kiss her again.

To keep on kissing her.

And that was a problem. A big fucking problem. He didn't *want* to want that. He didn't want that connection with anyone.

He had to focus on his music. He had to help keep Fractured at the top and get Crossfire there too. He didn't want to be distracted from those goals. He couldn't be. And Cassie was too damn selfless for her own good. She'd given herself without a second thought. Not just her body, her emotions, and the painful pieces of her past. All he'd given her was a few orgasms. She deserved more than that. She deserved someone who could give her exactly what she needed. She'd had enough people in her life who let her down. She deserved someone who would put her first.

And that wasn't him. He just wasn't capable of it.

The accusations he braced for never came. Or the questions. Instead, Cassie just stared out the window, a crease between her brows and a distant look in her eyes. Every now and again, she unconsciously touched her left hand where her engagement ring used to be. He noticed her doing it because he couldn't stop staring at her while he waited for her to just fucking *say* something. And every time he saw the gesture, he would grit his teeth and suppress the ridiculous urge to punch something.

The car ride to the concert venue was no better than the flight. Cassie still avoided looking at him while he couldn't keep his fucking eyes away from her. He jiggled his knee and shifted in his seat. He'd gotten used to talking to her. To hearing her voice and seeing her smile. He rubbed the heel of his hand against the pressure growing behind his sternum. Would she stop sitting up with him at night? He only had himself to blame if she did.

Would she leave if they couldn't get back to the way things were?

Fuck. He'd really screwed things up. He should have just talked to her when she'd been down on her knees in front of him instead of taking her into the bedroom and screwing her. Even if that was something he'd been imagining doing for far too long. Even if just the memory of being that close to her had him fisting his hands on his knees to avoid doing something stupid again.

Once he had himself under control, he looked at her—at her profile, the curve of her cheek, the softness of her lips. As if responding to the weight of his gaze, her stormy blue eyes met his. Several emotions flitted over her face before she looked away again. Zac's heart gave a hollow thump.

She gave him something when she shared her pain with him and he'd given nothing in return.

"My father thinks I ruined his life." He almost didn't recognize his own voice, it came out so low and rough.

Cassie's gaze jerked back to him. She shook her head. "*Why?*"

Zac expelled a breath. He hated talking about this. He didn't even talk to his friends about it. Even when they were kids, he hated the thought of them knowing. Which was why he'd avoided inviting them to his house as much as possible. They knew he wasn't close to his father. But he didn't think they had any idea the way things really were. That's how he wanted it. But he wanted Cassie to know. He wanted to give her something, even if it couldn't repair the damage he'd already done.

"It took me a long time to figure out why he hated me. I pieced it together from the screaming matches between him and Mom. From the things he yelled at me whenever I got in his way. From the gossip I overheard." He clenched his jaw and looked out the window.

"Zac, you don't have to—"

"He used to be a touring musician." He looked back at her and made himself keep going. "Lead guitarist. When Mom got pregnant with me, she got sick and ended up on bed rest. Dad was forced to stay home and look after her. He wasn't happy about it, but she didn't have anyone else. She needed someone, and he was it."

Cassie's eyes were soft as she listened, not pressuring him to talk, just letting him do it at his own pace.

"I figure he was probably always a big drinker. But no one cares about stuff like that when you're on tour, as long as you turn up and do a good job. It's part of the life, right? Not so much when you're working a regular job, trying to support yourself and your pregnant wife. He got a job bartending and occasionally playing his guitar. His drinking got worse. He stayed out late when he should have been home with Mom. You know, the usual." Zac shrugged, though his shoulders were so stiff, he was surprised they didn't crack at the movement.

"After I was born, Dad couldn't wait to get back out on the road, but he was out of the loop, drinking more heavily than ever. Having a needy wife and baby at home held him back. His words." Zac could hear the flat bitterness in his voice and cleared his throat before continuing. "He couldn't pick up gigs as easily, so he spent more and more time at the bar, working and drinking. One night, he drove drunk and had an accident. Single car only, thank fuck. And he was lucky enough. Only ended up with a brief hospital stay, a DUI, a hefty fine, and nerve damage in his left hand."

He looked away from the shock of understanding in Cassie's eyes. His dad had never let him forget that if it hadn't been for him, he'd still be out there living the dream. Instead, he could barely play the music he loved more than anything or anyone.

The same way Zac loved it.

Cassie edged closer but didn't touch him. He didn't blame her after what happened on the plane. But that didn't stop him from wanting her to.

"He should have never put that on you, Zac," she said. "None of it was your fault."

"It wasn't just me. He resented the hell out of all of us, Mom and Tori when she came along. God knows what they were thinking, having another kid. Maybe Mom hoped it would make things better between them." He gave a short laugh. "It didn't."

"Why didn't they get divorced?"

It was the million-dollar question. Why didn't his dad leave? How could his mom not have walked away? "Some kind of sick co-dependency? Not wanting to be alone? I don't know, they've always had a toxic relationship. Mom swore she loved him and he loved her, but they fought constantly. Dad was always angry. *Always*. He used to scare Tori when she was younger. She ran and hid whenever he started in on me. But if it was him and Mom going at it, I would take her upstairs to her bedroom, and sing to her. Nursery rhymes, silly songs. Anything to distract her from the words they were screaming at each other and the sound of dishes smashing."

"Did he..." She bit her lip. "Did he hit her? Did he hit *you?*"

Without realizing he was doing it, Zac found himself tracing the pick that lay against his chest under his shirt. He dropped his hand. He hadn't answered her, but his hesitation must have told her the truth.

"Zac..." It came out on a shaky breath.

"Not all the time." He cut her off before she could say anything else. Not wanting to meet her gaze, he focused on where he was now playing with his leather cuff. "Not Mom, as far as I know. And not Tori. That's the important thing. It was a long time ago, anyway. He stopped when he finally realized I was going to be bigger than him."

The featherlight touch on his arm startled him into looking up. Her eyes were glossy. "I'm so sorry, Zac."

With her this close, it was hard to remember that touching her was a mistake. Her warmth seeped into his skin, her scent filling the space between them. The tempting curve of her full lips made him want to lose himself all over again. To drown himself in the comfort she gave so freely.

He restrained himself. He refused to go there again. If he knew one thing, it was that his heart and soul were just as tangled up in the music as his dad's had been.

So instead of pulling her against him, he reached up and

stroked his thumb down her cheek. "I'm sorry, too." He wasn't even sure what he was saying sorry for. Her shitty childhood or what happened on the plane.

Or maybe he was sorry for his own history. Maybe without it, things could be different between them. Maybe he would be a different man. A better man. One who could love Cassie the way she needed. One who could give her the life she deserved.

Whatever she understood from his words, she accepted them. Her gaze softened, mouth turning up in a shaky smile. He hoped that meant they were okay. Because as much of an asshole as it might make him, he didn't want her to go. Not yet.

He dropped his hand from her cheek as the car pulled into the venue. They'd managed to make it back in time for the final sound check.

The first damn person Zac saw when they got backstage was Bryan, staring balefully at him as they passed. As pissed off as he still was at what Bryan had done, knowing he'd been there for Cassie when she needed someone softened his opinion.

Slightly.

Still, Zac didn't like the way Bryan watched Cassie. As if he was just biding his time. As if he knew this whole thing was a lie and was just waiting for it to be over so he could swoop back in.

Zac kept his gaze fixed on him. If the man wanted to grovel and try to win Cassie back after the tour, there was nothing Zac could do about it. As much as the thought pissed him off. But right now, fake or not, Cassie was his girlfriend.

Not Bryan's.

His.

Zac stepped closer to Cassie and slung his arm over her shoulders. It seemed to surprise her, but she didn't pull away. He didn't check to see if Bryan was still watching them, just guided Cassie up on stage where the rest of Fractured was gathered. He ignored the grin on Noah's face as they approached.

"How's your dad?" asked Connor when they got close enough.

"Alive." Zac dropped his arm from around Cassie's shoulders when Dan stepped toward him, holding out one of his basses.

"Wasn't sure if you'd be back in time, so I did the initial check," Dan explained to Cassie.

"Thank you. I appreciate it," she said. Dan gave her a grin and a wink.

Zac ran his fingers over the instrument and played a couple of verses. The heavy strings felt good under his fingers. Not as good as Cassie's body, though. He glanced in her direction. She had her head tilted down, her lips curved up as she listened to the music.

You ruined my life.

Tension knotted his shoulders. His dad may believe Zac had ruined his life, but true or not, he'd learned one thing from his father. If you can't commit your whole heart to someone, then don't commit it at all. He knew what happens when the people you're supposed to love come last. And he refused to be responsible for ruining anyone else's life.

Zac put his head down and kept playing.

Chapter Twenty-Eight

Cassie stood to the side of the stage as Fractured brought the house down. Watching them perform never failed to make her heart pound. Electricity surged through the air, crackling against her skin, making the fine hairs on her arms stand on end. As much as she used to love watching Bryan perform, she'd never experienced this kind of full body response. She wasn't the only one feeling it. The entire crowd was a shrieking, writhing mass, reaching and straining toward their idols.

The flare of the lights, the driving beat of Noah's drums, the oscillating screams of Tex's guitar, Connor's deep, whiskey-smooth voice, and under it all, the pulse of Zac's bass that vibrated through her bones. He didn't play to the crowd like the others did as he moved around the stage. He was lost in his own world, head down, the muscles in his arms and shoulders moving smoothly as he played.

Now and then, he looked out over the crowd, giving them the gift of his intense gaze. And every time he did, fans would scream and call out for him—desperate for his attention. Sometimes he'd catch someone's eye and flash them a smile, and even through the wall of sound surrounding her, Cassie could hear women calling his name.

They craved his attention. A moment of his time. A night in his bed.

She longed to hold him.

To be the person he turned to when he needed someone.

Cassie squeezed her eyes shut. She had to stop thinking that way. She and Zac were just... Well, she didn't really know what they were. More than boss and employee. Friends maybe? Whatever they were, she accepted it. Even though every time he looked at her, she felt it from the top of her head to the tip of her toes. It didn't mean anything. It couldn't mean anything. She didn't need more heartbreak. And Zac was heartbreak personified. Not because he was an asshole. It would be easier if he was. No, he wasn't an asshole. He was just so self-contained, it was like he existed in his own little world. He was an enigma to her. Maybe even to his friends. Sometimes when he was talking and laughing with them, she could almost see how he held himself back.

It was like Tori said—he didn't really seem to need anyone.

Noah smashed his sticks into his cymbals to end the song, and Zac made his way toward her, dragging the strap of his bass over his head. His white T-shirt was plastered to his body, outlining the hard ridges of his muscles. Muscles she'd run her fingers over. Muscles that had flexed over her again and again as he'd thrust into her. Her breathing quickened, her skin warming as he smiled at her.

He held out his bass, and she reached for it with her

empty hand, passing him the one she'd been holding. Their fingers brushed, and her eyes flicked up to meet his.

For a beat, they stood there, Zac staring down at her while the lights flared behind him, her frozen with her pulse going haywire. Then he slipped the instrument over his head and returned to the stage. With the exchange made, she could breathe again.

She just had to remember what this was, and she'd get through it with her heart intact.

Cassie turned away and did her best to focus on her job.

Later, after finishing the load-out, Cassie headed into the crowded after-party. She spotted Tex and Noah first, surrounded by a group of fans. Summer and Eden were nearby, and Cassie made her way toward them. Their warm smiles reassured her she wasn't intruding. It was the first time she'd seen them since they'd arrived from LA earlier in the evening.

They exchanged hugs. Although she wasn't completely used to their casual affection, she was getting there.

Tex and Noah were signing merchandise as they chatted easily with the excited fans. As the last few moved away, throwing lingering, yearning gazes over their shoulders, the two men turned their attention back to their women. Noah hooked his arm around Summer's waist and pulled her into him, smiling down into her upturned face and dropping a tender kiss on her lips. He murmured something in her ear. A lump formed in Cassie's throat at the joy on Summer's face. She looked away, only to be faced with Eden wrapped in Tex's muscular, tattooed arms.

She felt like a fraud standing with them, looking in at their happiness from the outside.

Cassie scanned the room, the air escaping her lungs in a rush as her gaze collided with Zac's. She couldn't look away from the heat of his stare. Warmth blossomed in her chest, licking out to her extremities as his eyes seared into hers. Memories surged to the forefront of her mind, echoes of pleasured gasps and moans. Her body thrummed with awareness.

Someone stepped into her line of sight, and the connection was severed. She took a deep, steadying breath.

Friends. Just friends.

She dragged her attention back to the others, but a too-familiar presence behind her had butterflies winging around her stomach. She squeezed her eyes closed. When she opened them again, Noah was watching her. The corner of his mouth quirked up, and he gave her a wink. God, how embarrassing that he'd seen her reaction to Zac's presence.

"Everything okay?" Zac's warm breath tickled her ear, and flames lapped across her skin. She looked at him over her shoulder.

His gaze was intent. Too intent. Her body pulsed with hunger—tingled with remembered caresses. She focused on his mouth as she recalled how it had felt pressed against hers. Without conscious volition, her tongue darted out to wet her lips.

Zac's eyes flared and his hand curled around her hip. He leaned closer. "Don't."

"Don't what?"

"Play with fire."

She hadn't meant to. But at his words, at the knowledge she wasn't the only one struggling with this, recklessness ripped through her. "What if I want to?" What if she wanted to burn under his touch again? What if she wanted to throw herself into the fire just to be with him for a few hours?

His fingers tightened, his head lowering until his mouth was right by her ear. "You'd regret it."

"Would you?"

For a few seconds, there was just the heat of his body enveloping her. Then his grip on her hip was gone, and her body cooled as he stepped back.

Disappointment cut through her arousal. She turned back to the group, ignoring the various raised eyebrows and knowing smirks directed at them.

"So, I was thinking," said Noah.

"You know how we feel about that," drawled Tex.

Ignoring him, Noah continued. "It's been ages since we've been to karaoke. We used to go all the time, but since Zac started satisfying his exhibitionist urges as Crossfire's front man, he's given up his favorite pastime. I think we should resurrect the tradition."

A chorus of agreements rang out. Cassie tugged at the hem of her T-shirt and shifted on her feet.

"You'll come, won't you, Cassie?" asked Eden.

Uncertain, she twisted around to seek confirmation from Zac. After everything that had happened, would he rather she didn't join them?

Zac's brows lowered, and the skin around his eyes tightened.

Cassie's stomach dropped. *He didn't want her there.* She glanced away, preparing to excuse herself for the night.

"She's coming," Zac said, and her head jerked back toward him. His lips were pressed together in a straight line, his gaze boring into hers. Was he angry at her?

He was so damn confusing. But she wanted to go with them, so she just turned back around and nodded.

The others didn't seem to notice the tension between them because they just carried on talking. The party was wrapping up, and they were figuring out where to go once it was over.

If Zac was angry, though, he didn't move away. She concentrated on her breathing, on resisting the urge to lean back against him. Because Zac was right. She was playing with fire, and she'd already been burned enough for a lifetime.

Chapter Twenty-Nine

"This is perfect," Noah said as they pushed through the slightly greasy-looking dark wooden door.

Noah was right. The dive bar in South Boston was exactly like the ones they frequented when they wanted to have some low-key fun. It had been way too long since they'd relaxed and let loose at karaoke. Even though Zac loved playing bass, he'd always had a thing for singing. It was the reason he'd formed Crossfire with Noah when Fractured went on hiatus.

One of the reasons, anyway.

About two dozen people scattered around the smoky interior were watching an embarrassed but smiling woman on the little stage sing a slightly off-key rendition of "Like a Virgin".

Only a few of the audience turned at their group's entrance. Most turned away without recognizing them since he and his bandmates all wore caps pulled low over their faces. But the attention of a few of them lingered. Drew wandered over to speak to the bartender. The man listened to him, then swiveled his gaze toward where Zac and the others were still standing by the door. He gaped at them for a second, then gave a wide grin. He nodded at Drew and went back to wiping down the bar top, with only a couple of surreptitious looks in their direction.

Tex led the eight of them to one of the largest booths at the back of the room. Drew made his way up to the side of the stage. He waited for the woman to finish her song, then climbed the steps and spoke to the bored-looking man sitting on the stool next to the karaoke machine. Another stunned pair of eyes found them and lit up with excitement.

Drew took the microphone and walked to the center of the stage, where he announced to the thankfully not massive crowd that the bar was closing for a few hours. He added that they were more than welcome to stay and listen to a once-in-a-lifetime performance by the members of Fractured, who would be happy to sign autographs and take photos. The caveat was that they refrain from letting anyone know the band was there, or posting any photos or videos on social media until after the band had left the premises.

It was his standard spiel. The last thing any of them wanted was to be mobbed by fans or paparazzi while they were trying to relax and have fun.

After the resulting rush of fan engagement, photos, and autograph signings, they all ordered drinks and chose their first songs. Zac let Eden and Lexie sit on either side of Cassie. He told himself he did it because it was nice for her to spend some time with the other women, but he knew the truth. If he sat next to her, he'd be tempted to touch her. To drag his fingers along her thigh, up underneath the skirt of that flirty little dress she was wearing, and listen to her breath hitch. To play the role of attentive boyfriend a little too realistically. And he refused to screw her around any more than he already had.

It had pissed him off back at the after-party when she looked at him for permission to come with them tonight—that she still saw herself as an outsider in their group. It pissed him off even more that she thought he might say no. If he'd spent more time making her feel comfortable in this situation instead of focusing all his efforts on trying—unsuccessfully—to keep his hands off her, would she have reacted differently?

He promised himself he'd do better from now on. He'd already told her there couldn't be a repeat of what had happened on the plane.

Or the hotel room...

He took a long pull on his beer and forced his attention to the stage.

Half an hour later, he was wincing at Noah's off-key rendition of "You are the Sunshine of my Life" by Stevie Wonder. The man could bang a drum set like nobody's business, but he couldn't sing to save himself. From the wide grin on his face, it was obvious he didn't give a shit. He was focused on Summer as he sang, and she turned red, even as she half-hid her face behind what apparently passed for a cocktail menu and laughed.

Zac couldn't help cracking a smile. At one stage, he'd honestly doubted the two of them could get past their issues. But they'd proved him wrong.

His eyes cut sideways. The corners of Cassie's mouth were curled up, her gaze moving between Noah up on stage and Summer laughing and blushing opposite her.

But it was the wistfulness in her expression that hit him in the gut. It was clear she wanted what they had. She wanted love. She deserved to be with someone who'd treasure her forever, keep her safe, show her exactly what she was worth. It was just another reminder to keep his hands to himself.

He swiftly returned his gaze to the front of the room, just in time to catch Noah's grinning salute to the now raucous audience. Before leaving the stage, he bent down to talk to the emcee. His eyes met Zac's across the room, the corners of his mouth sliding into a smirk.

Zac groaned internally. He knew that look. It didn't bode well.

A few seconds later, Noah walked back to the table, the smirk still on his face. The PA system crackled with the announcement of the next performance.

"Next we have Zac and Cassie, singing 'I Was Made for Loving You'."

Zac cocked his brow at Noah. Why the hell had the drummer chosen a KISS song? And why was he so smug about it?

Noah's smile only grew wider, and Zac narrowed his eyes. What was he up to?

Zac looked over at Cassie, who was staring back at him. He let out a heavy breath and stood, Cassie following his lead. She maneuvered her way out of the booth, and he grabbed her hand. They made their way to the stage to a backdrop of cheers and catcalls from his friends and their audience.

He realized his mistake once they got up there, and Noah's devilish expression finally made sense. It wasn't "I Was Made for Lovin' You" by KISS. It was the duet between Tori Kelly and Ed Sheeran. He should have known.

Cassie must have sensed his disquiet because her lips were pressed together, eyes searching his.

"Is this okay?" she asked.

"Of course." He forced his mouth into an insincere smile. And really, what the hell was his problem? He'd sung with plenty of women before. They were even planning a damn duet on the upcoming Crossfire album.

But in a very short space of time, playing music with Cassie, listening to her poetry, hearing her sing had become personal. Something she shared just with him. And singing this song with her? He just wanted to get it over and done with, then go back to the booth and order another drink.

He grabbed the microphones and handed one to Cassie. The music started, the notes of the guitar intro echoing in the suddenly quiet room. Cassie took a deep breath and looked at the prompter. She sang with her head tipped down, her lips almost touching the microphone. Her clear voice cut like a bell through the dim, smoky atmosphere of the bar.

Even though she was looking at the prompter, it was clear she knew the words because she didn't falter. She was deliberately avoiding looking at him.

Zac sought out his friends sitting at the back of the bar. They were staring, and he spotted a few raised brows. They were probably wondering why the two of them were acting so awkwardly. He was a damn professional, for fuck's sake.

He shifted, angling himself toward Cassie, drawing her attention. Their gazes met and locked. Her eyes shimmered in the low light as she sang the words of the song. The ones that told him she'd been waiting for him all her life. That she'd been made just to love him. That begged him not to hurt her.

Zac's grip tightened around his microphone.

He was so distracted by the emotion in her voice, he almost missed his cue to cut in on the second verse. She watched him, her lips parting as his voice deepened when he sang the lyrics asking her not to let him go, letting her know he'd been waiting for her too—promising he wouldn't hurt her. On the second chorus, her voice joined his, the harmony sending chills down his spine.

Without noticing when it had happened, he found himself closer to her. So close, she'd tipped her head back to look at him. Everything surrounding them faded, and all he could see was the lights reflecting in the depths of her sapphire eyes, the graceful arch of her dark brows, the faint spray of freckles over her nose. His gaze dropped lower to the soft fullness of her lips. She was almost whispering now. The catch in her voice made the words she was singing all too believable.

When it was his turn to join in again, the tightness in his throat caught him off guard. His voice cracked. *Fuck.* When was the last time that had happened?

Cassie's eyes were wide and dark as they sang the last line of the song. Their voices trailed off as they reached the end and stood, staring at each other. The last note faded into silence. Zac swallowed, then looked away from her to the audience. All he could see were stunned faces and cell phones held up, recording.

After a few long heartbeats, the place erupted in cheers and claps. Zac searched for his friends. The men were all grinning like idiots, while Lexie, Eden, and Summer were smiling and wiping their cheeks.

Feeling strangely exposed, Zac took Cassie's microphone and placed it down with his. He reached for her hand and headed for the edge of the stage.

"Zac, is something wrong?" she asked, as she almost had to jog down the stairs to keep up with his rapid strides. Zac slowed so that he didn't drag her off her feet.

"No, I just need a drink." She said nothing else as they wound their way through the tables to get to the back. A few people reached out to touch him as he passed. He gave them a tight smile and kept going. Being groped by random people was a hazard of the job. It didn't mean he had to like it.

When they got back to the booth, Eden jumped up and threw her arms around him, then Cassie. "That was so beautiful," she gushed. Lexie and Summer echoed the sentiment.

"Damn, you two have some fantastic on-stage chemistry," Noah said, a wide grin creasing his cheeks.

"Have you ever thought about becoming a professional singer, Cassie?" Tex asked once they settled back in the booth.

Cassie gave a little laugh and shook her head. "I love singing, but it's not really something I want to do professionally."

"You don't want to always be a guitar tech, though," Zac said.

She shot him a look.

"What do you want to do then?" Summer asked.

Zac kept his eyes on Cassie, enjoying the way her cheeks tinted pink as she spoke about herself to the others. As if she wasn't used to people taking an interest in her. And she probably wasn't, having been around Bryan all the time. He was sure her ex-fiancé probably sucked up all the attention in any room he was in.

He picked up his fresh beer and leaned back in the chair, catching Connor's eye across the table. The lead singer arched a dark brow and gave him a too-knowing look. Zac schooled his expression into practiced impassivity.

The last thing he wanted was to encourage his friends' speculation.

His eyes drifted back to Cassie, just as she twisted her hair off her shoulders and somehow pinned it on top of her head, exposing the smooth column of her neck. The memory of pressing his lips there as he moved inside her slammed into him and his body pulsed with sudden hunger.

Worse than that was the ache that grew deep in his chest.

He took a big swallow of his drink.

Fuck.

Chapter Thirty

Cassie tapped the end of her pen on her notebook and looked across the living room of the bus to where Zac sat with his guitar.

On the face of it, things seemed to have gone back to the way they were before the two of them had slept together. She still sat up with him, writing in her notebook, while he and his bandmates poured their hearts into trying to finish their album. She still watched him perform every night and ensured his instruments and equipment were working perfectly. She still enjoyed his presence a little too much. But now her skin remembered the touch of his hands, her body remembered how it felt having him inside her. And her heart... Her heart remembered how it had tripped and stumbled when he'd told her about his father. It remembered the look in his eyes as they sang together on that little karaoke stage—when she'd almost believed the words they were singing. She hadn't been the only one. Several people recording that night had uploaded the video, and it had gone viral, resulting in renewed media attention on their *relationship*.

Cassie couldn't bring herself to watch it. She didn't want to see what everyone else must have seen on her face as she sang. She knew developing feelings for Zac was a terrible idea. He was completely focused on his music, to the exclusion of everything else. He didn't *want* anything else. He'd told her that, and she believed him. After all, she'd met his parents. Having grown up with their example, she could understand how he wouldn't want to replicate it. But it hurt her to think he'd given up on love. That he'd convinced himself there was no value in it. Even though evidence of its beauty surrounded him every day, with his bandmates' relationships.

Zac channeled all his emotions into his music, but was that enough? Could that ever be enough to have a fulfilling life?

Now, they were sitting together on the bus once more. She watched him, cradling the guitar in his arms, a small half-smile on his face at something one of his bandmates had said on his screen. Her heart tumbled in her chest. She swallowed and willed herself to stay focused on her notebook.

But stubbornly, her mind went straight back to him.

It was funny, really. They had so much in common, yet they were so different. Neither of them had grown up with much—or any—love from their parents. He had his sister, but he'd spent his youth protecting her, not being supported by her. Both he and Cassie had grown up without a good example of a loving relationship. But he'd shunned the whole idea of love, and she'd thrown herself into the dream of knights in shining armor, soul mates, and happily ever afters. She'd believed in the fairy tale.

But maybe he had the right idea.

Maybe expecting true love that lasted forever *was* a

child's daydream. Maybe you were better off finding something you loved and throwing yourself wholeheartedly into it. Maybe *that* passion was what would keep you warm at night, not the familiar body of a lover lying next to you.

Her pen was poised over the page, but her hand didn't move. Her mind was blank.

She found her eyes back on Zac. She could hear raised voices coming from his phone. They were having a heated discussion about something. Some lyric they didn't agree on. A chord change one of them thought didn't fit. He was listening, no longer smiling. A line etched between his brows. He said a few words, and there was silence from the other end of the phone. Then, a few words from them, a nod from Zac, and whatever argument they were having was over.

He always came across as calm and collected—so in control of every situation. How did he do it? She always felt like she was teetering on the edge of one emotional cliff after another. The only time she'd ever seen him slip was when he'd kissed her, when he'd touched her in the hotel room, when he'd screwed her like a groupie in the back of the plane.

At least, that's how she should have felt about what had happened.

But it hadn't felt like that at the time. It didn't now, either. She didn't know why. Maybe it had been the way he'd looked at her, the way he'd been so focused on her, the intensity in those beautiful eyes. Or maybe it was how his touch had made her body come alive in a way she didn't think it ever had before.

She watched him push his hair off his forehead, the muscles of his forearm flexing. Her gaze traced over the width of his shoulders, admiring the way his T-shirt stretched over his broad chest.

Heat pulsed through her.

She wasn't supposed to want him.

But she did.

She wanted his touch. She wanted to come alive under his hands.

She wanted him to lose control again. She wanted to be the one who made it happen.

Cassie watched, heart crashing against her ribs, as he said goodbye and disconnected the call. She'd never done anything like what she was contemplating before. She'd never had to. She didn't even know if she'd be able to.

This wasn't the right time or place for what she wanted. But need suddenly had its claws in her. She needed something. Something to hold on to for the rest of the tour—for when she was alone again.

He looked up, and their eyes met. A hint of a smile flickered and died on his lips. He must have noticed something on her face because his gaze sharpened.

Cassie slid her notebook off her lap and stood, surreptitiously trying to wipe her damp palms on her thighs. She drew in a shallow breath, then walked toward him. Maybe she should have moved more seductively, swayed her hips or something. But seduction wasn't something she'd needed to practice with Bryan. The two of them had come of age together, taken each other's virginity in a fumbling, laughing tangle on his bed when his parents were out for the night. Sex between her and Bryan had always been fun. It had always felt good. But it had never filled her with fire the way just the touch of Zac's hand did.

She didn't know how to do seduction, but she was going to try.

He'd laid his guitar on the table next to his phone. As she approached, he swiveled on the bench seat to face her. She moved forward, so close he had to widen his legs, so she didn't run into them.

"What are you doing, Cassie?" His voice was low and tight. He knew what she was doing. She could see the knowledge in his eyes. In the way he held himself so still. Restrained.

Recklessness pulsed through her veins. Made her skin flush hot, then cold.

She licked her lips and swallowed past the dryness in her throat. "You're always in control," she said. "Of your emotions. Your music. Do you ever let go, Zac?" She didn't recognize the breathy, seductive tone of her voice. "Everyone needs to lose control sometimes." She reached out and trailed her fingers down the side of his face.

He stared up at her, his eyes flaring, hands clenching where they rested on his thighs. She dropped to her knees between his legs.

"What are you doing?" he repeated, but his voice rasped.

"I'm helping you to let go. Just for a few minutes. Let me do this for you." Her hands went to the button of his jeans, and she flipped it open. He inhaled sharply as she eased the fly down slowly. He gripped her wrist, and she thought he was going to tell her no. But he surprised her. "It shouldn't be here."

"Why not? Don't tell me there haven't been plenty of women down on their knees in front of you right where I am." She steeled herself against the stab of jealousy in her chest. She knew the reality of the rock star lifestyle.

Zac's jaw hardened. "It's not the same."

"It's exactly the same. I'm offering this to you."

He shook his head, a short, sharp jerk. "Those were just transactions. I got something, they got something."

"And?"

"And you're not looking for bragging rights, are you?"

"I want something all the same."

His fingers flexed around her wrist. "What do you want?"

"I want to see you let go again. I want to be the one to give you that."

"You give too much of yourself." Even as he said it, his hand loosened.

Cassie kept her eyes fixed on his as she hooked her fingers in the waistband of his jeans and tugged. Excitement thrilled through her when he gave in and lifted his hips. She dragged the jeans down over his thighs until he was sitting there in only his black boxer briefs.

Even though she'd been the one to push the issue, her skin prickled with heat at what she was doing. The others were only a few feet away in the sleeping area. Maggie was up in the front, driving. And yet, she couldn't have stopped for anything right then. The craving was too strong. The need to have her hands on him again, to give him pleasure, to see him lost to her touch, the way she'd been lost to his. He was so wrong if he thought she wouldn't get something out of this.

"Take your shirt off," she said. A surge of satisfaction flowed through her when he reached over his back, gripped his T-shirt, and pulled it over his head.

Cassie sat back on her heels to take him in. He was beautiful. The most beautiful man she'd ever seen, with his sculpted muscles and smooth, tanned skin. The enticing happy trail leading down toward the swell of his erection now only confined by his underwear.

The anticipation of what she wanted to do made Cassie's mouth water. Zac's breathing deepened as she took her time looking at him. She met his gaze again, wanting to see the same need filling her reflected in his eyes.

Her heart stuttered in her chest. There was more than need there. There was longing, frustration, anger—not at her. Maybe at himself. But it was need that was winning.

She peeled his briefs down, releasing his impressive length. It had been days since they'd been together, but she hadn't forgotten how perfect he was. She definitely hadn't forgotten that piercing.

She eyed it hungrily, and Zac's hands rose to her face, sweeping some strands of hair off her cheeks and tucking them behind her ears. Her blood whooshed loudly through her veins as his fingers pushed further back, tangling in the loose tendrils, tightening almost to the point of pain. It sent a bolt of lust through her. "Don't tease me, angel." His voice was tense.

It made her want to push him. It made her want to push herself.

She leaned forward until her lips hovered just above his piercing and let the heat of her breath wash over it. His cock jerked in response, and she smiled to herself, a thrill coursing through her.

She gripped him firmly at the base of his shaft and flicked her tongue over the bead of wetness at his tip, then over the metal barbell just below. A stuttered groan was his only reaction. She leaned down further, took the smooth, swollen crown into her mouth, then sank down until it nudged the back of her throat.

He swore violently as his hips tilted and his fingers flexed against her scalp. Arousal coiled in her belly.

She pulled back, swirled her tongue around the tip,

flicked his piercing again, then sank down even farther this time.

"*Fuck*," he hissed. She raised her gaze to find him watching her, mouth slightly parted, eyes hungry. The frustration, the anger, it was all gone. The only thing there now was white-hot need.

She let her lips rub over the satin-smooth skin of the tip, then glided her mouth back down, pulling a low rumble from his chest.

She shivered and moaned in response. His shaft pulsed against her tongue, so she picked up her pace, drawing him deeper, then pulling almost all the way off him.

One time she let him fall from her lips so she could stroke him from root to tip, lapping at the sensitive slit as she did.

"Cassie," he groaned, and she did it again, playing with his piercing, licking the pre-cum that beaded there until he yanked her head back. "Open," he growled.

And she did, chest rising and falling, body alive and crackling with wild energy. His whole body drew tight as he fed his cock back into her mouth.

Zac's eyes slammed shut as she took him back down. He was throbbing against her tongue, and she pressed her thighs together. This was what she wanted. Both of them lost to each other. She wasn't sure she recognized herself right then. But she didn't care. She liked it.

Letting go of her hair, he cradled the back of her head with one hand, using it to guide her up and down. "More," he panted, all control gone.

She didn't think it was possible, but he seemed to swell even thicker between her lips. It made her dizzy with desire. With the knowledge of what she was doing to him.

"Look at me." The pitch of his voice was so low, Cassie

shivered. She raised her gaze to his again. His fingers flexed in her hair as she sank down onto him, the tip of his shaft pushing into her throat. "You really are a fallen angel," he said through gritted teeth. "On your knees for me."

She wasn't sure what he meant, but she didn't care. All she cared about was that he'd let go. Let his control slip. A series of rough pants spilled from his mouth, and she sucked hard, took him deep.

His body coiled tight. "Cassie. *Fuck. Fuck.* I'm going to come, angel." And then he was, growling and cursing under his breath as he released shot after shot into the depths of her mouth.

The muscles of his thigh twitched under her hand as his cock spasmed against her tongue. She moaned as the taste of him filled her. She swallowed, then swallowed again.

Finally, the pulsing stopped. Zac was breathing fast. "Fuck, Cassie. You make me lose all control."

It was what she wanted to hear.

She pulled off him, her lips curling up in satisfaction until she saw his expression. His brows were lowered, his jaw tight. Cassie's stomach tumbled.

"Get on the couch," he demanded.

"Zac, I—"

"On the couch. Now."

She stood on shaky legs and backed toward the leather couch. His gaze burned into hers and her heart pumped furiously in her chest. Her legs hit the seat, and she sat down.

Zac stood, pulled up his boxers and jeans, leaving the fly undone, then stalked toward her. He reached her, bent over, and dragged her down so her hips almost hung off the edge of the seat.

His hands went to the waistband of her shorts, and he slowly inched them and her panties down her legs and off.

He pushed her thighs apart and dropped to his knees between them. Now it was *her* breath that was catching in her throat.

His gaze pierced her. "Don't you dare make a sound."

She shivered at the demand. "Why?"

"Because I'm the only one who gets to hear you come." The possessiveness in his voice caused a fresh burst of arousal, and she whimpered.

"Can you do that, Cassie?"

"Yes." Her thighs quivered.

"Good girl," he said, then dropped his head.

The heat of his breath washed over her just before he buried his face between her legs. His tongue raked over her clit, his palms on her inner thighs spreading her wide.

She was already halfway there from what she'd just done to him, and the tension in her core built rapidly as he licked and sucked. One long finger speared inside her, followed soon by a second as she writhed under him, trying desperately to keep quiet. A moan escaped her as he continued working over that sensitive bundle of nerves with his tongue, circling it, giving it light flicks and gentle sucks.

Her hips bucked up as her fingers threaded through his hair, pulling tight as he scraped his teeth over her tender skin. He growled against her, the vibration sending extra sensations rippling through her sex. He spread her wider, sucked harder. She slapped her hand over her mouth to stop herself from crying out.

He added a third finger and drove them back in.

"Oh god," she moaned, her legs shaking as he drew her clit between his lips and rolled his tongue over it again.

Cassie threw back her head, her eyes squeezing shut.

The familiar pressure was growing, liquid heat flowing through her, blood rushing in her ears.

With a final lash of his tongue, she came hard, squeezing around his fingers. A rumbling groan vibrated against her as Zac made his satisfaction known. It only threw fuel onto the fire. She writhed and bucked up against his mouth as ecstasy coursed through her in wave after wave.

When it finally began to fade, Zac pulled back. The pleasure he dragged from her was visible on his lips and chin. He ran his forearm over his face, then leaned forward, gripped the back of her neck, and pulled her toward him until their mouths crashed together. She didn't care that she could taste herself on his tongue as the kiss grew deeper, wilder, hotter.

He broke away, then dropped his forehead to hers. Their panting breaths mingled. His other hand came up and cupped the side of her face, his thumb brushing her cheekbone. Her eyes sagged shut at how good his touch felt. The hand on her neck tightened, then he let her go and stood.

Cassie looked up at him, standing so tall, the fly of his jeans hanging open. Even after the orgasm he'd just given her, she itched to peel that denim off his hips. To touch him, stroke him. He was hard again. She could see the telltale bulge, and she wanted him again too—in her hands, her mouth, her body.

But if she'd made him lose control, he was slowly gathering it back around him. Her chest tightened. As he ran his hand over his face, dropped his head, and zipped up his fly, she realized she wanted more than his temporary loss of control. She wanted *him*. She wanted him to want *her*.

But when he knelt and gently pulled her panties and

shorts back up her legs and helped her up, his expression once again shuttered, she knew she wouldn't get what she wanted.

Cassie stood on shaky legs, took a step forward, and placed her hand on his chest. His heart raced under her palm. No matter how calm he looked on the surface, it was clear what had happened between them had affected him.

"Cassie..." he started in a low voice. She shook her head.

"This was supposed to be for you," she said. "I don't expect anything more, Zac."

A pulse leaped in his jaw. "You deserve better."

"So do you."

He stared at her, then lowered his head and brushed his lips over hers.

Her heart squeezed tight, and she blinked back tears at the tenderness of his kiss.

But then he stepped back and raked his hands through his hair.

"Time to hit the sack," he said, voice gruff.

He turned away, and she let out a little breath before following him to the bunks.

Chapter Thirty-One

Cassie carefully wiped down and polished the last bass Zac had handed off to her, ready to pack it away for load-out. It was the newest of Zac's instruments, and she made a note to adjust the pickups the next day, since the tone during the last song had been a little damper than she liked.

Her eyes flicked out toward Zac, loving the sight of him on stage. But she forced her gaze away. Loving the sight of him wasn't doing her any favors. She hadn't done what she had last night with the idea it would change anything between them. But caught up in her need for him, she hadn't considered that her heart might not thank her for it.

She'd spent a restless night, reliving everything that had happened between them, getting herself all hot and bothered again at the memory of his touch. She'd had to ruthlessly suppress the desire to climb into his bunk and press herself against him. He wouldn't want that. She may have made him lose control, but she couldn't make him want to keep her.

Drew strode up to her side, jolting her from her

thoughts. She smiled at him, but his return greeting was distracted as he frowned out at the stage. He ran his hand over his mouth.

"Is everything okay?" she asked.

He turned to her, his frown deepening. He studied her for a moment, then blew out a heavy breath. "I have to talk to Zac. I'm not sure if I should pull him from the show. I don't know if he'd want me to."

Cassie's breath caught. Was it bad news? His dad? *Tori*? She looked back out at the man she was starting to feel far too much for. What would he want? She turned back to Drew, her heart in her throat. "It's not his sister, is it?" She was sure he would want to stop the performance if it was.

Drew shook his head, and she could breathe easier again.

"Let him keep going," she said. "There are only about fifteen minutes left."

Drew nodded, shoving his hands in the pockets of his jeans. The skin around his eyes was tight as he stared out at the men on stage. Considering he was only around five years older than them, he sometimes exuded a protective vibe that was almost fatherly.

She was glad they had him. Someone they could trust implicitly—who'd repeatedly proven that he had their backs. Someone who would always be there for them. Her heart hurt as she watched Zac pace around his side of the stage. What was he going to be walking into when the concert ended?

She desperately wanted to ask Drew what he needed to talk to Zac about so she could try to figure out what impact it would have on him. But she didn't have that right. Even if she was actually his girlfriend, she didn't know whether Drew would tell her. Guarding the band members' privacy was one of his top priorities. Maybe if she were his wife—

A sudden pang of longing pierced her chest. She squeezed her eyes shut.

God, she was such a fool.

They'd shared a couple of intimate moments. That was all. And none of it meant anything to Zac. Wanting to be the one who was there to comfort him when he needed it wouldn't do her any good.

He had Drew for that. His bandmates. His sister. Not her.

Nerves jangled around inside her for the rest of the performance. Drew either paced agitatedly next to her or stood with his arms crossed, tense and silent, waiting for the concert to finish. The worst part was when the men came offstage before their final encore.

They stood around the side of the stage, taking the opportunity to rehydrate and giving the unusually quiet Drew curious looks. Cassie's stomach churned with worry. When Zac came and stood next to her, it was all she could do not to put her arms around him. The fact that she didn't feel like she could, even after everything they'd done together, spoke volumes.

Fractured returned to the stage to perform their final two songs, and Cassie exchanged a look with Drew. She wondered if she'd made the right choice by suggesting he should wait to tell Zac.

A short while later, with the screams from the fans ringing through the arena, the men gave their final salute and jogged off the stage. Cassie pulled off her headset, and her eyes met Drew's for a second. Apprehension tightened his features.

Fractured Kiss

The band gathered around their manager. They were obviously aware something was wrong.

"I need to talk to Zac for a second." Drew looked at the others. "He'll see you back in the dressing room."

They nodded and walked off, shooting concerned glances over their shoulders. Drew took Zac a little off to the side.

Cassie busied herself with Zac's last bass, wiping it down, checking the strings, trying not to listen in on the conversation happening a few feet away. All she could hear was Drew's low voice. Nothing from Zac.

After a minute, Drew stopped talking and there was silence. Cassie's pulse thrummed erratically, as if she were the one hearing bad news. She wanted to be there, standing next to Zac. She wanted to wrap her arms around him and let him lean on her. Instead, she tried to go quietly about her work and not intrude on their conversation.

When it came, Zac's voice was more audible than Drew's had been. "Is Tori okay?"

In response to Zac's tone, Drew raised his voice enough that Cassie could hear his words. "She was composed on the phone, but..." Cassie imagined him shrugging. "I don't really know her well enough to say."

Cassie stole a glance in their direction. Zac was staring at the floor, his brows drawn. When he finally looked up, it was at her, not Drew. He held her gaze for a long beat and Cassie's breath stalled in her lungs. What was going through his head? Did he need her? She wavered in place.

She wasn't forced to make a decision about going to him. Zac turned his attention back to Drew. "Thanks. I'll give Tori a call and check on her." He strode off.

Drew scrubbed his hand over his mouth. When he

looked back at Cassie, his lips were pressed together. He came over. "I don't know how much you overheard…"

She shook her head quickly. "Just the last bit. But you don't have to tell me."

Drew sighed. "I think you should know."

Cassie clasped her hands together tightly and waited.

"His dad had another massive stroke in hospital. He didn't make it."

Her heart ached for Zac. His relationship with his father was practically non-existent, but she doubted the fact he was suddenly gone would have no impact at all.

Drew studied her. "It might be worth you talking to him. Because I doubt he'll be talking to the others. I'll get Dan to ask one of the other techs to finish up here."

"I'm not sure if he'll want to talk to me either."

"Maybe not. But it won't hurt to try."

Cassie hoped her expression wasn't as skeptical as it felt, but she nodded and turned to go. Drew's hand on her wrist stopped her. Deep lines bracketed his mouth.

"Do what you can, Cassie. I'm worried about him. He needs to get the fuck out of his own head."

"I'll try."

"That's all I'm asking."

She nodded again, then headed for the dressing room.

When she got there, she knocked quietly, reluctant to barge in.

"Come in." It was Connor.

Cassie slipped inside, closing the door behind her. Zac wasn't in the room with everyone else, but the worry in the air was palpable.

"Zac's in the shower," Connor answered her unasked question. "He just got off the phone with his sister."

Fractured Kiss

"Did he..." she trailed off, wondering if he'd told everyone what had happened.

"His dad," Tex stated.

Cassie breathed a sigh of relief. He'd told them.

"He didn't say much else," Lexie said. "Just that he was going to fly out to see Tori and his mom tonight."

Cassie wondered if he'd want her to go with him again. After last time, maybe he'd prefer to do it on his own. She looked at the door to the showers. She wanted to go to him. She wanted to wrap him in her arms. But would her presence make it better or worse?

The weight of everyone's stares pressed on her. They were looking at her as if she should know what to do. But they were the people he was closest to. What could she offer him that they couldn't? Her feet were frozen to the ground.

Lexie came over to her. "Go and talk to him, Cassie. He would never ask, but he needs someone right now. And I think you might be the person he needs the most."

Cassie wasn't sure if that was true or not. But she'd risk rejection if there was a chance she could help him.

She gave Lexie an uncertain smile, then headed for the shower room. Not bothering to knock this time, she stepped inside. Steam filled the air, but she could see Zac at the far end of the room. He was standing under the shower spray, forearms braced against the tiled wall, head hanging between his shoulders.

Her lungs compressed at seeing how alone he looked.

He didn't move as she approached. Had he even heard her come in? She stopped just short of the spray, debating what to do. It was a physical connection he'd sought out after their visit to the hospital. He might not want anything more from her right now, but she could at least give him the benefit of her touch, so he knew he wasn't alone. Acting on instinct, she stripped her clothes off until she was standing there completely naked. With a deep, fortifying breath, still not sure how he'd respond to her presence, she walked into the spray of the water. She stepped up behind him, slid her arms around his waist, and pressed herself to him.

He didn't react, so she rested her cheek against his back and let the warm water run over both of them. A few seconds later, he straightened, gripped her wrist, and pulled her around to his front. He wrapped his arms around her and hugged her tight.

They stood like that for a few minutes before his breathing deepened. He raised a hand to her chin and tipped her head back. His expression was so raw and full of need, it made her heart hurt.

Zac's gaze roamed over her face, dipping from her eyes to her mouth and back up again. He lowered his head slowly, so she had plenty of time to stop him. But Cassie didn't wait for him to close the distance. If it was her touch he needed to soothe his pain, she'd give it to him in whatever form he needed.

She went up on her toes and pressed her lips to his.

Zac immediately deepened the kiss as his arousal pressed into her. She whimpered in response to the slide of his tongue, and he curled his hands around her hips, lifting her and pressing her against the cool tiles. Cassie wrapped her legs around his waist and ran her hands down the warm, wet skin of his back. He rocked his erection against her sensitive core, and her head fell back against the wall. With one arm supporting her weight, Zac dragged the fingers of his other hand across her stomach until he reached her clit. His thumb stroked over it, sending jagged shards of pleasure radiating through her.

His breath shuddered hot against the skin of her neck.

She wiggled against him, tilting her hips. He ignored her movements, continuing to slide his thumb over her, to stroke himself against her needy center.

"Please... Please, Zac." She didn't know what she was begging him for. She wanted him inside her, but without a condom, there was no way they could risk it. She had an IUD and had always played it safe, even though she'd been in a long-term relationship, but now was not the time for that discussion.

Instead, she raked her nails down his back and arched toward him, thrusting her breasts into his chest.

Zac's breaths were uneven. He kept up the same pace, working her with his thumb, his thick shaft thrusting between her folds. It was good. So good. But something wasn't right. He was holding both of them on the edge, not speeding up, not giving them what they both needed to push them over. The muscles of his back were coiled tight under her hands.

Cassie blinked drops of water from her eyes and focused on his face. His pupils were blown wide as he watched her writhe against him, but his expression was distant, his jaw at a sharp angle.

Realization stole her breath. God, he must be so tangled up inside right now. His dad might not have been a good man, but that didn't mean his loss wouldn't deeply affect Zac. She doubted he would admit he was hurting, though, even to himself. Instead, he was seeking solace the best way he knew how, through physical connection. But for whatever reason, he was struggling to let go. Maybe his restraint was a way to regain whatever control over his emotions he'd lost at the news of his father's death. Or maybe he was holding back because what he really needed was an emotional connection. He just didn't know how to ask for it.

Cassie framed Zac's face with her hands, arched up, and pressed her lips to his. When his mouth opened, she deepened the kiss. The stubble on his cheeks was rough against her palms and she let herself sigh her pleasure into his mouth. She stroked his tongue with hers and tangled her fingers in his wet hair. When she tugged, she felt an answering rumble in his chest.

She pulled back. He'd lost that distant look. Now his eyes were dark, searching as he looked at her. She brushed another kiss across his beautiful lips, then feathered her way along his jaw before nipping lightly at his ear. His hips jerked against hers, causing her to gasp involuntarily.

She kept going, licking and sucking down the strong column of his neck. He had almost stopped moving, his hips gently rocking against hers, his thumb barely stroking her clit.

When she looked up at him again, his eyes had slipped half-closed. He bent his head, his mouth capturing hers in a long, searing kiss that pulled a whimper out of her. Then he gentled it, barely brushing her mouth with his for long, torturous seconds before taking possession again, his tongue thrusting deep.

Cassie rolled her hips, dragging herself up and down his erection. He groaned against her lips, and she did it again, sending a thrill of pleasure through her. His thumb pressed against her clit, sparking lights behind her eyes. They moved against each other as their kiss grew deeper again.

Cassie's legs were shaking where they wrapped around his waist. She was so close, but she wanted him to come with her. She needed them to be together at the end of this. His thumb slid over and around the delicate bundle of nerves at the apex of her sex, and the pressure in her core built, almost pushing her over the edge.

Fractured Kiss

Her head dropped back, and she let out a ragged breath that ended in a moan.

"That's it, Cassie. Are you going to give me what I need?" It was the first words he'd said to her since she'd entered the room.

His hips jerked harder, his thumb moving more rapidly. Cassie whimpered as her pleasure spiked.

"Make me come, Zac," she said between pants. "Please, make me come."

He bent his head and drew her nipple into his mouth. The suction and scrape of his teeth over her sensitive flesh pushed her higher, higher. Until his name was a wordless prayer spilling soundlessly from her lips as he rocked against her.

Just as the first tremor wracked her body, Zac crushed his lips down on hers again. His tongue thrust deep as she came apart in his arms. The movement of her hips stuttered to a halt as the ecstasy stole her ability to move. But Zac continued thrusting against her, dragging out her pleasure until he came, groaning low and deep into her mouth. Even then he continued to move, spurt after scalding hot spurt coating her stomach, landing on her clit, only to be immediately washed away by the water that still fell on them. Cassie pulled him harder against her. The fingers of her other hand tangled in the hair at the back of his head.

When their mouths finally parted, Cassie sagged into him, her breath coming in shallow gasps. Zac's movements finally slowed, then stopped completely, and she let her legs drop from around his hips. He moved back enough to allow her to slide down.

Loosely circling her neck with his hand, he brushed her jaw gently with the thumb that had just made her orgasm.

His eyelids slid shut, and he rested his forehead against hers.

"Angel." The murmur was so low, she almost didn't hear it.

Cassie's heart swelled and pressed hard against her ribs. She wrapped her arms around him. "What do you need from me, Zac? How can I help you?"

He pressed his lips to hers in one last kiss, then pulled back from her. "I'm going to fly out tonight and check on Tori. And Mom. I'll come back, then fly down again for the funeral."

"Do you want me to go with you?"

He was silent for a few seconds. "No, I think I'll go on my own this time." Her stomach plummeted, but he went on. "Can you come with me to the funeral?" He didn't look directly at her as he asked.

"Zac…" Her throat thickened with emotion. "Of course I'll come."

He nodded, then turned the tap off, leaving them naked as the steamy air swirled around them.

She studied his face. Most of the turmoil seemed to be gone. She was glad she'd been there for him. She'd be there at the funeral as well. And she'd give him whatever comfort he'd accept from her then, too.

Chapter Thirty-Two

Zac stood with Cassie on his right-hand side, looking at the bare earth of the grave. The one they were about to lower his father into.

Tori was on his left, next to their mom. He should probably have been standing between the two of them, but he'd wanted Cassie next to him. He hadn't let her move away when they'd approached the gravesite.

Drew and all of his bandmates were there, looking uncharacteristically somber in their dark suits. Lexie, Eden, and Summer stood next to their men, holding their hands. His friends had barely known his dad, except to know that he and Zac didn't get on. They weren't here today for his father. They were here to support him.

Connor caught his eye and gave him a nod. If anyone understood what Zac was feeling now, it would probably be him. His relationship with his father had arguably been worse than Zac's. He returned the gesture.

His eyes went to Cassie standing at his side. She wore a simple, black dress and looked beautiful as always. Her midnight hair done up in an elegant arrangement at the back of her head, and her smooth skin illuminated by the sunlight.

Movies always made you think it rained during funerals, and it would have matched his mood if it had been. But there was no rain today. The sun shone clear and bright, warm against his skin. Yet inside, he was cold. Shouldn't he feel something? Something more than indifference?

Yes, his father had been an asshole. But he was still his father. And now he was gone. Zac stared at the hole in the ground as the minister's voice droned on, reciting facts about his dad that someone—his mom or his sister—had obviously given him. He felt nothing.

Absolutely nothing.

Slender fingers intertwined with his. Cassie didn't look at him, her attention on the minister. But the pressure of her palm against his sent a pulse of warmth through him.

A hard lump grew in his throat, and he swallowed against it. Was this what a relationship was supposed to be? Giving without expecting anything back? Standing with someone for no other reason than you didn't want them to stand alone?

Zac's chest tightened, and he took a few deep breaths. At least he was feeling something now. Funerals were emotional, even when there was no good reason they should be. It was the finality of them. Knowing that even if you had hoped for things to be different, it was too late now.

Zac reached for the pick around his neck but stopped himself before he touched it. He curled his fingers into a fist and let his hand drop to his side again.

When the minister finally wrapped up, Zac's friends and Drew offered him their condolences. Lexie, Eden, and Summer gave him and Tori a hug and spoke soft words of polite sorrow to his mom. And the whole time, Zac just stood there, holding Cassie's hand and nodding mechanically.

A few minutes later, they made their way to where the cars were parked. When they got there, Zac's mom turned to him. "I don't know why you're not staying the night at the house." Her voice wavered.

"Cassie and I have a hotel room downtown, Mom. But we'll be back tomorrow to see you before we have to fly back to the tour."

His mom's red-rimmed eyes turned glossy again, but before she could say anything else, Tori stepped in. "I'm going to stay the night with you, Mom." His sister had a kinder heart than him.

"Yes, but we should all be together, remembering your father." Her tears welled again.

The thought of having to listen to his mom talk all night in glowing terms about the man who had considered him a waste of space turned Zac's stomach.

"I'm sorry, Mrs. Ford. I think it might have been my fault," Cassie said. Zac shot her a warning look, which she ignored. "I thought you might not be comfortable having a stranger staying in your house tonight."

He appreciated her efforts. His mom didn't. Her face flushed red, and she narrowed her eyes. "I don't know why he brought you, anyway. I know my son. He'll get rid of you soon, just like all the rest of them."

Cassie's flinch was small, but Zac felt it. Anger roared to the surface, but he couldn't let it out. Not here. Not now.

Instead, he tugged Cassie toward him and put his arm around her waist. "Don't start, Mom."

"Come on, Mom." Tori urged her toward the car. But his mom pulled away, fire flashing in her eyes. "You should have stayed. You knew he was sick. You knew he might not make it. You should have been there for him."

"He wasn't there for me. Not once," Zac growled. "Or Tori. Or you. Why the hell should I have cut my tour short to be there for him? He wouldn't have wanted it, anyway."

"Don't talk about him like that!"

"Mom." Tori's voice was firm. "You're upset. Let's get you home. Zac will come and see you tomorrow."

With a last scathing look at him and Cassie, his mom let Tori guide her into the car. Before following her, Tori turned and threw her arms around Zac. "I'm sorry, Z." She squeezed him hard and gave a watery laugh. "I feel like I say it every time I see you lately."

His sister surprised him by throwing her arms around Cassie too. She must have whispered something in her ear because Cassie nodded and gave her a small smile.

Then Tori followed their mom into the back of the black sedan, and they drove off. He watched them as they passed through the gate, where two security guards had been stationed in case any paparazzi or fans tried to get in. Luckily, they'd been able avoid his dad's death being publicised, and it seemed like they'd been successful in making sure no-one found out where they were and why.

The touch of Cassie's hand on his chest made him realise he was just standing there, with his arm around her.

"Let's go." He took her hand in his and led her toward the car that was waiting to take them to the hotel.

The ride was silent. Zac stared pensively out the window at the houses they were passing. Halfway there, Cassie unbuckled her seat belt and slid across to him. She rested her head on his shoulder. He put his arm around her again, her presence soothing him the way nothing else seemed to.

When they got to the hotel, the driver took them down to the underground parking garage to minimize the chance of him being recognized.

They made it up to their suite without encountering anyone. As soon as they got inside, Cassie removed the pins from her hair, letting it fall loose around her shoulders. She sat on the couch and watched him as he took off his black jacket, pulled off his tie, and rolled up his sleeves.

He wandered over to the bar. "Want a drink?"

It was the first words he'd said since the cemetery.

"Yes. Thank you." Her voice was soft.

He mixed their drinks, then walked over and handed hers to her, then sat down in the chair opposite and took a sip. The alcohol might as well have been water. It did nothing to relax him.

Cassie was watching him, her gaze soft and searching. Suddenly, he didn't want any distance between them. He wanted her right next to him, as close as possible.

It must have shown on his face, because she put her drink down, kicked off her heels, and crossed the space between them. She lifted the hem of her dress so she could straddle his lap. He pulled her down onto him and rested his forehead on her chest.

Cassie sifted her fingers through his hair. The warmth of her body and the sweet scent of her skin loosened a screw in his chest he hadn't even known was there.

"When I was fourteen," he said. "I used to sneak in and play my dad's guitar."

Her hands paused, then continued their lulling tug on his hair.

"He loved that thing. Whenever he wasn't around, I'd go in, take it out of its case, and practice. I taught myself to play on it. I think there was a small part of me that thought that one day, I'd show him what I'd learned, and we'd finally have something in common. Something to bond over. I thought maybe he'd finally be proud of me."

Cassie's breaths were shallower now. He lifted his head off her chest but kept his eyes down. He fixed his gaze on her pulse, where it throbbed at the base of her throat. Her heart rate was rising. She already knew the story wouldn't end the way he'd wanted it to. But she let him keep going.

"I must have gotten lost in the music one day, not heard Dad come in, because I was in the middle of playing when he burst into the room. He'd been drinking, and I don't think I've ever seen him so angry. He started screaming at me. How dare I touch his guitar. That if it wasn't for me, he'd still be playing. That I was the reason he could never play professionally again.

"That wasn't the first time he'd hit me, but it was one of the few times he hit me in the face. I wasn't expecting it, and he knocked me down. I dropped the guitar, and he picked it up and started swinging it at the set of drawers. He smashed it to pieces."

Cassie's hands dropped to cup his face. "Oh, Zac." Her voice wavered.

He closed his eyes. It was the only way he could finish the story.

"When he was done, he threw what was left of the neck of the guitar at me and said if he couldn't play it, no one could, especially not me. Then he left. Went straight back out the front door and, I assume, to some bar to keep drinking. After he'd gone, I realized I was still holding his pick. I'd been squeezing it so tightly, the edge had cut into my palm." He choked out a laugh. "I still have the scar to prove it."

Cassie's fingers traced over the pick where it hung from

around his neck. He nodded. Her palm pressed down over it, the warmth from her hand easing some of the chill radiating from his chest. She still didn't say anything, though, letting him continue at his own pace.

"Mom came up then. She'd obviously heard the noise, but she waited for him to go. She told me I should have known better." His laugh was tight. "She helped me clean up the blood, and I had a few days off school. Enough so that it wasn't obvious what had happened. When I got back, I went straight to the music room. I was going to play, whether or not he liked it. But when I got there, there were two other boys already using the guitars. There was only a bass left. I went in, picked it up, and started playing around with it. I liked it. I think I liked that I wasn't trying to follow in Dad's footsteps even more. It's why I kept the pick, to remind me of who I don't want to be."

He looked at her face for the first time since he'd started talking. Her cheeks were wet, her eyes huge pools of warmth and compassion he wanted to drown himself in. He reached up and wiped her tears away with his thumbs.

"Zac..." she started, her bottom lip quivering.

"Shh, it's okay. Don't cry. That was the day I met Tex and Connor. That was the day that changed my life. It might have never happened if things were different. I can hate my dad, but I'll never be sorry for that."

"Was he angry when he found out you were playing the bass?"

"He didn't find out for a long time. I'd stay late and play with the others after school. We didn't talk about it much, but we all needed each other. Connor was angry about being sent from Ireland to live with his aunt. He hated his dad about as much as I hated mine. Maybe more. And Tex had only recently moved to town, and I know it was hard for him without his mom. But it was only when Noah began hanging out with us that we started talking about forming a band. And then it didn't matter how pissed he was. We never looked back."

"I'm so glad you found each other," she said.

I'm glad I found you. It was on the tip of his tongue to say it. But he couldn't. He couldn't. Because that was making a promise he wasn't sure he could keep. Even if a part of him had started wanting to.

"How did he react when you got signed?"

Zac gritted his teeth, resisting the urge to touch the pick where it rested against his chest. "He laughed. Told me I was just the bass player, and us getting signed had nothing to do with my talent. That I just happened to be in the right place at the right time, and that was it. That I was just riding on the coattails of my friends."

She brushed her fingers over his cheeks. "You know that isn't true, don't you, Zac? You're so talented. So good at everything you do." He closed his eyes and let his head fall back against the chair. She followed him, her hands still warming the side of his face, her sweet breath washing over him. "Is that why you work yourself so hard? Is that why you're so determined to make Crossfire as successful as Fractured? You've been burning yourself to the ground because of the opinion of a bitter, jealous, old man."

He opened his eyes and reached for her wrists, tugging them away from his face. Her concern did something to him. It filled a part of him that had been empty for a very long time. He didn't know what the future might hold, but that didn't matter right now. What mattered was her. And he wanted her more than he'd ever wanted anyone. Right then, he wanted her more than he'd ever wanted anything in his life.

He let go of her wrists, slid his fingers through the silky strands of her hair, and tugged her face down to his. She came without a second thought. The salt on her lips made his heart constrict. This woman. She'd already given him her body, her compassion, her tears. She'd give him her heart if he let her. And there was a chance he just might take it.

Her lips parted, and he was lost in the taste of her.

His tongue stroked against hers, and she fisted her hands in his shirt and moaned.

The sound seared through him, warming him, heating all the cold places inside him. He wanted more. More of her moans, more of her taste, more of her touch.

More of *her*.

Zac ran his hands down her back and pulled her against his chest. There were too many layers between them. He had to have her skin against his, right fucking now. He found the zip of her dress and tugged it down, then dragged the top down to expose her. His hands were greedy on her body as he slid them up her rib cage, and he groaned as he cupped her unconfined breasts.

Her pebbled nipples pushed against his palms. "Cassie." It came out like a broken plea, but he didn't care. "I need you," he murmured against her skin. "I need you."

"You have me." Her fingers went to the buttons of his shirt, brushing against his heated skin and driving him a little mad. She pushed the material off his shoulders and let her hands roam over his chest down to his belt buckle, pulling it open and unbuttoning his fly.

Zac hissed through his teeth as her fingers wrapped around his dick. He circled her waist with his hands as she freed him from his pants.

Cassie lifted herself up, and he shoved her dress down

over her hips, followed by the silk slip of her panties. She slid off his lap and let her clothes pool at her feet.

Zac stared up at her as she stood in front of him like a fucking goddess. No, she wasn't a goddess. She was an angel. *His* fallen angel. Tempting him with everything he shouldn't want. Driving him crazy. Making him break his rules again and again. And he couldn't bring himself to care.

She tugged his pants down, and he kicked them off, then reached for her, his fingers pressing into the curve of her ass. He pulled her down until she straddled him again, using his grip on her to rock her against his length.

Her head fell back, and she whimpered, sending more blood to his engorged shaft.

"I want to have you with nothing between us," he said, his voice strained. "I've never gone bare before. Never even considered it." The slide of her hot center along his cock had his mouth struggling to formulate the words. "But we can get a condom if you're not okay with that."

"I want it too, Zac. I want everything you can give me. I've never done it before either."

"Are you sure you're okay with it?"

"Yes. So sure."

"What about—"

"I'm on birth control."

His whole body shuddered in anticipation. "Put me inside you."

She nodded, her eyes wide and glassy with arousal. She raised herself up and wrapped her fingers around his erection, rubbing the head through her wetness. A whimper fell from her lips as she deliberately ran his piercing over her clit.

"Now, Cassie," he demanded. Every one of his nerve endings was lit up and sparking. If he wasn't buried deep in her pussy soon, he couldn't guarantee he wouldn't come all over her instead of inside her where he wanted to be. Where he *needed* to be.

She finally positioned him at her entrance and eased down, taking the first inch of him into her body. He'd never felt anything as incredible as the way Cassie's hot, tight channel closed around the head of his dick. He didn't think he'd ever want to feel anything but that feeling ever again.

Cassie tilted her hips, trying to take more of him. He slid his hands up the outside of her thighs, staring down at where their bodies were joined. His heart hammered against his ribs as he took over, working her down onto him one inch at a time.

Her mouth hung open as he bottomed out. Zac almost came out of his skin at the feel of her wrapped so hot and slick around him.

He held her still, breathing heavily through his nose to control himself. He didn't want to rush this. He wanted to savor her, how he felt when she was in his arms, when he was buried deep inside her. He wanted to make sure she loved every single second of it. Her face was canted toward his, her dark waves like a curtain around them, tendrils fluttering with each of their breaths.

Rather than thrusting up into her the way his body was urging him to do, he glided his knuckles over the swell of her breast, then used his fingertip to circle the hard point of her nipple before giving it a light pinch. She jerked and whimpered as her body clenched around his. Involuntarily, his hips flexed up into her, and she moaned.

But he stilled himself, continuing to roll her nipple between his thumb and finger as his mouth went to the other hard peak. She writhed against him as he drew it between his lips and gave a sharp suck.

"Yes," she said. "Zac, please." Her hands went to his shoulders, as if she was going to use them as leverage to move on him. But he knew once she started, he wouldn't be able to stop himself from taking over. And he needed this to last. He needed to hold onto this moment with her as long as he could.

He took her wrists and pulled her arms behind her, transferring his grip so he clasped both in one hand. He held her still, impaled on his hard length, while he worked her breasts with his mouth and other hand.

He felt the first flutter of her body around him. "Let me touch you," she said.

"Not yet."

She tried to move her hips, but he tugged down on her arms to stop her from sliding up and down. Restricted from riding him, she rocked backward and forward, grinding her clit against his pelvis as much as she could, trapped as she was between his chest and his hold on her wrists.

Sparks of pleasure were shooting through him, pulsing out from where he was buried inside her. He didn't have much time before he lost complete control. He tugged and pinched on one nipple, flicking the other with his tongue before drawing on it hard and rhythmically.

Her body tightened, gripping him firmly. "Zac, I want... I need..." She couldn't finish, only able to roll her head back and thrust her breasts forward to give him better access. It only took a few more strong pulls on her nipple before she broke. A wild cry fell from her lips as her channel squeezed hard around him over and over. Her arms shook against his hold, and he let go so he could grab her hips and pull her farther down onto him. He wanted to be as deep inside her as he could get. Wanted to feel every last clench of her body around his. To experience every second of how she came apart for him.

"Good girl... you feel so fucking good... you don't know what you do to me." The words fell brokenly from his lips as he clenched his eyes shut and held onto the fraying edges of his control.

Finally, the pulsing of her inner walls subsided, and she was left trembling and gasping. He wrapped his arms around her and pulled her against his chest. He wasn't sure if the quaking of his own body was from the restraint he was only just clinging to or from something else—some emotion rolling through him he didn't want to acknowledge yet.

Cassie pushed herself upright, and he swore he'd never seen anything more gorgeous in his entire life. Her sapphire eyes glittered, her cheekbones were stained pink, and dark curls of hair stuck to the dampness at her temples.

"Zac," she begged. "Please. I want to feel you come with nothing between us."

"Take it then. Take what you need from me." His voice sounded feral to his own ears.

Her eyes flared, and she moved her hips against his tentatively. He didn't stop her this time, and freed from his hold, she began an intoxicating rise and fall that had him throwing his head back against the chair. But he soon jerked it forward again so he could keep watching her. The incredible sight dragged a guttural groan from him. "Fuck." He grabbed at her hips again. "Look at you, angel. You're so fucking beautiful."

Their gazes collided, holding as she moved on him. He couldn't stop staring at her. At the way her eyes changed color. The way her lips parted as she gasped. The way her eyelashes fluttered on every deep, driving downstroke. He couldn't get enough of her. Of the slide of her body against his. Of the silk of her skin under his hands. Of the way she made him feel.

She arched her back and rolled her hips and rode him. Pleasure so intense it was almost painful built at the base of his spine. He knew he didn't have long if he wanted to take her with him. He found her swollen clit with his thumb and gave it one rough rub. Then another, and she was coming. She cried out, contracting around him.

The control he was only just holding onto snapped. He banded his arms around her waist and pistoned his hips up into her. Fire raced along his spine, scorching its way up his shaft. He threw his head back and yelled out hoarsely as his orgasm exploded through him in shuddering wave after shuddering wave.

Even as he came, he couldn't seem to stop thrusting into her—addicted to the drag of her body over his cock as it throbbed inside her, filling her.

"God, Zac," she sobbed. "I can feel everything. It's so good. So good." The grip and release of her muscles around him extended his pleasure out almost unbearably.

He gave her everything he had. Poured it all into her. Drained himself dry. And he took everything she gave him in return. Their bodies were slick with sweat. He could feel his pulse pounding through every inch of him.

"Cassie..." His voice broke on her name.

He didn't even know what he wanted to say. He'd never experienced anything like this before. He didn't want it to end. And maybe it didn't have to. At least, not yet. Would it hurt for him to be selfish? To take what she was offering and enjoy it while he could? Would it really be so bad? Cassie knew what this was and that there was an expiration date. She knew, but she gave herself anyway. Because that's who she was. Would it be so bad for him to give in to it?

His hips jerked one final time, and then he forced them both to be still, though residual tremors still whispered through her as she clung to him. He kissed her, the slide of her tongue soothing the frantic pounding of his heart. The press of her body against him softened the jagged edges in his chest he hadn't even known were there.

Once you've had this, will you be able to let it go?

He shoved the thought back down. Let the feel of her in his arms, the sinfully, sweet taste of her mouth, the renewed swell of his body inside her, drown it out.

He wrapped his arms around her and stood.

Cassie pressed her lips to his neck as he carried her to the bed and laid her down.

He made love to her over and over, only letting her drift off to sleep hours later. That's when he allowed himself to test out the shape of the words that had been running through his head all night. The ones that had been there ever since she'd slipped her hand into his at the funeral.

He pressed his lips against her temple and let them out on a whisper.

"*Stay with me.*"

Chapter Thirty-Three

They flew back to meet the tour in Tampa, Florida, the next morning after a tense breakfast with Zac's mom and sister. Cassie had sat there in uncomfortable silence while Zac's mom had basically ignored her. Tori had tried her best to fill the gap, but it was a relief when Zac announced they were leaving.

At the last minute, Zac's mom threw her arms around him and sobbed into his chest. His shoulders had stiffened, but he'd held her, rubbed her back, murmured a few soothing words, then stepped away. After hearing how she hadn't defended him when he was a child, Cassie was inclined to think that was far more than she deserved.

Things had changed between her and Zac since the night before—since he'd shared a part of himself with her. She'd never experienced such an earth-shattering physical and emotional connection with anyone. His story had broken her heart, but he'd pieced it back together with every slide of his hands over her skin and stroke of his body inside hers.

It seemed to have affected him too, because in the morning, he'd roused and immediately reached for her, held her against him, then made love to her again. There had been an openness and vulnerability in his gaze when he'd looked at her, and a new level of intimacy between them. She didn't ask him what it meant, though. If she could ease some of his pain, even for a short time, she wanted to. Pushing him to acknowledge that something had changed might just destroy it.

Or maybe she was just a coward, who didn't want to find out that she was imagining things.

After they'd rejoined the tour, when it was time for Cassie to leave him and begin her pre-show checks, Zac surprised her by kissing her backstage, in front of everyone. He took his time, his lips firm against hers, his tongue claiming her mouth. She was breathless when he finally released her, and her legs shook as she walked away. Now, as she worked, she held the memory of that kiss close, letting it warm her, and fill her with hope.

She was absently setting up Zac's bass effects pedalboard while thinking about the night before and everything that had happened over the last few weeks, when Bryan stepped in front of her.

Cassie blinked up at him, surprised. She hadn't spoken to him in weeks. He'd kept his distance since the day she'd told him they were over, although every now and then she caught his eyes on her. Stella still directed nasty looks at her when they passed each other, which Cassie ignored. Whatever the woman's problem with her was, Cassie didn't want to give her the satisfaction of thinking she was affected. And considering Stella's apparent lack of remorse about what she'd done, Cassie figured she probably had some deep-seated issues of her own she'd eventually have to face up to.

But now, looking up at Bryan, Cassie felt nothing but a

dull pulse of sadness at the sight of him. Sadness that they'd obviously let things go on between them far longer than they should have. It took him hurting her in a big way for her to recognize there was something wrong in their relationship.

Bryan's brows were lowered, his lips pressed together in a thin line. "I heard something."

Cassie straightened, a zing of nerves racing down her spine. "What did you hear?"

"I heard that this thing between you and Zac isn't real."

Cassie's stomach dropped. How could that possibly have gotten out? She couldn't imagine any of Zac's bandmates or the other women talking. Drew? But he seemed trustworthy; she couldn't imagine it was him. Not to mention it had been his idea to start with. It was probably just an idle rumor started by one of the road crew with too much time on their hands. With the amount of gossip that usually went on during a months-long tour, it wasn't impossible to believe someone might have thrown the idea out there. Or who knew, maybe it had even come from Stella. Disparaging someone else's relationship seemed like something she might do.

It didn't matter, anyway. She kept her voice relaxed as she answered. "What Zac and I feel for each other is real." That was nothing but the truth. Whatever emotions Zac had about her were real, even if they weren't the same as she felt for him.

Bryan stared hard at her, as if trying to find the lie in her words. Then his shoulders slumped, and he ran a hand through his curls. His laugh was sad. "I got my hopes up for nothing, then. I got it in my head you were doing it to punish me for Stella."

Proof he didn't know her as well as she'd thought. "I

would never do that, Bryan. What you did hurt me badly, but I would never turn around and do something to you in revenge. Particularly not if it involved someone else."

"It was just so damn quick." There was a bite to his voice she didn't appreciate.

"As quick as you sleeping with Stella while we were still engaged?"

He looked away. "It was a mistake. I'm sorry. I don't know what else to say." His words were almost monotone. As if he was as tired of saying it as she was of hearing it.

"There *is* nothing else you can say. And sometimes sorry doesn't fix things, Bryan. You did something that you knew would devastate me, something that would damage our relationship beyond repair. You did it while I was on tour with you, at a time and place where you could easily be found out. I think you did it because deep down, you must have known we weren't meant to be together. I don't believe you really want me, Bryan. I don't believe you could do that to me if you loved me the way you keep saying."

"I do, Cassie. And if there's a chance—"

"There isn't."

His face flushed, mouth twisting up. She braced herself for him to say something hurtful, but he didn't. His lips softened, and he let out a breath. "The tour's over in a couple of weeks. What are you thinking about doing when we get home?"

She'd been trying not to think about it. But she was running out of time to make plans. She needed to book a plane ticket home, find somewhere to stay temporarily until she could get a rental of her own, and start looking for a job. Maybe she would even begin looking at different options in the music industry. She'd become a guitar tech to be part of

Bryan's world. Now she had the chance to figure out what made *her* heart sing.

A small seed of something like excitement blossomed inside her. For the first time in a long time, her life was her own, to do with what she wanted. If only that didn't mean she would never see Zac again. An ache grew in her chest. She let out a silent sigh. "I'll move my stuff out once I've found a place to live."

His expression was pained. "Cassie, I—"

She cut him off. "Bryan, please let this go. I can't keep talking about this with you. You need to live with the consequences of your decisions." Her heart lurched in her chest as a memory of Zac's body moving over hers flared to life. "And so do I," she said so softly, she doubted he heard her.

Bryan rubbed the back of his neck, studied the resolution in her face, then gave a sharp nod and moved away.

Cassie looked down at the pedalboard in her hands, and she swallowed hard. Then she took a deep breath and got back to work.

* * *

Cassie stood and stretched, arching her back to loosen the tightness from sitting curled up on the couch. With only a week to go on the tour, she was already struggling to imagine not having this time with Zac anymore. Things were still good between them, although there were times when she felt him pull away from her. She'd particularly noticed it the few times she'd tried to talk to him about his father's death. His face would shutter, and he would brush her off, assuring her he was fine, insisting there was no reason to mourn the loss of a man who'd never wanted him in the first place.

Maybe he actually believed that, but she wasn't sure she did. She knew from her own experience that emotions when it came to family were never simple. Even though her relationship with her mother was practically non-existent at this point, Cassie was sure if she found out her mom had died, she'd have some incredibly conflicted feelings about it. And Zac's reaction after he'd first heard the news of his dad's death told her he definitely had some unresolved emotions where his relationship with his father was concerned. And even if he didn't want to grieve the man his dad had been, he could still grieve the loss of the loving father—the loving *family*—he deserved, but other than Tori, had never had.

Her gaze was drawn to him on the other side of the room. He was in the middle of his call, but his eyes were on her, the intensity in them making her shift in her seat. As much as she might like to take advantage of the way he was looking at her, she was exhausted. She didn't think she could stay up much longer, and he'd be working on the album for a while yet.

Cassie picked up her notebook and walked toward him, prepared to let him know she was calling it a night. She consoled herself with the knowledge that at least he'd be joining her in her bunk when he finally finished up.

"Going to bed," she mouthed as she approached him.

"Wait." He reached out and grasped her wrist, then turned back to his phone. "I think I'm going to call it a night, guys."

Cassie blinked. This was the first time he'd ever cut off one of their sessions of his own volition. Apparently, his bandmates were equally surprised.

"Are you kidding me, man? I canceled a date with a Victoria's Secret model for this," said Devon.

Zac's lips quirked. "I'm sure if you call her, she'll be more than happy to fit you in."

"I'm sure she *will* be more than happy to *fit me in*."

The snorts of laughter from the other end of the call had her smiling and rolling her eyes at the same time. *Boys will be boys.*

Zac's thumb stroked over the back of her hand, and he tugged her toward him so she half-fell into his lap.

"Ah, it all becomes clear now," Beau said. "Hey there, Cassie. Looks like we have you to thank for our early night."

Her skin heated. "Hey, guys."

"We're almost out of time to get this finished," Zac told them. "Let's have an early one tonight and keep going tomorrow."

There were a few good-natured grumbles but grins all around when they signed off.

Zac gripped her hips and moved her, so she was straddling him. He fisted a handful of her hair and pulled her head back so he could drag his lips along her throat.

"Zac," she breathed, her exhaustion forgotten as his tongue flicked hotly across her sensitive skin. She rolled her hips, and he groaned, the rumble in his chest vibrating through her.

"Fuck, Cassie. You drive me crazy," he muttered.

"Good," she said, eyes drifting shut. "That way you'll remember me when this is over." She angled her chin to give him better access, but he froze.

Cassie tried to lift her head to see what was wrong, but his hold on her hair wouldn't let her. "Zac?"

"Come back with me." The words were whispered against her skin.

Cassie inhaled shakily. "What?"

"Come back to LA with me. After the tour."

Her heartbeat skipped, hope rising in her chest. She tugged at his hold, and this time, he released her.

They stared at each other. The tension around his eyes made it clear the question wasn't easy for him.

"You want me to go home with you?" She needed to make sure she understood him properly.

His nod was jerky. "I have to fly out to the UK two weeks after we get back from the tour. But you could stay with me until then."

No mention of anything after that, but she wasn't sure she cared right at that moment. He didn't want this to end. That was the important thing.

"What are you thinking?" His tone was casual, but there was a vulnerability in his expression she'd only seen once before, at the hotel after his dad's funeral.

"I'd like that," she said. He didn't smile, but the tension eased around his eyes.

"Good." He pressed a kiss to the corner of her mouth. "Because I'm not quite done with you yet, Cassie Elliot."

She smiled and tried very hard not to think about the moment when he *would* be done with her.

Chapter Thirty-Four

"You asked her to go back with you to LA?" Connor's voice was incredulous. "She's going to be staying with you? At your apartment?"

They were sitting around the card table in their dressing room, relaxing while Blacklite hit the stage to warm up the crowd.

"Just until I go to the UK," Zac replied to Connor's question, his voice gruff. "She doesn't have a place of her own to go back to yet. Or a job. She's free at the moment."

"So, is this a real thing between you two?" Noah asked.

Zac scowled at the excited look on the drummer's face.

"Because I think that's awesome. Cassie's great. She's perfect for you," the drummer continued.

Discomfort made Zac's breath shallow. He should have known his friends would try to make a bigger deal of this than it was. Yes, he liked Cassie. A lot. He knew asking her to come home with him was completely out of character. But he wasn't interested in analyzing or labeling it. Neither he nor Cassie was ready to say goodbye yet, and that was all this was. He was going to the UK two weeks after they got back, and he'd be gone on tour for three months. It made sense to make that the end of this thing between them, whatever the hell it was.

Before this, the thought of touring with Crossfire in the UK and recording at Abbey Road had filled him with excitement, but now there was only a strange sense of disconnect. He was just tired. That was all. It had been an intense tour with everything that had happened. The album, his dad, Cassie... And he only had two weeks of downtime before he had to do it all over again.

"Nothing's changed. This is still temporary. It just makes sense for us to stay together until she has a new job lined up."

He ignored the skeptical expression on his friends' faces. Yeah, he knew it didn't make sense. Coming to LA with him was only going to delay her finding a new job in Las Vegas. But whatever. They were going to think whatever they wanted to, regardless of what he said.

"Whatever you say, man," Tex drawled with a smirk, proving Zac's point for him. But his friend's grin fell away. "Just, for fuck's sake, don't be blind to what's going on between you two. You're very good at reading everyone else. Not so good at yourself. Don't make the same mistakes we did, okay? You didn't have a problem telling us when we were being fucking clueless."

He didn't want to keep talking about this. Yes, he'd had opinions when it had come to his bandmates' relationships. He was regretting sticking his nose in now, since it seemed to mean they thought they could do the same with him.

Wanting to end the conversation, he just nodded and took another sip of his beer. There were only a few performances left on this tour, and then they'd be heading home. No matter what the others thought, he and Cassie had this thing under control. Everything was going to be fine.

* * *

"Thank you, San Diego! You've been amazing. We'll see you again soon!"

All four of them gave their usual salute to the crowd and left the stage to a wave of screams and shouts that made Zac's ears ring. He made a beeline to where Cassie was waiting for him, her gorgeous smile making his heart thump erratically in his chest.

He took his bass off, but when she reached for it, instead of handing it to her, he wrapped his arm around her waist and pulled her toward him, claiming her mouth.

There were scattered cheers from the other crew, already dismantling equipment for the final load-out of the tour. Zac ignored them, focused on her taste. On the feel of her hands sliding up his chest and wrapping around his neck so she could pull herself closer.

This was the last time he'd get to do this. The thought struck him like a blow. She'd never again be waiting for him when he finished a show. He'd never be able to bask in the warmth of her smile or the press of her body against his. It wasn't as if he could keep her on as his guitar tech after everything that had happened. That would just be asking for trouble. Not to mention it wasn't what she wanted to do long term.

He deepened the kiss, trying to drown out the hollow ache in his chest the thought triggered. He still had two more weeks with her in LA. Apart from some sessions with the guys to finalize their album setlist and get some practice in, he'd have plenty of time. They could have their fill of each other before they went their separate ways.

Cassie broke away with a breathless laugh. "I have to finish getting your stuff packed up."

He grumbled but let her go. "See you at the after-party?" That was another thing he was going to miss. Having her there at the after-parties had made them far more enjoyable. Not that he didn't enjoy engaging with his fans. It was the other stuff that had started to get old. The groping, the constant flirtation, and groupies vying for attention. He hadn't realized how frustrating it had gotten over the years, never knowing if someone was going to talk to you about your music or just do whatever wild act they thought would get you to take them somewhere and fuck them.

She smiled. "I'll be there as soon as I can."

He dropped another quick kiss on her lips, then left, heading for the dressing room to shower and change. He was tired and looking forward to getting home tonight. But more than that, he was filled with a strange sense of adrenaline completely unrelated to what he'd just been doing on stage. Something that might have a lot more to do with the woman he'd just walked away from and the fact that tonight she'd be in his home.

* * *

Zac gripped Cassie's hand as he pressed in the code to unlock his apartment door. He swung it open and led her inside.

"Wow," she breathed, looking around at the huge open living room.

He looked around too, seeing his home with fresh eyes. With its light wooden floors, enormous windows, and modern, understated furniture, it was spacious and beautifully airy. "Hang on, I'll just get our bags, then show you around."

Cassie waited for him in the middle of the room, her hands twisting in the hem of her top. She seemed as unsure about being in his home as he was having her there.

Dumping the bags by the door, he went to her, cupped the back of her head, and kissed her. She relaxed against him, and some of his own uncertainty faded. He pulled back, grabbed her by the hand, and led her farther into the living room. All his Fractured bandmates lived in houses in Malibu, while he lived in an LA apartment. It was a big fucking apartment, though—more than big enough for him. And it had an awesome view over the city.

"Oh my god, Zac," Cassie said as she approached the floor-to-ceiling windows and saw the lights spread out in front of her. She reached out and touched the glass with her fingertips. "It's so beautiful."

"Yes, it is," he said, but he wasn't looking at the view. He took her hand again and pulled her away from the window. "Plenty of time to admire LA later."

He led her past the open concept kitchen that flowed off the living room. "Kitchen," he said, gesturing to it as they walked. When she slowed, as if she wanted to give the space a closer inspection, he tugged her hand and led her on. "Media room." He pointed it out as he kept moving.

"Zac?" she said.

"Music room." That door was closed. He didn't stop to open it for her. "Guest room, guest room." They passed two more doorways.

"Zac!" She laughed. "I don't know if this counts as showing me around."

It didn't. And he had said he'd give her a tour. But it had

been a long fucking day, and he was tired. There was only one room he was interested in showing her right now. The rest could wait until tomorrow.

"My bedroom." He pulled her into the oversized room.

Her breath caught as she saw the same view of LA through the wall of glass that made up one side of the room. "It's amazing," she murmured.

He hadn't turned the lights on, so she was only a slender form silhouetted against the glow of LA at night. His body tightened as he imagined walking up behind her, peeling her out of her clothes, and fucking her up against the window, her breasts pressed against the cool glass.

He pictured taking her on the balcony that ran off the living room, bending her over as she braced her hands on the railing and tried not to scream his name. He saw himself fucking her in every room, on every surface of the apartment, and hoped he'd have time to do it all before he had to leave.

Before *she* had to leave and go start her new life. Whatever that might be.

But tonight, there was only one place he wanted her. He stepped up behind her, brushed her hair away from her neck, and pressed his lips against the velvet of her skin.

Tilting her head to the side, she let out a sigh.

He pulled her away from the window and maneuvered her toward his king-sized bed. When the edge of the mattress pressed against the backs of her legs, she dropped down onto it.

Looking up at him through her dark lashes, her lips curved into a smile that drained all the blood from his body and pooled it in his throbbing dick.

He was going to take his fallen angel right here. He was

going to make her writhe and call out his name where no other woman had ever been.

It was all he could give her—to be the only woman he'd ever fucked in this bed. Even if it didn't seem like enough.

"Lie back," he said, voice hoarse.

She obeyed him, her dark waves fanning out around his head.

She looked so damn perfect lying there, like she—

He cut off the thought before it could fully form, distracting himself by reaching for her jeans.

Because thoughts were dangerous things. And letting that one loose was far too risky.

He'd have these two weeks with her, and then he'd let her go.

He peeled the denim off her legs and closed his eyes against the sight of her. She looked seductive, innocent, sweet enough to eat, dirty enough to spend hours defiling. She looked like… His treacherous mind got away from him. The thought he'd held himself back from thinking before slipped its leash before he could stop it.

She looked like she was exactly where she belonged.

Chapter Thirty-Five

"At last, we finally get to meet Cassie in the flesh!" Cassie blushed as Beau looked her up and down. He broke into a warm smile, and the next thing she knew, she was wrapped in his muscular arms. Taken aback, it took her a second to return his hug.

When he stepped away, another gorgeous dark-haired, blue-eyed man took his place. They looked so similar, they might have been brothers, but Beau and Devon were cousins.

"Nice to meet you, Devon," she said.

"It's *very* nice to meet *you*," he replied with a devilish grin. "So which guitar tech school did you come from, sweetheart? And are there more of you?"

Her eyes darted to Zac, who looked less than pleased with his bandmate's flirtatious tone.

Caleb, Crossfire's blond-haired, green-eyed drummer, was next. "Hi there, gorgeous. I can see why Zac doesn't want to let you out of his sight."

"Uh..."

"That's enough, guys. You can leave Cassie alone. She's just here to watch."

With big grins on their faces and a wink from Caleb, the three other Crossfire band members sauntered over to Zac.

"Okay," he said. "Let's get this run-through started."

The guys collected their instruments and made their way through to the studio's rehearsal room.

Zac came over to her, holding his guitar. "You going to be all right here?"

"Yeah. I'm excited to hear you play."

"Okay. It's set up so you can hear us, but we can't hear you. Just use the intercom if you need anything."

She nodded, and he headed into the room behind the others. It was a strangely distant interaction. This was only her third day in LA, but things had started to change between them almost as soon as they'd gotten back off the tour. He still surprised her with little signs of affection, and he'd been nearly insatiable sexually in the short time she'd been staying with him. But other times, he seemed to revert to keeping her at a distance.

Cassie sat down on the comfortable couch and pulled her legs up underneath her. She was going to try not to worry about it. He was under a time crunch to get this album done, so she couldn't expect him to be all about her. And this would be her first time hearing all four of them playing together in the one spot. She was really looking forward to it.

The guys joked around in the rehearsal room for a bit before Zac pulled them into line. They started the first song, and Cassie leaned back against the couch, a smile on her face as she listened to them practice the songs she'd heard them write.

Her eyes rested on Zac, her body warming. He was so

beautiful. His movements were smooth and efficient. His intensity as he focused on what he was doing such a turn-on.

That was even more true when all that intensity was focused on her.

Cassie gave a little shuddery sigh. She couldn't get used to this. He hadn't talked about what would happen after he left for the UK, and so far, she'd been too nervous to bring it up. She couldn't get her hopes up that there would be anything more for them. As much as she might wish there could be.

She forced her muscles to relax. She wanted to listen to him play and sing and not worry about what the future might hold.

But they weren't playing or singing at the moment. They'd paused mid-song and were discussing modifying the transition between the second verse and the chorus. Caleb said something that made Zac smile, and a tingle rushed through her. His smiles did something to her. Maybe because they so often seemed hard-won. He was always pushing himself. He really needed to relax more—to enjoy the incredible success he already had. She'd thought that without his father around to try to prove himself to, he might ease up a little. But that was apparently wishful thinking.

She wanted to be the one to ease his heart. She wanted to be the one to support him and show him he was enough. To show him how amazing and talented and beautiful he was. To let him know every day that he was loved—

Her breath stalled in her throat.

Loved.

She loved him. Of course she did. Deep down, she must

have known for a while. At least since the hotel room after the funeral. Maybe before.

Tears stung the backs of her eyes, and she swallowed past the hard lump in her throat. She was so screwed. In less than two weeks, he was going to head to the UK and forget about her. He didn't do relationships. He didn't do long-term. And if his father's death hadn't changed how hard he pushed himself, it wouldn't change how he felt about committing to someone.

What was between them wasn't real. Maybe it felt real. Maybe she'd convinced herself it was real. But reality was going to bite her in the ass when he said goodbye and walked away.

The rapid thumping of her heart had temporarily drowned out the sound of their playing. It was only when she closed her eyes and took a deep breath to calm herself that she noticed what song they were practicing. It was the one she'd helped Zac with during their first night staying in a hotel together.

Her eyes flew open and locked onto his. He must have been able to see something was bothering her, because he was watching her through the glass with a crease between his brows. He was focusing on her, not what he should focus on. His music. The thing that was most important to him.

She forced a smile to her face. She didn't want to be a distraction. Not when what he was doing meant so much to him.

For a second, his brows stayed drawn together, and she worried her smile hadn't been convincing enough. But then his expression cleared. He flicked a sexy little half-smirk in her direction, then turned back to his bandmates.

Cassie's pulse had kicked into high gear. The walls

suddenly felt like they were closing in on her. Her heart was going to end up broken again, and there was nothing she could do about it.

This time, she'd walked into the flames with her eyes open.

The ringing of her phone in her purse startled her. Grateful for the distraction, she fished it out. Lexie's name flashed on the screen.

"Hi, Lexie," she answered.

"Hey, Cassie. How are you?"

Cassie's gaze went to Zac, but he had his head together with Beau, discussing something to do with the next song.

"I'm okay, thanks. What's up?"

"Connor mentioned Zac was taking you to the studio today. And I know he'll probably be there all day, so I thought I'd check in with you and see if you wanted to come and hang with me, Eden, and Summer for a couple of hours. I thought you might enjoy a bit of girl time."

A tentative smile crossed Cassie's lips. Some time away from Zac might be exactly what she needed to sort her feelings out. And for someone who hadn't had a lot of girl time in her life, it sounded perfect.

"Let me just ask Zac if he minds if I don't stay. Can I call you back?"

"I'm going to jump in the car now. Just message me if you're in, and I'll swing by and pick you up."

"Okay. Thanks, Lexie."

They hung up, and Cassie waited for the guys to finish the run-through of the song they were working on. Then she hit the intercom button.

Zac looked up. "Everything okay?"

Cassie hoped he wouldn't be offended if she asked to leave. Hopefully, he'd understand. "Lexie just called and invited me to hang out with her, Eden, and Summer. I told her I wanted to check with you."

"Hold on," he told her.

He murmured something to the guys, then put his guitar down and came out. "Is anything wrong? You looked upset before."

"Everything's fine," she lied. "It's just, it was nice of Lexie to invite me, and while I love listening to you play, I thought maybe it would be good to..." Her voice trailed off. She hesitated to say it would be good to get to know the women better, because the truth was, she probably wouldn't see any of them again after she went back to Las Vegas. "Let you concentrate on what you're doing while I have some girl time." The words felt strange coming out of her mouth. When was the last time she'd had girl time outside the tour they'd just returned from? Had she ever, or had she spent all these years letting her whole life revolve around Bryan?

She held her breath, not sure how Zac would react. But he just searched her eyes, then nodded. "Yeah, I guess there's no point in you hanging around here. We're going to be a few hours. Is Lexie going to pick you up?"

"That's what she said."

"Okay, that's good. I assume she'll just drop you at the apartment afterward. You remember the code, don't you?"

She nodded.

"I'll see you back there later today, then."

He dropped a kiss on her head, then headed back into the rehearsal room. She felt the distance open up between them again and hated it.

Cassie let out a sigh, then messaged Lexie. A dull pain throbbed behind her ribs. A pain she had no one to blame for but herself.

Chapter Thirty-Six

Zac took a long pull of his beer, then leaned back in his chair, enjoying the warm evening sun on his face. A burst of laughter from across the table had a smile tugging at the corners of his mouth.

He was sitting with his Fractured bandmates and their women at an outdoor table in Connor and Lexie's cliff-top garden. Drew was down at the other end of the table, on the phone as always. Their manager was more work-focused than he was. Cassie was sitting to Zac's left, her forearm brushing his as she put her drink back on the table. They'd been home for almost a week now. And he'd adjusted more rapidly than usual to being off tour. Normally, it would take a few weeks to get used to not performing constantly. But maybe that was because this time, he had something to distract him.

Or someone.

Cassie was wearing a pretty yellow sundress, her hair pulled back off her beautiful face in a ponytail. The tip brushed the smooth skin of her back every time her head moved as she talked animatedly to Summer.

Lexie and Connor had invited them and the others over for dinner, and now they were all sitting outside, watching the sun set over the ocean. The view was beautiful. The darkening blue of the sky reminded him of Cassie's eyes. The sound of the waves crashing against the cliffs was soothing after another long day of rehearsals.

Cassie laughed, and something warm came to life in his chest. He wasn't used to having a woman by his side at one of these get-togethers. But sitting there with Cassie next to him felt good.

It felt right.

He extended his arm along the back of Cassie's chair, his wrist loosely draping over her shoulder. Distracted from her conversation, she turned to look at him, giving him a soft little smile that hit him dead center in the chest. He almost pulled away but forced himself not to. Because as unfamiliar as the emotions she evoked in him were, as much as he kept questioning what he was doing, he enjoyed touching her. He liked the way she made him feel. He liked being near her, hearing her voice and her laugh. He liked seeing how well she fit in with his friends. So instead of pulling away, he stroked little circles over the warm, bare skin of her shoulder with his thumb.

Her ponytail brushed across his forearm, and he let himself indulge in a fantasy of wrapping it around his fist and tugging her head back. He'd lean over, press his lips to her throat, and—

"Can I get everyone's attention, please," Connor interrupted Zac's daydream. He subtly adjusted himself in his jeans as he looked toward where their lead singer and Lexie were sitting. "So, we actually asked you all here today because Lexie and I have some news we wanted to tell you all in person."

Lexie's face looked a little flushed, but her gray eyes sparkled prettily.

"Do you want to tell them, baby?" Connor asked his wife.

"Uh, sure. Um..." She was a little lost for words, and a seed of ice grew in Zac's chest. "So, uh, Connor and I, that is..." She let out a breath. "Turns out I'm pregnant."

Everyone started talking at once, high-pitched squeals from Summer and Eden, congratulations all around from the men. He needed to congratulate them too, but the words stuck in his throat, the ice spreading through his chest.

His hand dropped away from Cassie's shoulder, and for one long beat, his mind stayed frozen on the word.

Pregnant.

The paralysis passed. "Congratulations," he managed to get out through a dry throat.

He didn't know why he was so shocked. He knew this was going to happen at some stage. Connor and Lexie had been married for two years. And although at one time he would've never believed Connor would get hitched, once he had, it seemed inevitable that he'd want it all.

And after Connor, who would be next? Noah and Summer were engaged. It didn't look like Tex and Eden would be too far behind. Soon he'd be the only man left standing. Wives *and* kids thrown into the mix changed everything for Fractured. It had to. His bandmates would be tied here, to their families. What would happen to their tours? To long days in the studio followed by PR events that lasted into the early hours of the morning? What would happen to the life he'd built around this band?

Over the too-loud thump of his heart, he stared at the grin creasing Connor's face. Everything he knew was changing. His father was dead—the driving force behind everything he'd ever fucking done suddenly gone. Now, who knew what would happen with Fractured—would it even survive? Or would it crumble around him as his bandmates got pulled in different directions?

He suddenly wondered if this was why he'd been so driven to set up Crossfire when Fractured went on hiatus. Maybe he'd seen the writing on the wall even then, after Connor had fallen head over heels for Lexie. Had he been preparing himself to let go of the one thing he'd always had to hold on to?

Fuck. He was dizzy, his lungs laboring as if he couldn't quite get enough air. He was an expert at putting on a good face, though. No one would know the panic scraping at his insides.

The rest of the celebration passed in a blur. He said all the right things, smiled, and laughed when expected. Shook Connor's hand and kissed Lexie on the cheek. But all he could think about was how quickly he could get away.

Finally, it was over. On the drive back to LA, he tried to talk to Cassie as if nothing was wrong. Apparently, he wasn't as successful as he normally was at pretending. Cassie leaned toward him and placed her hand on his thigh. "What's wrong, Zac?"

A confusing vortex of feelings left him reeling. The bolt of lust he always felt when she touched him. A warmth that filled the space behind his rib cage at having her near. And sheer fucking terror at the fact she was there at all. That he'd let himself stumble into the one situation he'd spent his adult life avoiding.

Lexie and Connor's announcement reverberated in his mind. Love, families, white picket fences. Those things went hand in hand, and they all pointed to the same thing.

He was going to lose Fractured. Maybe not this year. Maybe not next year. But it was coming. He could sense it.

His heart tripped and stumbled at the concern in Cassie's beautiful eyes. Eyes that were still filled with the same dreams he'd told himself right at the very fucking start meant he would never touch her.

But he had. He fucking had. He'd touched her and tasted her and hadn't been able to let her go. And now, all he could see were those fucking white picket fences. Love and marriage and kids—her open gaze promised all those things. This was why it was so much easier just to be with women who wanted the same thing he did. A fuck or two, bragging rights if that's what they were after, or just a no-strings-attached good time for a few weeks. He'd known from the very first moment he'd met Cassie that she wasn't one of those women. And he'd taken her, anyway.

Zac looked back at the road. "I'm fine. Just thinking about the UK tour." He stole another glance at her. Her lower lip was caught between her teeth, and her brow was furrowed.

She gave a slow nod. "Okay."

Her hand withdrew, and he wanted it back again. He wanted it too fucking much. He drew in a breath. There was only a week left, and then this would be over. He would have done what he promised her—fixed his mistake. She would go back to her life, find another job in the industry while he was away, and that would be that. They'd probably never see each other again.

Zac viciously suppressed the pain that sawed through his chest. His music, Crossfire, and Fractured—whatever might be left of it—those were the only things that mattered.

He just had to make sure he remembered that.

Chapter Thirty-Seven

Cassie stared out at the bright lights of LA. She sighed and slumped down on Zac's couch. Things were going wrong, and she didn't know how to fix them. Or if they even could be fixed. The distance between her and Zac that she'd noticed on and off since they'd gotten to LA seemed to be permanently in place now.

She'd tentatively tried to raise the issue with Zac that afternoon. She'd asked him if they could talk about what was going to happen with them when he left for the UK in just under a week's time. He'd basically shut the conversation down, claiming he had to head out for another rehearsal. She wasn't naïve. She knew what that meant. It wasn't like she hadn't been expecting it. Still, she'd let hope build. She let his invitation to LA mean more than it should have.

Zac had been gone for almost seven hours now. He hadn't called or messaged her. She'd composed half a dozen texts to him, then deleted them. She had no idea what to say. Or whether she should say anything at all.

Maybe she just needed to accept the inevitable.

The thought sent a lance of pain into her chest, and a breath shuddered out of her. Reluctantly, she pulled up some rental listings for Las Vegas and scrolled through them half-heartedly. It was hard to get excited by any of them because none of them were near Zac.

A tear slipped slowly down her cheek, and she absently brushed it away.

The beeping of the keypad startled her. She put her phone down on the coffee table and stood, smoothing her suddenly damp hands against her thighs.

Zac walked in, and her pulse sped up the way it always did when she saw him. She took a step forward before stopping as Beau, Devon, and Caleb strolled in behind him.

"Hey, Cassie. How's it going, beautiful?" Beau swooped down on her and gave her a hug. She smiled, but her heart had fallen. Her eyes met Zac's over his bandmate's shoulder, questioning. He looked away from her, his gaze dropping to the coffee table. His brows lowered, and his lips thinned. As soon as Beau let her go, Cassie followed his gaze.

Her phone screen was still on, Las Vegas rental listings showing on the screen.

When she looked back up, Zac's expression had smoothed away, and he was saying something to Caleb.

Cassie took a breath and tried to smile. "Can I get you guys a drink?"

"I've got this, Cassie," Zac said, looking in her direction, but not really looking at her. "You can go back to what you were doing." His eyes dropped to her phone for a second.

Well, she guessed she was dismissed then.

Beau's gaze darted between the two of them, and he frowned. "You're going to join us, aren't you, Cassie?" His tone told her he was less than impressed with Zac's comment.

That made two of them.

She gave Beau a grateful smile. "Thanks, but I've got some stuff I need to do. And I..." Her breath hitched, the reality of what was happening making the backs of her eyes sting. "I think I have less time to get it sorted than I expected."

She picked up her phone, avoiding everyone's gaze. "I'll leave you all to it." Throwing a smile around the room, she headed for Zac's bedroom.

She was still awake when the guys left a couple of hours later and Zac finally came to bed. She watched him as he undressed, and when he climbed in next to her, she rolled toward him, wanting to address the situation. But he surprised her by immediately wrapping his arms around her and pulling her tight against his chest.

"Zac, I—" she started.

He buried his face in her neck and released a ragged breath. Cassie froze in surprise, then slid her hands up his back. He was hurting. Whatever it was that was making him act this way, it was causing him pain.

Zac's lips found hers, and he kissed her, softly and tenderly. It was so at odds with how he'd acted toward her that she let herself luxuriate in the feel of him against her. His taste, his scent, he filled her senses completely.

He pulled back, but before she could say more, he slid the strap of her cami top off her shoulder, tugging it down, then skimming his knuckles along the sensitive skin on the side of her breast. She shivered.

The low light glimmered in his eyes as he looked at her. "I don't want to talk right now, Cassie. We can talk later, but right now, I just need your body against mine."

Her heart stalled, fell, then managed to pick itself up again. But its beat was uneven. She recognized the words, even if he didn't. It was almost the same thing he'd said to her on the plane, the first time they'd slept together.

He was deflecting. Exactly the way he had back then.

Zac brushed his lips over her neck, and she let her eyes slide shut. She tipped her head back and breathed out a sigh of pleasure. They had to talk. She knew that. But the uncertainty of how that conversation would end clawed at her. She had a good idea it wouldn't end the way she wanted.

He was right. Later was better.

She sat up and drew her top over her head.

* * *

Zac was gone when she woke the next morning. He'd left her a note on his pillow letting her know they were getting in an early practice session at the studio, and he didn't know how long he'd be.

Cassie flopped back down on the bed and stared sightlessly at the ceiling. Was this how it was going to be? Him avoiding the situation until he could escape overseas and be done with the inconvenience of her?

She had a long, hot shower, then looked at a few more rentals online. She made some inquiries and set up a couple of viewings for the next week.

After that, she sat down with her notebook and did some writing. But the flow of words quickly dried up. She sighed, then flicked back through the pages, looking at some of what she'd written during her time with Zac. She stopped at a poem she'd written a week before the tour had ended, after Zac had asked her to come to LA with him. A sad smile curved her lips at the hopefulness of the words.

The smile wobbled and fell. Zac had been gone for hours again. She debated calling Lexie, Summer, or Eden, but decided she was better off not letting herself get any closer to them. Leaving was going to be hard enough as it was.

She looked back at her notebook, then over at Zac's spare guitar case. She brought it over to where she'd been sitting. Carefully unlatching it, she pulled the instrument out and held it in her lap.

After glancing at the words in her notebook, she let her fingers skim over the strings. A tune emerged as she softly sang what she'd written. She grimaced. It wasn't great, but she kept going. Her eyelids drifted shut as the notes flowed from under her hands. Suddenly, her eyes popped open, and she repeated the chords she'd just played. She modified the arrangement slightly and played it again.

She smiled. It wasn't bad. The tune suited the hopeful tone of what she'd written. It wasn't perfect by any means, and she didn't know how the other instruments might fit in with it just yet. But it felt... right.

She frowned down at her notebook. Why had Bryan always dismissed her poetry? She imagined how it could have been, her sitting with him, both of them with guitars in hand, making music together. She should have figured it out earlier that things weren't right between them. There was too much imbalance. She'd loved him so much—or at least needed him so much—that she'd let her own hopes and dreams wither and die while she followed him on the path to fulfilling his.

But after watching Zac write his album over the last few months, seeing her own words come to life with his help, what she'd done on her own today—it felt like something she might like to do. Something she might just end up being good at.

The keypad beeped, the door opened, and Zac walked in. She half expected him to have invited the others back again to avoid being alone with her. But he hadn't.

Cassie's heart raced as he walked toward her. His gaze took in his guitar in her hands, and she suddenly wondered if she should have asked him if she could use it.

"I hope you don't mind," she said.

His brows pulled together. "Of course I don't mind. You can use anything of mine." He glanced at her notebook. "What have you been up to?"

"I tried putting one of my poems to music."

His eyes lit up with interest. "How'd it go?"

She gave a little laugh. "It could use some work. But I don't know. I guess I quite like it."

"Can you play it for me?"

"I'm not sure I'm ready for anyone else to hear it."

"Please, Cassie." His voice was low.

He always seemed to push her outside her comfort zone so easily. And for the first time in days, tension didn't tighten the air between them. She took a deep breath and picked up his guitar. She ran through the chords to refresh her memory, then sang.

When she finished, Zac's gaze was unfocused. She waited breathlessly until he nodded. "It's good."

She couldn't help but smile. Her man of few words.

"Can I have the guitar?" he said.

She handed it to him, and he sat on the couch, angling himself toward her, his knee touching hers.

He started with the same basic chord progression she had, then made some minor modifications. "Sing it for me," he said, and she did.

Her voice wove through the music he played as if those two things had always belonged together. They made changes, tweaked some words, some of the notes. When they finished, Cassie couldn't contain her smile.

His eyes held hers, an emotion she couldn't name glittering in them. "This is good, Cassie. Really good."

She smiled wide, feeling buoyant. Songwriting seemed like such a natural progression from her poetry. Why hadn't she done anything with it before? Because she'd been too nervous to share her words with anyone? Or because she'd been too busy trailing after Bryan to spend any time thinking about what *she* might actually want to do?

Zac leaned back on the couch, watching her with so much warmth in his beautiful hazel eyes it made her breath catch in her chest.

Her smile wavered, and she swallowed. She needed to get this out. No matter how painful it might be. She needed some clarity. "Zac, I really need to know where we stand," she said. "Things are so up in the air at the moment. I guess I'm nervous we're not on the same page."

He tensed at her words, his visage darkening. He stood and paced to the window. Then he twisted back toward her, shoving his hands in the pockets of his jeans. "What is it you want, Cassie?"

She blinked. "I want..." She took a deep breath. Now or never. "I want to be with you."

He looked away, his jaw working. The silence stretched on, and she felt compelled to fill it. "You haven't told me what you want from me. I thought..." She swallowed through a too-dry throat. "I thought maybe you felt the same."

"What specifically are you asking me?"

Frustration rushed through her in a wave. "I'm asking if

you're willing to commit. To see if this could be a real relationship."

He raked both of his hands through his hair, then laced them behind his neck, rocking on his heels. "I'm going to the UK for three months."

"I know that."

"You're going to wait for me here while I'm over there for months?"

"I'm not saying it will be easy. I know it won't. But I'd like to try. I think this is worth it. I think *we're* worth it."

"Cassie, I told you from the start I don't do relationships. We don't want the same things. I can't give you what you want." Some unknown emotion threaded his words.

Cassie's heartbeat thudded loudly in her ears. "Do you think I'm asking for a ring on my finger?"

Zac's jaw tightened. "You've already had a ring on your finger. So, you tell me."

Her fingernails dug into her palms. "So that's it? Because I might want to get married one day? Because I might want to have a family? That rules me out?"

"You know I don't want that."

As hard as she tried not to let it, her voice wobbled as she said, "So this is it? You go to the UK and we just... cease to exist."

"It was always the plan, wasn't it? You go back to Las Vegas and get a job, and then this is done."

Dread weighed her down. This wasn't going to go the way she wanted it to. She couldn't stop the words from tumbling out though. "That was the plan, but things change. *We* changed. And there's nothing fake about what I feel for you, Zac. Nothing. I love you. I've fallen in love with you."

His whole body was coiled tightly, eyes a blaze of green

and gold as he stared at her. "Cassie..." He took a step forward. Her breath stalled, heart leaping in her chest only for it to plummet when he stopped short. His hands went to the back of his neck again, gripping hard as he looked up at the ceiling. As if the answer to what he should do about her, about her inconvenient feelings for him, was written there.

When he dropped his gaze again, whatever he'd been feeling, whatever he might have been going to say, was locked up tight.

"You deserve better." He might as well have been talking to a casual acquaintance, there was so little inflection in his voice. "I should have never kissed you."

The familiar yawning chasm in her chest, the one she'd lived with every day before she'd met Bryan, cracked open. Zac was doing what he did so well—distancing himself.

Exhaustion dragged her shoulders down. The hole gaped wider. She could beg. She could plead. She could try to reach for him, to hold him tight and never let go. Her hands craved the touch of his skin. She wanted to bury her face in his chest and breathe him in.

But she didn't do any of that.

A single tear escaped and trickled down her cheek as he stared at her with those cool, unreadable eyes. The trail it left behind seemed almost to scald her skin.

Her voice was quiet when she spoke again. "Someone once told me that being alone is better than being with someone who doesn't value my true worth. And she was right. If all you see when you look at me is a burden—an obligation you don't want—then I'd rather be on my own, anyway." Her gaze caught on her notebook lying on the table. It was open at the song they'd been working on. She nodded over at it. "You can keep it or throw it out. I don't care. I don't want it anymore."

Fractured Kiss

"Cassie," he said, his voice tight. But she was done. She had nothing left to give him. Loving Zac wasn't good for her. For once, she needed to put herself first. She turned and walked out of the room, and he didn't follow her.

She called a ride-share service as soon as she got to the bedroom. Twenty minutes later, she was packed and out the door. And that was all the time it took to strip herself out of Zac's life.

Chapter Thirty-Eight

Cassie stepped out of the arrivals gate, the familiar sound of the slot machines scattered throughout the terminal welcoming her home to Las Vegas. Except, home wasn't really how it felt anymore. She was adrift—homeless, loveless, and currently jobless. She did have something she didn't have before, though. The small kernel of what might turn out to be a dream of her own.

She made her way through the crowded terminal to pick up her luggage. After grabbing her bags, she turned to head to the exit, but a sign with her name on it caught her eye. A man in a dark suit was holding it up. Cassie looked around, wondering if it could be a coincidence. She didn't see anyone else walking up to him, so she approached him tentatively.

"Hi. Um, I'm Cassie Elliot, but I'm not sure if—"

"Courtesy of Mr. Ford," he said with a smile.

She blinked. "Oh. Okay." He held out his hand, and she hesitated, then gave him her bags.

"Mr. Ford has asked me to drive you to your hotel. He's booked you a suite."

"Which hotel is that?"

He named one she could never afford on her own and a sob almost burst from her. Why was Zac doing this? Because he cared, or just because he felt guilty? She managed to hold back her tears and shook her head. "I can't stay there. Would you be able to take me somewhere else? If not, I can get a taxi."

His brows drew together. "I can take you wherever you need to go, Ms. Elliott. Just tell me where that is."

She named a budget hotel in Spring Valley, ignoring how his brows met his hairline. It was a significantly different destination. But it was closer to where she'd be searching for an apartment.

He nodded and reached for her bags. "I'll be happy to call and cancel Mr. Ford's booking on your behalf if you'd like."

Cassie thanked him and followed him to his sleek black car.

As they drove, she stared down at her phone.

She bit her lip, then typed out a quick message to Zac.

Cassie: *I appreciate you sending the car and booking me a hotel room, but I've decided to stay nearer where I'll be looking for an apartment. Thank you, though. And good luck with recording your album.*

She grimaced. It was awkward and stilted, but she wasn't sure how she was supposed to talk to the man she was in love with. The man who'd made it clear he couldn't love her back.

With a deep sigh, she gazed out the window, not seeing the passing cars and buildings as her mind drifted back through all that had happened in the last few months.

Zac hadn't replied by the time she pulled up at the hotel. The driver helped her out of the car, collected her bags, and walked her inside. She thanked him when he left her at the front desk, but he refused a tip, telling her that Zac had handled everything.

After checking in, she carried her bags into the elevator and ascended to the third floor. The room was basic, but clean and comfortable—better than many of the places she and Bryan had stayed in during the early years.

She sat down on the bed, her shoulders slumping as she thought about what her next step was going to be. Find an apartment, get her stuff from her old one, get a job. Maybe one where she didn't have to travel. The thought of going on tour again seemed to have lost its appeal.

Her phone beeped, and her heart surged into her throat at the sight of Zac's name on the screen.

Zac: *I just wanted to make sure you were comfortable and safe.*

Cassie: *I am. You don't have to worry about me anymore.*

She threw her phone down on the bedspread and fell back onto the mattress. She lay there, listening for another message notification until sleep tugged at her.

None ever came.

***

A few days later, Cassie had managed to lease a small apartment. Only then did she venture back to the one she had shared with Bryan for the last two years.

She asked the cab driver who dropped her off to come

back for her in an hour, then headed up in the elevator to the top floor, hoping that she'd get lucky, and Bryan wouldn't be home.

After letting herself in, she came to a sudden halt in the entryway. Her breath caught in her lungs as she was overtaken by a wave of memories: how excited they'd been when they'd first moved in, the furniture they'd bought together, the many nights of planning and dreaming over the dinner table.

But even with the onslaught of what had been happy memories, there was a different feel to the apartment now. Walking in here didn't fill her with warmth. It no longer felt like her safe little refuge from the world, with Bryan by her side. Even as regret over the way things had ended pierced through her, she felt a whole new world of opportunities opening in front of her. A world that no longer relied on having Bryan with her.

Cassie dropped her purse on the kitchen table. The apartment wasn't that big, and the silence told her that Bryan wasn't at home. She breathed out a sigh of relief and made her way to the bedroom.

Unfortunately, her relief didn't last. She was in the middle of packing a suitcase when she heard the front door slam. She looked through the open doorway to see Bryan staring at her. His lips were thin, his jaw as hard as granite. He didn't speak to her. He just walked into the kitchen, grabbed a bottle of beer from the fridge, and went out the sliding door to the balcony. It shut behind him with an extra hard thump.

Cassie looked down at the blouse she was holding, then let out a sigh and kept packing.

When she finished, she left her cases by the front door. Then she followed Bryan out to the balcony.

He was leaning back in a chair, his eyes half-closed against the brightness of the sun. The beer bottle dangled from his fingertips. He flicked a look in her direction before going back to staring out at the view.

Cassie sat on the chair next to him.

"Do you love him?" he asked before she could say anything.

Her hesitation must have answered for her.

"Does he love you back?"

"Not enough," she whispered.

He gave a raspy laugh. "I should be happy about that."

"Why?"

"Because that's the story of my life."

She blinked. "I loved you."

He slid his gaze her way again. "Not enough."

"What?"

"Cassie, you needed me far more than you loved me. You didn't love me the way I loved you. Not the way you love *him*."

Anger punched her in the gut. "You're saying you slept with Stella because you didn't feel *loved* enough?"

He tipped his head back, closing his eyes. "I slept with Stella because even though I knew you didn't love me the way I loved you, I still wanted to spend the rest of my life with you."

It took her a few seconds to get the words out through the tightness in her jaw. "So, you were punishing me for not loving you the way you thought I should?"

He shook his head. "It had nothing to do with punishing you. I never wanted to hurt you, Cassie. But just for once, I wanted to feel like I was enough. And that was easy with Stella because she didn't want anything more than a good fuck. And I was good enough for that."

The air left Cassie's chest in a rush. She leaned back in her chair and stared out at the view too, matching his pose. She didn't understand him. This person who had once been her closest friend. Now he was a stranger. Why hadn't he ever said anything to her about how he felt? Because he hadn't wanted to face what was wrong in their relationship?

"Do you love Stella?" she asked eventually.

His laugh was harsh. "No. But at least with Stella, I know we both feel the same way about each other."

The anger boiling inside her faded. What was the point? They were over. This whole part of her life was over. While it made her sad that she was losing the person who had been an essential part of her life for so long, she didn't wish it were different. She couldn't anymore. "I'm sorry if I made you feel you weren't enough."

"I know you didn't mean to. I used to think it was just the way you were. Because of your mom. That maybe you could never love someone with your whole heart. But when I saw you with him, I knew the truth. It wasn't you. It was us. It was that you didn't belong with me."

She nodded, and the silence stretched out between them as they both looked out at the view.

"I should go," Cassie stood.

Their eyes met, and in his churned a mix of sorrow, pain, guilt, and even relief. He may have gone about it the wrong way, but she was grateful things had ended between them before they'd tied themselves to each other and ended up miserable. Because she doubted he would have ever told her how he felt. Stella would have been just the start of it. The start of him taking the easy way out and finding validation in other women. She may have needed him too much, but he'd needed her just as much. Too much to just let her go. Like the words she'd written months ago, they'd been too entangled with each other to see the truth that need doesn't equal love.

How ironic that she'd ended up falling for a man who didn't need her at all.

And now she didn't have him either.

For the first time since she was fourteen, her life was completely her own.

It was up to her to make of it what she wanted.

Chapter Thirty-Nine

Being at Abbey Road never got old. Zac looked through the big window down into the studio on the ground floor. Studio Two was iconic; it was where the fucking Beatles had recorded most of their music throughout the 1960s. He'd been here before with Fractured, but there was a different thrill being here with Crossfire. His younger bandmates' expressions as they'd entered the hallowed space for the first time had brought a smile to his face.

The effort had exhausted him.

Sitting in the lounge room above the studio waiting for their guest to arrive, Zac's hands moved across the strings of his guitar, playing the song he and Cassie had been working on when he'd let her walk out of his life. His fingers slipped, the discordant note echoing through the room. Three pairs of eyes turned in his direction.

"Losing your touch, old man?" Caleb grinned at him.

Zac flipped him the bird. He closed his eyes, picturing Cassie's face as she sang the words she'd written. The delight shining in her expression, the beautiful smile on her lips. His heart constricted so hard, he had to rub his chest with the heel of his palm.

Fuck.

He didn't know what was worse: the memory of how he'd hurt her or imagining what would have happened if he'd never kissed her that night at the club.

He *missed* her. He missed everything about her. Her smile, her laugh, the press of her lips to his, her touch and compassion, the way he could turn to her when he needed someone.

But that was the problem. It had all been about what *he* needed. He'd never cared about what she needed. He was selfish, just like his father. Putting his bands and his music and his needs above her. The only unselfish thing he'd done when it came to Cassie was to let her go. Because he'd *wanted* to keep her. He'd wanted to ask her to stay with him. He'd even considered asking her to come to the UK. But that would make him no better than Bryan—expecting her to follow him around. To have it all be about him because he was too busy, too wrapped up in his music, to make her his priority.

"You keep playing that song. When are you going to share it with us?" Devon sat down next to him.

"I'm not," he said.

"It's good."

"It is."

"Is it Cassie's?" Devon asked.

Zac's gaze jerked up to meet the knowing look in his bandmate's blue eyes. His lips pinched together, and he looked away.

"What the hell happened?" Devon said. "You were happy. You were even relaxing a bit. We all saw it. Now she's gone, and you're miserable. You've been pushing us like hell to get to this place, and you look like you'd rather be anywhere else."

Zac swung his head back to face him. "Pushing you? You want to be here just as much as I wanted to get us here."

"Of course we do. What fucking musician doesn't? But fuck, man, we want to enjoy the ride getting to wherever we're going as well. And the last thing we need is to lose our front man because he's burning out trying to exorcise some demons he won't tell anyone about."

Zac jolted back in his seat. "What?"

Devon glanced over at the other two, who were watching with furrowed brows. He turned back to Zac. "We love you, man. But fuck, you're working yourself into the ground. One day, not too far into the future, you're going to realize it too. And then I'm betting you're going to decide you need to make a choice. Excuse us if we're left wondering whether we might not be the ones you choose. Unlike you, we don't have another mega-successful band waiting in the wings. We don't get to shrug our shoulders and say, oh well, guess it didn't work out."

Zac pushed to his feet, staring down at Devon, who didn't stand to match him. He just sat there, his forearms resting on his thighs, hands dangling between his legs as he held Zac's gaze. There was a touch of anger there, but he was resigned more than anything. Resigned to the fact Zac was going to let them down?

Zac dropped his guitar on the couch next to Devon and walked away. He headed through the control room and down the stairs to the studio, his boot heels striking hard against the parquetry floor.

He stood in front of their equipment, which had been set up ready for the morning's session. His hands were clenched so hard, his arms shook. What the fuck? Where the hell had this come from? They'd wanted this too—it hadn't been just him. The fact he knew Devon, Beau, and Caleb didn't have a backup plan was why he'd been pushing them all so hard. Why he'd been so focused on making this work.

And yeah, maybe he'd started Crossfire with the goal of proving something to his dad. But his father was gone now, nothing Zac did would ever be able to change his opinion. And he knew the weight of his responsibility when it came to Crossfire. He was their front man, the glue that held the band together. He was well aware of what that meant.

Footsteps approached across the studio. Zac didn't turn, but he could tell from the stride it was Beau.

"This might not have been the best time for Devon to bring it up, but he's not wrong," Beau started. "You're going to burn out, Zac. Two bands. Two *successful* bands. Touring, recording. I honestly don't think any of us expected to get where we are so quickly. If at all. And we appreciate everything you've done. You're Crossfire just as much as you are Fractured. But you're tearing yourself apart trying to be everything to everyone. You can't keep on this way, and we don't want to lose you."

He'd thought he'd been handling it fine. But apparently his bandmates were questioning his dedication. Were they right? Was he going to end up screwing them over because he wasn't making them his priority? "So, you want me to leave Fractured to concentrate on Crossfire?"

A flash of surprise crossed Beau's face. He tilted his head to the side, his eyes appraising. "Would you?"

Would he? Would he walk away from his friends? From their success. From their fans? With Lexie's pregnancy, things were going to change. Fewer albums, less touring, less of what he'd spent his life devoting himself to. Particularly when the other two inevitably followed in Connor's footsteps.

His chest felt hollow. Should he give up Fractured to focus on Crossfire? Was he being selfish trying to hold onto both?

"That wasn't meant to be a difficult question, man," said Beau. "It wasn't even a serious one. Why would you think—"

Before he could finish what he was saying, the door to the studio swung open. Bob, Hazard Records' UK rep, made his way over to them, followed by a woman. She was dressed in skintight jeans and a crop top that showed off a toned stomach. Long waves of cotton candy pink hair flowed over her shoulders.

"Damn," murmured Beau.

Still half-lost in his own head, Zac stepped forward.

"Zac, Beau," said Bob. "This is Talia."

"Hi, Talia." Zac reached out to shake her hand.

She gave him a slow, curling smile and squeezed his hand. "Hi, Zac, I'm so pleased to meet you."

He dropped her hand and was almost knocked off his feet by Beau shouldering him out of the way. "Hey, Talia. Beau."

She graced him with the same smile she'd given Zac. "Well, it's great to be here with you guys. I can't wait to get started on this duet today." Her refined British accent contrasted with her vibrantly colored hair.

"Zac, can I speak to you for a minute?" Bob asked, while Beau engaged Talia in small talk.

Zac nodded, and they took a few steps across the room away from them. "What's up?" he asked.

Bob's gaze darted over his shoulder toward Beau and Talia. "The label wants to add another song to the album."

Zac frowned. "What are you talking about? We've decided on the tracks for the album already. It's done."

"We want to include a cover of the song you sang with your little guitar tech at karaoke. The fans will go nuts for it." He nodded over at Talia. "And if you sing it with her, it'll break her wide-open in the US. The lawyers are already in talks."

"No." Zac's tone was low and firm.

"Zac, with Talia's voice, that song will be phenomenal. It'll be a sure number one hit."

"I said no. I'm not discussing this." From the sudden silence behind him, the snap in his voice had attracted Beau's and Talia's attention.

Bob's nostrils flared. "Look, your fling with the guitar tech is over, but we can capitalize on that viral video. And if we push the angle that you and Talia are a couple, this album will be a runaway success. You never know, it could even beat Fractured's sales from the last album."

The thought of their album reaching those kinds of sales numbers should have had him over the fucking moon. It would finally prove his dad wrong. But the only thing he could think about was Cassie hearing it and seeing tabloid rumors that he and Talia were together. Imagining the hurt on her face made icy anger flow through his veins.

He was about to cancel the whole damn session when Talia's melodic voice came from behind him.

"Bob, can I talk to Zac in private for a minute?"

Bob eyed her, then nodded. He and Beau left them, heading up the stairs to the lounge where the others were waiting.

Zac watched her coolly as she came and stood in front

Fractured Kiss

of him. He shouldn't blame her for this shit, but he couldn't help feeling resentful. She cocked her head, her big brown eyes curious. "So, I'm guessing the guitar tech wasn't just a fling."

It rubbed him the wrong way hearing her and Bob refer to Cassie that way. "Her name is Cassie."

"Right." She smiled. "So, this thing with *Cassie* isn't over like everyone is saying?"

He ground his teeth together but didn't answer.

She nodded slowly. "You know, even without the label putting it out there, as soon as we record this duet and release the video, people are going to be linking us. It's human nature."

She was right. He knew it, and he hated it. Hated the thought of hurting Cassie more than she'd already been hurt. By her mother. By Bryan. By him. By people who couldn't seem to love her the way she deserved.

An idea trickled through his mind. It took him by surprise—but it felt right. When he told Talia what he wanted to do, she just shook her head, laughed, and agreed to it.

He looked up at the window of the control room where his damn nosy bandmates were standing watching. He nodded to let them know everything was okay. They came traipsing down the stairs. When they were all there, he looked over at Bob. "There's been a change of plans."

Chapter Forty

Cassie lined up at the checkout with her groceries. Sweat stuck her tank top to her back, and she reached around and pulled the material away from her skin. It had been a long day at work. But even though she'd had a late finish, the heat still hit her on the walk from her car to the grocery store.

She'd ended up deciding not to continue as a touring guitar tech. She wanted to build something of her own. Something that wasn't based on Bryan's dream.

While she worked on her plans for the future, she'd gotten a job as a guitar repair technician at an independent music store that also had a small recording studio attached.

She spent her days repairing customer-owned guitars, while helping in the recording studio when needed. No one knew or cared who she was or that she'd supposedly been dating one of the biggest rock stars in the world until a few short weeks ago.

Cassie juggled the milk and bread and a box of mac and cheese that was going to be tonight's dinner. She was too tired to cook from scratch. Not only was she working long hours at the store and studio, but she was writing songs. Or at least, she was practicing writing songs instead of poetry. It was a slightly different skill, but one she was picking up quickly.

And she loved it.

She was almost at the front of the line now. While she waited, she scanned the shelves, her eyes catching on a magazine headline that had her heart shooting into her throat.

UK Pop Starlet and Crossfire Hottie Make Beautiful Music Together! (In and Out of the Studio).

The photo below it showed a tall, dark-haired man in a club making out with a curvy, pink-haired woman.

Nausea rushed over Cassie so fast, she almost dropped her groceries to clutch at her stomach. The line moved, but she didn't, her feet frozen to the floor as she stared at the photo. It was so painfully familiar. The memory of the first time she'd felt Zac's lips against hers came rushing back. She clenched her eyes shut against the pain, but an impatient cough behind her dragged her out of it and got her feet moving again.

She reached for the magazine with a shaky hand but snatched it back. She couldn't torture herself that way. She was still so raw from everything that had happened. Reading the details of Zac and Talia's rendezvous would pour so much salt on her open wound, it might end up with her a screaming, crying mess on the floor.

Cassie dropped everything on the counter and blinked hard, trying to hold back the tears. Her pulse throbbed painfully in her temples. When the cashier told her the price, she fumbled with her purse, passed her a crumpled note, then gathered up her groceries and practically bolted from the store.

She held on with gritted teeth until she got back to her apartment. But as soon as she dropped her bag on the countertop of the small kitchen, she slid down with her back against the cabinet door, dropped her head against her knees, and sobbed until her throat was raw.

She thought she was moving past it. Past *him*. Getting her life together. Making a future for herself.

On her own.

Yes, she was lonely. But she was getting used to it. This, though. This pain was a living thing inside her chest, clawing and shrieking to get out. If she'd thought finding Bryan and Stella together had torn her apart, this was far worse. Because it proved beyond a doubt that what she thought Zac had grown to feel for her was as fake as their relationship was always supposed to have been.

When the tears eventually ran out and her head pounded from all the crying, she pushed herself up off the floor and put away the groceries she'd left on the counter. She'd lost her appetite, so she stashed the box of mac and cheese in the cupboard.

Her eye caught on her laptop, sitting out on the bench. She'd resisted buying the magazine, but she had to fight the masochistic urge to look Zac up online. Or maybe she shouldn't fight it. Rubbing the truth of it in her face might cauterize the wound. It might be what she needed to force herself to let go. The way seeing Bryan with Stella had made her let go.

She wavered on her feet. Then squared her shoulders and sat down in front of the computer. After all, she was already cried out. Hopefully, she had no more tears left.

Cassie quickly typed in Zac's and Talia's names before she could come to her senses.

She clicked on the first link that came up, but it was just

an article about the fact Talia would be recording a duet with Crossfire, so she tried the next one. This article had the photo from the magazine up the top. Cassie's heart almost beat its way out of her chest as she made herself look at it.

She frowned. Zac's hair seemed slightly different. Longer, curling around his ears more. He might have just let it grow, but still, something seemed off in his proportions.

She steeled herself and scanned the article attached to the picture. Her shoulders sagged, and she slumped back against the chair, a sob falling from her lips.

It wasn't Zac in the photo. It was Beau. Beau was kissing Talia in some faraway British nightclub. Relief made her almost lightheaded, and she clicked out of the site. But not before reading that apparently it was Beau who had recorded the duet with Talia. Was that a mistake on the reporter's part? The duet had definitely been written for Zac to sing with the beautiful pop star. What could have changed that?

The throbbing in Cassie's head had eased, the sharp pain in her heart dulling to an ache. But the damage had been done. Zac was front and center in her mind again. Not tucked away where she tried to keep him. Her body felt bruised from all the emotions that had cascaded through it in the last couple of hours.

She stared out the window that overlooked the neighboring apartment block.

She should channel her pain. Try to write a song to get it out of her system. She'd resisted doing it before now. Too scared of digging into the hurt. But holding onto it wasn't helping. She was better off doing something with it. That way, at least her broken heart would be good for something.

But first, she needed a shower. She was still sticky with sweat. Her face felt stiff with all the tears she'd cried.

Cassie headed down the short hallway to her cramped bathroom. The taps screeched as she turned the water on in the shower and adjusted the temperature before stripping off and stepping under the spray.

She tipped her head back and let the water run over her face and down her body. Thinking about Zac hurt. Still. But with more time, she knew she'd get past it. She just needed to keep her chin up and get through each day. And eventually, after however many days it took, thinking about him wouldn't leave her feeling like she was a little shattered inside.

She had to believe that was true.

After a few more minutes, she reached for the taps and turned the shower off. She dried herself, put on her pajamas, and headed to the kitchen to pour herself a wine. She figured she'd probably need it.

Cassie grabbed a pen and her new notebook off the side table, opening it to a fresh page.

She forced herself to remember everything that had happened. From the first time she'd met Zac, to staying up nights with him on the tour bus, the kiss, the first time he'd touched her in the hotel room, the first time they'd slept together, to him making love to her after his dad's funeral. And then she remembered how it had all slid away from her.

The dream shattered by reality.

She let herself experience it all again, all the highs and lows, all the emotions, all the love she'd felt for him. Still felt. Tears trickled down her face, but she put her pen to the page and let it all flow out of her.

When she finished, she didn't look over it straight away. Instead, she let her eyes drift shut on a jagged exhale. It had

Fractured Kiss

been cathartic, letting her love and pain pour onto the page. She felt stripped bare but cleansed.

Cassie finally looked at what her heart had poured onto the page. A smile trembled on her lips. It read like a story. A love story. Just one without a happily ever after. Wasn't that what they called a tragedy?

Maybe it was. Maybe she could look at her life so far and label it a tragedy. But she wasn't going to. She wasn't going to depend on anyone else to make her happy anymore. She was going to rely on herself.

She'd write her own goddamn happily ever after.

Cassie closed the notebook with a snap, drank the rest of her wine, and went to bed.

Chapter Forty-One

Zac punched in the code to Noah's house and pushed the big wooden door open.

He wandered through to the backyard where he could see the three others outside, sitting around the table next to the pool. Zac slid open the glass door and stepped out. His friends looked up, grins spreading across their faces.

"Welcome back, man," said Noah. "Grab a beer and get your ass over here. It's been too long since we've seen your ugly face."

Zac rolled his eyes and smirked but pulled a beer bottle from the bar fridge and joined them at the table. He dropped into the chair next to Tex.

"So, how was it?" Connor asked.

Zac sat back and took a sip of his beer. Three expectant faces watched him, but he took his time deciding how to answer. "The guys loved it. The recording went off without a hitch, and the tour was good. The UK crowds are as insane as ever."

He didn't miss the look the three of them exchanged.

Tex rubbed his chin. "How about you? Had a blast?"

Zac narrowed his gaze at him. "It was fine. Great. Recording at Abbey Road is always awesome."

"Uh-huh. Don't overwhelm us with your enthusiasm."

"Heard from Cassie?" Noah jumped right in.

Zac's heart lurched. He'd spent the last three months trying to put Cassie out of his mind and failing miserably. He hadn't even been able to bring himself to get laid while he was away, turning down every proposition, rejecting every approach by groupies. Reverting to cheap, meaningless sex seemed too much like a betrayal of Cassie after what he'd experienced with her.

Which was ridiculous, considering he would probably never see her again.

He just needed a little more time to forget what he'd given up, that was all.

When he finally got his voice working, it was like sandpaper. "No." He cleared his throat. "Didn't really expect to."

"Really? Because you two were pretty close there for a while," Tex said. He pulled out his phone. "It's good, though, because I met a woman the other week who would be perfect for you—"

Zac shook his head, but he couldn't stop the corners of his lips turning up. Trust Tex to remind him of the words he'd said when he was trying to knock some sense into his friend about Eden. "You think you're funny?"

Tex just laughed.

Zac's mood soon sobered. "Actually," he began slowly, and the amusement around him faded. "There's something I want to talk to you all about." His heart battered his rib cage as he prepared to say the words out loud for the first time. "I've been thinking a lot lately. About how things are going with Fractured and Crossfire. With the three of you settling down, getting pregnant." His eyes went to Connor, whose brows had lowered. "Things are going to be changing for us. For Fractured. At some point, we're going to have to start making tough choices. And—"

"No." All humor was gone from Noah's face.

Zac eyed him. "I just think—"

"Not happening," said Connor.

Zac looked around at them all. Their jaws were tight, their expressions resolute.

He tried again. "Things are different now—"

"You don't think we saw this coming?" Noah broke in. "That at some stage you would think you needed to choose?"

"*You* made a choice," Zac reminded him.

Noah nodded. "I did. I made a choice based on what would make me happiest. Spending more time with Summer. That's what made me the happiest. She is the only thing I would choose over you guys. But *she* would never make me choose. Neither would Lexie. Or Eden. If you tell us that being in Fractured doesn't make you happy anymore, then you have the right to walk away. You can devote all your time to Crossfire, and there's no doubt you'll have a huge amount of success. But make that choice because it's what will make you happy. Not because you think you have to. Not because you think you can't have both."

Zac shook his head. Unsure what to say, sudden doubt cast on what he thought he had to do.

"We know things have been crazy for you," Tex said. "I don't think any of us expected Crossfire to take off the way it did. So, the fact things might be changing doesn't mean you have to walk away. It just means you have the space to do what you need to do with those guys."

"And if you think we're going to let you disappear on us, you don't know us at all," said Noah. "I haven't forgotten what you told me. That sometimes it hurts less if you choose to let something go than if you try to hold onto it and lose it anyway. So, don't think I don't know what you're doing."

Zac scrubbed his hand over his mouth, his eyes moving from one of his friends to the other. Was that what he'd been doing? Trying to give them up before the changes that were coming took them from him? He thought back to his conversations with Devon and Beau, wondering if he'd deliberately misinterpreted their concerns over how hard he was pushing everyone. Was he using them as an excuse to let go of Fractured before the choice was taken out of his hands?

"Look." Connor leaned forward, and Zac didn't know if he'd ever seen their lead singer look more serious. "I'm not sure if I've ever said this to your faces. But you and Tex and Noah are my family. The three of you, Lexie, and my aunt are the best family I could ask for. I don't think I ever really talked about how alone I felt when I arrived here from Ireland. That went away when I met all of you. I feel insanely privileged that I've been able to go on this journey with you all. And I know things are changing now. I know we're wading into unknown territory, and that's a little terrifying. For *all* of us. But that doesn't mean our journey is over. That doesn't mean *Fractured's* journey is over."

Had he ever really let himself think of his bandmates as his family? He didn't think so. He'd always been too busy trying to keep some distance—to keep *everyone* at a distance. When he was younger, he'd deliberately held part of himself back, because he didn't want his friends to know how much his dad hated him. Because deep down he'd been scared that maybe it was true. Maybe he *had* been responsible for ruining his dad's life. He'd been frightened, as only a child can be, that if his friends found out the truth, they might believe it too. That it might change the way they looked at him. And he'd needed their friendship and acceptance so badly he'd done everything he could to keep that part of his life hidden. But by doing that, he'd never fully let them in. As close as they'd all grown over the years, he'd never wanted to let himself be completely vulnerable in case he lost them.

Zac's throat tightened, and he had to swallow hard before he could talk. Something hit him with sudden clarity. *Right place, right time.* That's what his father had told him. Those were the words he'd been letting drag him down all these years. He'd spent all this time thinking of it as a bad thing. But it wasn't. It fucking wasn't. Because being in the right place at the right time, being in that music room at the same time as Connor and Tex had been a fucking miracle. It had changed his life in a way that had nothing to do with fame and fortune. It had brought him this family. Not just the three of them, but Lexie, Eden, and Summer. He'd spent his whole life caring too much about the opinion of a bitter old man, just because he shared his blood, instead of letting himself care as much as he should about the family he'd chosen to be with.

He took a deep breath as a weight lifted off his chest. He didn't have to choose. Whatever happened, whatever changed going forward, he would always have these men in his life. "Well, I suppose as brothers go, it could be worse." He squinted out at the ocean and took another sip of his beer. The others relaxed back in their chairs.

And that was that.

"So, Lexie's been keeping in touch with Cassie." Connor changed the subject.

Zac's heart stumbled again, and it took him a second to school his expression into one of pleasant interest. He wasn't sure what the others saw on his face in that second, but Noah snorted, then covered his mouth with his fist and pretended to cough when Zac cut his eyes in his direction.

"That's good. How's she doing?" he asked, hoping the hoarseness in his voice didn't give away the tension that filled him.

Connor gave a casual shrug. "You'll have to ask Lexie. She doesn't really tell me what they talk about." A flash of what looked suspiciously like amusement gleamed in his green eyes.

Zac nodded but didn't give Connor the satisfaction of reacting. Luckily, they followed his lead and moved on to other topics, and he spent the next couple of hours relaxing and enjoying his friends' company.

But even though he was having a good time, he kept finding his cell phone in his hands, his thumb rubbing over the screen. Once, he even opened his message app and clicked on Lexie's name. Started typing. But he came to his senses and deleted it. It had been three months. Three months with no contact. Cassie would have moved on by now. Inserting himself back in her life would be a dick thing to do.

That was why he deliberately put his cell phone in a drawer when he got home that evening.

That lasted about ten minutes before he convinced himself it was just friendly interest when he messaged Lexie.

Zac: *Hey, Connor mentioned you've been in touch with Cassie. I just wanted to make sure she's doing okay with her new job.*

The wait for Lexie to get back to him seemed to stretch on forever. Finally, his phone chimed.

Lexie: *Welcome back! Cassie's doing okay. She's working as a guitar repair technician, and part-time in a recording studio. And she told me she's doing some songwriting on the side.*

A broad smile spread across his face.

Zac: *That's great. I'm glad she's pursuing that.*

He hesitated for a long time, then tapped out another message.

Zac: *Is she happy?*

He waited impatiently for her reply and was surprised when his phone rang instead.

"Hey, Lexie," he answered.

"Hi, Zac." Her voice was warm, but he sensed concern in her tone. "Look, I just want to say that I appreciate you wanting to make sure Cassie is okay. And I know you care about her. But if there's anything more than casual interest on your part, you need to think really hard about what you're doing. She's just started to get herself together. And as much as I think you two make a great couple, her heart has been broken twice in quick succession. She doesn't need it happening again."

He gritted his teeth at the thought he'd broken her heart. "I wasn't planning to get in touch with her. That's why I'm asking you."

"Zac..." There was a long pause, and then she sighed. "I know this goes completely against what I just said—and I meant what I said. But, Zac, Cassie was really good for you. And I think you were good for her. You two could have something special. I want that for you. I really do—we all do. But you need to be committed. You need to choose her with one hundred percent conviction."

He shook his head, even though she couldn't see it. "You've got the wrong idea."

"Maybe I do. And if that's the case, then I'm sorry for overstepping. But I love you, Zac. You, Tex, and Noah are like brothers to me."

Zac startled. It was the second time today someone had called him family.

"Tex and Noah may have had their issues when it came to Eden and Summer, but they were never closed off to love the way you are. And the way Connor used to be. I worry about you. I want you to be happy. I want you to experience all the amazing things life has to offer, including love. Because take it from me, life can change in an instant. So, grab happiness when you can. You don't want to spend your life regretting what you missed out on."

He knew Lexie wasn't talking out of her ass. She'd lost her first husband only a few short years after they'd been married. She knew exactly what she was talking about. And she'd still taken a chance on happiness with Connor.

"Lexie, I can't give her what she needs. I don't have it in me. I've got too much else going on to have the time to devote to her."

"Is that what's holding you back? Do you think she's going to take you away from what you love?"

Something snapped inside him. "What if she does? What if I end up resenting her for it? What if I end up hurting her even more because I just don't have it in me to love her more than the music? What if I make her feel like she isn't enough again and again, until it breaks her heart and all that's left between us is misery?" He was breathing heavily by the time he finished pouring out all his fears.

Lexie waited patiently for him to finish. "You know, people talk about hearts as if they're fragile. But our hearts are the strongest things about us. They can endure unimaginable pain and still retain the capacity to heal and grow. You have room in your heart for more than just one thing, Zac. Your music, your career, those are important. But they aren't the only things that make life worthwhile. Love can be hard. It can hurt. Sometimes it's terrifying. But loving less just because you're scared is *not* the answer. Whatever you might have been led to believe"—she paused, tellingly, and he wondered what she might have intuited over the years—"love by its very nature is unselfish. You have an enormous capacity for love, if only you'd let yourself. And the very fact that you are so worried about hurting Cassie should tell you that what you feel for her isn't selfish. Which means you're more than capable of putting her first."

Zac closed his eyes, a deep shudder wracking his body. Had he gotten it so wrong? Had he spent all these years thinking he had to choose between the music and everything else he cared about when that wasn't true? He rubbed his temple. "Thanks, Lexie."

"I really am glad to have you back, Zac."

He let out a rough chuckle. "How are you anyway? With the pregnancy."

She laughed lightly. "I already feel like I'm the size of a house. I can't imagine what it's going to be like in three months."

"I'm sure Connor's taking good care of you."

She hummed in agreement. "Did you ever expect him to be a doting dad-to-be?"

He barked a laugh. "No. You definitely changed him."

"I didn't change him. He just let himself see the possibilities."

He groaned. "Okay, okay. I get it."

Lexie laughed again. "Good. Really think about it, Zac. Because in the months you and Cassie were together, you already changed her life for the better. And I think she did for you too. Imagine what you could do for each other in an entire lifetime together."

He nodded, staring sightlessly out at the view over LA and forgetting, for a second, she couldn't see him. "Yeah, okay. Thanks, Lexie."

They said their farewells, then Zac threw his phone down on the coffee table. His mind was all over the place after the day's conversations. But before he could start figuring out what it all meant, his phone rang again.

Half-expecting it to be Lexie calling back with some more sage advice, it surprised him to see Talia's name on the screen. They'd exchanged phone numbers while they were recording. They'd even hung out with her at a club one night when they'd crossed paths again during their tour. She and Beau had gotten a little cozy on the dance floor, which had played right into the label's hands for the release of their duet. The duet he was meant to have sung with her, but which he hadn't been able to bring himself to do, knowing how the tabloids would spin it.

"Hey, stranger," Talia said when he answered.

"Hey. What's up?"

"I'm in town, and I've got a proposition for you. Any chance we can meet?"

"You're in LA?"

"Yep, arrived last night."

Zac rubbed the back of his neck. If it would distract him from the whirlwind of thoughts flying around his head, he was game. "Sure. Since I'm assuming it's business-related, do you want to meet at Drew's office tomorrow morning? I've got to head in and see him, anyway."

Talia agreed, and they arranged a time, then said goodbye.

Zac spent the night tossing restlessly. Lexie's words had opened the floodgates. He was inundated with vivid memories of Cassie's beautiful smile, those gorgeous eyes, the rightness of her body wrapped around his.

Even more than those things, he'd missed talking to her, hearing her laugh, and making music with her. He craved the warmth of her presence. Having her near had made each minute of the day brighter, even when he'd been trying to pretend it didn't.

He eventually fell asleep, but it was a long time coming.

The next morning, he woke early and exhausted. He headed to Drew's office at nine, and they'd just finished running over their upcoming promo schedule for the release of Crossfire's album, when there was a knock at the door. Drew opened it and ushered in Talia and her manager. Zac stood, and Talia's pretty face lit up.

"Zac!" She walked over and threw her arms around him.

Zac gave her a quick hug, then stepped back, catching a flicker of a smile on her manager's face. The man held out his hand. "Zac," he said with a nod. They'd met once before, in the UK, when he'd dropped in on one of their recording sessions.

"Cameron." Zac shook the man's hand, then let go and shoved both of his into his back pockets, looking between Talia and her manager. "So, what's this about?"

Talia dropped onto one of the comfortable couches Drew had in his office and grinned up at him. She waited with her eyebrows raised until Zac followed suit and sat opposite her. "How are things with you and your guitar tech?"

"*Cassie*," he growled.

Talia gave him a coy smile. "That's the one."

"I told you before, we're not together."

"Mmmm." She leaned back and crossed one long leg over the other.

Zac shot a look at Cameron—who merely quirked his lips in response—then returned his attention to Talia. "So, are you going to tell me what you wanted to see me about?"

"Actually, it's not really you I want to see. Or at least not just you."

Zac kept looking at her, waiting for her to get to the point.

"Well, things might not be better between you and your guitar te... uh, Cassie." She smirked. "But that song you were playing all the time during breaks when we were recording—the one Beau told me you and Cassie wrote together? It was beautiful. I haven't been able to stop thinking about it. I want to buy it and record it."

Zac kept his gaze steady on her, even as a surge of pride rocketed through him. Not that it surprised him. He already knew Cassie was talented. "Yeah? Well, you'd have to talk to her about that."

"It's not just Cassie's song, though, is it?" Talia asked,

her eyes artificially wide and with a flutter of her long lashes.

Zac snorted. She wasn't as innocent as she appeared. "It's not, but it was mostly hers. And if you're serious about doing this, I don't want it to come through me."

Her brows arched. "Why not?"

"I don't want her to think she owes this to me."

Talia nodded thoughtfully. "Right, okay. Cameron can contact her directly." She looked over at her manager, waiting for him to confirm before continuing. "But she'll know the only way I could have heard it was from you, right?"

"As long as she doesn't think I've pushed you into it as a favor to her. She needs to know it's her talent that captured your interest, not my influence."

"Okay, we can make that work." She studied him. "You swapped out our duet with Beau because you didn't want Cassie to think something was going on between us. Now there's this. You obviously care about her. More than care, I would guess. Why the hell aren't you with her?"

"Because we want different things." The words felt wrong coming out of his mouth. He was starting to think he might have been telling himself a big fucking lie this whole time.

"Well, what is it you want Zac?" Talia asked.

He hesitated. For the first time, he didn't have a clear answer to that question. Things were changing. *He* was changing. A few months ago, he would have said he only wanted to focus on his music. He would have said he wanted to get Crossfire to the top as quickly as possible, regardless of the cost. But that had been because he thought he had something to prove. To his dad. To himself. And doing something when it was just to prove a point came at a cost too. One he wasn't sure he was willing to pay anymore.

A few months ago, he'd refused to believe he could be what Cassie needed. But now...

Now he was starting to see the possibilities.

Chapter Forty-Two

Cassie pressed a button to stop her laptop recording. She couldn't hold back the smile that spread across her face. After clicking a few buttons, she hit upload and gave a little squeal of happiness. She followed that up with a laugh at herself as she flopped backward on the bed.

It was the tenth song she'd uploaded to her various social media channels. She'd already gained a small but enthusiastic following. One of her fans had even contacted her to ask if she'd write a song for his band. And he'd offered her money! She was really starting to think she could make a go of this songwriting thing. She wished she could tell Zac.

Zac...

Her heart gave a single, pained thump.

Why did it still hurt so much to think about him? Surely she should be over him by now. Considering how much Bryan had meant to her, she'd been able to move on from him much quicker than this. And she was in a great place now. She had her apartment, which was small but neat, a job she enjoyed, even if it wasn't her dream job at the moment, and the possibility of doing something she could really be passionate about. She'd even made friends. Now that she wasn't wrapped up in Bryan anymore, she was finally taking opportunities to meet people.

And yet whenever she thought about the time she and Zac had spent together, her heart still hurt, and her eyes still burned with tears she tried hard not to shed.

At night, he still filled her dreams.

Cassie sat up and swung her legs over the side of the bed. She just had to keep reminding herself that even though what she'd felt for Zac was real, the scars of his past would never let him believe there could be something true and lasting between them. Not that she could talk about letting your scars have power over you. She'd clung to someone who didn't really love her just because she'd been scared to be alone again.

Her phone vibrating on the bed next to her pulled her out of her thoughts. She frowned at the unknown number.

"Hello," she answered.

"Cassie Elliot? My name is Cameron McAllister. I'm Talia Harrison's manager."

Cassie blinked a few times. "I'm sorry. *The* Talia Harrison?"

He gave a dry chuckle. "The one and only."

Cassie blew out a breath. "Wow. Okay. Um, what can I do for you?"

"Well, recently Talia heard a song that you wrote, and she liked it. She liked it a lot. So much so that she'd like to purchase the rights to record and release it."

"What?"

"Talia would like to buy your song."

Cassie's mind went blank, her heart almost punching

through her chest. An unwelcome thought occurred to her, and she sucked in a sharp breath. "Did Zac put her up to this?"

"She overheard Mr. Ford playing the song when he was in the UK recently. But he in no way influenced her decision. In fact, he insisted on not being involved in this process at all."

Hurt bloomed in Cassie's chest. Zac wanted nothing to do with her. If he had, this would have been the perfect opportunity for him to reach out to her. "Well, he helped write it, so doesn't he have to be part of this?"

"No. He's signing over all rights to you."

"He's what?"

"I have a document here from Mr. Ford that assigns all copyright of the music to you." He sounded vaguely impatient. "You own all the rights to this song. So, are you interested in meeting with Talia?"

Unwelcome tears sprung to Cassie's eyes. She should be over the moon that someone like Talia Harrison wanted to buy her song. And she was. But knowing Zac didn't want to be involved, that he wasn't interested in seeing her or talking to her, hurt far more than it should.

She brushed the tears away, swallowed past the lump in her throat, and answered him. "Yes. Yes, I am."

* * *

Cassie stared with wide eyes at the gorgeous pink-haired woman sitting opposite her.

"So, what do you think, Cassie? Are you interested in selling your song to me?"

"I honestly don't know what to say. I'm so honored. But..." She didn't know how to bring the topic up.

A smile flickered over Talia's lips. "Zac?"

She released a ragged breath. "I know Cameron said he signed over rights to me. Does that mean he won't be involved in this at all?"

Talia studied her. "Do you want him to be?"

Cassie froze for a second. "I—" She hadn't expected that question. "I—No, I suppose it would be better for him not to be involved. Obviously, he doesn't want to be." She stopped her fingers from tugging at the hem of her top.

Talia hummed non-committally. "Then you're all good because he won't have anything to do with this recording."

Cassie should be relieved not to have to worry about how painfully awkward it would be seeing Zac again. But she only felt sad. She didn't want Talia to know that, though. So, she just smiled as if everything was fine.

"I'm hoping to record in a couple of weeks," Talia said. "It would be great if you could be here for that. And I'd like to work with you to finish the song before then, as well. Are you able to spend a few days here in LA so we can work together?"

Cassie shook her head. Not in denial, just at the sheer ridiculousness of being in this situation. Talia seemed to understand because she just waited patiently.

"I'm sure I can get some time off work."

"That's great!" Talia stood, and Cassie assumed the meeting was over. She rose to her feet too.

She was surprised when the other woman pulled her into a hug. "I'm really looking forward to working with you, Cassie."

"I'm looking forward to it too. Very much."

A mischievous glint shone in Talia's doe-like brown eyes. "And I promise Zac won't be anywhere near the studio while we're recording."

Chapter Forty-Three

"I'll be there soon." Zac hung up his phone and smiled to himself. He caught Lexie's gaze and grinned at the curiosity brimming in her eyes.

"Who was that?" she asked.

"I've got another surprise for your baby shower. I was just confirming it was ready to pick up."

Lexie smiled. "You already bought the baby a mini bass guitar and a karaoke machine. What else could she possibly want?"

"You have to make sure she plays the bass. I know that miniature drum kit Noah bought her is pretty sweet. And Connor and Tex will definitely try to sway her toward a six-string, so I'm counting on you to guide her toward the best instrument. And I know you know that's the bass."

Lexie laughed, but then she cocked her head. "You seem very... happy. Is there something going on you want to tell me about?"

Zac suppressed another smile. "Why wouldn't I be happy? Look where I am." He gestured around them, and Lexie sighed and nodded.

They were sitting in Lexie and Connor's cliff-top backyard. The sun was shining, and his Fractured bandmates were over by the grill, arguing over who was the best cook. Drew stood back, watching with his arms crossed, a crooked grin on his face. Summer and Eden were in the house finishing off decorating Lexie's baby shower cake.

Lexie rested her hand on her bump and rubbed it. "We've got a lot to be thankful for."

"We do."

Zac felt a strange sense of calm, considering what today was. Not too long ago, he would have seen this as an ending. Even a couple of weeks ago, he'd been preparing himself to walk away.

Things had changed now, though. He'd opened himself to the possibility of more, as Lexie had said. As she and Connor had done. As all of them had done, in one way or the other. This wasn't an ending. It was a beginning. His family was growing. Their ability to create music together wasn't going anywhere. Music was who they were. It had shaped their lives, and it would continue to shape them, even if that shape was slightly different now.

He'd spent the two weeks since he'd gotten back from the UK figuring everything out.

Figuring *himself* out.

A week ago, he'd invited his friends to his apartment and had an honest conversation with them about how things had been between him and his dad. The three of them were furious at his father, and pissed with him for not sharing with them before. He got it. They would have been there for him if he'd let them, but he hadn't, and he figured that after everything they'd been through together, that probably hurt. But at the end of it all, they'd sat there together on his balcony overlooking LA, drank some beers, laughed and reminisced about their lives so far, and everything that was still to come.

Three days ago, the band's charitable trust had forwarded him a letter from Annika, the little girl he and Cassie had met at the hospital. The writing was her mother's, but the words were hers.

She had written to let him know that even though it looked like she was going to get to be a grown up one day after all, she was still okay with him and Cassie getting married. She also mentioned that she would like to be a flower girl at the wedding. Since she'd just been a flower girl at her aunt's wedding, she knew what to do and what *not* to do now. Apparently, there had been a slight incident where she'd dumped all the flower petals out of her basket at the beginning of the aisle, rather than scattering them as she was supposed to do. But her aunt had just hugged her when she cried, and everyone had clapped and smiled at her when she'd kept going, throwing pretend petals in the air. She was hoping to receive her invitation to his wedding soon so she wouldn't grow out of her flower girl dress and could wear it again since it was so pretty.

At the end of the letter was a note from Annika's mother where she'd expressed her eternal gratitude to him and the rest of the band. The nurse at the hospital had let it slip where the funding for her daughter's treatment had come from. She wanted to make sure she let them know that Annika was in remission and the doctors were optimistic about her chances of staying that way.

Zac had damn near shed a tear at that letter, then laughed at the drawing Annika had included, which showed stick figure versions of him and Cassie getting married, with a little stick figure Annika standing next to them throwing petals up in the air.

Fractured Kiss

He'd had to force himself not to pick up his phone to call Cassie so he could share the good news right then. But he'd held back. His first conversation with her needed to be in person.

When he stood, Lexie's gray eyes narrowed, even as she smiled. "What are you up to?"

"I have a gift I have to pick up. I'll be back soon, though."

Zac gave her a wink, then headed through the house and out to where he'd parked his charcoal gray custom Dodge Charger.

He drove through the traffic, winding carefully in and out of the other cars. He was eager to get where he was going, but he didn't want to speed and get pulled over. If he was late, it would ruin everything.

He checked the time and pressed his foot a little faster on the accelerator.

Chapter Forty-Four

Talia bounced over and hugged Cassie. "That was amazing. This song is going to be phenomenal. I can feel it."

Cassie laughed and returned her hug. In the days they'd worked together leading up to this recording session, the two of them had hit it off. And even in that short period of time, she'd learned so much about what it took to be a professional songwriter. "I still can't believe you wanted to record our song."

"*Your* song."

"It's not just mine, whatever the rights say," Cassie said.

Talia grinned. "I'll walk out with you."

Cassie picked up her bag and followed her out of the recording studio, looking around as they made their way through the building. A sad, hopeless, still-in-love part of her wished she could see Zac, even though she knew he wouldn't be there.

Talia opened the door to the gated parking lot and stepped out. Cassie came behind her, blinking in the bright California sunlight. In front of the door was parked a sleek, dark-gray car with a tall, broad-shouldered figure leaning against it. She stopped in her tracks.

"Well, I'll leave you to it," Talia trilled.

Cassie turned a narrowed gaze on her. "I thought you said he wouldn't be here." She wasn't angry, not really, but the blood was pumping so fast through her veins she needed a few seconds to regain her equilibrium.

Talia gave her a bright smile. "I said he wouldn't be here while we were recording. And it looks to me like he only just got here." She gave Cassie a kiss on the cheek, waved to Zac, and strolled off.

Cassie stood there and watched her go, willing strength into her body—and her heart. Then she turned to Zac, swallowing hard as her eyes drank him in.

He came toward her, and her pulse sped up even more. It had been over four months since she'd seen him in the flesh. She didn't want him to know how his presence was affecting her. She had more pride than that. She raised her chin and kept her gaze steady as he stopped in front of her.

He shoved his hands in the pockets of his worn jeans, his soft moss-green T-shirt that brought out the green in his hazel eyes pulling tight over the breadth of his shoulders.

She said nothing, just watched him warily.

"I'm so fucking proud of you, Cassie."

She blinked, not expecting that to be the first thing he said to her.

"For what?"

He huffed out a laugh. "You just sold your first song to a chart-topping pop star."

"With your help."

He shook his head. "The only thing I did was happen to play it where other people had the chance to overhear it."

"You helped with the music."

"Minimal. And there are always going to be tweaks to the music when you're writing songs. And anyway, it's not just that. Look how far you've come in the last seven months. Look where you are, Cassie. You chose to follow a dream all by yourself. And you're killing it."

A lick of warmth spread through her, and her defenses wobbled. She wrapped her arms around her stomach to strengthen them again. "What are you doing here, Zac?"

"I have something I need to show you."

She frowned. "What is it?"

The corner of his mouth lifted. "It's really something you need to see."

"I don't know if that's a good idea. I think it would probably be better for both of us if I just went—"

She forgot what she was saying when he stepped forward and touched his fingertips to her cheek. His brows were drawn together, his eyes dark and serious. "I hurt you, Cassie. And you don't owe me anything. You have every reason to walk away and not look back. But I'm asking you not to. I'm asking you to give me a chance to make things right."

His proximity had butterflies taking flight in her stomach. Going anywhere with Zac would be risky. She wasn't over him yet, and spending time with him would only fan those flames back to life. But his touch burned against her skin and his gaze never wavered from hers. There was such a depth of emotion there that something vibrant and hopeful blossomed in her chest.

"Okay." The whispered word was out before she could stop it.

His fingers brushed along her jaw as he dropped his hand, and she suppressed a shiver.

He stepped back, a smile curving his lips as he reached

behind him and opened the passenger-side door of his car, swinging it wide and gesturing for her to take a seat.

She slipped in and buckled her seat belt as he shut the door and jogged around to the driver's side. After buckling himself in, he started the car with the press of a button. She was acutely aware of him sitting so close beside her. The intoxicatingly masculine scent of him filled the confined space and brought back far too many memories.

"Where are we going?" she asked.

He gave an enigmatic smile. "To see some friends."

"Which friends?"

"It's Lexie's baby shower. I thought you might like to surprise her."

"Oh. Okay. Thank you, that's... that's kind of you."

She was happy at the thought of seeing Lexie. Of course she was. But she couldn't stop the disappointment that crashed over her in a wave. She'd thought he was there for her, a part of her hoping he'd realized he wanted her after all. But he was just being a nice guy.

She turned and looked out the window, sinking back into the deep red leather bucket seat.

Zac didn't talk for the rest of the trip, and neither did she. The silence should have been uncomfortable. But for some reason it wasn't. She felt almost as if she could finally take a deep breath, when she hadn't even realized she'd been struggling for air since she'd seen him last.

It wasn't too long before they were pulling up the long driveway to Lexie and Connor's house. Nerves made Cassie's stomach twist. Although she'd spoken to Lexie a few times over the last few months, this was the first time she would see her, or any of the others, since she'd left LA.

A sudden thought struck her. "Are they expecting me?"

He pulled the car in to park. "No."

"So, I'm crashing the party?"

He tossed her an unconcerned grin, then exited his side and jogged round to hers. She sighed and undid her seat belt. Zac opened her door for her, and she stepped out. He put his hand on the small of her back and guided her to the entrance of the house.

"Are you sure—"

"I've never been more sure of anything in my life."

She frowned at him. That was a weird thing to say about a baby shower.

He took her through to the back of the house, where they could look out onto the beautifully manicured backyard that overlooked the ocean. Outside was a long trestle table, with all of his Fractured bandmates, Lexie, Eden, Summer, and Drew sitting around it. The group was laughing at something, obviously enjoying themselves.

Instead of taking her out to join them, Zac stopped her with a hand on her wrist. She turned to him with raised brows. "Aren't we going out there?"

"I told you I had something to show you."

He *had* said that. She'd forgotten once he started talking about the baby shower.

"Right. And this something you want to show me is here?"

He nodded outside. "It's right out there."

Cassie turned to look, seeing only what she'd seen before. His bandmates, his friends, his manager.

"I don't know what I'm supposed to be looking at."

He stepped closer, his arm brushing hers. For a long beat, he was silent, watching the people outside. "Along with Tori, those people out there are my family." He didn't turn to face her as he spoke, and she kept her gaze on his profile. "I've spent all these years refusing to acknowledge

Fractured Kiss

it. I thought not letting myself get fully emotionally invested in them, or anyone, gave me some kind of control. I thought it would keep me safe." Now he did face her. "But all it did was keep me lonely. I just didn't know it until now. Until you."

Cassie's lips parted. "Zac..."

He cupped her cheeks, and his eyes searched hers. "I thought letting people in would force me to make choices I didn't want to make. I didn't want to have to make sacrifices. And I didn't want to resent the people I was supposed to love for forcing me to do it. I didn't want to hurt anybody the way my dad hurt us."

"You're not your father, Zac. I don't believe you'd ever be capable of hurting others the way he did."

He nodded. "Being with you made me happy, Cassie. For the first time, I felt what it was like to have someone by my side and be stronger because of it. And I realized I've actually had that all along. I just didn't appreciate it." He glanced back out the window. "I had these guys. They're my family, and I love them. But I want more. I want *you* by my side. I want to be by yours. I want what Connor, Tex, and Noah have. And I want it with you. If you're willing to take a chance on me."

Her heart beat a wild rhythm in her chest. "Zac, I don't know what to say."

"Well then, let me say something else. I love you, Cassie. Being with you makes me feel whole in a way I've never felt before. Your warmth, your sweetness, your beautiful soul—you are everything I always wanted and everything I told myself I could never have."

Zac's thumbs swept over her cheeks, brushing away the tears she hadn't noticed were falling. He let out a long, slow breath and his lips tilted into a smile.

"I think I knew I was going to love you from the moment I kissed you," he said. "I told myself that night that I was doing it to prove a point to Bryan, but that was a lie. I kissed you because I wanted to. Because I was looking for any excuse to touch you. To taste you. So I gave myself the excuse I needed. My father tried to hurt me by saying I was in the right place at the right time when it came to Fractured. And all this time, I thought it was a bad thing. But now I know the truth. Being in the right place at the right time brought me to this moment. I was in exactly the right place at exactly the right time when you ran into me in that hallway. If I hadn't been, none of this would have ever happened. I will be forever grateful for being in the right fucking place at the right fucking time. And I'm so damn sorry it took me this long to figure my shit out. I'm so fucking sorry I hurt you in the process. But I'll never be sorry for kissing you. And I will never, *never* be sorry for falling in love with you."

More tears spilled from Cassie's eyes. Her heartbeat was detonating in her ears, her whole body lighting up from the inside out. Maybe she should be more wary. Maybe she should hold out. But nothing in her life had ever felt more right, more perfect, than this moment. Maggie had told her months ago that sometimes it was good to be foolish because it meant you were taking a chance on something that could be amazing. And she wanted amazing with Zac. She wanted something unforgettable.

She curled her fingers into his T-shirt, just above the waistband of his jeans. "I love you too, Zac. I thought what I had before was love, but I was so, so wrong. That wasn't love. It was friendship that got twisted into dependency. I'll always be grateful to Bryan for finding me in that field, but we were never meant to be together forever. We didn't strengthen each other. I was following him around, not standing by his side and helping to choose our way."

His eyes searched hers as he listened. His thumbs continued stroking over her cheekbones, even though her tears had slowed almost to a stop.

"I needed to find my own self-worth not let someone else determine it," she said. "And I have. I finally know who I am and what I want. I want to write songs. I want to follow my dreams and have adventures along the way. And I want *you*." She stepped closer so that they were toe-to-toe and she had to tip her head back to look at him. "I want to stand by your side. More than anything in the world."

Zac gave her a crooked grin, but his beautiful hazel eyes blazed with intensity. "Does that mean I get to kiss you again?"

She gave a slightly hysterical laugh. "God, yes. I've missed your kisses. I've missed the way you touch me. I've missed everything about you."

He slid his hand into her hair and tilted her head farther back. "Are you going to be mine, angel?" His voice was low and rough.

Her pulse leaped. "I think I've always been yours."

Zac's lips brushed hers, a teasing pressure. She wasn't having it. She reached up, gripped the back of his neck, and brought his mouth down on hers.

Cassie's eyes fluttered closed, and her hands went to his hair, her fingers threading through the short, silky strands. She parted her lips and moaned when he deepened the kiss. Her blood heated in her veins, making her limbs heavy and pliant.

When he finally pulled back, his eyes were dark. "As much as I'd like to find the closest guest room and reacquaint myself with every inch of you. I promised you a party. All the things I want to do to you are going to have to wait."

Cassie let out a jagged breath as Zac slid the glass door open. "Shall we?"

She nodded and stepped outside.

Chapter Forty-Five

Zac guided Cassie out to join the baby shower with a hand on her back. The opening of the door attracted the attention of the others, but it took them a second to realize who he had with him. When they did, there was excited chatter and a whoop from Noah.

Cassie's smile was a little shy as they all came toward her in a group. Lexie was the first to pull her into a hug.

"Cassie, oh my god. Why didn't you tell me you were coming? I'm so happy you're here."

Cassie laughed at Lexie's excitement. "I didn't know I was coming until Zac came and got me."

Lexie hugged him next. She tipped her head back and smiled at him. "So, is Cassie our gift?"

"I said I had a surprise for your baby shower. The gift part was for me." He winked at her, and she laughed in delight.

"So, you two are together?"

Zac smiled. "Yeah." He looked for Cassie and found her being embraced by Eden while Summer waited her turn. "I finally let myself see the possibilities."

"I'm so happy you're happy," she said softly.

"Me too, Lexie. It's been a while."

Eventually, after everyone had said hello to Cassie and hugged her, they all sat back down at the table. The press of Cassie's arm against his sent warmth pulsing through him. This was what he'd been missing from his life. This contentment.

"It's about time," Connor spoke from where he sat on Zac's left.

The corners of Zac's lips slid up. "Is that so?"

"You know when I knew this was coming?" Connor tipped his chin toward Cassie.

"When?" Zac asked, amused.

"The first time I saw you hold her hand."

Zac huffed out a laugh. "Yeah?"

"Yeah." Connor smirked. "I'd never seen you do that before. I knew she'd be the one to break through that thick head of yours."

"You're one to talk." Zac's gaze landed on Lexie where she was leaning her head toward Drew, a beautiful smile on her face.

"I never claimed to not have a thick head." Connor's Irish lilt deepened as he stared at Lexie, his green eyes bright.

"Jesus." Zac laughed, tipping his head back and scrubbing his hands over his face. "How did this happen to us?"

Tex must have been listening in because he leaned across the table. "Fate works in mysterious ways, man. Don't question it. Just enjoy the fucking ride."

Zac dropped his hands and looked at Cassie, drinking her in. "I intend to."

He shifted in his seat and the pick hanging inside his

Fractured Kiss

shirt pressed against his chest. He reached for it, fished it out of his T-shirt, and curled his fingers around it.

Cassie's hand found its way into his other one. She squeezed. "Everything okay?"

"Come with me," he said, pulling her up to stand.

He tossed a smile at the others around the table, then led Cassie to the edge of the cliff that overlooked the ocean.

He took in the view. The sun was low on the horizon, the sky darkening shades of purple and pink and gold. "It's beautiful, isn't it?"

She turned to look at the view and let out a deep sigh of appreciation. "It's incredible. I feel like I could stand here for hours just watching the sun dissolve into the ocean and the colors bleed from the sky until all that's left are diamonds scattered on black velvet."

"Still a poet, I see."

She laughed lightly. "Not my finest work."

"So, what is your finest work?"

The corners of her lips curled up. "Nothing you'll ever see."

He turned to face her. "Why not?"

"It's in my head."

"You've never written it down?"

She smiled, her eyes still fixed on the horizon. "I don't need to."

He crossed his arms and studied her profile. "What's this poem about?"

She looked at him out of the corner of her eye. "You. It's the words that run through my head every time I see you."

His heart stalled as he took in the delicate lines of her face, her dark lashes, her sapphire blue eyes made temporarily lighter by the rays of the setting sun. She was so damn gorgeous, in body and soul. And she was his. She was giving him her heart, and he was going to treasure it the way it should be treasured. The way everyone else in her life should have treasured it. The way his father should have treasured the hearts that were in his care.

Suddenly reminded of what had brought him over there, Zac reached up and pulled the leather band from around his neck.

"I wondered if you still had that," Cassie said.

He held it up, watching it spin against the darkening sky. "I've spent too long holding onto painful memories instead of trying to make good ones of my own. It's about time I got rid of it."

He looked around and picked up a small stone, wrapping the leather band tightly around it. He pulled his arm back and threw it as hard as he could, watching with satisfaction as it arced out and down. It disappeared from sight before it hit the surface of the water. But he didn't have to see it sink to know it was gone.

Cassie put her hand on his back and smoothed it up and down. His gaze met hers, and there was so much love there, it hit him like a blow to the chest. He faced her, cupping her cheeks and brushing his thumbs over them.

"I love you, Cassie," he said. "I love you so fucking much. I don't know where this journey is going to take us. I just know I want you with me. I want it all. Everything."

Her lips parted, her eyes shimmering. "I love you, too, Zac. I think the journey is going to be amazing regardless of where we end up."

What he saw in her eyes didn't scare him now. Whatever was there, he wanted to be the one to give it to her. To share with her the home and family they'd hopefully build together.

He feathered his lips over hers once, twice, before deepening the kiss.

The holes in his heart had been filled. He had everything. His music, his bands, his family.

And Cassie. He had Cassie.

He'd been in the right place at the right time.

And now he had it all.

Epilogue

Cassie put down her latest notebook and watched Zac laughing with Tex and Noah. Connor was at the other end of the living room, FaceTiming Lexie and little Amelia, now six months old and the spitting image of her beautiful mom.

The rest of them had already said hello to mother and baby and spent far too long trying to make Amelia laugh. There was nothing quite like seeing three hulking rock stars trying to outdo each other pulling funny faces for the benefit of a very unimpressed baby. But it had been nice to see her and Lexie after being on the road for three weeks.

It hadn't been three weeks for Connor, of course. He'd flown back home twice on the record label jet to see his family, and he called them every day. Sometimes more than once. It was lovely to see how smitten he was. She hadn't known him before he'd met Lexie, but Zac had told her about the lead singer's difficult youth and how meeting Lexie and marrying her had made such a difference to him.

Cassie's eyes went to Tex. There was another man who was looking forward to a big change. Eden had announced her pregnancy and engagement not long after Lexie's baby shower. The big, long-haired, tattooed guitarist had almost looked like he was going to shed tears of joy when they'd announced the news to everyone. Cassie couldn't have been happier for them both.

And in a few short weeks, Summer and Noah were getting married. The two high school sweethearts were so blissfully excited, it was beautiful to see. Noah was bouncing off the walls even more than normal, while Summer seemed to be compensating by becoming almost Zen-like in her calmness. It might be because this would be her second marriage. But Cassie was inclined to think it had more to do with the deep happiness that glowed like the sun from Summer's eyes every time she looked at her husband-to-be. There was no fear or uncertainty in her at all. And no one who saw them together could doubt they were meant to be.

Cassie let out a deep sigh of contentment. Being able to go on the road with Zac and the others was amazing. Now that she was doing her songwriting full-time, she could mostly do that whenever she wanted. She only had to stay home occasionally, if she was needed in the recording studio. Over the past nine months, Talia had bought the recording rights to three more of Cassie's songs, and the two of them had become friends. In fact, once they got back from this mini East Coast tour, she and Talia were going to try writing an entire album together.

And Zac... A smile spread across Cassie's face as her eyes found him again. Being with Zac was incredible. She counted her blessings every single day that he'd been in that hallway at exactly the right time for her to run into.

Cassie's heart filled with love as she watched him. He was both the same and different from the man she used to sit here with all those months ago. He seemed lighter somehow, unencumbered by the weight of his past. With Fractured taking longer breaks between touring and recording, he could work with Crossfire without the pressure he'd been putting on all of them before. He was having fun with it. And she loved seeing his happiness. She loved being a part of it.

Connor finally said goodbye to his wife and daughter, then stood and stretched. "Hitting the sack," he said as he strolled toward the sleeping area.

"Yeah, right behind you," said Tex, and Noah nodded in agreement.

Zac caught her gaze. "I'm not tired yet. Fancy staying up for a while for old times' sake? I've been working on a song I'd like to get your thoughts on."

Cassie nodded and gave him a smile. She was a little tired, but not enough to say no to some one-on-one time with him. She didn't think she'd ever be that tired. Memories of what they'd done together on this bus during their first tour flitted through her mind and she pressed her thighs together. Since Lexie and Connor weren't using the rear bedroom this time, she and Zac had commandeered it. But the thought of reenacting what they'd done out in the living room previously was particularly appealing.

Once everyone had cleared out, he ushered her over to where he was sitting at the kitchen table. She walked toward him with a seductive swing of her hips and bit her lip as his eyes flared brightly.

She considered dropping to her knees when she reached him, but he didn't give her the chance. He wrapped his arms around her waist and pulled her down on his lap. She let out a laugh, which ended abruptly when his mouth landed on hers. As always, she lost herself in the taste and feel of him. She reached her hands up under his T-shirt, but when she tried to tug it up, he pulled back.

"I really do have a song I want you to look at," he said.

A little surprised, she blew out a breath and tried to refocus on his words. "Sorry. Being with you like this brings back a lot of memories."

"Me too, angel. And we'll definitely get to that." He drifted his lips down her neck and she shivered. "But first, what do you think of this?"

From somewhere next to him, he pulled out another notebook and placed it on the table, opening it to near the back.

Her eyebrows shot up. It was her old notebook. The one she'd left with him when she'd walked out. He'd hung on to it, telling her he wanted it as a souvenir of how they'd first gotten together. At the time, she'd thought it was touchingly sentimental on his part. But apparently, he'd been carrying it around and writing in it himself.

She quirked a brow at him, but he just smiled and drew her attention to the book by tapping his finger on the page. She looked down at the lyrics written in his neat handwriting and started reading.

Cassie smiled. The words were beautiful. The lyrics spoke about the transformative power of love and how fate can bring two lost souls together when they least expect it. She could hear in her head how the words would sound set to music as her eyes ran over them.

"Zac, this is beautiful." She twisted toward him and linked her arms behind his neck. "What was your inspiration?" She gave him a coy smile.

He grinned back. "It just came to me."

"Hmm, okay. Who's going to sing it, then?"

He shrugged. "Haven't thought that far ahead."

Cassie cocked her head to the side, wondering why he was being so evasive, considering he'd been so keen to get her thoughts. "Do you at least have a name for it?"

"That's the one thing I'm sure of," he said.

She waited for a few seconds, then let out a little laugh. "Okay. What's it called?"

"Will You Marry Me?"

Cassie blinked, taken aback. Then she smiled. "I love it. It's like the song is the story of how they meet, and the title is actually the ending of the story."

Zac nodded, looking serious. "Exactly. What do you think of the last verse? Do you think it's emotional enough?"

She looked back down at the notebook to reread the last verse and sucked in a sharp breath at the sight of the huge solitaire diamond ring he'd somehow, without her noticing, placed in the middle of the page.

"So will you?" he breathed against her neck.

A sob burst out of her as she stared at the ring, lying on the beautiful words he'd written.

"Hey. Hey." He caught her chin between his thumb and forefinger and turned her head, so she was looking at him. His hazel eyes were so full of love, it made her cry harder. "Not quite the reaction I was hoping for." He grinned crookedly.

Cassie flung her arms around him and pressed her face to his neck. He held her close, his hands smoothing up and down her back as she cried. After about a minute, she was able to gain control of herself enough to raise her head and press her lips to his.

He deepened the kiss immediately, sliding his tongue into her mouth and making her delirious with the taste of him, as always. But the poor guy had waited long enough for an answer. And more than anything, she wanted to give it. She'd just needed a moment to collect herself. To mentally pinch herself and believe what was happening.

Cassie pulled back and smiled at him through her tears. "You're like a dream. My personal dream come true. I love you so much, Zac. More than I even knew was possible." She placed her hands on either side of his face and brushed another kiss against his lips. "Yes, I'll marry you." Then she looked him in the eye. "As long as that's what you really want. Because I don't need a ring on my finger to be with you. You know that, right?"

A slow grin spread across his face. "I know you don't. But turns out, I do. I want a ring on your finger. I want everyone to know you're mine. And that I'm yours. Now and forever."

"I am," she said. "I am yours, Zac. In every possible way."

He slid his fingers through her hair and tugged her down to him. She went willingly. Just like she always would. She'd follow him, and he'd follow her.

And together they would make this journey through life an unforgettable one.

Keep in Touch

Join my mailing list at www.lmdalgleish.com/newsletter for news and updates, as well as to be the first to hear about new releases, sales, and giveaways. Or if you'd prefer not to receive any newsletters, you can follow me or contact me below:

Website: www.lmdalgleish.com
Facebook: www.facebook.com/DalgleishAuthor
Instagram: www.instagram.com/lmdalgleishauthor,
Bookbub: www.bookbub.com/profile/l-m-dalgleish

About the Author

L. M. Dalgleish is a lifelong book lover whose passion for romance novels began in the long sleepless nights following the birth of her first baby. Two more babies later and she's still in love with strong, sassy heroines and sexy, but emotionally unavailable (at least to begin with) heroes.

She lives in Canberra, Australia, with her husband, three kids, and a very large, very fluffy cat. In her spare time, she enjoys hanging with her family, reading, eating too much pasta, and watching horror movies.

Also by L.M. Dalgleish

Fractured Hearts

Fractured Dreams

Fractured Trust

Printed in Great Britain
by Amazon